...TILL IT'S OVER!

ROBERT M. KERNS

Knightsfall Press

———

Published by Knightsfall Press
PO Box 280
Mineral Wells, WV 26150
https://www.knightsfallpress.com

ABOUT THIS BOOK

Claim an inheritance.

It's a simple goal, right?

Nothing is simple when Cole returns to Centauri, the seat of Coleson Interstellar Engineering. Challenges at every turn (including an attempt on his life), with no idea who he can trust. And then...the Solar Republic gets involved.

Will Cole find the people working against him in time? Will they succeed in ending the Coleson line once and for all?

Read Now to find out!

DRAMATIS PERSONAE

- Cole: Bartholomew James Coleson is the heir to the immensely wealthy Coleson Trust; indeed, some star systems compare their GDP to estimates of the Trust's worth as a metric of economic growth and achievement. The source of this wealth is his family's ownership of Coleson Interstellar Engineering (CIE), the company that owns and maintains the interstellar jump gate network used for transit between star systems, and he is captain/owner of the battle-carrier *Haven*.
- Srexx: Srexxilan is the self-aware AI inhabiting the computer cluster aboard the battle-carrier *Haven*.
- Sasha: Sasha Thyrray is the middle child and oldest daughter of Paol and Mira Thyrray. She is the first officer aboard the battle-carrier *Haven*.
- Harlon: Colonel Harlon Hanson commands the marines aboard the battle-carrier *Haven*.
- Emily: Commander Emily Vance is the daughter of Sevrin Vance and the commander-air-group (CAG) aboard the battle-carrier *Haven*.
- Sev: Sevrin Vance is the second child and oldest son of Carl

and Lindsay Vance in Tristan's Gate. He is Cole's Director of
System Infrastructure.

- Painter: Julianna Painter is the former owner/captain of the
  freighter *Beauchamp*. She is now Cole's Director of
  Everything Else; if it's not related to the actual construction
  process of re-building Beta Magellan (which is Sev's
  responsibility), it falls under Painter's aegis.
- Garrett: Garrett is Cole's oldest friend. He found Cole
  shortly after the massacre of Beta Magellan and raised him
  until Cole was ready to go out on his own. Garrett now
  serves as Cole's spymaster... er, that is... Director of
  Intelligence.
- Lindrick: Draketh Lindrick is a former general in the
  Aurelian Commonwealth ground forces. Responsible for the
  attempted coup that led to a general civil war in the
  Commonwealth, Lindrick is also the man who led and
  perpetrated the Massacre of Beta Magellan many years ago.

CHAPTER ONE

Briefing Room, *Haven*
    Docking Slip 12, The Gate
    Tristan's Gate
    24 April 3000, 09:15 GST

Cole leaned back against his seat as he scanned the faces looking back at him. Sasha, Emily, Garrett, Sev, and Painter occupied seats around the table.

"So," Cole said, calling the meeting to order, "I know I told everyone that the purpose of this meeting was to discuss the plan for the Alpha Centauri trip, but there are a couple of things I need to cover beforehand. Sev, what's the status of our construction project at the shipyard?"

"As we've discussed in the past, the biggest bottle-neck was working through getting the materials from the fabricators aboard *Haven* to the shipyard where the craft are actually built. It took us most of November and a week or so into December to work through that. Since then, though, we've been churning out one per day, handing them off to the test-pilots. Srexx has also been helping with diagnostics and certification."

Cole grinned like a small child faced with a mountain of presents. "So... I have my air wing?"

Sev looked like he wanted to sigh. "We're still waiting on two bombers to be produced today and tomorrow. Then, we start the testing and certification process for the dropships. If everything with those goes well, we should have *Haven* up to its full complement in a little over two weeks."

Cole nodded and shifted his attention to Emily. "Well, the wrench jockeys have done their part, CAG. How are my pilots?"

"You do realize that calling this your 'air wing' and calling me 'CAG' is such a misnomer it's almost sad, right?" Emily asked.

"And just what would you call them, then? I haven't exactly seen an abundance of modern carriers from which to draw inspiration. Have you?"

Emily heaved a heavy sigh, leaning back as she gave into her defeat. "Okay. You have me there. I've been running everyone who passed basic qualification for pilot status through the simulators. Some have washed out, but most haven't. There are enough that I've decided we're going to rotate pilots through the maintenance and support crews. I've looked up some of the pilot culture stuff you've referenced from the wet navies back on Earth, not to mention my own experiences with Aurelian SDFs, and I'm not having that pilot-elitist crap in our unit. The past week or so, I've been running them through the scenarios you've been using for the HES ships, just a day behind."

Cole blinked. "You've been... oh, damn. How'd that work out for them?"

"Not so well, at first. The HES ships didn't really put up much defense in the sims, but *Haven*'s point defense shredded them. It was almost embarrassing. The upside is that they can now fly and fight in formation without any collisions. That's always a plus."

"I'd say so," Cole agreed, nodding. "Would you trust them at your side in combat out in space?"

"Yes, I would, and I'm not just saying that because they're *my* people. They've come a long way in two months, and they're as good as they'll get without flying actual sorties. There's only so much you can learn in simulations."

"Okay, then. Don't post it yet, but I want you to establish two rosters for each ship's shift: combat area patrol and ready alert. Anytime we're moving in a system, the combat area patrol is out and about. True, *Haven*'s sensors make it wicked difficult for anything to surprise us, but if the fighters are already out there, that just means less time to active engagement if we need them. The ready alert roster will be the patrol's reinforcements, for want of a better term."

Emily nodded once and made some notes in her data tablet.

Cole shifted his attention to Garret. "Okay, Garrett. It's your turn. What's the word on Lindrick? Have you found him yet?"

Garrett shook his head. "He is either a very slippery fellow or so busy it's almost beyond belief. We seem to be chasing his coat-tails more than anything else. When my people arrive in a system, he just left or he was never there. I do have some unconfirmed reports that he has linked up with some deserters from Aurelian armed forces, but I have no corroboration on that nor any significant detail, really. My people and I will keep doing what we do. Don't worry; we'll run the bastard to ground eventually."

Just as Cole was turning to Sasha, the overhead speakers chirped and broadcast, "Bridge to Cole!"

Cole frowned at the urgency in Mazzi's tone and pressed the key on the control pad by his right hand to accept the call. "I'm here, Mazzi."

"A fleet just arrived via the jump gate to Ruusae. From what we can see at this range, it appears to have corvettes, frigates, destroyers, cruisers, and battleships. The ship's sensors also detected a message broadcast from what we believe to be the fleet's flagship."

Cole smiled. "Can you play that message for us?"

"Srexx just finished piecing it together. Playing it now."

"*People of Tristan's Gate, I am Draketh Lindrick, and I have come to apprehend the terrorist, Paol Thyrray, and his family. If you choose to resist our lawful efforts, I will blockade this system and raid any shipping flagged by your star system.*"

"Hey, Cole?" Garrett said.

"Yeah, Garrett?"

"We found Lindrick."

"Thanks for the update," Cole replied. "I appreciate all the difficult work you do."

Grins threatened to escape the others seated around the table.

"Mazzi," Cole said, "bring the ship to alert status. Issue an immediate recall of any personnel aboard the station, and start bringing up the TacNet with the SDF we've practiced in the simulations. What HES ships do we have in-system?"

Mazzi was silent for a moment before answering, "We have most of them. Prioritizing the air wing pushed back their refits, so they've been running jobs as convoy escorts."

"Okay. Good. Have the cruisers start moving into a transit formation centered on us as soon as we undock. Split most of the destroyers and frigates off to be close protection for any non-combatants in the system, but I want a decent screen on *Haven*. Has the station seen the arrival or the message yet?"

"No, sir. The light from their arrival won't make it here for another five-and-a-half hours, give or take... with the message right after that."

"Right then," Cole said, adding a sigh. "I'm going to need a conference call with the head of the SDF and the Defense Minister, then. You should probably page our SDF liaison to be here for the call, as well."

"Yes, sir. Anything else?"

"Not at the moment, Mazzi. Thanks. Cole out."

The overhead speakers chirped again, and Cole looked to Painter and Sev. "Unless you two want to rack up some combat hours, you'd best head back to the station. Hey, Srexx... you with us?"

"Of course, Cole."

"You've had time to scan through the ship schematics for Aurelian ships. How would you rate the effectiveness of our air wing against their corvettes?"

"Honestly, Cole, they should abandon ship to save us the effort."

"All right, then. How about an Aurelian frigate?"

"Our fighters will take some hits, but I anticipate the shields and armor will provide ample protection."

"Okay. What about destroyers, then?"

Silence.

"That would be... unwise, Cole. The destroyers—especially if any are *Dawn*-class—possess extensive point-defense batteries. While the shields and armor on the fighters are the best I and my schematics can provide, they simply do not have the amount of protection an actual starship possesses."

"Good to know. Thanks, Srexx." Cole turned to Emily. "Start preparing your people. Their role will be taking out as many corvettes and frigates as they can, to keep our destroyers and frigates from needing to work."

Painter and Sev both stood. Sev directed a look at his daughter that seemed to carry all manner of unspoken communication, the most obvious of which was the ages-old parental 'be careful.' He followed Painter out of the briefing room.

Five minutes later, the briefing room hatch opened once more to admit Lieutenant Commander Brianna Vance, resplendent in her SDF working uniform. She stepped to the table and snapped to attention.

"Lieutenant Commander Vance, reporting as ordered, sir!"

Cole wanted to growl and grind his teeth. Despite the best efforts of people like Sasha and Mazzi, he'd managed to keep a much more relaxed atmosphere aboard *Haven* than he was sure he'd find aboard any other ship just about anywhere, and Brianna Vance was as much a bad influence as they were. Oh, he knew discipline and structure and all that was important, but Cole wasn't military. And what's more, he wasn't going to *be* military.

"I believe we've already had this talk, Commander Vance," Cole said. "I appreciate the respect, but saluting and 'Attention on deck!' and all that rot is *not* who I am. Have a seat."

"Aye, sir," Brianna said.

A sound reached Cole's ears from Sasha's direction, and he thought it sounded suspiciously like a snicker. Ah, well... one must always pick one's battles.

"You sent for me, sir?" Brianna asked, drawing Cole's attention back to the matter at hand.

Cole nodded. "A fleet arrived through the Ruusae jump gate. Lindrick is commanding it, and he's come for the Thyrrays. Even if I *were* inclined to let him have two of my people, I'll be dipped in tar and lit aflame before I give *anything* to the man who oversaw my families' massacre. The ships that answer to me are going out there, and we're going to pound Lindrick's fleet into scrap until they surrender and turn over Lindrick to me. I'm just waiting on a conference call with the SDF commander and the Defense Minister to update them on the plan."

Brianna's eyes looked like they wanted to bulge. "Uhm, sir... what if they decide to handle this differently? What if they activate your SDF credentials?"

Cole shrugged. "I never wanted those credentials in the first place, and while I do consider myself to be a team player, the only team I play for is mine. I'm not calling them to ask their permission, Brianna. I'm calling them to explain how this will happen."

Now, Brianna looked like she wanted to find a safe place to hide. "Uhm, sir... I'm not sure that's the best tack to take on this. I can't tell my ultimate commanding officer and the civilian head of the SDF that we're not going to listen to them."

"I wasn't asking you to, Brianna. I'll handle the conversation. If you feel this puts you in an untenable position, you're welcome to return to SDF Command aboard the station."

"I can't do that, sir," Brianna countered. "I was assigned as your liaison by SDF Command. My duty station is here."

"Look, Brianna, I get it. You're an SDF officer. That's your thing. The small problem is that no one ever *asked* me if I wanted an SDF liaison officer, and quite frankly, things were moving too fast when this little bombshell was dropped for me to care about giving your commanders the proper response of 'Go to Hell.' It's nothing on you. These last few months, I've forgotten you were even aboard. I'm sure that's exactly what you love hearing, but I do appreciate how you've kept yourself out from under foot. Though, I have been meaning to ask you if you enjoyed those sparring sessions with Srexx, where you tried to hack your way into the protected schematics for this ship."

"Brianna?" Sasha almost shouted.

Brianna turned equal shades of an embarrassed red and a frightened pale as she squeaked, "You knew about that?"

"We're getting a bit far afield, but since Mazzi hasn't called with that conference link... yes, I knew about it. Srexx works for me, and even if he didn't, we're friends. There is zero chance something like that would happen and he *wouldn't* tell me about it. It was my idea to let you find that archive you downloaded. Did you ever hear anything back from that?"

"Uhm, no? They just said to stop trying to steal information."

Cole grinned. "I'm glad they didn't hold it against you. The archive you downloaded was—in truth—a sophisticated virus. It gave Srexx access to the data-net of whoever put you up to it and allowed him to replace all their research data with audio files of animal farts. He asked for my input on what to do, and I thought animal farts would be the best illustration of my thoughts on the matter. I'm pretty sure he even got their backups, too."

Sasha and Emily couldn't maintain their composure any longer. They both erupted in howls of glee and mirth.

"Cole, you didn't!" Sasha said, between fits of laughter.

"Of course I did, and you should be very glad Srexx asked me for input. He was just going to set up a logic bomb that would've shredded the entire government data-net beyond salvage. I thought that was a little extreme for a first offense. If they hadn't given up, though, we might have reached that point."

Cole's words ripped all mirth out of Sasha. Memories of Srexx offering to begin preparations to take over the entire data infrastructure of the Aurelian Commonwealth went through her mind.

"Thank you for your restraint," Sasha said.

Just then, the overhead speakers chirped, broadcasting, "Bridge to Cole."

Cole tapped the comms control by his right hand again. "I'm here, Mazzi."

"I have that conference call for you, sir."

"Thank you, Mazzi. Put it through."

The speakers did a double chirp, and the briefing room's holo-projector activated to display the two people on the call from their shoulders up. General Elizabeth "Beth" Trumball was a straight-forward, no-nonsense woman who didn't care for any beating around the bush; Cole rather liked her, except for how rigidly military she was. Defense Minister Mattias Stone made Cole think of an old-Earth weasel; his slicked-back dark hair and pointed nose almost proclaimed his untrustworthiness. That assessment, however, couldn't have been farther from the truth, as all Minister Stone wanted was the best defense for Tristan's Gate.

"Hello, General, and Defense Minister," Cole said. "Thank you for taking my call."

"What can we do for you, Coleson?" General Trumball asked. "I have a meeting in ten minutes."

"I just thought you might like to know that a fleet commanded by Draketh Lindrick arrived through the Ruusae jump gate about a half-hour ago, and he sent the message I'm passing over now." Cole accessed his implant and attached the message to the conference call.

Moments later, General Trumball scoffed. "Now, do you see why I keep arguing for the system leadership to nationalize that damned ship, Defense Minister? The sensors aboard that thing reported the fleet's arrival when we haven't even seen its light yet. We won't even get updates from the outer forts for another four hours at best. We *need* that technology!"

"Now, General," Defense Minster Stone said, "this isn't really the best time for that, and besides, the system leadership has already voted down your numerous requests and proposals in this matter. The potential for failure and negative outcomes far exceeds the potential for success."

"And let me be very clear," Cole said. "That's not something you want to fail on the first attempt."

"No, Mr. Coleson, it isn't," Stone replied. "The system leadership understands that very well. Thank you for your notification of this issue, sir. I shall bring it to the Prime Minister's attention, and we'll have a course of action shortly."

"With all due respect, Defense Minister," Cole countered, "I wasn't calling to play 'Mother, may I.' I'm taking my ships out there, and I'm going to deal with that fleet. When *Haven* returns, Lindrick will be dead or in my brig. You should issue a travel advisory for the combat that will be occurring shortly."

"Now, see here!" General Trumball growled. "This is an SDF matter. Don't make me activate your commission, *Colonel*."

"General, I think—" Defense Minister Stone began.

Cole interrupted him. "General, like I told your so-called liaison that could better be termed a spy, I never *wanted* that commission. The way it was explained to me, it was a fig leaf to allow me to hire the military portion of the shipyard to repair the ships that defected from the Commonwealth and build my small craft, and my bank records indicate the projects have been very beneficial for Tristan's Gate. If you think you can use that commission to bludgeon me, General, you're a fool. Defense Minister, as soon as we close this call, I'm taking *Haven* out to meet them. Keep the citizens at a safe distance; I don't want anyone hurt. Cole out."

The conference call ended on the image of General Trumball almost spitting fire and Defense Minister Stone looking resigned. Brianna bent her head toward the tabletop, her eyes closed and her lips pursed; Cole wasn't sure, but she might've looked a little pale, too.

Cole stood and said, "Let's go, people. There are ships waiting for us."

CHAPTER TWO

Haven took up its position amid the thirty-four ships waiting just beyond the near-station traffic patterns. The status lights around the bridge glowed amber, proclaiming the ship to be at alert as everyone throughout the ship worked to ensure *Haven* was as battle-ready as possible.

The moment *Haven* slid into position at the center of the formation, Cole called for a fleet conference, specifically asking for Emily Vance and Harlon Hanson to join himself and Sasha in the flag briefing room. Unlike the bridge briefing room, the flag briefing room had the capability to conference hundreds of captains in an almost VR-like environment. As close as all the ships were, the comms wouldn't have any latency.

"Mazzi, you have the bridge," Sasha said as she followed Cole.

Mazzi nodded once, saying, "Aye, ma'am," and moved to the center seat.

Stepping through the port hatches, Cole turned left and walked aft. The flag bridge occupied the compartment just aft of the bridge briefing room, and the flag briefing room was just aft of that.

Emily and Harlon stood by the hatch to the briefing room. Cole nodded in greeting to each and led the way into the space. This wasn't the first time Cole had entered the flag briefing room, but it was the first time the space was put to its intended use. Cole wasn't sure how he felt about that. On one side, combat wasn't good, no matter how you looked at it. On the other side, though... if a fight had to happen, Cole didn't mind doing what needed done to ensure he or his people walked away from it. Out of all the possible reasons to lead his ships into a fleet action, taking down Draketh Lindrick was a task to which Cole harbored no objections.

As Cole assumed his seat at the head of the table, he couldn't help but marvel at the capabilities of the flag briefing room. The holo-cameras in the room would record the images of everyone present for transmission between the other ships in the fleet, and holos of the other captains and their first officers would soon appear in a hemisphere facing the physical occupants.

Cole didn't have to wait long. It seemed he had no sooner planted himself in the seat when pairs of holos began appearing, becoming a half-circle of faces hovering over the briefing room table. Cole recognized everyone; after all, he'd run them ragged through simulated fleet maneuvers over the past few weeks. Truth be told, it was more for his sake than theirs, as almost everyone looking back at him had at least a decade of naval and ship-driving experience.

"Hello," Cole said. "I want to thank all of you for coming. Is everyone aware of our reason for assembly today?" When no one spoke up to the contrary, Cole resumed. "Good. You will be receiving your unit assignments shortly. One could hope that the ships in Lindrick's fleet will surrender when I call for it, but I think we all know the odds of that happening. I have one goal for this engagement: kill or capture Draketh Lindrick. To that end, I will be asking Srexx to devote as many resources as he deems appropriate to verifying Lindrick's presence in the fleet and identifying the specific ship Lindrick inhabits. Once that is accomplished, that ship's IFF code in our TacNet will change to 'Do Not Engage.' This gentleman on my left is the commander of the ground forces aboard *Haven*. He will launch a mission to board Lindrick's flagship and capture him... if not the whole ship. I will leave the minor details up to him and his people. I just want Lindrick.

"The order of battle for this engagement is as follows. You're welcome to engage your size class and down. Leave the two battleships to *Haven*. They will pound anyone else in our formation to scrap in no time. I'm anticipating a number of frigates and corvettes to break off and attempt a rush for the shipping lanes. Let them. I have a surprise for them."

"If I may," one of the cruiser captains said, "would you care to elaborate on this surprise? It's all well and good to surprise the opposition, but we're not the opposition."

Cole grinned. "No. You are certainly not. Ladies and gentlemen, *Haven* is a Class I Battle-*Carrier*, as I've said many times in the past. We are only short two bombers and the dropships based on *Haven*'s technology before our small craft complement is complete. For the first time since Humanity left Earth, we will deploy fighters in a naval engagement." The expressions looking back at Cole ranged from disbelief to eagerness and, in a couple cases, outright glee. "Are there any other questions?"

No one spoke.

"Oh... one last item of note. I would like to hope this last topic will not be needed. That being said, we live in an uncertain galaxy. I know it's all spelled out in your employment paperwork, but if the topic should arise among your crews, know that I *will* stand by my commitment to ensure the welfare of the families of any we lose today. Each and every one of you is part of the collective I label as 'my people,' families included, and those families don't stop being 'my people' just because the direct employee is no longer with us. For anyone who treats with me in loyalty, I will return that loyalty ten-fold.

"Okay. Rest your people, and be ready. I'll call the fleet to battlestations thirty minutes from contact. Thank you."

Cole nodded once and stood from the table, ending the conference.

"Harlon, prep your teams. Emily, I want them to have the best pilots flying escort for the dropships. As soon as we confirm Lindrick's presence and verify a location, Harlon, you're on the clock."

Harlon nodded. "We'll be ready."

"All right, then," Cole said. "Let's do this."

. . .

Emily and Harlon broke off from Cole and Sasha, disappearing into a transit shaft. Sasha walked with Cole.

"You want to pilot one of the assault ships, don't you?" Sasha's tone made it sound more like a statement than a question.

Cole nodded. "It feels wrong to be back here, sitting on the bridge, while they go out there. I understand the whole 'burden of command' thing. It's all over the courses I've been studying to attain the Captain certification from the ISA, but that doesn't mean I have to like it."

Sasha stopped, turning to face him and drawing Cole to stop as well. "I know, Cole. The best leaders never do like it."

"I never wanted to be a leader, Sasha."

"We don't always get what we want, Cole, but if we're lucky, we have what we need. My sister and I would be dead if not for you. Yeleth and Wixil also, probably. Maybe even my parents and brother. Have you ever stopped to consider just how many lives you've impacted in the past nine months?"

Cole resumed walking. The bridge hatch was less than five meters away now. "I know, Sasha, and if I had it all to do over again, I can't think of one thing I'd honestly change. Besides, if the massacre had never happened, I still would've most likely ended up a leader. I was an only child, after all, and I don't remember my parents ever discussing more kids."

"So, I think it's time you took the center seat," Sasha said. "You handle yourself well in the simulations, and... well... I think it's time."

Cole sighed. "I don't get to pilot even *Haven* now?"

"Nope," Sasha rejoined. "Time to put on those big boy pants, Cole. You're the captain."

Cole did his best to return a very put-upon sigh, but the effect was marred just a bit by the hints of a smile at the corners of his mouth. "Yeah, I suppose I am."

Turning into the hatch, Cole led Sasha onto the bridge, and for once, he didn't frown or sigh when Mazzi called out, "Captain on the bridge!"

"I have the conn," Cole said as he moved to occupy the center seat.

Sasha moved to his right side as Cole continued, "Wixil, would you come here, please?"

Wixil looked up from where she occupied her customary seat at Mazzi's elbow and moved to stand before Cole and Sasha. The young Ghrexel stood in place, not quite coming to attention; her tail languidly swished from side to side. Cole knew her well enough to see the concern radiating off her, but to anyone who didn't know her, she appeared relaxed and almost unconcerned.

"Wixil," Cole said, "the time has come for me to become the ship's captain in truth and not just the owner who pilots the ship and acts the role for video comms. That leaves a vacancy at the helm I want filled by the best person possible. You have the highest scores in piloting, spatial awareness, and reaction time... of the *entire* crew. The position of First Shift Helmsman is yours if you want it."

Wixil's ears perked up, and her tail went ramrod-straight. Cole couldn't miss the gleam in her eyes. In an instant, though, that gleam faded, and her tail drooped. She looked to Mazzi. Cole didn't miss the barely perceptible nod Mazzi gave her, either, and the happy adolescent was back.

"Yes, Cole, I want it!"

Cole grinned and nodded once. "Take your station, then, Wixil."

Mazzi summoned additional crew to assist her with the weapons stations, the starboard recession soon filling with two more people.

Wixil pivoted and almost dashed to the helm, sliding into the seat there as if it had been made for her. "Helm ready, Captain!"

"Mazzi, do we have the fleet's TacNet up?"

"Yes, sir. All links are showing green."

"Wixil," Cole said, "plot an intercept course to Lindrick's fleet, and send it to the TacNet for distribution throughout the fleet."

From Cole's vantage point, he could see Wixil's fingers dance across the helm console. Two minutes passed, and she announced, "I have the course, Captain, and I've copied it to TacNet."

A minute later, Jenkins at Comms said, "All ships report the course locked in, Captain."

"Thank you, Jenkins. Wixil, take us out."

"We're about thirty minutes from contact, Captain," Wixil announced.

"Thank you, Wixil," Cole said and looked at the port-side recession.

For the first time since *Haven* carried a full complement of people, crewmembers occupied the stations of the port-side recession: Flight Ops and Marine Ops. Cole didn't have their names memorized yet, but both junior officers looked eager to contribute.

"Flight Ops, my compliments to the CAG, if you would please. Begin launching fighters."

Cole watched the tactical plot as dots far smaller than their smallest frigate began leaving the bow of *Haven* four abreast. Even though the space overlooking the flight deck was the domain of the position Cole had termed 'Air Boss,' Cole knew Emily would be there, too, watching her people leave the ship for their very first combat deployment. In fifteen minutes, sixty fighters took up their respective positions in the fleet, creating a ring around *Haven*.

"Flight Deck signals all fighters launched, Captain," the lieutenant at Flight Ops reported. "They are starting preparations to launch the boarding parties now."

Cole nodded. "Thank you, Lieutenant. Sasha, I'd like you at my side for this next part." When Sasha was standing at Cole's right elbow, he said, "Jenkins, record a message for transmission. Make sure Sasha is in the video."

"You're on, sir."

"Attention, incoming fleet. My name is Bartholomew James Coleson, and I command the Battle-Carrier *Haven* and this battle-group. I do not recognize Draketh Lindrick's claim to the Thyrrays, and I myself have unfinished business with Lindrick. Surrender and turn over Lindrick to me; this doesn't have to be any more unpleasant than it already is. If you force me to engage your fleet, I can assure you that none of your ships will escape unscathed. Coleson out."

"Message recorded," Jenkins said, "and it's ready to transmit."

"Send it, please, all channels and frequencies."

Jenkins replied, "Sent, sir."

"Mazzi, battle-stations, please. Jenkins, please signal the fleet to assume combat formation," Cole said.

Klaxons blared throughout the ship as status lights shifted from amber to red.

"Also sent, sir," Jenkins said.

Cole watched the fleet re-arrange itself into a series of formations in which the destroyers and frigates centered themselves around the cruisers that pulled away from *Haven*.

"Mazzi, your primary targets are the two battleships. If—no, when —this goes down, split our torpedoes between them. The cruisers are your secondary targets. Srexx?"

"Yes, Cole?" the AI responded via the overhead speakers.

"If Lindrick is over there, I want to know where."

"Yes, Cole."

"Mazzi, as soon as Srexx provides a location on Lindrick, shift the targeting priority on that vessel to shields, weapons, shuttle bays, and engines... in that order."

"Aye, sir," Mazzi replied.

Just then, a mass of dots appeared around the enemy ships on the tactical plot.

"Missile launch!" Mazzi announced. "Tracking seven-hundred-fifty —repeat: seven-five-zero—incoming birds. Flight time is six minutes."

"Coordinate missile defense through TacNet," Cole said, his voice calm and unworried. "All ships, weapons free."

Cole watched his own ships launch a full complement of missiles and—from *Haven*—torpedoes.

"Cole," Srexx said.

"Yeah, buddy?"

"I have confirmed Lindrick's location aboard the battleship *Vanren's Despair*. I am highlighting it in the tactical plot."

"Thank you, Srexx," Cole replied, grinning. "Feel free to have fun now."

"Yes, Cole. Thank you."

"Marine Ops, my compliments to Colonel Hanson. Please advise him we have identified his target, and ask him to give us a few minutes to thin the herd before he launches."

"Aye, sir!"

"Flight Ops, send our deployed fighters to thin those corvettes and frigates. They are to avoid any targets too close to destroyers or cruisers; the larger ships' point-defense is too heavy."

"Aye, sir!"

Cole watched the battle unfolding in the tactical plot. He held no illusions that he was some kind of tactical genius; it was his first action in full command, too. The enemy missiles were just reaching interception range, and his fleet's interceptors were wreaking havoc. There wouldn't be too many left for the point-defense batteries, at the rate things were going, but that was a good thing.

"Sasha, do I see a gap forming in the enemy formation? Right there. It looks like the destroyers and frigates along this line are re-positioning for... are they moving to intercept our torpedoes?"

Cole stood and stepped to the tactical plot, lifting his hands to zoom in on the space in question. Sure enough, a group of frigates and destroyers were re-positioning to serve as a shield wall for the battleships against the seventeen incoming torpedoes. The slowest moving projectiles on the field continued to close, and Cole watched as they first fired a volley of interceptors. Two torpedoes vanished. Now, those ships opened up with their full energy armament, including the point-defense batteries. Six more torpedoes vanished. One frigate took a torpedo almost square amidships and became an expanding cloud of debris. A destroyer took a torpedo about three-quarters back from its bow, and the aft third of that ship ceased to exist, its reactor not even having time to go critical before it vaporized. Another destroyer took a torpedo almost square amidships like the frigate, but *unlike* the frigate, some of it survived... the forward third and aft third drifting and trailing sparks as they vented gases and water.

Six torpedoes still remained.

"Mazzi, re-target the remaining torpedoes to *Vanren's Despair*. Focus on shields and weapons. Wixil, get us in there. Energy batteries free on targets of opportunity until we're in range of the battleships; then, focus on subduing *Despair*."

A chorus of "Aye, sir," echoed from different stations around the bridge. Cole zoomed the tactical plot back out to see how the overall engagement was going. Just as Srexx had predicted, his fighters were shredding the corvettes; the frigates were slower to go down, but they were faring no better than their smaller counterparts. The other ships of his fleet hammered opposing vessels with both missiles and energy emplacements.

Cole knew when they'd crossed into 'enemy territory.' The ship started shuddering, taking hits on the shields.

"Outer shields at sixty-eight-percent and holding," Mazzi announced. "We have two-percent bleed-through to the next layer, but it's manageable. Energy batteries report ready."

"Fire at will until we reach those battlewagons," Cole said.

Cole blinked as a sphere of enemy ships—mostly frigates and destroyers this far from the enemy core—vanished from the tactical plot around *Haven*. That sphere became more of an oval as *Haven* bore down on the two battleships at the center of the enemy's formation. Cole couldn't keep from grinning when he saw three of his formations fall in behind *Haven* and push out the edges of the debris sphere in their wake.

An enemy formation made up of two cruisers and several destroyers made a firing run across *Haven*'s bow, and even on Deck Three, Cole felt the ship shake.

"Outer shield—forward arc—is down to forty-five-percent," Mazzi announced, "and the fourth layer is down to ninety-two-percent."

"Engineering reports they're directing additional power to the forward shields," Jenkins said.

Just then, Cole saw two of the dots representing his ships blink twice and fade out.

"Captain, the destroyer *Achilles* and the frigate *Erinyes* report they've taken heavy damage," Jenkins announced.

Cole shifted the tactical plot to focus on his wounded ships. He could see several frigates moving in to finish the job... but those two wounded ships weren't alone. A cluster of pin-pricks—no more than single pixels in the hologram—flitted around nearby frigates and corvettes.

"Flight Ops," Cole said, "divert some nearby fighters to the *Achilles* and *Erinyes* until we can get a few more ships in there for support."

"Aye, sir!"

Cole watched several of the fighters break off from the frigates they were harrying and shift to defend their wounded comrades. Two formations of destroyers were also moving to assist, and they'd arrive in time to shore up the defense against the incoming frigates. That situation handled, Cole shifted the tactical plot back to the 'beachhead' *Haven* was establishing in the enemy formation... just in time to experience his ship reaching energy range of the two battleships.

The deck heaved beneath Cole as the battleships unleashed their energy weapons, and Cole was glad he'd put his feet in a wide stance. Flexing his knees, he managed *not* to face-plant onto the deck.

"Outer shields in the forward, port, and starboard arcs are down," Mazzi announced. "Fourth layer at fifty-percent and dropping fast."

"Well, I guess we're in range of the battleships," Cole remarked dryly. "Mazzi, focus your fire on preparing the *Despair* for boarding. Give the other battleship everything that won't help you subdue *Despair*. Srexx, can you put a read-out for the shields, armor, and hull on the tactical plot for me, please?"

The requested information appeared, and Cole watched the numbers as the battleships hammered *Haven* with everything they had. An eternity later—but only seven minutes and thirty-two seconds in reality—Mazzi called out, "Fire mission complete, Captain! Shifting weapons to second battleship."

"Flight Ops," Cole said, "launch the boarding parties with full fighter escort."

A glance at the numbers on the plot showed Cole the starboard shields were down to the third layer, with a ten-percent bleed-through to the inner-most shields. *Haven* was giving as good as she got, though. The second battleship had already lost its shields facing *Haven*, and gases and water vapor vented through several deep rends *Haven*'s energy batteries gouged into the battleship's hull.

Six assault shuttles—surrounded by eighty fighters—sped to the battleship off *Haven*'s starboard bow, which was left mostly intact lest a stray shot kill the one person on the other side Cole wanted to capture most. Those shuttles locked on to airlocks around the battleship as the fighters broke off to destroy any energy emplacements *Haven*'s weapons had simply deactivated.

"Jenkins, record a message for transmission," Cole said.

"Ready, Captain," Jenkins replied.

"Attention, enemy vessels. You have taken two—no, three—of my ships out of the fight, while my fleet has reduced your numbers by a full third. I have active boarding operations occurring on your flagship, and my weapons crews are hammering the other battleship to scrap as I speak. Please... do not needlessly throw away the lives of your people. I will honor the surrender of any ship that does so. Coleson out."

"Ready to transmit, sir."

"Send it please, all channels and frequencies."

Cole watched as enemy ships continued to disappear in puffs of holographic destruction. Cole feared his people would have to cripple every ship arrayed against them, which he very much didn't want to do.

"Captain," Jenkins called out, "we're getting a flood of surrender requests!"

"Put me on live."

"You're on."

"This is Cole. Surrendering ships, set your transponders to strobe, and cease hostilities. If you're mobile, leave the engagement area. Any ships that have emergency needs, send that information, and I'll do what I can. That is all."

It wasn't long before every transponder in the field was flashing, except for the battleship *Vanren's Despair*.

"Captain," the Marine Ops officer called out, "the boarding party reports a cessation of all resistance. The first officer is asking to surrender in exchange for Lindrick."

Cole grinned. "Accepted, and ask the marines to deliver Lindrick to the brig once they're back aboard. That bastard and I need to have a conversation."

CHAPTER THREE

Tristan's Gate System
    24 April 3000, 14:43 GST

The aftermath of the battle played out much as Cole's previous actions had... except, this time, Cole was in command. Stepping *Haven* down from battle-stations to alert status, Cole asked the ships of his fleet to start moving through the surrendered vessels and wreckage, performing Search And Rescue wherever appropriate. It was a grim task, wrapped in clouds of hope. Cole insisted on bringing any in need of urgent medical attention aboard *Haven*. One question kept coming from among the survivors:

"What will happen to us now?"

The people on the front line didn't have an answer. They kicked the question up the chain until it reached Cole, but Cole didn't have an answer, either. At one time, he would've jumped at the chance to interview people with the Kiksaliks present to determine if they were viable recruits. *Haven* was full-up now, though. Sadly, however, several of the HES ships were *not*... not anymore.

Cole announced that he'd have an answer for the survivors once they'd returned to The Gate and conducted an after-action analysis. Cole's attention to after-action matters evaporated, however, at a simple text message from Harlon sent directly to Cole's implant: We have him aboard.

———————

Cole entered the common area of the brig. Several of his ground forces milled about, discussing the boarding operation. Everyone snapped to attention at Cole's entrance, but he didn't notice. Cole only had eyes for one man. He walked straight to Harlon and lifted his hands in question.

"Well? Where is he?"

Harlon turned and appraised Cole's expression and stance for a moment. Then, he nodded his head toward the corridor that went to the maximum security cells. "This way."

Harlon led Cole down the corridor. They passed through two check-points that required DNA verification before proceeding. Cole approved. At last, Cole stood before a cell with a single occupant. The cell contained a bed, a combination sink/toilet, and a sonic shower with a partition that went up to a short person's shoulder. Everything was a painful shade of bright white.

The cell's occupant paced like a caged animal, though it wasn't much of a circuit. Step, step, turn. Step, step, turn. Step, step, turn. He looked young for a general, and Cole thought he noticed some slight signs of rough treatment. Heh. Lindrick wasn't lying on the floor, a bloody mess clutching his ribs, so Cole's concern was largely non-existent.

"Can he see us?" Cole asked.

"Nope. Right now, the barrier is opaque on his side and totally sound-proof. We could set off a bomb over here, and he'd never know it."

Cole nodded. "I want him to see me... hear me, too."

Harlon lifted his arm and keyed a couple commands into the panel beside the cell's entrance. Cole thought he heard a faint hum, but he wouldn't have sworn to it. Lindrick stopped pacing, turned to look directly at Cole.

"So... you're the young pup who got away," Lindrick said, his voice rough and worn. "How'd you manage that? We burned that planet's surface almost down to glass."

"I wasn't *on* the planet," Cole replied. "I slipped out to teach myself how to pilot Dad's newest shuttle. I was in the asteroid field when you arrived."

"Ah," Lindrick responded. "Watched it all, then, did you?"

"Not really. I did see what was left."

"For what it's worth, I'm sorry you had to see that. You were... what... ten? Twelve, maybe?"

"I was thirteen," Cole replied, his jaw clenched.

"So, this is it, then? Time to torture me to death for all my crimes against your family? Have me die screaming like they did?"

Cole took a deep breath and pushed the rage and hate from his mind. "Nope. My people will ask you questions, and you will answer them."

Lindrick scoffed. "You have no concept of the interrogations I've survived. What makes you think your people can break me?"

Now, Cole allowed himself an almost-predatory grin. "Who said anything about breaking you?"

With that, Cole turned and left. Harlon took that as the cue to blank the barrier once again. Cole stopped at the first checkpoint he reached and turned to Harlon.

"Let him stew for a few hours. Garrett will handle his questioning, and there will be a Kiksalik or two plus an Igthon and a Ghrexel in the room. The Kiksaliks will get us everything we need."

"There's another option," Harlon said.

"Oh? What's that?"

"Start flooding his cell with any of several dozen gases that ensure compliance. He'll be so eager to talk by the time Garrett gets around to asking him anything, he'll probably volunteer stuff we never thought to ask."

Cole turned over that idea in his mind a couple times before nodding once. "I'll mention it to Garrett. Since he's in charge of this kind of thing, he can decide how to proceed."

———

"Cole?"

Cole looked up at the overhead speakers as he walked down the corridor toward the bridge and smiled, saying, "Yeah, Srexx? How are you doing, buddy?"

"I am quite well, Cole. My status does not have the inherent variability present in organic life-forms."

"Fair enough," Cole replied. "What's on your mind?"

"Have you given any thought to the fate of the wreckage?"

Cole stopped at the bridge's port hatch. "Not really. Why do you ask?"

"The ship's supply of raw material is low, as we used most of what we'd accumulated plus purchasing even more regolith and unwanted ore to make the parts for the air wing. It might be wise to apply for salvage rights on the wreckage and, once it's broken up, feed the pieces to the recyclers. Doing so would also provide what we need to stock up on munitions for the air wing."

"Okay. I'll see to it."

"Thank you, Cole."

Cole pivoted and stepped across the corridor to the hatch that led to his office. It opened at his approach and revealed Akyra Tomar sitting at her desk. She looked up at the hatch's opening and smiled at seeing Cole.

"Hello, sir! How'd the battle go?"

"We're towing three of our ships back to the shipyard, and many more are making provisional repairs. Lindrick is in the brig."

Akyra smiled. "I'll bet you're happy about that. I mean the 'capturing Lindrick part,' not our ships needing repairs," she rushed to add.

Cole grinned. "It's okay, Akyra. I translated. Srexx brought up a very good point. We're low on material for the recyclers and fabricators. Would you prepare a salvage claim for filing with the system authorities?"

"Of course, sir! I'll get right on it and forward the completed claim to you for review once I'm finished."

"Oh, you don't need to do that. Send it to Painter on The Gate and ask her to hire enough salvage crews to get the job done before we leave if the claim's approved."

Akyra nodded once. "Aye, sir! Consider it done."

"Thanks, Akyra," Cole replied and stepped back through the hatch to the corridor.

Sasha looked up as the hatch cycled to permit Cole's entrance to the bridge, and she smiled as she vacated the captain's chair.

"You're just in time."

There was far too much gleam in her eyes for Cole's liking. "I'm just in time for what?"

"A message just came in from the surrendered ships. I haven't reviewed it yet."

"Kicking the can up the chain, are we?"

Sasha grinned. "Why not?"

"Jenkins, my first officer tells me a message just arrived," Cole said.

"That's correct, sir."

"Might as well get it over with," Cole replied. "Put it on the forward viewscreen."

The viewscreen sprang to life, displaying the visage of woman just a few years older than Sasha. Her dark hair was in slight disarray, and grease spots dotted her forehead, left cheek, and what Cole could see of her uniform's shoulders.

"This message is for Captain Bartholomew Coleson. I'm Commander Brenna O'Keefe, and I've been chosen to represent the survivors among the surrendered ships. Please, forgive my appearance; it's been an all-hands operation just to keep life support going on my ship.

"It's impossible not to recognize the ships now moving throughout the remains of our fleet, broadcasting transponders starting with 'HES.' We don't know what 'HES' means, but all of us saw Sasha Thyrray at your shoulder during your initial communication. The survivors of our fleet have directed me to ask if you have a place for us within your organization. I understand that you probably want nothing to do with us, since we were exchanging fire not too long ago, but we're good people over here. We've never fired on life pods or block-aded jump gates. All we ask is that you give us a chance. Thank you. O'Keefe out."

Cole sat in the center seat and leaned back against it, his expression thoughtful. He looked to Sasha, asking, "Thoughts?"

"The biggest question is whether we can or should use them to fill the crew complements aboard the ships we already have."

Cole looked up at the ceiling for a moment before returning his eyes to Sasha and shaking his head. "No. As much as I'd like to think the people on our ships would be stand-up individuals, these potential recruits did just try to hammer all of us to scrap. It won't be easy for a lot of people to forget that. Besides... if they were going to hit me up for a job, why the hell didn't they surrender straight away? Why force us to reduce so many of their ships to floating graveyards... or just debris fields?" Cole sighed and pushed himself to his feet. He walked to the helm station—or at least the back of its chair—and turned, walking back. "But if we don't take them in, what happens to them? I can't imagine the people of Tristan's Gate are going to be so welcoming. I mean, the Commonwealth used to be one of their best trading partners from everything I've read. Now... now, the Commonwealth is just a source of refugees flooding their system and overloading their infrastructures, whether social, mechanical, or what have you."

"So what do we do?" Sasha asked.

"Would the SDF have been able to fight them off, if we hadn't been here?"

Sasha frowned. "Do you mean us as in *Haven* or us as in all our ships?"

"All our ships, including *Haven*."

Sasha frowned. She angled her head to the right, almost like halfway shaking it 'no,' as she grimaced. "I don't want to say 'yes,' but I don't want to say 'no,' either. Cole, Lindrick brought *a lot* of firepower. It wasn't quite the fifty-odd ships we adopted—for lack of a better term—but this wasn't a task force or task group. Not at all. This was a battle-group, an actual *armada*. The SDF would've made a valiant fight of it, and they might have delivered enough damage that Lindrick would've developed cold feet and pulled back. But if he had pushed through? He had *two* battleships, Cole. They could have taken the SDF's ships almost on their own."

Cole nodded. "Okay. Next question. You just said the SDF can't field anything larger than a light cruiser. Are they going to want any of these ships? Is General Tree-Up-Her-Ass going to give us any flack if we roll these ships into the 'HES' fleet?"

"General 'Tree-Up-Her-Ass?' Really?"

"Hey, I'm standing by that assessment. As foul as her disposition is, there's no way it's just a stick... not even a barbed stick."

Sasha pinched the bridge of her nose and sighed. "There are days when I think you're showing so much progress, and moments when you utterly remove all hope."

Cole lifted his hands as if to shrug. "What? At least I'm honest."

"I think the best thing is to escort everyone back to the station and ask for a meeting with the Prime Minister and the Defense Minister to see if they want any of the ships... and Cole? Please, *do not* refer to the commander of the SDF as 'General Tree-Up-Her-Ass' during the meeting."

"No promises."

CHAPTER FOUR

Conference Room, The Gate
   Tristan's Gate
   25 April 3000, 09:27 GST

Cole looked over the mass of people gathered in the ballroom-size space. He stood at the head of the group, at a portable table someone had provided. At the rate he was going, Cole thought he should maybe just go ahead and purchase the space, along with the offices where the interviews would be conducted.

"Is everything ready?" Cole asked.

Painter nodded. "Yes. Just like before, the interview staff—interviewers, guards, and Kiksaliks—will rotate out every four hours... four hours on, twenty hours off."

"All right. Let's get this party started." Cole lifted his right hand to his mouth and produced a shrill whistle. "Listen up, people! Thank you for coming. We will begin the interviews shortly. The finding of each interview is final; there is no appeals process. Don't lie. Don't prevaricate. We don't hire liars. We have your comms codes, and you have your scheduled timeslot for the interview. We'll have food and drinks for you shortly, but don't feel like you have to wait here. And yes, just in case anyone was about to ask, I'm ensuring everyone still aboard your ships is getting food, too. Painter, here, is in charge of the process. Disrespect her, and you won't be hired. Disrespect any of my people, and you won't be hired. That is all."

Cole turned to Painter, asking, "You good?"

"Yeah. I know how much you love public speaking. Go on, get out of here."

She didn't have to tell Cole twice. He pivoted on his heel and strode to the hatch. When it opened, he found Sasha waiting for him. He started to make a joke, then took in her expression.

"What's wrong?"

"Dad sent me a message," Sasha said. "He'd like to speak with you."

Cole nodded. "Okay. Did he say why?"

Sasha shook her head. "I mean, I could guess... but that's all it would be."

"Did he sound distressed in any way? Did he give you the impression he or your mother were in any danger?"

"Not at all. I wouldn't have bothered you if that had been the case. A detachment of Marines and I would already be on the way. He sounded... nervous. Not 'I have a laser pistol to my head' nervous, though."

Cole shrugged. "Well, no time like the present. I'll head over to their apartment now. Anything else happening I need to know about?"

"I don't think so. We still need to find someone to serve as Operations Officer. I've been kind of filling that role, but I'm supposed to be overseeing the department heads... not the department heads and one department."

"Okay. Ask Mazzi if she wants it. She'll need to recommend someone to take over as Weapons Officer if she does, though."

"I'll take her to lunch and see what she says about it in an informal conversation," Sasha said.

Cole nodded. "All right, then. Anything else?"

"I don't think so."

"Okay, then. I'm off to see your folks."

Sasha sighed. "Sometimes, Cole... you're incorrigible."

"Yeah, but life's too short to be serious all the time."

The address for Sasha's parents led Cole to one of the better residential decks several levels above the docks. Typically, the further one lived above the docks the more affluent and respected the person was. Paol Thyrray, his wife, and their son lived just two decks below the 'top' of the station.

Cole approached the apartment's hatch and pressed the chime control on the hatch panel. He didn't wait long at all. The hatch opened, the door sliding back into the bulkhead and revealing Sasha's brother. He stood just inside the hatch, dressed in a 'casual' suit made of a fabric that cost more credits per yard than some people spent on food in two months. He held a snifter in his right hand, and for the briefest moments, Cole saw a sneer before Nathyn schooled his features into a welcoming smile that didn't touch his eyes.

"Ah, Captain Cole! Do come in. Father said he'd summoned you."

"He 'summoned' me, did he?" Cole asked.

"Well, yes. Didn't you get the message?" Nathyn asked, missing the tone in Cole's voice.

"Sasha said your father asked if I had time to speak with him, but she made no mention of a summons."

Nathyn waved away Cole's statement. "Well, of course! It's always better to approach matters with the velvet glove instead of the iron gauntlet beneath it. We *are* Thyrrays, after all."

"Yes... I suppose you are."

"We need to sit down and discuss where we will be of most bene-fit," Nathyn continued, still oblivious to Cole's tone and darkening expression. "After all, we are exceptional people with enormous name recognition. Frankly, I'm surprised you haven't called upon us sooner."

"Excuse me?"

"Well, of course, we excuse you. You're a peasant freighter pilot who got lucky. You can't be expected to understand the nuances of leading people. That's why you need us in positions of authority and leadership. We will guide your growing empire and build it into the best version it could possibly be."

Cole scratched the left side of his jaw as he glared at the back of Nathyn's head. The longer he thought about the situation, the angrier he became. The last thing he wanted, though, was to alienate Sasha. She was his first officer, and he needed her far more than she needed him, even if there were few places she was safe from the bounties and warrants still levied against her by the Commonwealth. But Cole wasn't the type to hold that over a person's head.

"I don't think we have much to discuss," Cole said, putting all his willpower into diplomacy. "I'll just be on my way."

"Now, see here! You were summoned by Paol Thyrray," Nathyn said, his voice rising, "and he hasn't given you leave to depart. We are your *betters*, you jumped-up pirate."

"Nathyn? What's going on?" a voice asked, right before Paol stepped into the room.

Cole glared at Nathyn, his visage fit to melt a starship's armor. "I have never *once* considered being a bounty hunter, but I will not tolerate your attitude. I have half a mind to ship your entitled, worthless ass back to the Commonwealth, and damn the consequences. If you have even a shred of the wisdom possessed by an errant street child, you will go a damn long time before you contact me again."

Cole pivoted on his heel and headed for the hatch.

"Cole, please! Wait!" Paol said as he stepped past his son.

Cole stepped through the hatch and stopped in the corridor, turning to face Sasha's father as he said, "Give me one reason why I should."

Paol stopped. His mouth moved as if he meant to speak, but no words came. After a moment, Paol sighed. "I don't have one. I apologize for my son's behavior. He wasn't always like that... or at least, I didn't *think* he was. If you can find forgive—"

"Father!" Nathyn cried, aghast. "There is no reason to debase yourself before—"

Paol pivoted to face his son. "You've made enough of a mess of this. Be silent, or go elsewhere." Turning back to Cole, he continued. "If you can forgive me, I would like a few moments of your time."

Almost every fiber of Cole's being screamed for him to turn and leave without another word. Nathyn's conduct thus far demonstrated he was the exact *opposite* of the type of people Cole wanted on his team, and Cole didn't feel even slightly calm enough to summon a clear head for any kind of important discussion. Still, though... there was Sasha. She was one of his people, and Cole would crawl over ground glass for one of his people.

"Fine," Cole said, adding a sigh. "Your son has done an excellent job of predisposing me against whatever you have to say, so I advise you to be rather eloquent."

"Could we... step inside?" Paol asked. "I'd prefer not to broach the topic in a public corridor."

Cole stepped toward the hatch by way of an answer. Paol turned, leading Cole back into the apartment and gestured toward the available seating, saying, "Please, be seated."

Cole sat, and Paol followed suit.

"I asked Sasha if you had time to speak with me to discuss a... delicate... matter. Cole, we survive at the sufferance of my wife's parents. This apartment is theirs, an artifact of a time they routinely traveled to the station. It's no secret that you're building a rather impressive organization. Sev has spoken more than once of the work you've given him. I asked Sasha if you had any time for me, because I was hoping to discuss employment with you."

"Paol, I'll be honest with you. You don't want me to answer that right now. I'm not exactly in the most neutral frame of mind. Work up a resume with your skills, talents, and interests, and send it to Akyra Tomar."

"Are you *insane*? Drunk on power?" Nathyn exploded. "Paol Thyrray *does not* write resumes. You should be explaining why we should consider working for you!"

Paol sighed, lowering his head for a moment before returning his gaze to Cole. "Yes, I see what you mean. I'll send something over as soon as I can."

"Then, I think we're done here," Cole said, standing.

. . .

Cole departed the Thyrrays' apartment and went straight to O'Shaughnessy's. It was just 10:47, but Cole didn't care. He was in the foulest mood he could remember in recent weeks, thanks to Sasha's brother.

The pub was just opening for the pre-lunch and lunch crowds when Cole arrived, and he wasn't sure there was another customer in the place. He sat on a stool in front of the bar and waited the few seconds for the bartender to arrive.

"So, what'll it be?"

Cole grimaced. "I'm not sure. I just spent about a half-hour with the most conceited, entitled jackass I've had to endure in recent memory. What do you recommend?"

The bartender stood there for a moment. "You're Cole, right? That captain who rescued the Howlers and the Thyrrays?"

Cole nodded.

"I imagine a lot of people are wanting a piece of you after all that success."

"I'm not exactly short of applications."

The bartender turned, pulled a bottle off a shelf, and filled a shot glass almost to the brim. He placed the glass in front of Cole.

"On the house. I feel kind of sorry for you."

Cole picked up the glass and threw it back, swallowing the entire drink in one gulp. It was rather smooth, all things considered. He placed the glass back on the bar and nodded.

"Thanks," Cole said, standing up from the bar. He slipped his hand into his pocket and fished around, withdrawing a palm full of credit chits. He saw one marked '50' and dropped it on the bar by the empty glass. "Keep the change. I don't like 'on the house,' too many ways for good people to get into trouble. I appreciate the thought, though."

Cole turned and left the pub.

———

Painter looked up as Cole approached her table. The lunch carts ran down one bulkhead, presenting a buffet of incredible variety.

"How goes it?" Cole asked.

Painter nodded. "Oh, it goes. We've only had five so far that the Kiksaliks straight-up refused."

"A part of me wonders what we're going to do with all these people."

Painter shrugged. "We need experienced ship handlers to collect resources to build the station and shipyard in Beta Magellan, not to mention construction workers with zero-g experience. They may not have construction time, but everyone here is a veteran spacer with all kinds of zero-g hours. It won't be glamorous, but it will be a job. And they'll be safe. What brings you back here? I thought you went back to the ship."

"Don't get me started. Sasha waylaid me with a ringer of a meeting."

"That doesn't sound like something Sasha would do," Painter replied, frowning.

"Oh, I'm sure she had no idea how it would go down. That doesn't change the fact that I think the last hour would've been better spent shooting myself in the foot several times. Okay. I'm going back to the ship to check on the other irons in the fire. Call me if you need me."

Cole trudged back to the ship, his head down and his hands in his pockets. The past couple days circled through his mind. Jumped-up pirate? Ha... if that twit only knew. He'd met *real* pirates during the Jax years. Some of them, you'd never know. Others? Yeah, they looked the part.

Cole's mind drifted to Red Pattel, the Pirate Lord of Sector 82. Oh, yes. Cole met her once. He'd even had her comms code for a time, but that piece of information didn't survive Srexx melting his old implant. Fewer than ten people even knew Red Pattel was a *she*, and she'd wanted Cole—well, Jax—to join her crew. Not to mention she was rather pretty.

Turning down the corridor that led to his airlock, Cole sighed. No. Red had been right. Cole wasn't a follower. It just wasn't in his make-up. Whether it was something he'd absorbed growing up at the knee of the most powerful businessman in Human space or perhaps just a part of who he was, Cole was a leader. He charted his own course. He believed loyalty was a two-way street. Take care of your people, and they will take care of you. Nathyn Thyrray wouldn't take care of his people. Cole knew that for sure and certain.

Which put him in a serious fix. *Paol* Thyrray was a statesman, the latest scion of a long line renowned for their work in lifting the Aurelian Commonwealth to the greatness it enjoyed not all that long ago. Cole needed a statesman for what he wanted to achieve in Beta Magellan. But he *didn't* need a conceited, entitled twit who would prey on others. Not at all.

All of which meant the question of hiring Paol Thyrray would be very tricky, indeed.

CHAPTER FIVE

"Cole, do you have a few moments?" Srexx asked as Cole stepped through the inner hatch of the airlock.

Cole smiled, entertaining thoughts of turning Srexx loose on Nathyn. "Sure, buddy. What do you need?"

"Could you come to your office, please?"

"On my way."

Cole arrived at the hatch leading to his office just as one of Srexx's bots arrived with a box. Cole eyed the box with curiosity and led the bot through Akyra's office to his.

"Okay, Srexx... what do you have?"

"Since becoming aware of the jump gate network, I have examined several methods of improving it. My preliminary scans gave me sufficient information to hypothesize it might be possible to modify the jump gates to act more like *Haven*'s hyperdrive. I rejected this idea, however, because every society's economy we have encountered seems built upon the framework that the jump gates are a point-to-point infrastructure, instead of point-to-multipoint. Introducing such a modification, while an improvement for ships traveling, would create more problems from an economic standpoint."

The bot placed the box on Cole's desk and opened it. The bot then withdrew a device that looked very much like an old-style computer terminal.

"This, Cole, is my solution to helping you improve Human society. It is a quantum communications node. The jump gates already serve as a communications relay system. By adding a quantum comms node to each jump gate, we will make it possible for messages to traverse vast distances in miniscule amounts of time. I designed this particular unit to serve as a testing platform. *Haven* already possesses the equivalent to a quantum comms node, as does anyone with one of my implants. This device will permit a person or persons we designate to communicate with any quantum-comms-enabled location at will."

Cole stared at the device, blinking.

"Wow, buddy. This is... this is nice. We need to test it."

"Yes, Cole. I thought you might want to leave this unit with Painter and Sev, perhaps in their offices, when we depart for Alpha Centauri. We can then test it by calling them at various points in our journey."

Cole nodded. "I've been thinking about that. I don't think we're going straight to Alpha Centauri."

"Where are we going, then?"

"Aurelius."

Silence.

"You believe interrogating Lindrick will provide sufficient information to exonerate the Thyrrays."

"There's no 'belief' about it," Cole countered. "He already has. Garrett decided to use the 'truth gas' plan Harlon mentioned. Lindrick has been volunteering information right and left—not to mention cussing himself for doing so—and we've been recording it. He's given us a number of places to look for information to corroborate his answers, even if those places are in the Aurelian data-net. So, yeah... we're going to Aurelius. I haven't told Sasha, yet, though. I'd appreciate it if you kept this to yourself."

"Of course, Cole. Will you be taking Nathyn Thyrray with you?"

Cole snorted. "Not hardly. I'm going to Aurelius to get the warrants and bounties on Sasha and her family removed. It makes no sense to offer up Nathyn for the bounty I would then be demanding they vacate. Besides, serving up Nathyn for a bounty would probably cost me my first officer anyway. Not really something I want to happen. This comms node is good work, though. Thank you, Srexx."

"You're welcome, Cole."

The bot spun and left Cole's office. Cole followed it as far as Akyra's office.

"So, anything happen I need to know while I was gone?" Cole asked.

Akyra shook her head. "Nope. All quiet. The system authorities approved the salvage claim on the wreckage, and I forwarded the approval to Painter. She's covered up in interviews right now, so I'm helping her sort out the salvage before someone jumps our claim."

"You really think we need to worry about that?" Cole asked.

Akyra's eyes drifted over her surroundings for a few moments before she shook her head. "No. Probably not. No one around Tristan's Gate would be crazy enough to try stealing from you." She blushed and looked away.

"What?" Cole asked. "There was a thought, there."

"Oh... uhm... well... I still kinda keep an ear to the ground in the shadier parts of life."

Cole nodded as he processed that. "So, you're saying you still keep up with criminal underworld?"

"Yes. I don't *do* anything, just visit bars on the L decks and listen to people talk. You have those people completely cowed, you know. Yesterday, I was getting a drink after we docked from the battle. There was a guy from out-system, not really sure from where, but he kept trying to work up a crew to raid the wreckage... specifically because our salvage claim application was already public. Whoever this guy was, he *wanted* to steal from us."

Cole grinned. "Oh? What happened?"

"Eight guys kicked his ass and threw him out. The last thing I heard them say to him was, 'We don't mess with the Lone Marine around here, jackass. Go commit suicide somewhere else.' I almost snorted my beer when I heard that."

"It's nice to have a reputation, I guess," Cole replied with a slight shrug. "You doing well, otherwise?"

"Yes, sir! It was a little rough right after I signed on. That's why Yeleth assigned me as your yeoman, after all, but things have evened out. Turns out, I enjoy the work more than I expected I would. Who would've thought I had a talent for executive-assistant-type stuff?"

"I'm glad you enjoy it. I appreciate all your effort and time."

"You're very welcome, sir. I appreciate you not leaving me in Iota Ceti. Don't forget you have a meeting with Juliana Painter and Sev Vance aboard the station. You have forty-five minutes, but I didn't want you to get side-tracked."

———

Cole and Sev looked up from their holographic cards and the holographic pile of match-sticks in the center of the table when Painter entered the conference room. She was thirty minutes late.

"Don't say it," Painter almost growled as she almost collapsed into a seat. "The interviews are going well, and I was wrapped up in starting the next round. I'm here as soon as I could be."

Cole and Sev each looked to one another, and Sev made a miniscule movement Cole took for a gesture that he should handle it. Cole smiled, waving the matter away.

"Don't worry about it, Painter. You're overworked; everyone is to a degree. If you ever think you're unappreciated or underpaid, tell me at once, and I'll complain to the management."

Painter looked at Cole, her expression unreadable. "You *are* the management, Cole."

"So, I can't kick the can up the chain?"

"Nope. The credit chit stops at you."

"I guess I need to re-think my business model. I'm not sure it's working out as I intended." Cole scrunched his face into an absurd grin.

Painter smiled, which led to a chuckle.

"Feel better?" Cole asked.

"Actually, yes."

Cole nodded once. "Good. Anything else I can do?"

"Thanks, but I'll manage. So, who's winning?"

"Who do you think?" Sev asked. "He's a mean bluff, and he has no tells that I've been able to find."

Cole shrugged. "You could always assume I'm bluffing every time."

Sev scoffed, and Painter laughed.

"Yeah, that would work *so* well," Sev replied. "At least you talked me out of playing for real credits."

Cole smiled. "You're welcome. So, any updates on the refugee situation?"

"The refugees already here are growing restless," Sev said. "There aren't enough jobs for the number of people the system has now, and ships are still arriving almost daily with more refugees aboard."

"I've spoken with a few of the freighter captains," Painter said, "and they paint a pretty scary picture of what's going on inside the Commonwealth. The Provisional Parliament is suppressing dissenters and imprisoning opponents in the systems they completely control. They don't seem to be blockading the jump gates anymore, but they have taken up searching ships leaving planets and stations, trying to stem the tide of people fleeing their territory. They've had to institute state-owned freighters to transport trade goods, because independent freighters aren't staying. They're leaving the Commonwealth in droves and not coming back... all the while taking as many people as they can. There are even some brave souls going *back* for more refugees. I don't know how they're keeping from getting imprisoned and their ship impounded, myself."

Cole nodded, shifting his attention to Sev. "How's the system leadership? What's their stance in all this?"

Sev grimaced. "They're caught in the middle, Cole. They really are. On the one side, they abhor what these people are facing back home, and they don't blame them at all for wanting to go somewhere—anywhere—else. On the other side, though, there are something like seventeen thousand Commonwealth refugees in the system, and the system's economy and institutions were stable before the refugees' arrival. There wasn't a lot of growth, but it was stable, organic growth. The sudden influx of seventeen thousand people in weeks is straining every aspect of the system. The leadership doesn't want to turn anyone away, but they don't know how they can accept many more people before things start collapsing."

"Well then... I think they'll be receptive to my plan. What's the status on the construction company? How close are they to starting the assembly of the temporary station in Beta Magellan?"

"That's going fairly well. We're nearing completion on staging the materials, and the company is eager for us to canvass the refugees for anyone with construction and zero-g experience. The job's foreman says we should have the habitation modules ready for occupancy inside of six months if we start soon, with the industrial yards not too far behind that. Say... maybe eight months till we can start working toward permanent infrastructure for the system. These are all estimates, though. It could go better, or it could go worse. We won't know until it happens."

"That sounds like things are proceeding well. Can one or both of you set up an appointment for us to meet with the system leadership? I'd like their permission and support in meeting with the refugees."

Sev and Painter nodded, Sev saying, "We'll keep Akyra in the loop as things develop."

"Good," Cole said. "Is there anything else?"

Sev and Painter looked to each other, both finally shaking their heads.

"No," Painter said. "I don't think so."

"Sounds good. Find me if you need me." Cole pushed back from the table and stood, leaving the conference room.

———

O'Shaughnessy's, The Gate
25 April 3000, 18:22 GST

The sounds of a busy and populated common room settled around Cole's shoulders as he entered O'Shaughnessy's. He waved at the bartender as he passed, but Cole didn't stop at the bar. It was packed, anyway. Threading his way through the tables filled with people and servers on the move, Cole approached his destination: one of the semi-private booths in the darkened back of the common room. Garrett waited for him.

Cole slid into the booth across the table from Garrett and nodded in greeting.

"From what I'm hearing, you've had a busy time of it," Garrett said, "or at least, Painter has."

Cole grinned. "She has indeed. She isn't ready to quit on me yet, though. Well, I don't think so, anyway."

Garrett chuckled. "No. She's not even entertaining the thought."

"Oh? How do you know?"

"She has received a number of offers from various mercantile concerns. The offers always praise her business acumen, but the under-lying message is they want her to bring whatever she can of your secrets with her. The pay they're offering—both in signing bonuses and salary—is impressive."

Cole blinked. "Do I want to know how you came into that information?"

Garrett shook his head. "No. Probably not. Intelligence work is a lot like making laws and sausages. Everyone wants it done, but no one wants the full details."

"Fair enough. How goes everything?"

"Our guest is being *very* cooperative. Harlon was right. He's volun-teering stuff I would've never thought to ask. And yes... I've been recording it all. What are you going to do with all this?"

"We're not heading straight to Alpha Centauri when we leave. I'm taking the ship to Aurelius, and I'm not leaving until those warrants and bounties on the Thyrrays are quashed. I promised Sasha I'd make them go away when we first met. Lindrick's testimony and whatever we dig up when we arrive in Aurelius will give me the leverage I need."

Garrett nodded, sipping his beer. "Speaking of the Common-wealth... I'm picking up whispers that the Rigellian Alliance and the Sirius Imperium might enter the fray. The partisans already engaged in the conflict have been trying to use it as a cover to settle old scores, and both the Rigellians and the Imperium have lost shipping over the past few weeks. I don't have concrete information on who pulled those triggers, but this mess is going to get *a lot* worse before it gets better."

"All that does is spread the misery around," Cole replied, pursing his lips and shaking his head as he sighed. "The average citizen doesn't want this war. They prove that by trying to flee wherever and whenever they can."

"I know," Garrett agreed. "Tristan's Gate is almost to the breaking point. If something doesn't change soon, things will have the potential to get nasty. There are already anti-refugee groups starting to pop up. It won't be long before they start campaigning."

The conversation flagged as Cole gave his drink order to their server.

Garrett watched the server leave, waiting for the individual to pass out of earshot.

"I want you with us when we go to Alpha Centauri," Cole said. "Will that pose a problem for your operations?"

Garrett shook his head. "Most of my people use message drops. I just make the digital rounds and collect whatever's waiting. The ones who normally don't can start. Oh... Lindrick gave me a piece you'll want to know; he mentioned it in our last interview, right before I came here."

"What?"

"He told me the people who hired him to massacre Beta Magellan were Solars."

Cole's eyes bulged. "Did he know who they were? What made him so certain?"

"He said the ship they arrived in to meet with him broadcast a Solar Republic transponder... and that he verified it as legitimate. Whoever they were, they weren't professional spies."

Cole nodded. "Guess it's a good thing we're going to Alpha Centauri soon. You'll be much better positioned to follow up on that."

"You can bet the ship on that," Garrett agreed.

The rest of the conversation drifted to other topics, and soon, Cole and Garrett returned to the ship, laughing over old times when Garrett had been teaching Cole how to survive as Jax Theedlow.

CHAPTER SIX

Docking Slip 12, The Gate
  Tristan's Gate
  26 April 3000, 08:35 GST

Cole entered Akyra's office, a drinks carrier holding his cup of tea and Akyra's coffee in his left hand and an asiago-cheese bagel in his right. He approached the desk and placed the drinks carrier on the corner, removing Akyra's and handing it to her.

"Thank you, sir," Akyra purred, just before taking a sip. She closed her eyes, a smile curling her lips. "Mmm... that's good. Just what I needed."

"I asked the personnel in the mess hall what you normally grabbed for breakfast, but no one had an answer for me."

Akyra smiled. "I normally don't get breakfast, sir, and if I'm thirsty, I'll just get something from the dispenser."

Cole saw something in her eyes he wasn't sure he liked... some kind of veiled hurt or discomfort.

"What about lunch?" Cole asked.

"Oh... I put an order in and the mess-hands deliver it when they bring the orders from the bridge watch-standers."

Cole's eyes narrowed. "We're going to talk about whatever *that* is. I've had the feeling for a quite a while now that you almost hide out in here, and I won't have it. This ship is just as much your home as anyone else's, and if there's a reason you don't feel welcome in any of the mess halls, I want to know about it."

Akyra's eyes widened until she looked like a small animal facing an apex predator.

"Oh, no, sir," she stammered. "There's nothing wrong. I didn't want... I mean, I didn't... there's no reason for you to think that, sir."

Cole eyed her for a few moments more before nodding. "Very well. If you would, please pass my compliments to Sasha and Yeleth, and ask them to meet with me at their earliest convenience. Make it clear they should coordinate to arrive together, please."

Akyra almost trembled as she jerked a nod. "Yes, sir."

Ten minutes later, Sasha and Yeleth arrived in Cole's office.

"You wanted to see us, sir?" Sasha asked.

Cole regarded her with a single, raised eyebrow, and the silence extended.

Sasha sighed. "You wanted to see us, *Cole?*"

Cole smiled and nodded, enjoying Yeleth's suppressed amusement at their dance.

"Please, be comfortable. A matter of concern aboard this ship has risen to my attention, and I want the source investigated."

"What is it?"

"Akyra Tomar doesn't feel welcome aboard this ship. She hides out in the yeoman's office and gets drinks from the dispensers. She doesn't eat breakfast and orders lunch with the bridge watch-standers. Stars only know what she does for dinner. Admittedly, the 'no breakfast' thing might not be a symptom of whatever this is. I usually just eat a bagel, myself." Cole took a breath and shook his head. "Long story short, whatever this is stops now. Today. I named this ship *Haven* for a reason, and I expect

everyone aboard to get with the program or get another job. You have
one week. If the situation persists after that, Srexx and I will take over the
matter, and the person or persons responsible—even if it's half the
bleeding crew—will be summarily dismissed and blackballed from any
organization over which I have authority or influence. Am I understood?"

Sasha regarded Cole with barely disguised surprise, and Cole understood why. She'd never seen this side of him. Yeleth, on the other hand,
bore the look of a predator with an opportunity to hunt... a very satisfied predator.

"Yes, sir," Sasha said, and for once, Cole didn't feel like sparring
with her about the 'sir.'

"If the matter is resolved within the week, I don't need names. I
don't care who was behind it, and I'm not interested in flogging anyone
before the crew. But... you make sure and certain every sentient aboard
gets the message that these fools have used up my patience and
forgiveness for *everyone*. Any future incidents like this will result in
that summary dismissal I mentioned, and the offending individual will
find him, her, or itself standing in whatever port is closest to us at the
time. I consider the next seven days to be the second chance. There
will not be a third." Cole took another breath and nodded once. "Okay.
That's it. Thank you."

Both replied with, "You're welcome," though Sasha's was more
tentative, and they vacated the office.

The hatch to the outer office hadn't been closed more than five
minutes when it irised open once more, and Akyra peeked in.

"Sir, do you have a moment?"

Cole smiled. "Of course, Akyra. What do you need?"

"I just received a message from Paol Thyrray. He attached his
resume to it and said you told him he should send it to me."

"Huh... he actually did it." Cole blinked a couple times, shaking his
head. "Well, lost that bet."

"Sir?" Akyra asked, frowning.

Cole waved it away. "Just vocalized mental chatter, Akyra. Nothing
note-worthy. Copy that resume to me, please."

Akyra nodded. "Yes, sir."

Not even a minute later, Cole's workstation beeped to alert him about a new message. He checked, and it was Akyra sending him Paol's resume. Jotting a quick 'Thanks!' off to Akyra, Cole opened the file Paol had sent.

Cole had no idea what a resume was supposed to look like. He'd never written one. Still, though, the document displayed in holographic screen told him a lot about Paol's skills and experience. Cole's focus landed on Paol's time in the Commonwealth Judiciary and Parliament.

A chime drew Cole's attention, and the accompanying alert informed him he had a meeting scheduled with the leadership of Tristan's Gate in just under an hour. Cole closed the resume and stood, closing down his workstation.

He stepped through the hatch to Akyra's office and stopped beside her desk.

"I have that meeting with the system leadership," Cole said.

Akyra nodded. "I was just about to remind you, sir."

"Good. Please, forward that resume to Painter and Sev, and ask them for their availability for an interview over the next couple of days. Pick a day that's not today, and schedule it with Paol. Things are winding down for us here in Tristan's Gate, so don't push it too far out."

Akyra nodded. "Consider it done, sir."

Cole nodded once, smiling. "Thank you."

He turned and left to meet up with Sev and Painter.

———

The meeting room bore many similarities to a hearing room. Rows of seating for spectators formed a gallery that occupied almost half of the space. A thigh-high divider—tastefully disguised as a stylized wooden barrier complete with a swiveling gate like those in ancient, Old Earth court documentaries—separated the gallery from a space containing a single table with a single chair. All this faced a raised semi-circle of seats in three rows of stadium-style seating behind a barrier that bore an eerie resemblance to a judge's bench. Only Cole, Sev, Painter, and Sasha occupied the room.

At the appointed time, doors on either side of the semi-circle opened, admitting several people. Cole recognized the Prime Minister and the Defense Minister. The rest Cole didn't know. The Prime Minister sat in the center seat of the lowest row. The Defense Minister sat to his right. Everyone else filled the remaining seats.

"Okay," the Prime Minister said. "Let's get started. I'm going to ask you to introduce your party, and fair's fair. As most of you know, I'm Geralt Hanson. To my right is Defense Minister Stone. The people with us are representatives of the System Legislature, coming from several different committees and sub-committees. Your turn."

Cole stood. "Thank you for agreeing to meet with me today. I am Bartholomew James Coleson, but I prefer 'Cole.' This is Juliana Painter, Sevrin Vance, and Sasha Thyrray. Painter and Sev are my local managers, and Sasha is my first officer."

"Thank you," Hanson said. "So, why are we here today?"

"I need people. My information leads me to believe that Tristan's Gate has a refugee problem. I think we can help each other."

"Succinct and to the point," Hanson said. "Please, elaborate."

"I imagine most of you know that my family colonized Beta Magellan, ending in a massacre almost fourteen years ago now. What many of you might *not* know is that my father intended to relocate Coleson Interstellar Engineering to Beta Magellan, as the basis for the system's economy. I've since learned my father and grandfather believed innovation within the Solar Republic is waning, and soon, this region of space would surpass the Solar Republic. He wanted CIE positioned to capitalize on that.

"I have a system that could support billions—if not trillions—of people and the capability to ensure their safety. You might have noticed my ship."

"Many of us have noticed you have a 'fleet' that outnumbers the SDF by a considerable margin," one of the legislative representatives said. "More than one of us are wondering if—or when—you'll decide to use them."

"With all due respect, ma'am, I already have," Cole said. "Two days ago, I defended this system and its citizens from Draketh Lindrick and his people. In November, I assisted in fending off a would-be occupation of this system as well. Those ships I have accepted were instrumental in both actions. Beyond defending this system, I have funneled millions of credits—possibly billions—into your economy, buying regolith and unwanted ore as well as hiring the shipyard to repair and upgrade those very ships as well as build the small craft needed aboard *Haven* and paying for outfitting and supplies through the chandlery."

"I would argue that Cole's commitment to friendship toward Tristan's Gate is beyond reproach," Defense Minister Stone said. "He has done nothing but serve as a role model for others."

"Please continue," Hanson said, gesturing to Cole.

Cole nodded. "As I was saying, I asked for this meeting to seek your support and permission to present the refugees with an alternative to Tristan's Gate. I'm putting together a colonization initiative for Beta Magellan, which will be very supportive of early signatories. I offer homes and jobs."

"Just for the sake of discussion," another legislator spoke up, "let's say you're successful in building up Beta Magellan. Let's say you become a power in your own right, as I believe the ship you command almost guarantees. What will be your position toward unaligned systems like Tristan's Gate?"

"Approach me and mine in friendship and trade, and we will do the same. Approach with violence and hostility? Well... may the stars have mercy on you, because I certainly won't."

Several among the leadership smiled. The legislator who asked the question said, "You're not much of a politician, are you, son?"

"Sir, I don't believe any of us have the time not to say what we mean. No one will ever have the occasion to question where they stand with me."

"So, what I'm taking away from your proposal," Hanson said, "is that you would like our support and permission to present an offer to the refugees in the system to be a part of your initiative to re-colonize Beta Magellan. Is that correct?"

Cole nodded. "That is correct, sir."

"And if you're successful, not only will you lessen the strain on our infrastructure by taking the refugees, but we just might have a new trading partner in a few years."

"That is also correct, sir."

Hanson scanned the faces of those around him, before saying, "I think the next step is for you to forward your proposal for that colonization initiative. No one should agree to support something they haven't seen with their own eyes."

Cole grinned. "Of course not, sir. We need to finalize some of the verbiage," more like write the stupid thing in the first place, "but we can provide that to you rather soon."

"Excellent, Mr. Coleson. Let's adjourn for now. We'll be in touch after seeing that proposal."

Hanson stood, leading the others to follow suit, and everyone left the conference room.

CHAPTER SEVEN

Docking Slip 12, The Gate
  Tristan's Gate
  27 April 3000, 10:13 GST

Akyra brought up the comms function of her workstation and went through her list of contacts, selecting 'Paol Thyrray' from the list and keying the command to place a holo call. The workstation's interface shifted to an oval viewing area, and the text 'Initiating Call' flashed in the center. Within moments the text vanished, replaced by a view of Paol Thyrray from his head to his shoulders.

"Hello?" Paol asked.

Akyra smiled. "Good morning, Mr. Thyrray. I am Akyra Tomar, and I work with Cole as... well... an executive assistant, for want of a better term. He asked me to call and schedule an interview with you. I have Cole's schedule open here, as well as the schedules of the other parties involved. There is an opening this afternoon, if that's not too short notice, but there is also some time tomorrow. I'm afraid I can't offer any times further in the future. Cole is intent on departing within three days."

Paol blinked. "Oh! Oh, my. I honestly didn't expect to receive this call. This afternoon works for me. Where should I be, and when should I be there?"

"If you didn't expect to receive *this* call, may I ask what call you expected to receive?"

A faint blush colored Paol's cheeks as he answered, "Well, to be truthful, I was expecting an impersonal message saying there were no positions available at this time. I'm afraid Cole didn't have the best experience when he called on me the other day."

"Ah," Akyra replied. "I can assure you that is not the case. Cole was *very* interested to see you'd sent the resume. Had the visit been more congenial, I strongly suspect he would've bypassed the bulk of the interview process altogether."

Paol nodded. "I suspected as much. So... where do I need to be, and when do I need to be there?"

"How does 2:30 this afternoon sound?"

"That sounds fine."

Akyra nodded once and keyed the commands to add the meeting to all four schedules she had open. "Very good, sir. The interview will take place in Suite E—as in 'Echo'—of Office Complex Seven on U-Three. Do you have any further questions?"

Paol shook his head. "None, thank you."

"Excellent! I look forward to meeting you, and I recommend you not be late. Goodbye."

Akyra closed the comms call and locked the meeting into the schedule for herself, Cole, Sev, and Painter. She'd make sure a Kiksalik accompanied her from the ship.

———

Cole entered the outer office where Sasha's yeoman would be—if she had a yeoman—and proceeded through to her actual office. The hatch irised open at his approach, and he peeked inside the compartment.

Sasha sat at her desk, manipulating the holo display of her workstation, and she looked his way when he peeked inside.

"Hi," Cole said. "Have a minute or three?"

"Cole, you're the captain. I have all day if that's what you need."

Cole grinned and stepped inside the office. Sasha gestured to the chairs across from her, and Cole sat.

"So... do we have an Operations Officer yet?"

Sasha shook her head. "No. I haven't had time to speak with Mazzi yet. Have you spoken to her about it?"

"Nope," Cole replied. "Number One, I didn't want to step on your toes, and Number Two, it's usually the middle of the night when I remember it."

"Yeah... good call on that; waking her up to ask about her career plans probably isn't the wisest choice." Sasha keyed a command on the panel near the right corner of her desk, and the overhead speakers chirped. "Sasha to Mazzi."

The speakers made a double chirp and broadcast Mazzi's reply, "Mazzi here, Commander."

"Do you have a few minutes available so you could stop by my office?"

"Of course, ma'am," Mazzi answered. "I'm on the way. Will there be anything else?"

"Not till you arrive, thanks. Sasha out."

The speakers chirped once again, and Sasha shifted her eyes back to Cole. "Now, we wait."

Just out of fun, Cole started a timer in his implant. At three minutes, sixteen seconds, the hatch irised open to admit Mazzi. She stepped to the edge of the desk and said, "You asked for me, ma'am?"

Cole moved to the chair in the corner created by the bulkhead and Sasha's desk, and Sasha gestured for Mazzi to sit.

"What are your career goals?" Sasha asked.

"Excuse me, ma'am?" Mazzi asked. "I'm not sure I understand."

"It's not a trick question," Cole stated, entering the conversation. "Where do you see yourself career-wise in... say... five years? Or maybe ten years?"

Mazzi blinked. "Uh... well... before the Commonwealth imploded, I thought I'd work up the ranks to command an SDF ship. I hadn't gotten around to deciding what my dream ship was."

"Do you still like the idea of commanding a ship?" Cole asked.

Mazzi chuckled. "With all due respect, sir, that's not going to happen. The Commonwealth is imploding. Besides, I resigned from the Caledonian SDF."

Cole resisted the urge to slap his forehead with his palm. "Mazzi, I want you to think about something for me. This ship now has a full complement of small craft, what the wet navies of our distant, distant past would call fighters and bombers. That's not even mentioning the assault shuttles for the marines aboard. I hired the shipyard in this system to build those craft from schematics Srexx had from the civilization that built this ship. I also have the schematics for almost *every* starship they designed. Several types of frigates. Destroyers. Light Cruisers. Cruisers. Heavy Cruisers. Oh... and let's not forget the Battle-Carriers, or the utterly terrifying Dreadnought. I'm not all that certain I want to crack open the schematics on the Dreadnought, though; it's a whole lot of ship, practically a station with a hyperdrive. Depending on how well Sev Vance does his job, we may be laying down keels for the ships that will become *Haven*'s carrier battle-group inside two years. So, I'll ask you this time. What are your career plans?"

Mazzi stared at Cole. "You mean they built a ship *bigger* than this one?"

Cole nodded. "Srexx told me he knew of four on operational status, and there may have been more under construction."

Mazzi grinned. "So, what you're saying is that you have plans to build a fleet."

"Right this moment, I'm just planning for Beta Magellan to have a 'home guard' and for *Haven* to have a full battle-group. I figure that's enough right there."

"I want in, sir."

"We have an opening for Operations Officer," Sasha said. "The Operations Officer is third-in-command, after Cole and me. All departments involved in the day-to-day operations of the ship that are not part of Support, Engineering, or Flight Ops report to the Operations Officer. It's the next step toward a command of your own."

Mazzi grinned again. "I accept."

"*Haven*?" Cole asked, angling his face toward the overhead speakers.

"Yes, Cole-Captain?"

Cole frowned while the ladies smirked. "As of this date and time, log Alessandra Mazzi's promotion to Lieutenant Commander and assignment as Operations Officer, per my authority."

"So logged, Cole-Captain."

Cole shifted his attention back to Mazzi, saying, "You'll be able to obtain proper rank insignia from any dispenser."

"Your first task as Operations Officer," Sasha said, "is to select and train your replacement Weapons Officer. We're expecting light duty over the coming weeks, so you should have no problem getting the selectee—and yourself—acclimated to the new duties."

"Yes, sir, and ma'am," Mazzi said. "Thank you for your confidence in me. I won't let you down."

"You're welcome," Cole said, "and besides, you've earned it by my evaluation. Now... if you ladies will excuse me, I have somewhere I need to be."

———

Suite E, Office Complex Seven
    U-Three Deck, The Gate
    27 April 3000, 14:00 GST

Cole, Sev, and Painter waited in seats placed in the center of the table. Akyra occupied a seat off to the side with a Kiksalik beside her, and ship's marines were ready at both corners on Cole's side of the table, their arms and armor on prominent display.

Cole, Sev, and Painter chatted amongst themselves while Akyra made sure everything was ready to record the interview. The Kiksalik and marines waited in silence.

At 14:15 on the dot, the hatch opened to admit Paol Thyrray. He wore 'business casual' attire and carried a folio. He crossed the short distance to stand at the back of the sole chair on his side of the table and held the folio in front of him, both hands side-by-side near the folio's center.

"Good afternoon," Paol said. "I'm here for the interview."

"Please, be seated," Painter said.

Paol sat and placed his folio on the table in front of him, placing his hands in his lap after that.

"As everyone is here," Sev said, "does anyone mind starting a little early?"

No one gainsaid the idea.

"Very well," Painter said. "I am Juliana Painter, head of shipping for Haven Enterprises. The gentleman to my far left is Sevrin Vance, head of infrastructure for Haven Enterprises, and Cole is the sole owner of the company. To give you a better understanding of what we're doing, Haven Enterprises is working to establish a thriving system in Beta Magellan. The system is very wealthy in resources as well as available land; there are two Earth-type planets in the habitable zone, and they have already been terraformed to support life. Beyond that, we have two task groups surveying the unclaimed systems near Beta Magellan and placing claims markers in those systems. Thus far, we have claimed four systems; our primary intent with those systems is sourcing materials for the construction projects we will be undertaking in Beta Magellan. Any questions so far?"

"No, ma'am," Paol replied.

Painter nodded, and Sev took over, saying, "We are preparing a recruitment proposal to submit to the system leadership. If they approve, we will then present that proposal to the refugees here in Tristan's Gate. We hope to gain the bulk of our initial colonists and workforce from these refugees. If you've followed the exploits of Cole's ship, I think it goes without saying protecting the system won't be a problem. With that in mind, we need a... statesman. We need someone to draft a Constitution and preliminary code of laws for the system that will scale as we grow. Is this of interest to you?"

"Possibly," Paol answered. "What type of government did you have in mind? There are certain forms of governance I do not approve of and will not support."

"I was thinking a representative republic," Cole said, "with protections built in against empire-building and vote buying."

"What protections were you thinking?" Paol asked.

"The government can't vote itself raises in pay, for one thing. If an elected official wants a raise, it should go before a vote of the people directly represented. I don't have any other concrete examples at this time; that's just the first thing that popped into my mind. I and my heirs will be chief executive, and the position is hereditary. In cases where someone has multiple children, he or she will choose his or her successor."

"Why you?"

"Excuse me?" Cole asked.

"I mean, why are you and your descendants the chief executives? Why not make it an elected position?"

"Because I own the system, as will my heirs," Cole replied.

Paol blinked. "But I thought... " Paol's voice trailed off as his eyes went very wide.

"Yes?" Cole asked.

"You're the Coleson Heir, aren't you?" Paol asked, his voice barely above a whisper.

Cole nodded once. "Yes."

The color drained from Paol's face in less than a second.

"Oh," Paol whispered. "Oh, my. You really could blackball my son, couldn't you?"

Cole nodded again. "I don't need to expend the effort, though. As long as he keeps his attitude on such a loose leash, he'll blackball himself. I can't imagine many people would *choose* to associate with such a conceited prig who has no money to pay them for their slavish devotion."

Paol sighed. "He never seemed this bad, back in the Commonwealth. I don't know if his mother and I just weren't exposed to it or if it's something he's cultivated trying to hold on to the so-called 'glory days.' I know I didn't raise him—any of my children—that way."

"Do you have any further questions?" Cole asked.

Paol shook his head. "If you decide to offer me the position, I would gladly accept. Leaving aside the matter of pay, it's the kind of challenge I thrive on. I miss working on the laws and governance of the Commonwealth."

"Do either of you have any further questions?" Cole asked, addressing Painter and Sev.

Both remained silent.

Cole nodded once. "Very well. We'll inform you of our decision."

"Thank you," Paol said, retrieving his folio and leaving.

When the hatch closed, Cole turned to the Kiksalik and asked, "Your thoughts?"

He is driven and hopes against hope you will offer him this task. He is stagnating here, a slow and painful death. His son's actions trouble him. He is a good person and will be loyal to you if you give him a chance.

"Thank you," Cole said. "I appreciate your assistance in this. Please, offer my respect and compliments to your queen. Sev? Painter?"

"I concur with the Kiksalik's assessment," Sev said. "Paol is and always has been an idealist. He took his family's role as a kind of steward of the Commonwealth very seriously, and I don't think anyone will ever know how much the war and break-up of the Commonwealth has hurt him."

Painter nodded. "I have nothing to add, Cole."

"Okay. Hire him. He has free reign to pick a team, but he has to provide the list to Painter, who will handle the hiring and vetting. Anyone he wants to hire must go through both of you and a Kiksalik review. Be very clear that I don't want his son within a parsec of what we're trying to build."

CHAPTER EIGHT

Conference Room, Office Complex Seven
U-3, The Gate
Tristan's Gate
29 April 3000, 08:00 GST

Cole leaned back against his seat as he chatted with Sev. Painter wasn't there yet, but he and Sev were early. No need to razz her... yet. A small package occupied the seat beside him. Well... it wasn't really a package. It was more of a cubic briefcase, but still, it was a container for conveying multiple items from point to point.

"Our side of the family is—frankly—just a bit appalled at Nathyn's continued conduct," Sev said. "He wasn't always like this, and it bothers Paol and Mira. For all that they've spent most of their lives in a position of privilege, both of them—and their families—have worked to stay grounded and in touch with the people they're supposed to be helping."

Cole shrugged. "He's a grown man; as far as I'm concerned, he acts like that because he *chooses* to act like that, and I'm not wasting any more time on him. I meant what I said to Paol. He'll blackball himself, the way he's going, saving everyone else the trouble."

Just then, the hatch cycled, admitting Painter. She froze upon seeing Cole and Sev sitting at the table.

"What... I'm not late again, am I? I was sure I left on time."

Sev and Cole grinned, Cole saying, "No, you're fine. We're just early and chatting in the meantime."

"Oh," Painter replied, the tension leaving her shoulders. "Okay, that's good. I hate being late, but it seems like there's not enough of me to go around anymore."

"You too?" Sev asked, after a slight chuckle.

"Since the topic came up," Cole said, "I expect you to hire people you need. You have an account set up for your tasks, and the funds should be *more* than sufficient for whatever you need. I put another couple hundred million in there, just the other day. Along with the credits side of things, I've arranged for a young queen to establish a local nest of Kiksaliks here. She's the third queen, after the current queen and the heir, so she probably needs to make herself scarce if she wants to survive. I don't know for certain when we'll be returning, so there's no reason to hold up your hiring process indefinitely."

Sev and Painter nodded. Painter said, "Oh, I heard back from the system leadership. They liked our proposal and have set up a meeting with the refugee council two days from now."

Cole grimaced. "That's good... but also bad. I need to be bending space for Alpha Centauri. I've dallied long enough as it is. Heck with it. I trust you guys. It's your baby now. So let it be written, so let it be done, and all that. Have you hired Paol?"

"Yes," Sev replied, "and he understands his task and that he doesn't have hiring authority. He also understands that his son is not welcome in our business space."

"Good." Cole took a moment to send a message to Sasha, asking her to notify all crew of an April 30th departure. "Sorry. I just sent Sasha a message to begin preparations to depart tomorrow. The ship's stores should be topped up, so the most we'll need to do is download entertainment and training libraries... or perhaps just update them in the case of the ISA training library. Do you have anything you need to discuss with me?"

Sev and Painter looked to one another before turning back to Cole and shaking their heads.

"Right then. Let's talk Beta Magellan. While the surrounding systems have been claimed by Haven Enterprises, Beta Magellan itself was claimed by a several-times-removed great-grandfather, and as such, *I* own it... all of it. It has two life-bearing worlds—green worlds as the explorers like to say—and mind-bogglingly rich asteroid fields, and there are even a couple large gas giants if we decide we want to export reaction mass. None of *our* ships will use what the populated galaxy considers 'conventional' drive systems, but everyone else still does, so let's capitalize on that.

"Hire—or outright buy—a reputable surveying firm; they're going to be busy for a long, long time. My family's settlement is on Beta Magellan IV. I want all the real estate around that settlement for a thousand kilometers in any direction to be private, protected territory. No one—and I mean *no one*—touches it. I'm going to have to decide what to do about it eventually, but I'm just not there yet. Garrett and I buried everyone, but it was a very rough and improvised process. Hell... I was crying so bad I could barely see the whole time; he probably did more of the burying than I did.

"Aside from that restriction, the only other thing is that I don't want any land barons claiming huge swaths of land and then charging exorbitant prices to refugees for it. Write up land contracts where the refugees pay me 1 credit per year for the first ten years. At that point, we will re-visit the matter for them either to buy the land at market rates or roll the contract into a real lease agreement. Hmmm... you'd better hire a law firm or two, now that I think about it; get with Paol on that, since I'm guessing he knows which firms are reputable. I'll take a look at your operating account, run some numbers, and maybe drop a little more in there. Don't go crazy with it, but at the same time, I want you to be able to accomplish everything I've laid out for you. Any questions?"

"Sitting here, talking about everything," Painter said, "it seems like the most daunting goal I've ever been aware of, let alone been associated with. When I break it down and look at all the moving parts individually, it doesn't seem so bad."

"It's not," Sev responded. "Besides, there's a lot of 'have to complete A before starting B' types of jobs, so even though it's a huge mountain to climb, we don't have to start at the bottom and sprint our way to the summit."

"Oh... before I forget, I have a parting gift for you two," Cole said, lifting the case onto the table. He flipped the latches, and the case came apart to reveal the quantum comms node Srexx had prototyped. "This is a quantum comms node Srexx designed. He is developing a module to be added to the jump gates that should improve our interstellar communications by a significant margin. This is keyed to your DNA, and whatever you do, *don't* crack the case to see how it works. There's an anti-tampering mechanism that will go *BOOM!*"

Painter looked at Cole with wide eyes. "How big a boom?"

"I didn't ask, but knowing Srexx, I'm certain you could describe it with the phrase, 'overkill is underrated.' It's probably tied to the power source somehow, if he powered it with a tiny singularity. Don't worry, though. He assured me it's one-hundred-percent safe to move and carry with you. I expect one of you to have it with you at all times. You don't need to keep it on your person, as your implants can route through it, just keep it in your general area. Bring it to work with you and take it home when you go... that kind of thing. Okay?"

Painter still looked at the device a little bit askance, but Sev gazed at it with a child-like grin. No one said anything, so Cole stood.

"Right, then. This meeting is adjourned." Cole nodded at the comms node. "Call me if you need me."

————

Sasha and Talia approached the apartment where their parents lived. The ship was leaving the next day, and they wanted some time with their parents and brother. Sasha keyed the command to ring the hatch chime, but the hatch opened without ringing the chime.

Sasha took a tentative step inside, saying, "Mom? Dad? We're here. The hatch just opened when I tried to ring the chime."

Mira, their mother, peeked into the parlor that doubled as an entry space. "Oh, honey... you should know by now you never have to ring the chime with us. It may not be the house where you were little, but as far as your father and I are concerned, you will *always* be 'home' with us. You'd better hurry, too. We're setting the table now."

Sasha led her sister into the apartment and followed the warm smells of food. Unlike many members of upper echelons of Commonwealth society, the Thyrrays always shunned the practice of maintaining large household staffs. If they entertained, they would hire some temporary help to assist in the kitchen and serving the guests, but otherwise, Mira and Paol did everything themselves.

"Oh, wow, Mom," Sasha said as she and Talia entered the dining area.

"That smells divine," Talia added.

Mira looked up to regard her daughters. "If you react like that over one of our casseroles, I almost want to ask just what they're feeding you on that ship."

Sasha smiled, and Talia grinned.

"It started out pretty rough," Sasha said, "but back then, it was just me, Cole, Yeleth, and Wixil on a ship capable of carrying almost twelve thousand people. None of us were true cooks, and we didn't have much to work with anyway until we reached Andersoll. By the time the ship had a full complement, Cole made certain that the mess deck staff was well trained, and these last few months we've been sitting around Tristan's Gate, he's actually sent them off to various culinary schools. Sure... we could use food dispensers, but Cole prefers culinary staff."

Paol walked in and stepped over to the sink, washing his hands before turning back to his family. "Well, the dessert's chilling and should be ready for us right about the time we're ready for it. How are my girls?"

"You would not believe what it's like working in a cross-species medical team," Talia said. "I'm learning *so* much! I haven't seen any Moq'Dars or Thurians yet, but we don't have any in the crew, either.

There's no way I'd ever have had the kind of experience I do now if I'd stayed in the Commonwealth."

"Of course not," Sasha said, breaking into a grin. "We rescued you from a detention center; not sure how much medicine you'd be practicing in solitary."

Talia responded by sticking out her tongue at her sister.

"How about you, Dad? What have you been doing to spend the time?" Talia asked.

Mira and Paol were just returning with the dishes for the evening meal, laying them out in the center of the modest table and arranging them between the place settings.

"Uhm... well... I started a new job."

"You did?" Talia gasped, her eyes wide and alight. "Is it something with the system council, or did you find a place with a firm? Oh... did you start your *own* firm?"

"Are you going to take a breath so I can answer sometime tonight?" Paol asked, regarding his youngest daughter with a thinly veiled smile.

Talia gave her father a flat look but remained silent.

"It just so happens that I've accepted a position with Haven Enterprises," Paol said. "I'm going be in charge of developing the civics for the system... the Constitution and basic laws, that kind of thing."

Sasha smiled.

"Haven Enterprises," Talia repeated, frowning. "I'm not sure I've heard... " Her eyes shot wide. "... *Cole* hired you? You're working up the *government* for Beta Magellan? Dad, that is so cool!"

The hatch cycling echoed through the apartment, and not even thirty seconds later, Nathyn entered the dining area. Talia moved to him and enfolded him in as close to a bear hug as a young woman of average height and lithe build could manage.

"You're right on time, big brother," she said, her face partially buried in his shoulder. "If you'd been any later, we'd have started without you. Dad was just telling us about his new job with Cole."

"What?" Nathyn rasped. "I thought we discussed that, Father."

Talia pulled back and frowned at her brother. "What's the issue, Nate?"

"That's *Nathyn*, Talia, and the issue is that your guttersnipe captain has no respect for our proper station. Father *asked* him for job, when by all rights your Cole should have been begging us to work with him. If you had been here when he visited, I daresay you'd no longer have anything to do with him, and for the life of me, I cannot understand why Father persists in thinking this *employment* is such a major opportunity."

Sasha pivoted on her heel, moving Talia aside to get right in her brother's face.

"How dare you! Cole has *always* put his people first, and there are no such things as class distinctions as far as he's concerned. In his view, the Thyrrays of Aurelius are no different—or better—than the 'Akyra Tomar's of the galaxy."

"Of course, he doesn't admit to class distinctions! He's just some bottom-dwelling, jumped-up pirate who lucked into that ship! You told me yourself he *found* it... probably stole it, more like."

Sasha's jaw tensed as her nostrils flared. Her hands clenched into fists.

"*Bottom-dwelling, jumped-up pirate?* You are such an utter fool, Nathyn. What I'm about to tell you is no longer a secret, so don't think I'm betraying any confidences. Cole's name is Bartholomew James *Coleson*. His father was Jack Coleson... as in Coleson Interstellar Engineering. The dividend payments into the Coleson trust—not to mention the interest—amount to more than the GDP of some star systems. You need to get your head on straight, Nathyn. If he were anyone else, I'd be worried he'd blackball you across this side of the galaxy."

"Cole already said he had half a mind to ship Nathyn back to the Commonwealth," Mira said, her voice not quite a whisper.

"I can only imagine the kind of conduct necessary to provoke such a response," Sasha said, shaking her head.

"Besides," Paol interjected, "Cole told me during the interview he'd never blackball Nathyn; he said Nathyn will do it to himself and save him the trouble and effort."

The heat and tension drained from Sasha as she struggled not to laugh. Talia didn't bother trying to hide her giggles.

"Yeah," Sasha said, "that sounds like Cole."

"Enough of this," Mira said. "Dinner's getting cold, and no matter what else, we're still a family."

Mira directed her husband to the head of the table and sat at the opposite end, like she normally did when the family ate together. Nathyn sat at his father's left, Sasha at Paol's right, and Talia sat between her sister and her mother. Soon, the sounds of a good meal shared among family dominated the apartment.

CHAPTER NINE

Bridge, Battle-Carrier *Haven*
Docking Slip 12, The Gate
30 April 3000, 08:47 GST

Cole leaned back against the captain's chair and took a drink of his tea. He and everyone else awaited Docking Control's permission to depart. The past few minutes had seen a lessening of near-station traffic around their dock as the station shifted the shuttles and other small craft away from their flight path.

"Captain," Jenkins at Comms said, "Docking Control signals we are clear to depart. They said, 'Fair winds and safe travels.'"

Cole smiled. "Please, extend my thanks and compliments for their hospitality, Jenkins. Wixil, undock, please, and take us out. Maneuvering thrusters only till we clear the near-station traffic zones."

"Aye, sir," echoed from behind and in front of Cole.

Wixil had been practicing her piloting, and while she started as a capable—if inexperienced—pilot, she still had yet to develop the flair for maneuvers Cole made look effortless. Under her guidance, *Haven* edged backward out of the docking slip and moved through a much slower pivot and rotation like Cole often executed at speed before edging out of the near-station zone.

Five minutes after undocking, Wixil announced, "Captain, we have left the near-station zone and are free to navigate."

"Thank you, Wixil. That was a superb job. Set our course for Aurelius, please, and punch it. We have places to be."

Wixil's fingers flew over the helm as she locked in the ship's destination as Aurelius. She set the engines for half-lightspeed to the system periphery, and *Haven* rocketed out of the area, leaving many smaller and fleeter craft in its figurative dust.

A little over fifteen hours later, the ship arrived at the system periphery. The helmsman keyed the command to engage the hyperdrive, and *Haven* vanished from Tristan's Gate.

————

En Route to Aurelius
    Cole's Office
    3 May 3000, 10:18 GST

Sasha and Yeleth entered and moved toward the guest seating at Cole's gesture. Cole leaned back against his seat and directed an expression that mixed both a question and an expectation.

"Okay," Cole said, once Sasha and Yeleth were seated. "You've had your week. What's the status of that matter we discussed?"

Sasha glanced at Yeleth before replying, "It took a little investigating, but we managed to identify the problem and its source. The issue was a few of the Iota Ceti slaves organizing a clique against Akyra, as she was one of the pirates guarding the slaves. Yeleth and I had a few words with the clique, and Red had a few more. The people responsible have since approached Akyra and apologized for their behavior. Srexx was kind enough to provide us a recording of the encounter, and Akyra has started slowly edging into social events and groups aboard."

Cole nodded. "Excellent. Thank you for handling this. Is there anything I can help with?"

Sasha and Yeleth looked to one another, both starting to shake their heads at the same time. They turned back to Cole.

"No. I don't think so," Sasha replied. "Thank you."

"Very well," Cole said. "I'll consider the matter closed."

Sasha and Yeleth stood, leaving Cole's office.

———

System Periphery, Aurelius

13 May 3000, 13:17 GST

Haven appeared on the system periphery about 12 AU from the nearest jump gate. Within moments, the sensors populated the system plot, displaying a very active system, and most of the traffic broadcast military transponders, even the freighters.

"Painter mentioned something about this," Cole said as he looked at the system plot.

"Oh?" Sasha asked.

Cole nodded. "Yeah. Independent freighters have pretty much fled the Commonwealth, what with the Navy stopping and boarding them to look for refugees, and even the established shipping firms are reticent to enter warzones. With no other recourse, the Commonwealth instituted state freighters to ship goods. It's not the best, but it's the best they have."

Sasha just sighed and shook her head.

"Wixil," Cole said, "set a course for Aurelius, but let's not scare anyone. No faster than a quarter-light."

"Aye, sir," Wixil chirped, her fingers dancing over the console.

Haven was half-way to the planet when a cruiser flanked by two destroyers approached. Cole was still on the bridge, along with Sasha.

He didn't know about his first officer, but he didn't like the idea of leaving the transit of the system to Delta Shift's Officer of the Deck. That worthy was a rather young, untried lieutenant—in Cole's eyes anyway—and Aurelius held too much potential to explode.

"Captain," the comms tech said, "we're being hailed by that cruiser approaching us."

"Hmmm... we made it farther in-system than I thought we would. What's the comms lag now?"

"Thirty seconds and falling, sir."

"I can work with that," Cole replied. "Record for transmission, please."

The comms officer said, "You're on, sir."

"Greetings! I am Bartholomew James Coleson, aboard the Battle-Carrier *Haven*. I have come to request an audience with the Provisional Parliament."

"Ready to transmit, sir."

"Thank you. Send it."

A minute passed.

"Message coming in, sir," the comms tech announced.

"Put it on the viewscreen, please," Cole replied.

The image of a woman little older than Sasha appeared on the screen.

"Mr. Coleson, I am Captain Patricia Valane, commanding the Aurelian cruiser *Dauntless*. Based on your own message, you are harboring a fugitive of the Aurelian Commonwealth, wanted for High Treason, among other charges. You will surrender Sasha Thyrray to us at once or face the consequences."

Cole sighed. "How close to weapons range are they?"

The officer at the weapons station keyed commands into her console and replied, "They're on the edge of powered missile range right now, sir."

"This is *not* how I wanted this visit to go," Cole mumbled, adding another sigh. Lifting his voice, he said, "Bring the ship to alert status, if you please."

The status lights throughout the ship flashed amber as klaxons alerted the crew to the change. Two minutes later, the rest of the Alpha shift bridge crew slid into their seats. Three minutes after that, Sasha turned to Cole saying, "All decks report secured and at alert status."

"Thank you," Cole responded. "Jenkins, record for transmission, please."

"You're on, Cap."

"Captain Valane, I do not recognize the warrants levied against Sasha Thyrray. I have terabytes of irrefutable data that proves those charges and their associated warrants are frauds. That's *why* I'm trying to speak with the Provisional Parliament. I did not come to this system to start a fight, Captain, but I will protect my people. How this ends is up to you. Coleson out."

"Ready to send, sir," Jenkins reported.

"Go," Cole replied and looked to Sasha. "Do you think it will—"

"Missile launch!" Mazzi announced from the weapons station. "We have two-hundred-fifty incoming birds from the destroyer labeled H-Two. That is, two-five-zero birds. Flight time is six minutes."

"Well, whoever that captain is, he or she is an idiot," Cole growled. "Mazzi, sound battle-stations, please, and weapons free on H-Two."

"Launching missiles," Mazzi responded. "Flight time is ninety seconds."

Of the one-hundred-plus missiles *Haven* could've launched, Mazzi returned fire with just fifty. Almost before the Aurelian crew knew they were under attack, *Haven*'s missiles battered first the destroyer's shields and then raked its hull. Missile detonations walked back the ship from bow to stern, the ship soon looking like a strip of land after a carpet bombing. The very last cluster of five missiles bore into the drive sections and gouged deep rends in the ship. Not even five seconds after the final missile detonated, a massive explosion ripped through the port-aft quarter of the ship, and the destroyer started drifting out of control.

"Anti-missile interceptors launching," Mazzi reported. "Point-defense batteries locking on and firing. All incoming missiles destroyed, Captain."

"Thank you, Mazzi. If you please, show us the tactical plot."

A hologram coalesced into view, hanging in mid-air between the center seat and the helm station. The view centered on *Haven* and showed all contacts in the ship's immediate vicinity, color-coded based on IFF. The cruiser and remaining destroyer were red, and the destroyer marked H-Two was now colored gray.

"It looks like the destroyer is angling for a strafing run on us," Sasha remarked, standing at Cole's side.

"That's even more stupid than firing missiles at us." Cole growled and followed it with a sigh. "I brought us here to end those warrants against you and your family, Sasha. It doesn't look like I'll be able to do that, just yet... not without fighting the entire Aurelian Home Guard. I hope it goes without saying I don't want to do that."

"I know, Cole," Sasha replied, her voice soft.

Cole glared at the tactical plot, his eyes locked on the gray dot representing the destroyer they'd just hammered into scrap. It was that moment that Cole realized his mistake. He knew going into the confrontation that those three ships posed zero threat to *Haven*. When the destroyer launched missiles, what he *should* have done was turn the ship around and leave. Sure, the Aurelians would probably cheer far and wide how they'd run off the great Battle-Carrier *Haven*, but truth be told, Cole didn't care about that.

"Mazzi, take us down to alert status, please, and Wixil, bring the ship about. Set course for Alpha Centauri."

A chorus of "Aye, sir," came from the two stations. *Haven* came about in a tight arc more appropriate for a cruiser—if not a light cruiser—than something more massive than a battleship and pointed its bow toward Alpha Centauri.

"Captain," Mazzi said, "they're accelerating on an intercept for us."

"They're ordering us to heave to and prepare to be boarded, Cap," Jenkins announced. "Captain Valane was rather nasty about it, too."

Cole chuckled as he settled back into the center seat. "Two words, Jenkins: make us. Wixil, let's see what they've got; three-quarters-light, if you please."

Wixil keyed the commands, and *Haven* erupted in speed. Even maxing out their engines, the Aurelian ships couldn't keep up, let alone out-distance them. When sensors didn't show any ships within interception range, Cole ordered a stand-down from alert status. When *Haven* reached the system periphery, Cole asked Wixil to engage the hyperdrive, and the ship vanished from Aurelius.

CHAPTER TEN

En Route to Alpha Centauri
   17 May 3000, 12:32 GST

The overhead speakers chirped and broadcast Sasha saying, "Bridge to Captain."

Cole keyed the command on the panel of his desk and replied, "Cole here."

"Sir, Chief Engineer Logan is on the bridge and would like a word. Do you have a few minutes?"

"Of course," Cole answered. "I'm in the office across from the bridge, so I'll be nice and wait for you."

"You're so kind, sir. Bridge out."

It wasn't long at all until Sasha led Logan into his office. Cole gestured to the chairs.

"Would either of you like some refreshment?"

Both Sasha and Logan declined.

"Right then. What's on your mind, Chief?"

"I'd like us to drop out of hyperspace for some unscheduled, non-critical maintenance on the hyperdrive," Logan replied. "I saw some odd readings in the engine room, and when I consulted Srexx, he recommended immediate maintenance on the systems involved. No part of our conversation leads me to believe we're in any danger, but Srexx was very clear that we should do this sooner rather than later."

"Sounds good to me. Srexx knows this tech better than I do."

"Heh... better than *I* do, even at this point," Logan agreed.

Cole tapped the control to activate the intra-ship comms, saying, "Captain to Bridge."

"Bridge, Mazzi here."

"Mazzi, what star system are we closest to right now?"

A couple seconds of silence passed before Mazzi replied, "It'll be Aquilae by the time I finish answering, sir."

"Very well. Divert to Aquilae and bring us out of hyperspace."

"Aye, sir."

"Thank you, Mazzi. Cole out." The speakers chirped, and Cole shifted his attention to Logan. "Will that do? Is there any other way I can help you?"

"No, sir. That'll be just fine. I'd better get back to Engineering."

Logan stood and left the office.

Cole motioned for Sasha to wait, and he waited until Logan would be well away from the office. Then, he said, "Srexx?"

"Yes, Cole?"

"First off, I want to thank you for helping Chief Engineer Logan. I appreciate you working with the crew."

"You are welcome, Cole."

"Second, I've never heard of any maintenance rated as immediate but non-critical. Was there something you *didn't* tell Logan?"

Silence.

"Cole, the odd readings Chief Engineer Logan mentioned often resulted from a generator containment system migrating out of polarity. The odd readings are, in fact, the earliest tell-tale that the containment system needs maintenance."

"Generator containment... do you mean the containment system for the singularity that powers the ship?" Cole asked.

"Yes, Cole. While the description of 'immediate but non-critical' might sound odd, it is just as I described. If left unchecked, it would be at least several days before the matter warranted a 'critical' rating. By doing the necessary maintenance now, we avert that necessity."

"I see. So... what you're saying is that we're *not* in imminent danger of dying?"

"Not according to the data available to me at this time. Would you like me to access the hospital deck's subsystems for a more thorough analysis of the crew?"

Cole grinned while Sasha just looked alarmed. "No, thanks, buddy... but I appreciate your willingness to put forth the extra effort."

"You are welcome, Cole. It is... nice... having people aboard again. I would prefer not to lose any more of you than is absolutely necessary."

"Me, too, Srexx... me, too."

Sasha closed her eyes and pinched the bridge of her nose. After a couple heartbeats, she looked at Cole again. She started to speak, but the overhead speakers chirped.

"Bridge to Captain," Mazzi said.

"Cole here, Mazzi. What do you need?"

"We just arrived in the Aquilae system, and there's a small vessel drifting a dozen AU or so from us broadcasting a distress call."

"Wait one, please," Cole responded and keyed the command to mute the call. "Srexx?"

"Yes, Cole?"

"Will that maintenance Logan needs to do prevent us from responding to a distress call?"

"No, Cole. The maintenance is restricted to the containment field, and maneuvers or even a minor skirmish would not impede Chief Engineer Logan and his people."

"Thanks, Srexx." Cole keyed the command to unmute the call with Mazzi. "Mazzi, thanks for waiting. Put us on a course to intercept the vessel. Sasha and I are on the way."

Cole entered the bridge, and Mazzi vacated the command chair, saying, "Captain on the bridge!"

Cole exerted the effort not to frown or grimace at Mazzi's actions as he crossed to the command chair and sat.

"Okay. What do we have?" Cole asked.

"It appears to be a Commonwealth Security ship," Mazzi replied. "It's the class used for high-security prisoner transports. There's scoring on the hull and residual radiation indicative of weapons fire."

"So, they were attacked," Cole said. "What kind of weapons does it have?"

"None, sir."

"What? Then, where is their attacker?"

"According to the schematics Srexx decrypted from Aurelian computer cores, most of the scoring on the hull corresponds to the prisoner transport cells," Mazzi said. "Whoever did this may have thought they killed the prisoners being transported and went on their way. Otherwise, I have no idea why the vessel isn't floating debris."

"Hail them, please."

Five minutes passed, and Jenkins announced, "No response, Cap!"

Cole swiveled the command chair to catch Jenkins's eye and smiled, nodding once and giving him a thumbs up. Then, he swiveled to face the port recession, saying, "Marine Ops, my compliments to Colonel Hanson, if you please, and ask him to prepare a boarding party. We need to check for survivors. Flight Ops, my compliments to Commander Vance as well, and ask her to arrange for an escort and area patrol while we have people aboard that vessel."

Each person responded, "Aye, sir," and Cole sat back to wait.

An assault shuttle surrounded by ten fighters soon left the ship via the bow egress and bore down on the drifting vessel.

"Captain," the officer at Marine Ops said, "the assault shuttle is reporting a hard seal on the vessel's starboard airlock, and the boarding party reports no response at the airlock. They are attempting to cycle the airlock. The airlock cycled, sir, and the boarding party is moving into the vessel. They're reporting all kinds of internal damage, sir; someone shot up that ship pretty bad. So far, they've found five casualties and no survivors."

"Has anyone accessed the cockpit?" Cole asked.

"Yes, sir. There was no one there."

"I am able to confirm the comms system still operates," Srexx said via the bridge's overhead speakers. "I have accessed the vessel's computer and am copying the data storage, including all surviving logs."

"Any indication in those logs of who did this, Srexx?"

"Yes, Cole. Three pirate cutters overtook the transport and fired on her without warning or communication. It is unclear why they stopped and left the area. The distress call had been broadcasting for several minutes when they left."

"Captain," the officer at Marine Ops said, "the boarding party reports all aboard the vessel are dead, except for one prisoner, and they're asking for instructions."

"Have them bring the prisoner aboard. I cannot justify leaving someone to die of thirst, starvation, or worse...no matter what they've done."

Marine Ops relayed the orders, and the waiting resumed. Less than ten minutes later, the assault shuttle undocked from the vessel, and the fighters resumed an escort formation around it as they returned to the ship.

"What are you planning on doing with the prisoner?" Sasha asked, her voice low.

Cole shrugged. "Haven't thought that far along yet, to be honest."

"Cole?" Srexx asked via the overhead speakers.

"Yeah, Srexx?"

"I believe I have identified the prisoner."

"Okay. Who is it?"

"It is the individual Aurelian authorities in Onyx believe to be Red Pattel, the Pirate Lord of Sector 82."

The tension left Cole as he slumped against the back of the command chair. He lifted his left hand and scratched his jaw. "Huh. Well, I'll be damned. Never thought I'd hear that name again."

Cole looked to Sasha, who stood to his right, and found his surprise or perhaps disbelief mirrored in her expression.

"You know Red Pattel, sir?" Mazzi asked, turning to stare at Cole.

"Jax Theedlow did," Cole said, adding a shrug.

"Captain, the Air Boss reports all fighters and the assault shuttle recovered," the officer at Flight Ops announced.

The officer at Marine Ops added, "The boarding party reports they are transferring the prisoner to the brig."

"Thank you," Cole said, but his voice was distant. He stared at nothing, his mind reliving a memory from another life... a life he thought he'd left behind. Cole didn't have a clear idea of how long he sat there, but when he became aware of his surroundings again, he knew what he had to do.

Cole stood and directed his attention to Sasha once more, saying, "Put us on course back to the system periphery. If I'm not back by the time Chief Engineer Logan finishes that job, let me know." Cole turned toward the port hatch.

"Sir?" Sasha asked.

Cole stopped and turned back to Sasha. "I have to know, Sasha. You have the bridge." Pivoting on his heel, Cole left without another word.

———

Haven's brig occupied a sizeable portion of Deck Five. A prison in miniature all on its own, it had two-hundred-fifty dual-occupancy cells and fifty single-occupancy cells. Stepping into the brig from the corridor opened to the entry and processing area. From there, five corridors left the space, each corridor being twenty-five cells deep with a row of cells on either side.

The single-occupancy cells extended out from the entry area in five corridors of their own. Each single-occupancy corridor was five cells deep with a row of cells on either side of the corridor. As these were the high-security cells, however, there was a security hatch to enter each corridor and after every pair of cells.

The two marines in the entry space for the brig snapped to attention when Cole stepped through the hatch. Cole didn't personally recognize them, but he was having far less success meeting all the marines than he did the regular ship's complement.

"As you were," Cole said. "How's our newest guest?"

"Honestly, sir?" the marine wearing sergeant stripes asked. "It's odd. She's docile, sir. She doesn't give off the kind of vibe you'd expect for a maximum-security prisoner. She didn't resist us or talk back or... anything."

Cole nodded. "Okay. That's good, I guess. Which one?"

"She's in Number Ten, sir. Since she wasn't resisting or anything, we put her in one of the regular cells."

"Thanks," Cole replied, adding a nod. He turned and walked down the indicated corridor and stopped at the cell labeled '10.' He lifted his right hand and keyed the command that would turn the partition transparent and allow the occupant to hear him.

A woman lay on the cot in the cell, her hands cradling her head. Aside from the garish yellow jumpsuit, the first thing Cole noticed was the unruly mass of curly hair, the fiery-red of open flame. She turned her head to look toward the partition, and her jaw dropped as her eyes went wide. She shifted to sit on the edge of the cot, facing the partition, and shook her head.

"Well, I'll be... if it isn't Jax Theedlow! Damn! You're looking good."

"If I deactivate the partition to come inside and sit with you, you won't attack me, will you? I'll accept your word on it, Red."

A mischievous smile curled her lips. "Well... I suppose that depends on how you define 'attack.' I always regretted not testing your resistance to my feminine wiles... or lack thereof." She added a simple wink that spoke for itself.

Cole chuckled and keyed the command to deactivate the partition. He stepped inside and sat on the small stool fixed to the decking in front of the writing desk anchored to the bulkhead.

"Damn, Jax! I never thought I'd see a friendly face again." Then, her face fell. "Are you? A friendly face, I mean... "

"Red, you saved my life. Need I say more?"

Red shook her head. "Sorry, Jax. I... well, I thought I was all alone now."

"What happened?"

Red took a deep breath and eased it back out as a heavy sigh. "Biggest damn mutiny anyone never saw coming. Everyone closest to me died, Jax. They took their time with Jemma before they killed her."

"Seriously?"

Red nodded. "With everything happening in the Commonwealth, a bunch of my captains apparently got together and decided to try going mercenary. I almost felt sorry for them. Anyone will tell you pirates *can't* stand up to or compare against veteran spacers, but they didn't believe that, I guess. They brokered a deal with the Onyx authorities that they received immunity for past crimes if they gave me up, and you see how that ended. I guess someone *else* in my organization didn't want to take the risk I'd talk; that's the only explanation I have for the attack on the transport." She looked up and held Cole's gaze for a few moments. "Look... I know I'm no saint. I deserve whatever the Commonwealth gives me. I just thought I'd have a longer run, you know? Thanks for coming to see me."

Red leaned over and pulled Cole into a hug, resting her head against Cole's shoulder. Cole let Red break the hug, and when she did, he blinked at seeing her eyes glistening with moisture. Cole held her gaze for a few more moments before he offered her a slight smile and nodded his head toward the open partition.

"What?" Red asked. "You want me to leave with you?"

"We're going to talk and catch up, and I'm not going to spend that time sitting on a stool that makes 'uncomfortable' feel like a compliment. Let's go."

"But... what about those marines?"

Cole broke into a grin. "Yeah, about that. Before we go too far, there's something you should know. 'Jax Theedlow' was a fake identity. That's not who I am."

"Well then, spacer... just who *are* you?"

"My name is Bartholomew James Coleson, but I prefer 'Cole.' I own this ship and double as her captain."

Red's expression was blank, her jaw slack. "Coleson? You mean like the jump gates Coleson?"

Cole nodded. "My father was Jack Coleson."

"Bullshit!"

CHAPTER ELEVEN

The marines in the entrance to the brig looked up as Red and Cole stepped out of the corridor. The first thing Cole noticed was there were now four marines as opposed to the two when he'd first arrived. The second thing he noticed was how three of the four moved their hands to their sidearms.

"Sir?" the sergeant asked. "Everything okay here?"

"Huh," Cole vocalized. "You know, we should probably work out code words for brig visits just for situations like this. Probably should've thought of that sooner."

"Answer him, already," Red hissed, though loud enough for everyone to hear. "I don't want to get shot."

"Sergeant, everything's fine. Red's someone I knew years ago. She saved my life, actually. I'm getting her some decent clothes, and we're going to the mess deck for some food. She'll never be a prisoner on this ship, as far as I'm concerned... unless she forces the issue... but I don't think that'll happen. Are we going to have a problem?"

The sergeant remained immobile for several moments before he shook his head, and the other three marines removed their hands from their side arms.

"It's your ship, sir," the sergeant said. "If you say she's not a prisoner, she's not a prisoner."

Cole nodded once and led Red out of the brig. They walked the short distance to the nearest transit shaft, and Cole took Red's hand, leading her inside.

"We're going down to Deck Seven. The recreation deck is where the shops are, including tailors."

"I still can't get over the lifts this ship has," Red said, not quite gaping at the open-air shaft they descended.

"Yeah, my first officer screamed like a terrified child the first time she rode in a transit shaft."

Red looked up to meet Cole's eyes and gave him a suggestive smirk as she said, "They must make skirts and dresses fun for the boys."

Cole laughed. "Maybe that's why everyone wears a ship-suit or pants."

———

Just finished with her after-shift workout, what Sasha wanted most was a good meal. The food on the mess deck was excellent, better than some five-star restaurants she'd visited, but sometimes, a person wanted a different atmosphere. The pubs and other eateries on the recreation deck catered to those desires.

Sasha stepped into Chromosphere, one of the recreation deck's pubs known for their food. Looking around the common room, Sasha's eyes settled on the second booth along the bulkhead, and she stopped cold. Cole sat in the booth with a woman Sasha didn't know but recognized from Cole's description: Red Pattel. They talked and gestured animatedly... like close, long-time friends catching up after an extended separation... and Sasha's eyes narrowed—her teeth grinding against each other—when she saw the woman lean into Cole's side as they laughed. She pivoted on her heel and left the pub.

———

"Oh, that's just priceless!" Red said, catching her breath after laughing. "How long did Srexx address her as 'Madam?'"

"No idea," Cole said. "I don't think it lasted too long after we learned what happened with her family, but for a couple days at least, it was 'Madam Sasha.' He even had the ship's computer doing it. When she came to the bridge to ask about joining my crew, the computer announced her as 'Passenger Madam Sasha.'"

After a moment, the laughter faded, and Red regarded Cole in silence. It dragged on until Cole lifted an eyebrow and asked, "What?"

"I heard about the Lone Marine even out in the backwater of Sector 82. If someone would've told me it was the guy I knew as Jax Theedlow, I never would've believed it. You're not who I thought you were, and I'm not just meaning the whole 'Cole vs. Jax' thing."

"It has been eight years, Red," Cole countered. "A lot can happen in eight years, and when we met, that was my first time out on my own. My friend Garrett and I had just parted ways, and I didn't even have my feet under me yet."

"You've done well for yourself. Everyone aboard this ship loves you, you know. I can see it."

Cole shrugged. "I don't know anything about that. I just want to pay them what they're worth and fulfill my side of the loyalty. There's so much I need to do, Red. No... that's not right. There's so much I *want* to do. That's why I'm going to Alpha Centauri. I need the credits in the Coleson Trust. It's the *only* reason I'm going."

"Well, I for one am glad you are. I'd probably be dead or dying by now if you hadn't shown up in... I don't even know the name of the system where you found me."

"Aquilae."

Red blinked. "Aquilae? Really? What the bleeding hell were you doing in Aquilae? There's nothing there. It's so desolate it gives backwater planets a bad name."

Cole chuckled. "We were en route to Alpha Centauri from Aurelius, and the chief engineer needed to do some maintenance that required us to leave hyperspace. Aquilae was the closest system."

"Damn. But for the grace of an engineer's whim, I'd be dead... or on my way to a prison planet or death row. That's a very sobering thought. It's almost enough to give a girl religion."

"I'm glad we found you, Red. I've always wished I'd kept in better touch."

Red chuckled.

"What?" Cole asked.

"As long as we're being all honest and sharing, 'Red Pattel' isn't my name, either. I was born Scarlett O'Donnell in a farming community on Gamma Seven. It was named Pattel after the caravan leader who founded it. I hope I don't need to explain how I came up with 'Red.'"

Cole laughed. "No... I'm pretty sure I know your inspiration for 'Red.' Scarlett, huh? Scarlett O'Donnell?"

"That's me, or at least, it used to be me... a lot of years, lightyears, and sins ago."

"Do you want to be Scarlett again?"

"Part of me says there's no way I can be. It says that naïve girl died a long time ago."

"Heh... you think I'm the Bartholomew James Coleson I was when I was twelve? Or even the Bartholomew James Coleson who cried over his family's graves? You can be the person you want to be."

"How? When the Commonwealth finally locates that transport, they'll plaster my face all over this quarter of explored space. Come to think of it, they might not be the only bounty on me by then, either."

"I named this ship *Haven* for a reason," Cole countered. "I don't care about who a person's been. I honestly don't even care what they've done. All I care about is who they want to be. Say the word, and I'll arrange an entrance interview for you to join the team."

She shrugged. "I don't know, Cole. This is all coming at me too fast. What happens if I don't want to decide right away?"

"Take all the time you need. I don't want anyone joining up if they're not one-hundred-percent certain it's what they want."

"There's one thing I do know I want."

"Oh? What's that?"

"It's time for Red Pattel to die, Cole, just like Jax. Call me Scarlett, please."

Cole smiled. "I'd like that very much, Scarlett."

———

Talia approached the hatch to her sister's quarters and keyed the hatch chime. The hatch opened almost before she'd pulled her finger from the panel. She stepped inside to see Sasha sitting on the sofa, a throw pillow clutched to her chest.

"Are you okay, Soosh? I thought we were meeting at Chromosphere."

"I know, sis. I'm sorry."

"You don't realize what you missed," Talia said as she sat in a chair across from her sister. "Cole was there, and he had someone with him nobody knows. She was gorgeous, too. Do you know anything about that?"

Talia looked up and froze at her sister's expression. Sasha's hands clenched the throw pillow in fists, and Talia thought she detected a slight flush in her sister's cheeks.

"Soosh? What is it?"

Sasha blinked and shook her head, releasing the throw pillow. Her movements looked a little forced to Talia, like they were a conscious and deliberate choice.

"It's nothing, Talia," Sasha said, her voice too even.

Talia moved from the chair to sit on the sofa with Sasha, putting her arm around her sister. "It's *not* nothing, Soosh. You looked like you were going to wring that poor throw pillow's neck. Not sure where its neck is, but still... "

"I said it's nothing," Sasha responded, her tone edging toward her 'command' voice for a moment. "My workout was more tiring than I expected, that's all. I dragged myself back to my quarters to recuperate."

Talia didn't believe that for a second, but she also knew the tone Sasha had used first. A professional, veteran interrogator after several days of breaking her down might—*might*—get whatever it was out of Sasha, but nobody else would.

"Well, if you're sure," Talia replied. She leaned over and put her head on Sasha's right shoulder. "You know I'm here for you, right, Soosh?"

"Yeah, I know," Sasha said. "Thanks."

"Okay. I'll leave you to it, but the second you decide you want to talk, you'll call me, right?"

Sasha nodded, confirming Talia's suspicions about her sister's less-than-truthful statements moments before.

Talia stood and went to the hatch. When she turned back to tell her sister goodbye, Talia saw Sasha once again clenching the throw pillow, staring blankly at the bulkhead. Talia keyed the hatch and stepped into the corridor. Once she'd stepped far enough away that the hatch irised closed, Talia stopped, considering everything she'd just seen.

"If I didn't know better, Soosh," Talia whispered as she resumed her walk down the corridor, "I'd think you were jealous."

———

Scarlett leaned back against the seat, a soft smile curling her lips. "Forgive me, Cole, but the last couple of days are catching up with me. I think, maybe, I should ask where I'm supposed to sleep."

"Hmmm... ," Cole said, "that's a good question. I'm pretty sure we're full up on crew, so a bed in crew berthing is a long shot. Oh... I know. I'll put you in the captain's quarters."

"You sly dog, you," Scarlett responded, her soft smile shifting to a smirk. "I know I said I was glad to see a friendly face, but it takes more than releasing me from the brig, giving me a set of clothes, and providing me an amazing meal and evening."

Cole frowned, not understanding. Then, his eyes went wide as he connected the dots, and he felt his face heat.

"Oh, my... you certainly are handsome when you blush," Scarlett purred. "You need to do that more often."

Cole blinked and shook his head as if to clear it, saying, "The piece of information you're missing is that I don't use the captain's quarters."

"Oh? Where *do* you sleep then?"

"The captain's day-cabin on Deck Three. It's across the corridor from the port access hatch to the bridge. Besides, the captain's quarters on Deck One are something obscene... like four thousand square meters. If you took out the dividing bulkheads, you'd almost have enough room for a professional sports match with a few stands for spectators."

Now, it was Scarlett's turn to blink. "Really? It's that huge?"

Cole nodded. "There are multi-million-credit condos in the upper levels of stations that are smaller. We'll pull some bed linens, towels, and pillows from stores, and you'll be all set. You ready to call it a night?"

"Yes, please. This has been the best evening I've had in a long time, but everything seems to have caught up with me. I'm so tired right now."

Cole smiled and moved out of the booth, extending his hand to her. "Well, then... let's get you some sleeping quarters."

CHAPTER TWELVE

The Centauri Trinary System (of which Alpha Centauri was a member) was an average of nine-hundred-twelve lightyears from Aurelius. At the normal cruising speed of eighty-percent on the hyperdrive, a one-way trip would take just shy of one-hundred-thirty-one and one-half days. After consultation with Srexx and Chief Engineer Logan, Cole decided to run the hyperdrive at eighty-five percent, shaving fifty-one days off the trip.

Still, eighty days was a long time without shore leave. Cole discussed that with Sasha, and they arrived at the plan of scheduling five days of shore leave every two weeks at the closest port. That plan would add fifteen days to the trip, but both Cole and Sasha thought it would make for a happier, more relaxed crew.

The trip passed with little incident, and almost every stop, Cole found some reason to draw Scarlett off the ship for at least a few hours.

System Periphery, Centauri Trinary System
    21 August 3000, 09:22 GST

. . .

"Could we get a system plot on the holo, please?" Cole asked.

No one verbally acknowledged Cole's request, but the hologram most often used for the tactical plot during combat appeared to display a plot of the system. The still-mysterious sensor technology *Haven* possessed recorded radio broadcasts like transponders long, long before those broadcasts had a hope of reaching *Haven*, so all manner of mobile and stationary dots populated the plot, beyond the star, planet, and asteroid locations.

Cole's eyes locked on one dot in particular. He stood and approached the hologram, tapping the focus of his gaze with his left index finger. The hologram zoomed in and displayed the dot's transponder data: the Coleson Clanhold. Arthur Coleson and his team had chosen the station's location very well. Balanced between the gravitational forces of Alpha Centauri and Proxima Centauri, the station floated through space pulled along by the trinary system in one of the most stable positions known in Human space.

Movement at Cole's side drew his attention, and he turned to see Sasha standing at his elbow.

"Fond memories?" she asked.

Cole shook his head. "No... no memories at all. My parents always told me I was born here, but they left for Beta Magellan when I was *maybe* two weeks old, if even that. I have no idea what we're sailing into."

Cole zoomed the plot back out to display the entire system again. None of the dots representing ships appeared to be on an intercept course for them... yet. *Haven* wasn't exactly a recognized design, and beyond that, she was *huge*, half-again the size of a Solar Republic Dreadnought. There was no doubt in his mind that *someone* would soon notice them and want a chat.

"Wixil," Cole said, "access the system plot, please, and put us on course for the Coleson Clanhold. Let's not disturb the natives, though; no faster than thirty-percent-light."

Wixil responded, "Aye, sir," her fingers flying over the helm console. They had 96 AU to travel before they arrived, and even at thirty-percent-lightspeed, that still meant a transit of slightly more than forty-four and a third hours. Nothing for it, though... all Cole could do was wait.

———

Coleson Clanhold
　Centauri Trinary System
　23 August 3000, 05:20 GST

Cole sat in the command chair, scratching his chin. *Haven* approached his family's station, and *no one* had challenged them the entire trip into the system. It was enough to give him a twitch between his shoulder-blades as he waited for the other shoe to drop.

"Comms," Cole said, "signal the station's docking control and request permission to dock."

It wasn't Jenkins at the comms station. They were still on Delta shift, and Alpha wasn't supposed to start for another forty minutes. But Cole couldn't sleep.

Not even ten seconds passed before the comms tech announced, "We're being hailed, sir... standard Solar Republic frequency on Channel Seven."

"Open a channel," Cole replied.

The overhead speakers chirped.

"Hello, I am—"

"Who gives a shite who you are? Just where do you think you're going to dock that big bastard you're riding in here? What in the nine hells is a 'Battle-Carrier,' anyway?"

If Cole was offended by the person's demeanor, he didn't show it, replying, "A Battle-Carrier is a battleship with a flight deck and small craft wing."

"Bullshit, sonny," the voice said. "Everyone knows fighters and bombers and the like are impractical and straight-up unfeasible at our current level of technology... even here in the Republic. Whenever you're ready to stop pulling an old man's leg, you go ahead and call us back."

"Hang on a second," Cole said, an unpleasant tone creeping into his voice.

Cole swiveled the command chair to face the comms station and gave him the signal to mute their audio. The comms tech keyed a couple commands and reported, "Mute."

Cole swiveled to face the port recession. "Flight Ops, do we have a squadron on ready alert?"

"Yes, sir, we do."

"Launch them... standard escort formation on *Haven*."

The ensign at Flight Ops looked at Cole with wide eyes. "Sir?"

"You heard me. Launch them."

The ensign bent over his console and started relaying Cole's orders. Within five minutes, thirty fighters surrounded *Haven*.

Cole swiveled back to face the comms station, asking, "Is that call still active?"

"Yes, sir."

"Unmute, please."

The overhead speakers chirped again.

"You still there, old man?" Cole asked. "Can you read a sensor plot, or are you too senile?"

"Well, I'll be damned," the same voice said, his voice hushed and laced with awe. "Just who are you, sonny?"

"You didn't seem too interested in that before," Cole replied, his voice almost a growl. "I'm Cole, and I command this ship. Now, I have business with CIE. Do you have a place for me to dock or not?"

"It'll have to be one of the freighter arms," the man said. "You're just too damn big for anything closer."

"That'll be fine," Cole said.

"Transmitting your docking assignment now. Docking Control out."

The speakers chirped again, and Cole turned to Flight Ops. "Recall the fighters. We'll dock once they're back aboard."

————

Cole led Sasha, Yeleth, Wixil, and Red the Igthon through the corridors of the station. Cole carried the dispatch pouch Leland Graf had given him in Zurich, all those months ago; it contained the sealed writ that verified his identity as the Coleson Heir. Everywhere Cole looked, what he saw evinced an eeriness that made him uncomfortable. The thought that he was standing in the place where he was born— where so many of his ancestors had been born—without feeling any connection to it at all might have contributed... maybe just a bit.

The corridor they traveled ended in a set of double doors. The stylized logo of Coleson Interstellar Engineering arced across the bulkhead over the doors. Cole slowed to a stop and took a deep breath. The culmination of his decision in the ISA office to step forward and claim his birthright was just in front of him, and Cole noticed his palms were clammy.

"You okay?" Sasha whispered, even though everyone else in their party had no difficulty hearing it.

Cole shrugged. "I'm not sure, but I will be."

Squaring his shoulders, Cole resumed his stride, the doors *swishing* open at his approach.

The reception area of CIE conveyed the company's stature as Number One on the Solar Republic's Fortune 250 list in a subtle and understated opulence. Cole didn't need to ask to conclude the carpet he crossed was beyond expensive, and the paneling over the bulkheads wasn't faux wood or even local Centauri flora. It was stained oak from the region where Arthur Coleson grew up in North America on Old Earth, and Cole didn't even want to hazard a guess as to how old it was.

Cole pulled his attention back to his objective and approached the reception desk. A woman sat behind the desk, an earbud in her right ear. She looked up at Cole's approach and speared him with exquisite baby blue eyes.

"Welcome to Coleson Interstellar Engineering. How may I help you?"

"I need to speak with the CEO," Cole said. "There's a matter of business we must discuss, and I've traveled quite some distance to have the conversation."

"Do you have an appointment, sir?"

"No. I wasn't certain when I would arrive, precisely."

The receptionist shook her head, the movement laden with regret. "I'm sorry, sir. CEO Jefferds is very busy, and it's doubtful I'll be able to fit you in. If you like, I can take a message and see that he receives it."

Cole nodded. "Very well. May I borrow a message tablet and stylus? Oh, and I'll need a certified delivery pouch. The message I carry is from Leland Graf at Credit Suisse."

The receptionist frowned. "I'm not aware of a Leland Graf at the local branch. Is he new?"

"Hardly," Cole replied, chuckling. "He's an executive at the Zurich branch."

"Ah. I wouldn't know anyone at the office on Earth."

Cole was rather proud of himself for maintaining a straight face. "My apologies. I meant the star system, not the city in Switzerland." Even though he kept his non-expression, Cole felt like smiling at the sight of the receptionist paling.

"I'll send for that sealed delivery pouch and a confidential message tablet right now, sir."

When a young man jogged up to the reception desk to deliver the items, Cole accepted them and set the delivery pouch aside for a moment. He activated the confidential message tablet and set a read timer of five minutes. Then, he wrote his message:

> I bear a sealed writ from Leland Graf in the Zurich system.
> The writ regards the Coleson Heir.
> Call at your earliest convenience.
> Comms code: Omega-5543297

Message complete, Cole opened the personnel directory and selected the CEO as the only DNA record that could activate the tablet. Then, he placed the tablet inside the delivery pouch and sealed it, once again selecting the CEO as the only person who could open it. All finished, Cole extended the pouch to the receptionist.

The receptionist eyed the pouch like a live snake and nodded to the young man. Cole turned and extended the pouch to him. The young man accepted it, his expression wary as well, and disappeared into the expanse of the CIE offices.

"Thank you for your assistance," Cole said, nodding once and turning to leave.

CHAPTER THIRTEEN

"Well, what are we going to do now?" Sasha asked as they stood outside the CIE offices.

A grin erupted across Cole's face. "I know. How about we go by my house?"

Sasha turned to look at Cole, but he and everyone else were already a few steps ahead, leaving her behind. She jogged to resume her place at Cole's right side.

"So... what house?"

Cole shrugged. "I couldn't think what else to call the part of the station that was always maintained as the family residence. 'House' was the best I had on short notice."

Minutes later, they stood in front of the massive blast door that prevented anyone from traversing from the company side of the station to the family side of the station. At first glance, there didn't appear to be a way past.

"This has probably been sealed since my family left for Beta Magellan," Cole remarked.

"If it's sealed, we're not getting in... right?" Sasha asked.

"Well, if it were just you guys, that would probably be true. But it's not just you guys," Cole said. His eyes landed on a panel cover. The cover was on the bulkhead to the right of the blast doors, and Cole saw hinges on one side. He moved closer and hooked his fingernails under one side. The panel came loose with a click and swung wide on silent hinges. It revealed a touchpad for DNA verification. Cole pressed his hand to the touch-plate.

At first, nothing happened. Without warning, a massive *clack* reverberated through the corridor, like a latch the size of Boston releasing after years of inactivity. The blast doors parted, sliding back into the bulkhead on either side of the corridor.

———

It was Joe's first day on the job. He was the newest analyst in CIE Security, and apparently, 'analyst' was synonymous with 'chair-warmer' or 'monitor-watcher.' His duty station was called the Pit. The Pit was the nexus of all security monitoring for the entire station, supported by over thirty employees.

A screen just to Joe's right sprouted a red border around its display that started flashing. Joe leaned just enough to read the text on the screen, and he slapped the large button on his left to summon his supervisor.

Ms. Engville approached his shoulder, and he pointed to the flashing screen. She leaned close enough to read the text and went pale. She snapped ramrod straight and urgently whispered into the comms microphone on her left sleeve. Not even two minutes later, the Chief Security Officer—the Head of CIE Security—stood at Joe's back. He leaned close, read the screen, and spoke five words.

"Get me a team... *now*."

He pivoted on his heel and left the Pit at a near-sprint.

The flashing alert reported the authorized access of the Coleson Family Residence by someone matching the last recorded DNA profile the system had for the missing Heir.

———

"Yeah... so this isn't as impressive as I expected it would be," Cole said. He stood in the center of a foyer that led to several rooms, and everywhere Cole looked, white sheets of canvas covered the furniture.

Sasha chuckled. "What were you expecting, Cole? No one's been here in... how old are you? A quarter century?"

"Ha! I'll have you know I turned twenty-seven on the way here."

"So, it's been even *longer*. People normally do stuff like this when no one's going to be in a residence for a long time." Sasha stopped and turned to glare at Cole. "Wait a minute. You're saying you had a birthday, and you didn't tell *anyone*?"

"Garrett knows. He wished me 'Happy Birthday.'"

Sasha's eyes narrowed. "Does Scarlett know? I'll bet she *wished* you a happy birthday."

Cole frowned. What was with Sasha all of a sudden? "No, Scarlett doesn't know my birthday. It's not something I talk about."

Sasha had another snipe ready to go when understanding settled on her shoulders like a ton of regolith. The last time Cole probably had a birthday party was in Beta Magellan. "Sorry, Cole. I... that wasn't like me."

Cole made a dismissive wave with his left hand. "Heh... don't worry about it. Well, I suppose we should go back to the ship. There's not as much here as I thought there'd be."

They turned to leave just in time to see seven people enter from the way they had come.

"Oh, hello," Cole said. "Who might you be?"

"CIE Security," the man at the front of the group said, his hand hovering near his sidearm. "Which one of you is the Heir? I know it's not either of the Ghrexels or the Igthon."

"How do you know one of us is the Heir?" Sasha asked, stepping forward.

"The DNA pad reported a successful authorization to the Nexus, Ms. Coleson. If you had bypassed the pad, it would've sent a different message." He took a couple steps forward, extending his left hand. But his right hand still hovered close to his sidearm. "Ms. Coleson, you need to come with us, please."

"Now, just hold it right there," Cole said moving forward to stand beside Sasha. "We don't know you people from Adam. It's all well and good to say you're CIE Security, but what have you shown us to verify that? Jack Coleson and all of his family were massacred, and there's no evidence all the threats to the Heir disappeared with time."

Cole accessed his implant to call the ship for a squad of marines, but before he could access the comms function, an alert popped up, advising him of an incoming call.

Hello? Cole answered the call non-vocally.

Mr. Coleson, this is Vince Jefferds, CEO of your company. Are you still on the station?

You could say that. My friends and I came to visit my family's residence, and we're currently facing seven people claiming to be from CIE Security. Their hands are hovering far too close to their sidearms for my comfort, and I was just about to summon a squad of marines from my ship.

I'll handle that. Please, wait right there for me... and also, please don't do anything rash.

No promises, unless you hurry. I don't handle threats to my people well.

I'll hurry.

The comms function informed Cole the call ended. Not even two seconds later, every comms device the seven security people had started blaring. The man in the front scowled and tapped his left ear as he spoke into his sleeve.

"What now, Vince? We're in the middle of a situation here." He listened for several moments, his eyes narrowing at last. "Stand down? Who the hell are *you* to tell *me* to stand down? Company security is *my* responsibility."

Okay. That tears it, Cole thought as he brought up his comms menu. He had no idea what he looked like as he navigated his implants menus, the way his eyes darted all over the place, but he didn't care. He addressed the message to Mazzi and Harlon.

He sent, *Confronted by station security. Refusing to stand down at CEO's order. Scramble the active-ready unit of marines. Activating my beacon now.*

The moment after he keyed 'send,' Cole accessed his implant again and navigated the menus to reach the command for his locator beacon. Without a second thought, Cole activated it.

"Vince... dammit, listen to me!" the man in charge of the security team growled. "Whoever these people are, they've spoofed the Heir's DNA! I don't care what that delirious fool in Zurich wrote."

He and the CEO continued to argue for several more minutes... right up until red lights started flashing to the accompaniment of a shrill whistle.

"Vince, I gotta go. Some dipshit triggered the security alert. We'll finish this later," the man said. It seemed he'd forgotten all about Cole and his people as he pulled a device from a pocket, tapped a couple commands, and stowed it once more, bringing his left sleeve back to his mouth. "Report! Who the hell triggered the security alert?"

Cole watched the man's eyes bulge at whatever he heard.

"What the blazing fires of hell do you mean, there's a quick reaction force moving my way? No... I don't believe you. This station is sovereign territory, despite being deep in the Solar Republic. Their own Constitution *prevents* them from boarding this station."

Cole and his people were in a perfect position to watch two of the ship's marines shoulder-roll across the doorway, coming up in a crouch with their stun rifles raised. Two more marines leaned around the corner, one low and one high.

"Freeze!" one of the marines shouted. "On your knees, now!"

The security team pivoted, their collective hands going to their sidearms. Cole saw which way *this* wind was blowing and dropped to the deck, the rest of his people following him.

"You stand down!" the man said, storming through his six people. "I am the head of CIE Security, and this is *my* station! I don't know who—"

Three stun bolts struck the man in rapid succession, and he collapsed like a puppet with its strings cut.

"On your knees... now!" the same marine shouted. "Hands on your heads! Last warning!"

Cole saw six heads angle down, and he guessed they were looking at their boss, who was now twitching sporadically. The faint smell wafting toward Cole suggested the man had fouled himself, too. The six security people dropped to their knees and placed their hands on their heads.

"Secure them," the marine said, and two broke off to move through the kneeling people, removing their sidearms and binding their hands behind their backs.

"Secure, Sarge," one of the two said.

"Team One to Base," the sergeant said. "All clear. Principal is secure and unharmed, all hostiles neutralized."

Cole's implant reported an incoming call, labeled as 'urgent.' It was Vince Jefferds.

"Hello?" Cole said, answering the call.

"Why is my office in lockdown with reports of armed marines storming the station?" Cole's implant conveyed the CEO's voice to the auditory center of his brain, making it sound like Jefferds was within speaking distance, and he didn't sound happy.

"It was apparent to me that your guy wasn't responding to your orders, so I handled the situation. While we're on the subject, it's not *your* office. It's *mine*. Just like I'm pretty sure this whole station is mine. It certainly has my name on it. Oh, and you need to send someone to collect your head of security. He mouthed off to my marines and took three stun shots, and I think one of them struck his head. He's on the deck twitching and doesn't smell so good. End the lockdown and gather the company leadership. It's past time I met everyone."

"I can't end the lockdown. Only the Nexus can do that, and they're shouting about calling in the Centauri Police."

Cole sighed. He angled his head up and spoke in a slightly raised tone. "Computer?"

"Acknowledged," a digital, feminine voice broadcast from unseen speakers. "Please state your request."

"I am Bartholomew James Coleson. Do I have the authority to end the station lockdown?"

"Yes, Mr. Coleson," the computer replied. A panel opened on a nearby bulkhead, revealing a DNA touchpad. "Please, touch the test-pad for identity verification."

Cole stepped over to the panel and placed his left hand on it. Within a second, it beeped.

"Identity verified, Mr. Coleson. Executing Coleson Override. Lockdown is cancelled."

"Is there something like a station-wide address system that I can use?"

"Of course, Mr. Coleson." The speakers played an odd tone that sounded familiar to Cole for some reason. "You're live, Mr. Coleson."

"People of Coleson Interstellar Engineering, may I have your attention please? I want to apologize for the recent excitement. I did not intend for your first experience with me to be something as unsettling as armed marines in your corridors. However, the head of security refused a direct order from the CEO, and I felt it imperative to act. You are in no danger, and my people will be leaving the station in moments. Once again, I apologize for the unforeseen excitement. Thank you. Coleson out."

Cole removed his hand from the DNA panel.

"Well, you've certainly painted me into a corner," Vince Jefferds said in Cole's ears.

Cole shrugged, even though he knew the CEO couldn't see it. "He brought it on himself. Dock him one month's pay, and make two things very clear to him. Number One: his employment is at your will and pleasure followed very shortly by mine, and Number Two: it's *my* station, not his. Now, send someone over here to scrape him off my deck before whatever's coating his underwear seeps through. He stinks. Call me back when you have the company leadership in a conference room."

Cole ended the call.

"Sergeant," Cole said, "I'd like for you to leave four marines to secure this area until CIE personnel arrive to take charge of these people."

"Aye, sir!"

"Computer," Cole called.

"Yes, Mr. Coleson?"

"Once there are no more people in the family residence, can you seal it once again?"

"Yes, Mr. Coleson. I can also arrange for cleaning bots to scrub the decking."

"That would be good, thank you."

Cole looked around the space, taking in the six security personnel with their hands secured behind their backs, the unconscious and twitching security chief whose smell continued to worsen, the marines he could see, and his friends.

"Right," Cole said. "I think we're done here for now. Back to the ship."

CHAPTER FOURTEEN

Executive Conference Room, CIE Offices
Coleson Clanhold
24 August 3000, 09:15 GST

Cole entered the conference room with CEO Vince Jefferds and walked straight to the head of the table, where he sat. Jefferds looked like he wanted to speak, but Cole held his gaze with a silent non-expression. Jefferds backed down and sat at Cole's right.

The door opened to admit Sasha, Yeleth, Wixil, and Red. Sasha led the group to where Cole sat, then took her place at his immediate left, Yeleth at her other side. Wixil and Red took up positions on either side of Cole but standing back against the bulkhead, their expressions blank as they scanned the room with their eyes.

"Are they really necessary?" Jefferds asked in a soft voice, eyeing the Ghrexel and massive Igthon.

Sasha chuckled, saying, "After the stunt your security chief pulled yesterday, you should consider yourself lucky there isn't a marine fireteam securing every intersection from here to the airlock where the ship's docked."

Jefferds grimaced. "I apologize for that. I don't know what got into him. He's never given me a problem before."

"How is he, by the way?" Cole asked, more out of curiosity than any real concern for the man.

"He's conscious, but that's about it. He's still regaining certain voluntary muscle control."

Cole chuckled. It was dark, no mirth whatsoever... edging toward malicious. "Maybe the next time armed marines tell him to stand down and kneel, he'll be a good boy and do as he's told. Otherwise, I foresee a lot of twitching and soiled clothing in his future."

"Are you saying they *aimed* for his head?" Jefferds asked.

"I'm sure I can't say, but per the standing orders I gave when I returned to the ship yesterday, they will from now on. You might want to pass the word to your people."

"They're your people, too," Jefferds countered, frowning.

Cole shook his head. "They have no idea who I am beyond a voice on a loudspeaker. In time, they might become my people, but that won't happen any time soon. I'm not going to be around here long enough for it to happen right now."

Jefferds blinked. "What does that mean?"

"You'll find out in the meeting. Where is everyone, anyway?"

"Ah," Jefferds replied, "well... I tend to run a rather relaxed policy about meetings. Since I'm usually running late myself, the meeting time is usually more of a fifteen-minute window."

"Okay. You need to make them understand that, while *you* might be just fine waiting on them, I'm not. They need to understand that ten minutes early for one of my meetings is five minutes late. The third time it happens, they can expect a written warning and one week's forfeiture of pay. There *won't* be a fourth; they'll be looking for other employment. Am I understood?"

"Yes," Jefferds said.

"Excellent. If you would, please step outside and chivvy them along."

Jefferds stood and left the conference room.

"A little harsh there, weren't you?" Sasha asked. "You're not usually so iron-fisted on the ship."

Cole frowned. "No one on the ship has ever tried to abduct you thinking you were me and refused to stand down when ordered to do so by relevant authority. Until these people demonstrate that they've earned 'nice and laid back Cole,' they get to enjoy the company of 'Bartholomew James Coleson, the Coleson Heir.' Besides, I'm not going to be an ass to the average person here. I'm sure most of them have a good head on their shoulders."

Sasha nodded. "I can see that. So, that's why you asked Harlon to have a company on ready alert before we left?"

"Yep. After that little stunt yesterday, I just can't shake the feeling that we've walked into a snake pit. Until we know who's a mongoose and who's a cobra, we're going to assume *everyone*'s a cobra."

The next seven minutes passed in a companionable silence, and Jefferds returned with a group of people. Each and every one of them seemed taken aback by the presence of Sasha, Yeleth, Wixil, and Red, but they filed into the room and took seats at the conference table. Jefferds returned to his seat at Cole's right.

"Hello," Cole said, almost before Jefferds's butt came into contact with the seat. "As you may or may not have guessed, I am Bartholomew James Coleson. I am Jack's son. A number of you should be old enough to remember my father. I have decided to claim my inheritance, and I came to Centauri to meet the company my family built. I am not pleased by the Chief Security Officer's insubordination yesterday, but I consider three high-power stun bolts to be sufficient expression of my personal displeasure and will take no further action in whatever discipline CEO Jefferds deems appropriate. Now, as much as I'm sure we all love the exercise, let's go around the table, so you can introduce yourselves."

"I'm Vince Jefferds," Jefferds said. "The officers at Credit Suisse overseeing the Coleson Trust brought me on-board when the previous CEO had to retire due to medical reasons. I've been with the company for three years now."

The woman at Jefferds's right lifted her head and looked Cole right in the eye. "I'm Trisha Townsend, Chief Legal Officer. I've been with the company for eight years."

The older gentleman on her right said, "And I'm Carl Bachman, the Chief Financial Officer. I've worked here for over thirty years, and yes, I do remember your father... your grandfather, too."

The gentleman to Bachman's right wore a white lab coat and seemed to be constantly unaware of his surroundings. Bachman nudged him with his elbow.

"Huh?" the man said, and Bachman nodded toward Cole. "Oh. I'm Lyle Chesterton. I've been the Chief Research Officer for... what year is it now?"

"3000," Bachman replied in a stage whisper.

"Oh. I've been here nine years already? My... how time flies."

The other CIE personnel at the table shared slight smiles or outright smirks.

"I'm Cara Stanwick," said the woman at Chesterton's right elbow. "I'm the Chief Operations Officer, and I started here six months ago. I've worked for other Fortune 500 companies, but it was an education coming here. I've seen why CIE is the Solar Republic's highest-grossing company."

"Thank you," Cole said. "Beyond meeting all of you, my primary goal for this meeting was to inform you that Coleson Interstellar Engineering will relocate *all* operations to Beta Magellan within five years." All of the CIE personnel stared at Cole with wide eyes. "As of this moment, that goal is the number-one priority of every department in the company."

"May I ask about your reasoning for that directive, sir?" Jefferds said.

Cole nodded. "Of course. First of all, my father and grandfather saw the rate of innovation waning within the Solar Republic. They believed that the expansion areas would soon overtake the Republic in developing new technologies, and they wanted the company positioned to take advantage of that environment. Secondly, I have no interest to live in or around Centauri. My life, my operations, my interests are centered out there... in the triangle of space created by Beta

Magellan, Zurich, and Tristan's Gate. While it would be possible to oversee the company with its business operations still in Centauri, it is not an ideal situation.

"I understand this is quite the shock, people. You just met me, and you have no idea what business credentials I have. I'll be honest. I have none. Most of my experience is in the cockpit of a freighter, but I have people building a functioning economy and population in Beta Magellan right now. By the time you're ready to move, the system *will* be ready to receive you. And one more thing. Mr. Jefferds, draft a company-wide memo for immediate distribution. In the memo, announce the new corporate priority and advise anyone who *does not* want to relocate to Beta Magellan to resign within two weeks; I will provide a generous severance package out of my own funds for anyone who resigns. Anyone who doesn't resign and actively works against this goal will be summarily dismissed. Any questions?"

The conference room was so quiet, a person could've heard a stylus strike the decking three compartments away.

"Right then. Good meeting. Mr. Jefferds, would you please arrange a tour of the company facilities for me, including all areas of the Research department? My assistant chief engineer is a major fan of CIE, and besides wanting to tour the company myself, she'd crawl across ground glass to see this place."

———

Jefferds arranged for an immediate tour, and Cole called the ship, asking Myrna to meet him in the reception area. For the next four hours, Jefferds and Chesterton took Cole and his group on a tour of CIE that spared no nook or cranny. Cole thought Myrna spent the entire time striving not to swoon.

Cole and his group slowly traversed a corridor en route back to the ship. Myrna chattered non-stop about everything she'd seen, and every third statement was a 'thank you' directed toward Cole. They were approaching the intersection where they'd make the last turn before the ship's docking slip.

Without warning, Wixil screamed, "Cole," and launched herself at Cole's back. Her impact staggered him and, as Wixil fell to the decking, Cole processed the other sound he'd heard: a laser weapon. The *next* sound he heard was Yeleth's rippling war cry. She pivoted, her claws already out on both her hands and feet, and erupted into a four-legged sprint in pursuit of the shooter.

"Go with her, Red," Cole said. "She might not be thinking clearly right now."

"I've called the ship," Sasha said, kneeling at Wixil's side. "They're scrambling a trauma team and the ready squad of marines."

Cole nodded. "Those marines had better hurry if they want a piece of whoever fired that shot. I wouldn't give two centicreds for his life if Yeleth catches him."

"Dammit, Cole, we need the shooter alive for interrogation," Sasha growled.

"Hey, I'm not the mother whose child was just shot. Chase Yeleth down and tell *her* we need him alive."

Sasha looked off in the direction Yeleth and Red had run, at last releasing a heavy sigh. "Yeah, you're probably right. If she catches him, she'll rip his throat out."

"Cole?" Wixil whispered.

Cole knelt and took her left hand in his. "I'm right here, Wixil. Help's on the way. You're going to be just fine."

"My back burns," Wixil whispered.

"I know. The shooter used a laser weapon of some type. I'm pretty sure you saved my life."

"That's good," Wixil replied. "I love you, Cole."

Wixil pulled Cole's hands to her cheek and leaned into them as she closed her eyes. Her tail still swished side to side every so often, and her chest rose and fell as she breathed.

· · ·

The teams from the ship arrived within a second of Yeleth and Red returning. Yeleth's expression and her lashing tail told Cole everything he needed to know about whether she'd caught the shooter.

"I was not successful in my hunt," Yeleth said, her jaw clenched.

"Don't worry; we'll get him. This station just became Srexx's playground."

CHAPTER FIFTEEN

Cole watched the team take Wixil away on a gurney. Sasha went with them. Red and thirty of *Haven*'s marines stood with Cole. It was a safe assumption the shooter *hadn't* been aiming for Wixil.

"Computer," Cole said.

"Yes, Mr. Coleson?" the computer asked, via speakers in the ceiling of the corridor.

"I need to implement a station-wide Coleson Override."

"Yes, Mr. Coleson." A panel ten meters away opened in the corridor's bulkhead. "Please, approach the DNA tester and verify your identity."

Cole walked to the panel, Red and everyone else moving with him. Cole pressed his left hand to the tester panel, and a short, double-beep sounded.

"Identify verified, Mr. Coleson," the computer said. "Please, state your directives for the Coleson Override."

"First, initiate a station-wide lockdown immediately, including all maintenance airlocks and life pods. All CIE Security personnel are hereby suspended with their credentials and access revoked until such time as they've been vetted by my people. Second... effective immediately, all station security tasks are the responsibility of the marine contingent aboard *Haven*. Interface with Srexx aboard *Haven* for any and all identity verification of my people. Third, you now report to Srexx. Srexx has full, unrestricted access to all station information systems and databanks. Any and all requests for information will go through Srexx for approval. Fourth, no ship currently docked at this station is allowed to leave without a full search by *Haven* marines. Any ship that violates this directive will be subject to forced boarding by assault shuttles. Fifth, any directive by CIE personnel that would negate, override, or otherwise modify any of these directives is to be flagged and referred to Srexx without implementation. Do any of these directives conflict with your core programming?"

"My core programming explicitly states I have no directives which supersede the safety of the Coleson line. Your new directives all work to support that core programming. There will be no conflicts."

"Implement my directives at once, please."

"Yes, Mr. Coleson. New directives now active. I have locked the docking clamps of all ships and craft currently docked until such time as you, Srexx, or your designee grants individual vessels permission to depart."

"Thank you, Computer." Cole turned to the marines around him. "Pass the word to Colonel Hanson. This station is his now. Find me that shooter, and get Kiksaliks to vet the CIE Security personnel as soon as possible. Oh, and have him designate a ready alert squad and assault shuttle to intercept any runners." Cole accessed his implant's comms functions, selecting Emily Vance. "Cole to CAG."

"CAG here, Cole," Emily's voice responded in his ears.

"Emily, launch our ready alert squadron with orders to patrol the near-station space and maintain a blockade. No departures that have not been personally approved by Harlon, Srexx, or me. I'll leave the shift design up to you, but I want constant coverage."

"Aye, sir," Emily replied. "They're launching now, and I'm activating the next squadron on the duty roster to begin prepping for launch."

"Thank you, CAG. Call me if you need me. Cole out."

Cole leaned against the corridor bulkhead, almost against the DNA tester panel, turning the situation around in his head and looking for what else he should be doing. He couldn't think of anything. He cast his mind back to the emergency management courses in the ISA training for the starship captain qualification.

Sighing, Cole righted himself and accessed the comms function of his implant, placing a call to Srexx.

"Yes, Cole?" Cole heard Srexx's voice in his ears as if Srexx were a person standing right beside him.

"Are you aware of the shooting?"

"Yes, Cole. I... I think I feel sad."

"I know, buddy. Me, too. Whoever did it probably aimed for me, instead of Wixil."

"Are you safe, Cole?"

Cole smiled. "Yeah, buddy. I am. I have Red and thirty of Harlon's finest standing around me. Srexx, the station's information network is now yours. Find me that shooter. If that isn't possible, find me any information on the shooter you can."

"I will, Cole. I shall devote my full resources to the task."

"Thanks, buddy. Cole out." Cole sighed and shook his head.

"May I ask, sir?" One of the marines said.

Cole grinned. "Srexx just told me he's going to devote his full resources to uncovering any and all information within this station involving the shooter."

Every marine turned to look at Cole before sharing a look between each other. The marine who'd first asked gave a low whistle and shook his head. "Well... *that* sorry bastard is thoroughly screwed."

Footfalls preceded a group of people coming around the corner where the shooter had fired. Every marine readied his or her laser carbine. Red growled; for Red, that was sufficient. The new arrivals froze, and Cole saw CEO Vince Jefferds in the middle of ten CIE Security personnel.

"Mr. Coleson, may I have a word?" Jefferds shouted.

Cole and his entourage approached the group. "Are these people CIE Security?"

"Yes, they are my personal detail," Jefferds replied. "I demand to know why the computer informs me all CIE Security personnel are on suspension pending review. No one discussed this with me."

"Marines, secure them and remove their sidearms," Cole said. The

CIE Security personnel started to move, but Cole's next words caused them to freeze. "If they resist, use any force you feel appropriate."

"Mr. Coleson, this just isn't done!" Jefferds protested.

Cole shifted his attention to his CEO. "Vince, someone just injured a very dear friend taking a shot at me. Well... I don't have conclusive evidence the shooter wanted me, but the other members of the group were Sasha, two Ghrexels, and Red here. I'm going with Occam's Razor on this. At any rate, given the attitude I saw in the Chief Security Officer, I'm not about to assume that CIE Security as a whole isn't compromised. Anyone who doesn't like it is welcome to leave *after* they've been reviewed by my people and absolved of all complicity."

"You can't do that!" one of the security personnel growled. "We're citizens of the Solar Republic! We have rights!"

Cole smiled. "Congratulations, but that only matters within the Solar Republic. On this station, my word is *law*."

Jefferds shoulders slumped. If Cole hadn't been looking right at him, he wouldn't have noticed. The motion was *that* slight.

"He can't do this... right, Mr. Jefferds?" Another security person asked.

Jefferds shook his head. "No, Adam. Mr. Coleson is entirely correct. Under the provisions of the Solar Republic Constitution, this station and any CIE holdings in the Centauri Trinary System are sovereign foreign territory. The Solar Republic has no authority or jurisdiction within thirty light-minutes of the station."

Cole looked to the marines. "Detach a few people to take these individuals to their quarters. I'm going back to the ship, and between Red and whoever remains, I should be safe enough."

"Sir... Colonel Hanson ordered us—all of us—to stick to you like molecular-bonding adhesive," the senior marine present countered.

Cole frowned. "I'll handle Colonel Hanson. I'm sure these people would rather await their interviews in their own quarters instead of *Haven*'s brig, because that's the only bed-space we have."

It turned out the marines were more afraid of Harlon Hanson than they were of Cole. The security personnel accompanied them back to

Haven, where they awaited transfer from the brig to their quarters aboard the station.

———

Cole arrived in the waiting room where Yeleth paced within seconds of the doctor. The doctor overseeing Wixil's care was none other than Yralla Hrrsh, the Ghrexel Cole had hired to be the chief of Ghrexel medicine aboard *Haven*. Hrrsh had also been Clanless when she came aboard, but Yeleth accepted her into the ranks of Clan Haven within minutes of her arrival.

"How is she?" Cole asked, moving to stand with Yeleth.

Hrrsh regarded Cole in silence a moment before nodding once. "As I was saying, Wixil's condition—while serious—is no longer life-threatening. Commander Sasha was correct that the weapon used was a laser device of some kind, and given the tissue damage I observed, you should consider yourself fortunate she blocked the shot, Captain. It would have killed you."

"So, she'll be fine?" Cole pressed.

Hrrsh nodded once, her tail languidly swishing side to side behind her. "Yes. She is resting now. We've started a series of therapies that will repair the tissue damaged by the laser shot. She won't even have any scar tissue when the therapies are complete. Once she is well enough for visitors, we will inform you."

A low growl rumbled deep in Yeleth's torso. "I am going to my young one and will sit with her."

"It may be some time—"

"I do not care."

Hrrsh looked to Cole. Cole lifted his hands and shook his head. "Hey... I'm just the captain. Even I have sense enough not to come between a mother and her child. This one's all you."

"Very well," Hrrsh replied. "Follow me."

Hrrsh turned to leave, and Yeleth gave Cole a silent nod and followed her.

CHAPTER SIXTEEN

Executive Conference Room, CIE Offices
    Coleson Clanhold
    Centauri Trinary System
    25 August 3000, 08:50 GST

Cole entered the conference room and smiled at seeing all the C-level executives waiting for him. Nice to see they 'got the memo' about punctuality at his meetings. He ignored their uneasy expressions at the five marines taking up position outside the conference room to match the five marines plus Red following Cole into the conference room. Cole wondered if Red's sheer size intimidated any of them, as the tips of the Igthon's ears brushed the ceiling.

"Good morning," Cole said as he strode to the head of the table. "Thank you all for coming. First order of business," looking directly at CEO Jefferds, "have you handled the matter of the Chief Security Officer's insubordination?"

"No, not yet. He's not even out of the infirmary."

Cole nodded. "I said I'd leave the matter in your hands, but if you wait too long, I may change my mind about more than just the insubordination. Understood?"

Jefferds jerked a nod.

"Excellent," Cole replied and shifted his attention to the executives en masse. "As most of you are probably aware, someone took a shot at me yesterday. Whoever it was missed, injuring one of my closest friends instead. My marine commander, Colonel Harlon Hanson, will be assigning a team to investigate this. You will cooperate fully with this investigative team. Anything less than your full cooperation—as judged by the investigators, not you—will be insubordination and grounds for summary dismissal. Do you understand?"

Several nodded, but a few looked down or away.

"I didn't hear you," Cole said. "Since you people insist on being children, we'll go around the table... just like in school. Jefferds, do you understand what I've said here today?"

"Yes, Mr. Coleson."

Cole proceeded around the table, calling each person out and requiring a verbal response. After the last person announced her understanding, Cole nodded once and started to leave.

"We should not be treated like this," one gentleman said. "We are highly respected members of the business community, and we have served this company for years."

Cole stopped, turned to lock gazes with the man who had spoken. "If your professional dignity is so put upon, submit your immediate resignation. I have zero concerns about filling your seat at the table." Cole held the man's gaze until *he* looked away. "No? If you're not prepared to follow through with your convictions, don't waste my time with pointless posturing. There is far too much to do."

With that, Cole left the conference room, the marines outside taking up lead positions.

Instead of returning to the ship, though, Cole went back to his family's residence on the station. He hadn't explored much of it the last time he'd been here, before Security interrupted. As he stood just inside the main door, Cole accessed the station schematics for the residence and shook his head, marveling at its size. The Coleson residence was easily a third of the station's total volume.

Cole chuckled. There was no way he'd be able to explore the whole space in a couple hours... not unless he made it a whirlwind tour. One location on the schematics drew his attention, though, and he used the schematics as a map to find his way there.

The Hall of Remembrance was as grandiose as its name implied, but tastefully so. Starting at the left side of the hatch into the space and going around the bulkheads, Cole saw images and artifacts of every direct ancestor of his family... all the way back to Arthur Coleson. Seven hundred years made for a lot of people.

Cole spent two hours working his way through about a quarter of the space, when he had a realization. He pivoted on his heel and strode from the Hall of Remembrance, leaving the Coleson residence without missing a step. The marines and Red shared looks that questioned Cole's motives, but they hurried to take up their positions around their captain, lest the Colonel find out they allowed Cole to lead the way.

In minutes, Cole entered the lobby of CIE and approached the reception desk. The person was the receptionist Cole interacted with when he first arrived. She looked up when he approached, blushed, and noticeably forced herself not to look back down again.

"Hello, Mr. Coleson," she said, her cheery tone forced. "How can I help you?"

Cole smiled. "Do you have access to Jefferds's schedule? I was hoping to steal five minutes, but if he's covered up, it can wait."

"No, I'm sorry. I don't have that information. May I have just a moment please?"

"Sure," Cole replied, nodding once.

The receptionist keyed commands into her workstation and touched a fingertip to the earbud in her right ear, saying, "Katrice? Hi, it's Sera up at reception. I have Mr. Coleson here asking if the CEO has five minutes he can steal, but he said it can wait if the CEO's covered up. How's his schedule?" The receptionist nodded, making Cole assume she was listening to what Katrice had to say. "Oh. Okay.

Give me just a moment, then." The receptionist shifted her attention back to Cole. "The CEO's exec says he left about twenty minutes ago for a meeting at one of our charitable organizations on Earth. He's not supposed to return until tomorrow, but she asks if there's anything she can do to help."

"Possibly," Cole replied. "I was going to ask Jefferds about hiring a team experienced in packing and transporting artifacts, along with a trusted moving company. I want everything in the Residence packed up for transport back home aboard my ship when we leave, and I figured it would be better to start sooner than later."

"Okay," the receptionist said, lifting a fingertip to her earbud once more. "Katrice? Yes. He's looking to hire people experienced in artifacts handling, packaging, and transport, plus a moving company we can trust. He wants to take everything in the Residence with him when he leaves." The receptionist winced and looked up at Cole. "Katrice. Katrice! Slow down. I don't think he's leaving anytime soon. He said he figured it would be easier to start sooner than later. Okay. Thanks, Katrice. I appreciate it."

"Is everything okay?" Cole asked.

"It is now," the receptionist replied. "Katrice thought you were fed up and leaving, and she was working on a minor meltdown before I stopped her. She's a little high-strung. She said she'd look into it, since the CEO would probably end up asking her anyway, and she's also going to get you some staff for your time here. For the staff, she's thinking one of our better admins and a hotshot or two from Legal. Pass me your comms code, please, and I'll see that she gets it."

"Omega-5543297."

"Wow. That's pretty high in the Omega chain. I didn't realize there were that many issued."

Cole grinned. "There probably aren't, and I doubt you'll find records of it being issued to me."

The receptionist looked up at Cole once more, her expression appraising. "There's a story there."

"You have no idea," Cole replied. "Use that code if you need me. I'll be around."

With that, Cole turned to leave. The large Igthon fell into step behind him as the marines arranged themselves in a mobile perimeter. Cole didn't really like it, but he liked the idea of being shot even less. As the entire troop departed CIE's offices, Cole's primary thought was how much he looked forward to being back home.

CHAPTER SEVENTEEN

Exercise Room 4, Recreation Deck
    Battle-Carrier *Haven*, Docking Slip F-Seven
    Coleson Clanhold, Centauri Trinary System
    27 August 3000, 09:45 GST

Cole moved through the stretches following his workout and sparring session. His sparring partner and instructor did likewise about three meters away.

"You've always been serious about this, sir," the marine regarded as the best hand-to-hand fighter on the ship said, stretching almost in unison with Cole, "but lately, you've really taken the dedication up a notch. I think you landed some very good hits today."

"Thanks," Cole said, then grinned, "but I think I received some, too."

The marine shrugged. "It's all about experience. I came to this a long time ago, so I've seen a few things. One day, you'll be in my place with someone looking at you pretty much like you're looking at me now."

"You think so?"

The marine nodded. "It was that way with me. I think, maybe, it's one of those cosmic trends that gets repeated over and over again. The good news, though, is you're getting better. Keep doing that."

Cole took a breath to respond, but the ship's intercom annunciation blared over the speakers, followed closely by a voice Cole didn't recognize saying, "Bridge to Captain."

Sure, Cole could've responded through his implant, but Cole never had liked captains who felt the need for compartmentalization. He always thought crews who knew the whole score were better prepared than crews who didn't. He took the few steps necessary to bring him to the room's comms panel and pressed a command.

"Cole here."

"Sir, the 'lock team report some interesting people, and they all want to see you."

Cole looked at his sparring partner and lifted an eyebrow in question. The marine shrugged as if to say, 'How should I know?'

"Did the 'lock team say who those people are, Bridge?" Cole asked.

"There are four, sir: two CIE personnel, and two people who appear to be Solar Republic Navy."

"Yeah, that doesn't match at all. What is SRN doing here?"

"No idea, sir. Station Customs reports passing them aboard twenty minutes ago."

Cole sighed. "Okay. Have them escorted to Akyra's office, and leave a guard or two in the room. I'm not concerned so much with the CIE personnel, but I don't want the SRN people trying anything. Alert Akyra that she's about to have guests, and pass all this on to Srexx, too, please. He probably already knows, but I like to keep him informed."

About twenty minutes later, Cole sat at his desk and sent Akyra a message to pass the CIE personnel through. Moments later, the hatch irised open to admit a young man whose expression betrayed his eagerness and a calm, professional woman carrying a folio. Cole stood to greet them.

"Hello, Mr. Coleson," the woman said. "I am Nadia Perez, and I work in CIE's Legal department. Katrice Nelson indicated you needed a small staff during your time here in Centauri. This is Mark Blumenthal; he's from the admin pool and very highly regarded. I understand his previous supervisor was most unhappy with Mark's reassignment."

Cole nodded, shaking Nadia's hand first and then Mark's. "It's nice to meet you both. Were you informed on what led to the assessment I needed a staff?"

"Yes," Mark replied. "I already have several candidates for the moving teams lined up. The artifacts team is proving a bit more challenging, but I'm thinking we'll find the people we need among University scholars looking for transport to the expansion zones for research. If they sign on with you for pay and a one-way trip, it becomes a mutually beneficial arrangement."

Cole nodded. "Works for me. We're not exactly set up for passengers aboard, but as long as they don't mind common ship accommodations, we can take care of them."

Mark smiled. "Sir, most of these people sleep on the ground for a living. Anything beyond that is pure heaven to them."

"Fair enough," Cole replied with a smile. "You should introduce yourself to Akyra out front. She's your counterpart aboard-ship." Mark nodded once. "Okay. Do either of you have *any* idea what the SRN people are doing here?"

"They are remarkably tight-lipped about their task, Mr. Coleson," Nadia replied. "Very reluctant to say much of anything beyond discussing such scintillating topics as the weather."

"Well, I suppose I might as well see what they want. Thanks for stopping by."

Mark left, but Nadia did not.

"Mr. Coleson, if I may, I suggest not meeting with the SRN personnel without legal advice until we have a better understanding of why they're here. Their unit insignia identifies them as members of the Judge Advocate General Corps."

Cole blinked. "So... they're lawyers?"

"Correct, sir."

"Do I need to give you a credit chit or something before they get in here?"

Now, Nadia blinked. "Why... whatever for?"

"So, there's a fiduciary relationship to establish attorney-client privilege."

A slight smile curled Nadia's lips, much like what she might allow for an amusing child. "Mr. Coleson, your company—CIE—is a private entity owned in whole by you, upon the execution of your father's will. We've had a fiduciary relationship since I started at CIE seven years ago."

"All right, then," Cole said. "Let's do this."

Cole gestured to a chair on his side of the room as he moved back to his desk. He sent a note to Akyra, asking her to send in the SRN personnel. Within moments, the hatch irised open for a man and woman in the uniform of the Solar Republic Navy. The man's dark hair showed some slight graying at the temples, while the woman appeared to be several years his junior. Cole moved to stand by his desk to greet them.

"Hello," Cole said, extending his hand. "I'm Cole, and this is Nadia Perez."

The man stepped in to shake Cole's hand first, as the woman twitched at Nadia's name.

"I'm Commander Patrick O'Connell, and this is my associate, Lieutenant Masters."

"Please," Cole said, "have a seat. Would either of you like something to eat or drink? I came straight here from my morning workout, and... well... my desk or one of these chairs is looking rather tasty right now."

The SRN officers shared a glance, and Commander O'Connell replied, "Well, since you're offering, I think we might enjoy something. They bundled us on a fast packet out of Earth so fast, we hardly had time to grab our notes."

Cole tapped the comms control on his desk, activating a direct link to Akyra.

"Yes, sir?" Akyra answered after the speakers chirped.

"Do you mind sending down to the mess deck for some refreshments? I'd like my normal morning fare. Nadia, Commander, Lieutenant... sound off on what you'd like."

The three looked at one another and somehow sorted who'd speak first, because Nadia said, "Some tea would be nice."

"Milk, honey, sugar?" Akyra asked. "We have the equivalent of a five-star coffee house."

Cole saw the commander and lieutenant perk up at the mention of the coffee possibilities.

"No, thank you," Nadia said. "I prefer straight black tea, hot."

"We have you covered, then. Who's next?"

"Coffee for me with hazelnut creamer if you have it," the lieutenant said, "and a pastry of some kind if possible."

"We have just about every additive for coffee and tea you could imagine; the captain likes to take care of his people. Might as well state your preference on the pastry, too," Akyra replied. "We have just about every variation you could imagine."

"Uhm, apple danish?"

"We have that. Too bad you're not here tomorrow. It's the pastry chef's monthly Apple Day, and you could choose from about fifty different varieties of apple for your danish."

The lieutenant's eyes seemed to glaze over for a moment as she smiled, whispering, "Oh, wow."

"I'd like coffee with cream and sugar, please," the commander said, "and two bagels with cream cheese."

"Any preference on the bagels or cream cheese? Like the pastries, you have some choices."

"Sesame seed bagel?"

"Have it," Akira replied.

"Uhm... strawberry cream cheese?"

"Have that, too. Would anyone like anything else?"

Cole looked around to everyone in the room, who shook their heads, and said, "We're good here. Don't forget to get something for yourself."

"I never do, sir. Akyra out."

The speakers chirped to indicate the closed comms channel.

Cole leaned back against his seat, eyeing the SRN personnel. "So... why are a couple of Solar Navy lawyers here to speak with me?"

The lieutenant didn't hide her surprise fast enough, but the commander maintained his non-expression.

"We were hoping to discuss an incident in which we believe this ship was a participant," Commander O'Connell said.

Cole nodded. "You're definitely a veteran lawyer. That's both informative and not... all at the same time."

"We were sent by the Board of Inquiry convened to investigate the Caernarvon Incident. When word reached the members of the Board that the other ship involved appeared to have arrived in Centauri, they expressed unanimous interest in your take on what happened."

Cole frowned. "You're going to have to give me more information. I'm drawing a blank on 'Caernarvon Incident.'"

"A sophisticated, simultaneous intrusion rendered an entire battle-group of the Solar Republic Navy ineffective for combat by engaging the reactor core ejection systems. The event occurred in the Caernarvon system, and our ranking officer on the scene was Admiral Himari Sato."

"Oh," Cole said, drawing out the word. "*That* Caernarvon Incident. Yeah... I bet your Admiral Sato and I have very different views on what happened."

"Are you willing to discuss the matter with us?" Commander O'Connell asked.

Cole chuckled. "I don't have a problem with it. The whole discourse doesn't paint your admiral in a very good light, though, and Sasha said she's one of your best."

"A moment," Nadia interjected. Cole, the commander, and the lieutenant turned toward her. "If this is to be a formal deposition, I require some time to discuss the incident with my client. It seems I am the only person present who is unaware of what transpired, beyond the bare summary you offered."

"I don't know that we need to go to trouble of performing a formal deposition," the commander countered.

Nadia lifted her left eyebrow, allowing the silence to extend before saying, "I am well aware of SRN JAG's reputation for... creative... interpretations of interview laws and evidentiary procedure. The only circumstance in which you will discuss any matter under review by a Board of Inquiry with my client is a formal deposition."

"That sounds like there's something here I'm missing," Cole said.

Nadia turned her attention to Cole, replying, "Under both the Uniform Code of Military Justice *and* Solar Republic Criminal Code, formal depositions must be entered into the case records in their entirety with no redactions or just cherry-picking what to include. More than one individual in the past has faced circumstances where they held an informal interview with JAG or representatives of the Republic's Ministry of Justice that reflected very poorly on them in the end, because the interview was not fully disclosed in the case. Any formal depositions submitted *must* be complete and without tampering. Deposition recorders imbed integrity checks in the file that verify its authenticity."

"Right, then," Cole said. "Formal deposition it is."

Nadia turned back to the JAG officers. "I trust you have the necessary equipment. If not, I am happy to contact CIE Legal. We have a number of the devices available."

Commander O'Connell sighed. "It's nice to see your reputation isn't exaggerated, Ms. Perez, and yes, we would appreciate the use of a deposition recorder."

"Your reputation?" Cole asked, shifting his attention to Nadia.

A slight blush colored her cheeks as Nadia answered, "Yes. It seems I'm regarded rather well in the legal community."

"Seriously?" Cole asked.

"'Rather well?' Ms. Perez, you're one of the apex predators in the legal field. I've seen the mere mention of Nadia Perez send long-established and well-respected firms with dozens of people on their legal teams into full retreat," Commander O'Connell said. "I also remember the considerable gnashing of teeth among the top-shelf private firms in the Republic when she chose to accept a position with CIE Legal."

"Well, then," Cole replied, smiling, "I'm glad she's on my side."

"You have no idea, sir," the lieutenant said. "You really don't."

Just then, the overhead speakers chirped and broadcast Akyra's voice, "Sir, refreshments have arrived. Is now a good time?"

Nadia regarded the JAG officers with a non-expression for a

moment before saying, "Without intending to appear rude, it might be the best use of our time if you excuse us. I can confer with my client regarding the event in question while we wait for the deposition recorder and enjoy our refreshments."

"That works," Commander O'Connell replied. "Where should we go?"

"If you don't mind sharing space with Akyra, I would imagine that would be sufficient," Cole said, directing a questioning glance at Nadia.

Nadia nodded. "If you are certain they will not be able to overhear or record our discussion, that's fine with me."

Cole chuckled. "They could leave recording equipment in the room, and it'd be blank when they retrieved it."

"Your sound shielding is that advanced?" Commander O'Connell asked.

"No," Cole replied, grinning. "My information security team is that good."

"Our recording devices utilize top-of-the-line Solar Republic military encryption," O'Connell countered.

Cole still grinned. "I didn't doubt it for a moment. Doesn't change my mind."

O'Connell looked a bit uneasy as he and the lieutenant stood. They moved to leave the office as a steward stepped in with Cole's and Nadia's orders.

Within moments, the hatch irised closed, and Cole and Nadia were alone with their refreshments. Nadia moved to the seat just vacated by Commander O'Connell.

"So, tell me everything about this Caernarvon Incident."

"Well, it was just after Iota Ceti... "

Several minutes later, Cole completed his narrative. Nadia sat in the seat, totally relaxed as far as he could tell, holding her cup of tea in her hands.

"So, what you're telling me is that this Srexx person hacked the computers—the military-grade computers with military-grade protections—of a Solar Republic battle-group and activated their core ejection mechanisms?"

Cole nodded. "That's exactly what I'm telling you."

"I've never heard of a Solar Republic ship getting hacked, not even something minor like their entertainment library. Just who is this Srexx?"

"Srexx... well... there's no point in hiding it from you. Srexx is an AI. His core architecture is a quantum computing cluster of three nodes, with each member of the cluster made up of at least two-hundred-fifty-six individual nodes themselves."

"That... is impressive. I know just enough to have a vague idea of Srexx's capabilities."

"Yeah," Cole said, "he decrypts protected military files for fun. We're still working on the concept of privacy."

Nadia almost dropped her tea. "You *must* be joking. He seriously decrypts military archives for fun?"

"Srexx? Care to weigh in?"

"Thank you, Cole," Srexx replied via the overhead speakers. "Yes, Ms. Perez, Cole's statement was accurate. I find unused compute cycles to be... inefficient... and I prefer to have data available on which I can maintain as few unused compute cycles as possible."

"What he's not saying," Cole opined, "is that he likes to copy the entire contents of a ship's computer core when we encounter them at the bit level. I imagine he uses the ship's external sensors to do so; we haven't really discussed the exact mechanics involved."

"And you're okay with this?" Nadia asked.

Cole shrugged. "From our discussions, he approaches it with a very 'Us vs. Them' attitude. He protects 'us,' without caring so much about 'them.' Morally, I admit I should have problems with it, but ethically and philosophically? My people come first in my eyes. Always and without question. So... it works."

"Am I one of 'your people?'" Nadia asked.

"I don't know yet," Cole admitted. "Everyone aboard here has been vetted in such a way that I have zero doubts where their loyalties and interests lie. Someone aboard that station took a shot at me. See the difference? But... we should probably carry on with that deposition unless you have further questions?"

"What level of threat did the Solar battlegroup pose to your ship?" Nadia asked.

"Srexx?" Cole said.

"That question is difficult to answer, Ms. Perez," Srexx replied. "At the time in question, *Haven* only possessed three of its five shield layers and didn't have any dorsal or ventral turret emplacements. As such, we were restricted to 'broadsides,' as you put it, but battleship-grade armaments make up those broadsides. It is unlikely that the battlegroup could have destroyed the ship; however, odds favored *Haven* sustaining significant damage in an engagement... possibly to the extent that we could not have departed the system without making repairs."

"And what were the chances of the battlegroup's survival in such an engagement?" Nadia asked.

"One one-thousandth of a percent," Srexx replied without hesitation, "plus or minus two ten-thousandths."

"So, by ejecting their reactor cores, you saved most of their lives, if not all, in addition to the people aboard *Haven* at the time."

"Yes, Ms. Perez."

Nadia nodded. "I think we're ready, then. I'm very interested to see how they approach their questions to you, Mr. Coleson. I see one of three approaches: pro Sato, against Sato, and neutral. If they're even a little wise, they'll be neutral. If they approach the matter with any hostility toward you at all, I'll neuter them... figuratively speaking, of course."

CHAPTER EIGHTEEN

Cole invited the SRN officers back in, as Nadia moved to her original seat. A thought occurred to Cole as the SRN officers stood, and he looked first at them and then at Nadia, asking, "Would you like to do this somewhere with more space? I don't care either way, but I thought you guys might find the office a bit cramped."

"What options do you have?" Nadia asked.

"The hatch to the bridge briefing room is just a few meters aft and around a corner. It has a larger table. Don't get your hopes up, though; the chairs are the same as what's in my office."

Nadia nodded. "That sounds nice, and it would provide everyone a work surface."

Cole looked to the SRN officers.

"I have no problem with it," Commander O'Connell replied.

"This way, then," Cole said, moving toward the hatch that led from Akyra's office to the corridor. He was about halfway through Akyra's office when the speakers chirped.

"Bridge to Captain."

Cole accessed his implant and routed the call through the ship's audio system without thinking about it, saying, "Cole here."

"Sir, the 'lock team reports a runner from CIE Legal with some stuff for a Ms. Nadia Perez. Do you know anything about that?"

Cole directed a questioning expression to Nadia.

"I sent a message to my staff via my implant while we consulted on the matter," Nadia replied.

Cole nodded. "Bridge, could you have someone escort the runner to the bridge briefing room, please? We'll be in there for a bit."

"Of course, sir. Will there be anything else?"

"Once the runner delivers Ms. Perez's materials, please make sure we're not disturbed unless whatever it is warrants an alert status," Cole replied.

"Of course, sir."

As Cole led the group to the briefing room, the voice followed them in the overhead speakers. By the time Cole arrived at the hatch to the briefing room, Nadia *and* the SRN officers looked a little wild around the eyes.

"Thanks. Cole out." When Cole turned to invite everyone to have a seat, he noticed their expressions. "Is something wrong?"

Commander O'Connell pointed toward the ceiling with his right index finger as he asked, "Was that normal?"

"Was what normal?"

"The call following you. Was that normal?"

Cole nodded. "I didn't want to hang around in the office or make the bridge wait until we arrived here, so I accepted the call with my implant and routed the audio through the ship's system. Don't your ships do that?"

The SRN officers didn't respond, but Nadia shook her head 'no.'

"Huh. Okay. Please, have a seat. The runner should be here shortly... unless they have problems with the transit shaft."

"That was a rather... new... experience," Commander O'Connell said.

Cole grinned. "Yeah, my first officer screamed like a terrified child the first time she used one. There seems to be an adjustment period sometimes."

"Your first officer," Commander O'Connell said. "Am I correct that she is, in fact, Sasha Thyrray, late of the Aurelian Navy?"

"Commander O'Connell, we have not yet begun the deposition," Nadia interjected before Cole could reply. "Please, reserve all questions potentially related to your investigation until such time as the deposition has started."

"I was just making conversation," O'Connell replied.

"Perhaps," Nadia said. "However, personnel assignments aboard the ship that embarrassed one of the most highly decorated battle-groups in the SRN tread alarmingly close to investigatory preliminaries, especially if those assignments have not changed since the incident."

Just then, the hatch irised open, and Red leaned his head inside. Both SRN officers paled; Commander O'Connell's eyes widened just enough to notice, while the lieutenant's jaw dropped.

"Cap, there's a runner out here from CIE," Red said, his deep voice almost a natural growl. "The little guy says he has materials for Nadia Perez."

Cole chuckled. "Everyone is a 'little guy' to you, Red. Pass him inside, please."

"Sure thing, Cap."

Red pulled back out of the hatch, allowing entry for a young man who looked barely old enough to shave. The young man carried a satchel and walked straight to Nadia, handing the satchel to her.

"Thank you, Charles," Nadia said. "That will be all."

"You're welcome, ma'am."

Nadia opened the satchel, placing a hardcase and several file folios on the tabletop before setting the satchel aside.

"You need anything, Cap?" Red asked, leaning back inside.

"Not at the moment, Red. Thanks."

"We'll be right outside if you do," Red replied, before withdrawing and allowing the hatch to iris closed.

Nadia, meanwhile, had opened the hardcase. Inside, Cole saw a device reminiscent of the old conference phones he'd seen in ancient movies and what looked like a collection of satellite microphones. She placed a microphone in front of each person before connecting them to the device. That done, Nadia activated the device, keying a couple commands before nodding once.

"We're ready here, sir," Nadia said.

Cole looked to the SRN officers and found them still staring at the hatch. "Is something wrong?"

"That... " Commander O'Connell stopped and cleared his throat. "I think he was the largest Igthon I've ever seen."

Cole grinned. "Yeah, he is, but he's a big softie... until you make him mad."

"Shall we begin?" Nadia asked.

The SRN officers turned toward the table and sat, opening their folios and laying out their materials. It took them right at a minute to organize everything, and Commander O'Connell looked up and nodded once.

"We're ready," the commander said.

Nadia keyed a command on the recorder and spoke in a strong, projecting voice. "This is Nadia Perez, legal counsel for Mr. Bartholomew James Coleson. The date is August 27th, 3000, and we are located in the bridge briefing room on Deck Three aboard the Battle-Carrier *Haven*. This is a formal deposition of Mr. Coleson in regard to the events of 27 July 2999, occurring in the Caernarvon System and hereafter referred to as the Caernarvon Incident. Let the record reflect that Mr. Coleson is the individual known as the lost Coleson Heir and has recently arrived in Centauri to finalize claiming his inheritance, specifically the sole ownership of and full executive authority over the independent corporate entity Coleson Interstellar Engineering. Would the deposing counsels please state your respective ranks, full names, and organization for the record?"

As Nadia finished stating Cole's full identity, Cole didn't miss the lieutenant starting to look a shade intimidated.

"Commander Patrick O'Connell of the Solar Republic Navy Judge Advocate General's Corps."

"L-Lieutenant Tiffany Masters of the Solar Republic Navy Judge Advocate General's Corps."

"Thank you," Nadia said. "Please state the case from which your request comes, Commander."

"It's not a case as such. As per standard regulations, a Board of Inquiry was convened upon TF-27's return to the Solar Republic to investigate the matters surrounding the incident. SRN JAG recently became aware that a ship matching the configuration of the opposing vessel mentioned in Admiral Sato's statement docked at the Coleson Clanhold, and the Judge Advocate General dispatched us to determine what we could learn about the incident here."

"Ah... and TF-27 is?" Nadia asked.

"TF-27 is the common usage for Task Force 27, a unit assigned to maintain the security of the Caernarvon system in response to increasing instability within the Aurelian Commonwealth. The continued presence of Solar Republic military assets in the Caernarvon system is stipulated under the two entities' trade agreement, which I can provide if you wish. Admiral Himari Sato was assigned to command the task force."

"Very well," Nadia said. "Now that we have the basics out of the way, do you wish to enter a formal summary of the events in question into the deposition's record?"

"When Admiral Sato challenged an unknown ship approaching the Caernarvon station at a significant fraction of lightspeed, TF-27 was rendered combat ineffective via a cyber-attack, utilizing an as-yet-unidentified vulnerability in the ships' information network to eject the reactor cores of every ship in the task force."

"Excellent," Nadia said, her voice almost a purr. "Commander, as this is an unscheduled deposition without the normal handshaking that occurs prior to such an event, I reserve the right to veto any question at the moment it is asked. If you disagree with this, the deposition is over, and you are welcome to attempt obtaining a subpoena for my client, let alone enforcing it. If you agree and wish to continue, please state your agreement for the record."

"As senior officer present, SRN JAG accepts your stipulation for this deposition."

"Very good," Nadia replied. "I think that's all the preliminaries handled. Mr. Coleson, do you wish to make a statement before the deposition begins?"

"I can't think of anything," Cole said, looking at Nadia. "Is there some kind of statement I should make?"

"Not as such, no. Usually in the case of a pre-deposition statement, it's more of a declarative than anything else. I have seen the three-way verification of your identity myself, and I can produce certified copies should SRN JAG request such."

"Well, then," Cole said, "let's hear what they came all the way out to Centauri to ask."

"Mr. Coleson," Commander O'Connell began, "are you in fact the individual who identified himself as 'Cole, the owner and captain of the Battle-Carrier *Haven*?'"

"Yes. I prefer 'Cole' over either of my given names or 'Mr. Coleson.' 'Mr. Coleson' always makes me think of my father or grandfather."

"How would you characterize the events of July 27th, what we're calling the Caernarvon Incident?"

"In two words, a colossal overreaction," Cole replied. "I told Admiral Sato we were just in the system to re-supply our food. I think we had like a day's worth of food left by the time we arrived in Caernarvon. She started the conversation on the hostile side of neutral, and matters spiraled from there. I never understood why she chose to commit the actions she did, but I have a responsibility to my people that far outweighs any consideration of her motives. I had an option to avoid combat, and I took it. I doubt Sato even understands how many of her people's lives we saved that day, too."

"May I ask how you figure you saved Solar Republic Navy lives? TF-27 had ninety-two ships. You had one. That suggests the outcome of any conflict to be a rather foregone conclusion."

"Yes, Sato had ninety-two ships, but even though my ship looks like a battleship with a flight deck, it is a grievous mistake to equate *Haven* with a battleship in the SRN. At the time of the Incident, *Haven* possessed three shield layers and considerable broadside armament. She lacked dorsal and ventral turrets, which anyone with basic sensors or a half-decent telescope if they're close enough will see is no longer the case. Members of my crew advised me that we had a significant chance of surviving any conflict, though we would be heavily damaged.

"Here's how it breaks down. Eighty of those ninety-two ships were destroyers and frigates, sixteen and sixty-four respectively. One torpedo from *Haven* will reduce a frigate to an expanding cloud of debris, and against a destroyer, there might be a quarter of the vessel left. *Haven* has seventeen torpedo launchers, and that's not even counting our missile launchers. The four battleships and eight cruisers would've taken longer to defeat, and we'd be taking damage in the meantime. Still, though... if I'd had no other choice, I would've fought them and won."

"I'll set your assessment of the potential conflict aside for the moment, if I may, and ask why you needed to put into Caernarvon for re-supply in the first place."

Cole grinned. "We had just departed Iota Ceti. When we arrived in Iota Ceti we had one-hundred-seventy-eight people aboard. When we left Iota Ceti, that number was eight-hundred-thirty-five. I went into Iota Ceti ill prepared for such a dramatic increase in the number of mouths to feed. With careful rationing, we might—*might*—have made it two more days beyond Caernarvon until no food remained on the entire ship."

Both SRN officers blinked, and the lieutenant voiced what they both had just realized, "Oh, shit. You're the Lone Marine."

"Whether my client is or is not the Lone Marine is not germane to the deposition," Nadia said. "Please, restrict yourselves to questions involving the Caernarvon Incident."

"What evidence can you provide that will corroborate your account of the Caernarvon Incident?" Commander O'Connell asked.

Cole leaned back against his seat as he considered the question. "It's possible I have bridge logs of the Incident. I know I have the communications logs. Hmmm... I think my official answer at this time should be that I'm not sure and need to investigate that matter myself."

"My question," Nadia interjected, "is why my client even needs to *present* evidence in the first place. Do your own ships not record logs of all spaces aboard, just for situations such as Boards of Inquiry and courts-martial? It is my understanding of the UCMJ that a ship must maintain a protected, tamper-proof archive of all log entries for the duration of its deployment. One would think my client's logs of the Incident and those retrieved from TF-27 would present the exact same record of events... simply viewed from different perspectives. Are you stating for the record that SRN archives aboard-ship are not tamper-proof?"

"I am stating no such thing," Commander O'Connell countered, a little too quickly to Cole's mind. "It's all well and good for someone to say, 'this is what happened,' but it's another matter entirely to back up those statements with evidence."

"Ah, I see," Nadia replied. "You are implying my client is a liar. I shall make a note of that libelous position for a future discussion with the SRN Judge Advocate General."

"It is in no way libelous, Ms. Perez, and I can't say I approve of your position."

"I disagree, Commander. Would you like me to cite relevant case law in which charges of libel stemming from official depositions have been upheld at all levels of the judiciary, both civilian and military? And isn't it also a matter of precedent that committing libel during an official deposition is grounds for charges of Conduct Unbecoming an Officer under the UCMJ? I would need a minute or two of quick research, but if you like, I will cite the relevant case law in that matter as well."

"I think we're done here," Commander O'Connell said, standing up and shoving his materials back into his folio.

"Very well, Commander," Nadia replied, the tone of her voice calm, pleasant, and unconcerned. "To where shall I forward a certified copy of this deposition?"

"For all I care," the Commander growled, "you can keep the damned thing."

Without another word, the commander pivoted and walked out of the briefing room, leaving a rather bewildered lieutenant behind. Nadia keyed the commands to stop the recording and looked to the lieutenant.

"We are no longer recording," Nadia said. "It appears something got a bit under the commander's skin."

"I-I've never seen him like that," Lieutenant Masters said, "but then, I've only been assigned to JAG for a couple months. This was my first case."

"Well, the SRN loves for their shit to roll downhill, dear," Nadia replied, producing a small data chit from a jacket pocket. "If you find yourself in an untenable position, that has my comms code. You have good marks from law school and a good reputation in the Bar Association. You might want to think about other opportunities to excel, outside of SRN JAG."

Just then, the hatch irised back open.

"Lieutenant!" Commander O'Connell growled. "Did you join a knitting circle?"

Lieutenant Masters mouthed 'thank you' as she stood, saying, "On the way, sir!"

Silence reigned in the briefing room for several moments after the lieutenant's departure, before Cole turned to Nadia.

"Is it just me," Cole asked, "or was there something going on with the commander? It seemed like he got a little hot under the collar awfully quickly."

"Hmmm... yes, you may have something there, sir. I shall reach out to a few of my colleagues and see what there is to learn about this Board of Inquiry. I will follow up with you when I know more."

"What are you going to do with the so-called 'official deposition?'"

Nadia gave Cole a predatory smile. "Oh, it *is* an official deposition, Mr. Coleson, and as it is regarding an active Board of Inquiry at the Solar Republic Navy's Judge Advocate General Corps, I feel it is my duty—both as an attorney and as a citizen of the Republic—to ensure this deposition reaches the appropriate officers."

"Do you really have an 'in' with the Judge Advocate General?"

"The current Judge Advocate General of the Solar Republic Navy is Admiral Sir Lucien Ortega, Mr. Coleson, and my mother's maiden name just happens to be 'Ortega.'"

"Well, I'm sure 'Ortega' is a fairly common name in certain regions," Cole replied.

"Oh, it is, Mr. Coleson, but it just so happens that the man in question is my mother's older brother. After he listens to this deposition, I daresay Uncle will answer any questions I have."

CHAPTER NINETEEN

Battle-Carrier *Haven*, Coleson Clanhold
    Centauri Trinary System
    28 August 3000, 11:15 GST

Cole walked down a corridor of the hospital deck. He reached the entrance to the patient ward and turned right, passing through the hatch. From the hatch, he walked ten meters to one of the patient rooms and pressed the hatch chime control. The hatch opened at once.

Entering the room, Cole saw Yeleth standing at the foot of the bed, her tail swishing languidly from side to side as she watched him enter. Cole nodded his greeting to her and stepped into full view of the bed. He had the barest impression of Wixil crouching on the bed, before a happy shriek tore his attention away from Yeleth.

"Cole!" Wixil cheered as she launched herself at him. Cole had all of two seconds to prepare, but he caught Wixil and held her. Wixil curled into Cole's arms and snuggled close, purring as she nuzzled Cole's shoulder. "Are you okay? I was worried about you."

"You were worried about me?" Cole asked, and Wixil nodded.

"Wixil, I'm fine. You're the one who took a laser beam for me. How are you?"

"I'm good. Dr. Hrrsh said I get to leave soon, like today. I missed you, Cole. I missed the bridge, even though we're docked. Has anything exciting happened?"

"Uhm... we're still searching for the shooter. The marines have cleared most of the ships scheduled to leave the station, though. I think Harlon is overseeing everything from the Nexus over on the station. Most of the marines are deployed over there, right now. I had a formal deposition by the Solar Republic Navy yesterday over what happened in Caernarvon last year. That was fun; the senior SRN officer lost it and stormed out. I'm not quite sure what's going on there, but the lawyer from CIE said she'd look into the matter. That's about it, I think."

"It sounds like I haven't missed much, then," Wixil said, still nuzzling Cole's shoulder.

"Nope. I'm glad you're okay, Wixil. I appreciate what you did, but if you're going to keep doing that, we're getting you some armor... okay? I don't want you getting hurt for me. I'm supposed to be getting hurt for you."

"I don't like that, either," Wixil said. "How about we just not get hurt?"

"Okay. Let's work on that," Cole agreed.

Spying two chairs in the corner of the room, Cole walked over and sat in one, still holding Wixil. Yeleth followed them and sat in the chair beside Cole. He said, "I'm sorry it took me so long to visit."

"That's okay. I don't know if they would've let you see me. Mother had to threaten to claw a few people before they'd let her stay with me. One of the orderlies tried to call the marines, but Colonel Hanson overruled it. He said something about 'anyone keeping a mother from her child deserves a little clawing.'"

Cole chuckled. "It's just as well no one tried to escalate that up the chain. I would've told Yeleth to save her claws and offered my sidearm."

Wixil giggled. "I missed you, Cole."

————

Cole sat with Wixil and Yeleth until Dr. Hrrsh released Wixil. Hrrsh specified light duty for a week and for Wixil to return for evaluation at the end of that week. Once all the forms were filed to release Wixil from the hospital deck, Cole scooped her into his arms and carried her to the quarters she shared with her mother.

Cole was just delivering Wixil to her bed when the speakers chirped, broadcasting, "Bridge to Captain."

Cole used his implant to accept the call and routed it through the overhead speakers, saying, "Cole here."

"Sir, the 'lock team reports a Nadia Perez is requesting to speak with you."

"I'm on Deck One right now. I'll swing by the airlock to meet her if she doesn't mind the minute or two waiting."

"Aye, sir. Is there anything else, sir?"

"I don't think so, Bridge. Thank you. Cole out."

The speakers chirped again, and Cole turned back to Wixil. Wixil's ears drooped a little, and her tail lay flat on the bed. She said, "I'm sorry you have to go."

"I know. I'm sorry, too. How about I visit later and take you and your mom to dinner?"

Wixil's eyes lit up as her ears perked. "Can we, Mother? Please?"

Yeleth smiled. "Of course, dear one."

Wixil almost tackled Cole again, hugging him. Cole returned her hug, careful of where she'd been hit by the laser beam.

"I'm sorry, Wixil," Cole said, breaking the hug, "but I have to go. I'll see you later for dinner."

"Okay."

Cole turned to Yeleth, saying, "Find me if you need anything," before he left the quarters.

————

Arriving at the airlock mere minutes after leaving Yeleth and Wixil, Cole nodded his greeting to Nadia Perez, shaking hands with her.

"Is there somewhere we can speak?" Nadia asked.

Cole nodded. "Sure. Let's go to my office."

He turned and led Nadia to the nearest transit shaft, going down to Deck Three. From there it was a short walk to the hatch leading to Cole's office.

As the hatch irised open, Akyra looked up from her workstation, saying, "Hello, Captain. Is Wixil doing well, then?"

Cole nodded as he led Nadia through the hatch. "I left her in the quarters she shares with Yeleth, though I wouldn't be surprised to wake up tomorrow with her curled against me. I still haven't figured out how she gets into my quarters."

"I'm surprised Yeleth doesn't have something to say about that, sir."

"I mentioned it the first time it happened, and Yeleth didn't seem concerned. She told me Wixil always makes sure she knows she's doing it."

Akyra smiled. "Well, at least you don't need to worry about being clawed by Mom, then. That's always nice."

Cole chuckled. "Nadia and I need to discuss a few things. Mind seeing that we're not disturbed?"

"Of course not. Do you want anything from the mess deck?"

"I'm fine for right now," Cole replied. "How about you, Nadia?"

"I would enjoy another cup of that tea, if it's not too much trouble. It's a blend I've never encountered before."

Akyra smiled. "I'll order a carafe and full tea service... just in case Cole decides he's thirsty."

"Thanks, Akyra," Cole said and led Nadia into his office.

Entering the office, Cole sat at his desk as Nadia took a seat across from him. Once she was seated, Nadia regarded Cole in silence a few moments.

"Mr. Coleson, as your attorney, is there anything I need to know about your relationship with who I assume to be a minor?"

Cole grinned. "You mean Wixil?"

Nadia nodded once.

"She adopted me as her surrogate father, and apparently, Ghrexel family units sleep together... as in curled up together. I found out about that part when I woke up from a nap on the bridge with an adolescent Ghrexel on me. Ever since, she randomly finds her way to me and curls up at my side or on me."

Nadia gaped at Cole. "You nap on the bridge?"

"When there were just five people aboard, sure. The computer could wake me if there was a reason."

Nadia's eyes roamed the office space. "This is a very large ship for just five people."

"Tell me about it. It felt so empty, even the head had an echo."

Nadia's lips quirked in what might have become a smile if given enough time.

"So," Cole said, "you wanted to discuss something?"

"Yes," Nadia replied. "I've heard back from Sol. What is your availability to visit Earth?"

Cole blinked. "I don't understand."

"After the deposition ended, I sent my uncle a certified recording. I received a reply, asking if you would be willing to speak at the Board of Inquiry and provide certified copies of your bridge, communications, and sensor logs involving the Caernarvon Incident. I wasn't about to commit you to anything, especially when there was an underlying urgency to my uncle's message I didn't like. I sent back a question of why he'd need you, and not twenty minutes ago, I received his reply. There is roughly a twelve-hour comms lag between here and Earth."

"What was his reply?" Cole asked.

Nadia's lips twitched before she said, "He told me SRN technicians were unable to recover any logs from TF-27 involving the Caernarvon Incident."

"What?" Cole almost gaped at Nadia. "Isn't that impossible? Commander what's-his-name said yesterday that those protected archives are tamper-proof."

"Quite. Uncle couldn't go into too much detail, but he did communicate that it's TF-27's position that whatever you did to eject their cores interfered with a number of additional systems, including the logging."

"Srexx?" Cole asked. "You there, buddy?"

"Of course, Cole," Srexx replied via the overhead speakers.

"What's your take on that? Would what you did to eject those cores have had any collateral effect on other systems?"

"Unlikely, Cole. By that point, I was sufficiently familiar with Human information systems that my actions were more like a scalpel than a hammer. The only system affected in the so-called Caernarvon Incident was the core-ejection mechanism, in that I activated it. The mechanism itself prevented any override, as it was not coded to activate unless the core was in danger of losing containment."

"If it wasn't coded to activate except in the case of the reactor nearing containment failure," Nadia said, "how were you able to activate the mechanism?"

Silence.

Cole suspected he understood the situation, and he said, "It's okay, buddy. She's with us."

"Are you certain, Cole? I have not yet finished vetting all CIE personnel. In the limited time I have had since beginning this conversation, I have found no data to suggest she is working at cross purposes to us, but neither have I found any data proving she is not."

"In this one instance, Srexx, let's extend a modicum of trust and see what she does with it. If someone we haven't spoken with discusses how you activated the ejection mechanism, we'll have our answer."

"Very well. Ms. Perez, I activated the core ejection mechanism by modifying the data feed from the engineering subsystem to trigger the sensors that monitored the reactor core."

Cole watched Nadia, and he knew the moment she fully processed what Srexx had done.

"You mean to say that you modified live data streams on ninety-two vessels simultaneously? You have the compute resources to do that?"

"My logs indicate the operation required seven-point-eight-five-nine-nine percent of my total resources." Now, Nadia gaped. "And there were anywhere from five to thirty-six sensors that required data modification per ship. The frigates had five, and it scaled up to thirty-six aboard the battleships."

Nadia paled, which given her olive complexion was something to see. "Srexx, have you encountered an encryption the Solars call 'Ultraviolet?'"

"I have."

"May I ask how long it took you to decrypt archives using that encryption algorithm?"

"My logs indicate the initial decryption required eight-point-two-six-one hours, but to be clear, I only devoted five percent of my total capacity to the task. I had nothing better to do at the time."

"And if you had devoted your full resources to it?"

"One moment... " Silence. "If my calculations are correct, under the conditions you specified, initial decryption would have required six-point-three minutes."

Nadia sagged back against her seat, her expression shell-shocked. When she lifted her eyes to meet Cole's, she spoke in an almost hushed tone, "Ultraviolet is the current top tier of military encryption for the Solar Republic. They believe it would require a planetary super-computer over one-hundred-fifty years to crack a file encrypted with it."

"Do I want to know why or how you know that?" Cole asked.

Nadia's lips curled into a smile. "Let's just say I have a reserve commission in the Solar Republic Marines and leave it at that."

Cole nodded. "Fair enough. So, someone tampered with the tamper-proof archives in TF-27?"

"It seems that way. My uncle would very much like to have you testify before the Board of Inquiry and provide certified copies of your logs."

"What's the downside of that?"

Nadia looked up at the ceiling. After several moments of silence, she pulled her eyes back to Cole, saying, "None, really, that I can think of."

"Even in light of the attempt on my life?"

Nadia shook her head. "I wouldn't think so. I won't reply to my uncle either way, so if you're able to go, it should catch everyone off guard. Given that you seem to travel with a short company now, between them and the sudden move, they shouldn't have enough time to put anything together."

"Okay," Cole said. "I need to consult with Colonel Hanson about it, but if he says he's good to operate here without the ship, we'll head out today. Reply to your uncle that you'll see what you can do but can't make any promises."

Nadia nodded once. "Very well. May I accompany you to Earth?"

"Of course. I'm not about to go there without my attorney."

"Will there be anything else, Mr. Coleson?"

"Not unless you have something."

"I'll send that reply right away and prepare for the trip. As I'm attached to your staff for the duration of your time in Centauri, I won't even have to check in with CIE Legal and risk a leak there."

Cole nodded. "Thank you. Akyra can get you an escort back to the airlock."

Nadia nodded and left.

CHAPTER TWENTY

Battle-Carrier *Haven*, Coleson Clanhold
  Centauri Trinary System
  29 August 3000, 06:17 GST

Cole sat in the command chair in the center of the bridge. The calm eye in a storm of activity. As the storm settled into a quiet calm, Sasha approached Cole's right elbow.

"All decks report ready for departure, sir," Sasha said.

"Thank you," Cole replied. "Take us out."

"Comms, contact Clanhold Docking Control, please; inform them of our intention to depart."

Five seconds later, Jenkins announced, "Docking Control wishes us well, ma'am. They'll hold the docking port for us."

"Thank you, Comms. Helm, undock the ship, please," Sasha said.

"Undocking," Wixil said, her tail swishing side to side like a lazy metronome. Five minutes later, Wixil announced, "We are clear and free to navigate."

"Set course for Sol, please, half-light to the system periphery," Sasha instructed.

Wixil's fingers danced over the helm console before she replied, "Course plotted and locked in."

Sasha looked down at Cole, a slight smile curling one side of her mouth. "Sir?"

Cole grinned. "Punch it."

Wixil keyed the command to execute the programmed course and speed settings.

Haven executed a stately one-hundred-eighty-degree flip away from the station with a one-hundred-eighty-degree roll midway through the flip. As soon as the bow pointed toward the departure point, the sublight engines activated, starting a steady climb to half the speed of light. The acceleration was such that, from the Clanhold, the massive starship shot away as if fired from a cannon.

On the bridge, Wixil's fingers flew over the helm console once more before she reported, "We are on course and approaching four-tenths'-light. We will arrive at the system periphery in thirty-one hours and change."

"Thanks, Wixil," Cole said, leaning back against the command chair. He lifted his gaze to Sasha and offered a rakish smile. "Any bets on our reception when we arrive in Sol?"

Sasha shook her head. "Fortunes will be won and lost on that question, sir. I'm sure the books are already going full tilt."

Cole's rakish grin turned down-right evil. "People, may I have your attention for a moment, please?"

Everyone on the bridge turned to face Cole. Cole slowly swiveled the command chair until he'd completed a full circle.

"If there happened to be one or more books running on the Solars' reaction to our arrival and if the Alpha shift bridge crew were to pool their available funds into one bet... or perhaps one bet for each pool... I would suggest any enterprising souls put their credits on 'No reaction at all... until we reach Earth.'"

"What are you planning, Cap?" Jenkins asked, earning a frown from Sasha for his abbreviation of 'captain.'

"But that would be telling, Mr. Jenkins. It's time to see how much you and your associates trust me." Cole stood and headed for the port hatch. Just as he neared it, Cole said, "Sasha, you have the conn."

————

Cole spent the rest of the shift that day in his office, studying the materials for the Fleet Command certification offered by the ISA. Having achieved his certification for Captain just prior to the Tristan's Gate shipyard completing the construction of the small craft, Fleet Command was the next rung on the ladder. Ever since he read the initial survey reports of the star systems neighboring Beta Magellan, for which Haven Enterprises was quick to register full system claims, the stray thought of operating multiple battle-groups built around battle-carriers had not left Cole's mind. It was one of the reasons he'd been so looking forward to the Centauri trip; Cole wanted to dig into his grandfather's archives for anything relating to naval tactics and strategy that included small craft he could find. Otherwise, he and his people would have to write their tactical doctrines from scratch.

When the tone that signified the end of Alpha shift blared through the office speakers, Cole looked at the time, stretching his shoulders. He had enjoyed dinner with Yeleth and Wixil the night before, and he made a mental note to make that a regular occurrence. In the meantime, though, lunch felt like a good idea.

The next day passed much the same for Cole. He occupied the command chair for the switch-over from Delta to Alpha shifts, and once nothing arose that required his immediate attention, he went to his office and resumed his studies.

Thirty-one hours and fifty-three minutes after departing the Coleson Clanhold, *Haven* reached the system periphery. Cole ordered one-hundred-percent on the hyperdrive, and *Haven* vanished from the Centauri Trinary System.

————

Battle-Carrier *Haven*
System Periphery
Sol
30 August 3000, 16:19 GST

Haven winked into existence half an AU beyond Pluto. Cole sat in the command chair. Sasha stood at his right elbow. The Beta shift bridge crew occupied the stations around them. A hologram of the system dominated the area between the command chair and the helm.

"I've only *read* about Sol," Sasha said. "I never thought I'd actually *be* here."

"To think... a thousand years ago, Humanity existed only on one little planet and had for its entire existence up to then," Cole said, "and a thousand years before that, we were struggling to pull ourselves out of the collapse of the largest empire Earth ever knew. It almost doesn't seem real, does it?" Cole took a breath. "Activate full stealth, please."

Status lights all over the ship became a bright blue, accompanied by a slight dimming of the general lighting. With full stealth, there were no klaxons.

Sasha spun to stare at Cole, her accusatory expression marred by a smile threatening to break free. "Sir?"

Cole shrugged and grinned. "I told them it was time to see how much they trusted me."

"You're evil," Sasha hissed, finally giving into a mischievous grin.

"Of course, I am," Cole replied. "I have the membership card to prove it."

"Damn," a voice from the port recess carried across the bridge.

Sasha locked on the offender, but Cole held up a hand, still grinning.

"Something wrong, Lieutenant?" Cole asked.

"The Alpha shift bridge crew is going to be cleaning up, sir. They took the long odds and bet on 'No reaction at all until Earth.' You didn't happen to discuss your plan, did you, sir?"

Cole chuckled. "Of course not. That wouldn't be sporting. Review the bridge logs if you like."

"No," the lieutenant at Marine Ops said, his voice almost a sigh, "but thank you, sir. We trust you. Did you have any skin in the game?"

"No offense, Lieutenant, but I could run the table on every book running aboard this ship, and if I were extremely lucky, the combined sum might—just *might*—equal a rounding error for me. Besides, those credits you're betting were mine before they were yours, and I value your hard work and expertise. Why would I want to take the credits back, especially by cheating? Just be sure to pass the word I don't want anyone going overboard with it. If anyone starts acting out trying to come up with creds to gamble... well... laid-back and easy-going Cole will go right out the airlock at that point. Clear?"

"Very clear, sir, and I'll pass the word."

Cole nodded. "Thank you, Lieutenant. Helm, lock in a course for Earth, please; it's the third rock from the star. I want to come in below the ecliptic, and make your speed thirty-five-percent-light."

"Course for Earth coming in below the ecliptic at thirty-five-percent-light. Roger that, sir," the Beta shift helmsman answered.

Cole fought the urge to sigh. Whoever normally had the watch for Beta shift must be a devotee of Sasha or Mazzi.

"That will bring us to Earth in just a hair under eleven hours and twenty-three minutes, Captain," the helmsman reported.

"Very good," Cole replied. "Proceed, please."

Sasha leaned close to Cole, whispering, "What are your plans once we reach Earth? Is it feasible to keep the stealth up?"

Cole shook his head, grinning. "I thought we'd just drop the stealth close enough to Earth to attract some attention but outside the traffic patterns, so we're not an immediate danger."

"Sir, this ship is larger and more capable than a Solar Republic battleship. From their perspective, we're going to be an immediate danger, no matter what we do. The professional way to do it would be to drop the stealth and come into the system like we belong here."

"I know," Cole said, sighing. "You're right, of course. I shouldn't be playing so fast and loose with everyone's lives, but the Solars are going to flip out when they see this ship, no matter what. Maybe this way, there will be enough compound flipping out that something will shake loose."

Sasha sighed. "I really hope this doesn't come back to bite us."

"It probably will," Cole replied. "We just have to be ready to bite back."

———

The passage of eleven hours and thirty minutes had *Haven* sitting in an observational blind spot at an odd angle and distance from Earth's L5 Lagrange point. After all, even with full stealth systems active, the ship wasn't invisible to the Mark One eyeball; it would still occlude stars, if nothing else.

Cole sat in the command chair and fought a serious yawn. He wasn't supposed to be on the bridge for another ninety minutes yet (plus or minus). Nadia Perez stood at his left side, with Sasha on his right, and he marveled that the ladies were so put together. They looked like they were used to being awake at this hour all the time.

Cole directed a thoughtful expression toward Sasha.

"What?" Sasha asked, noticing the expression.

"Let's go ahead and signal a shift change for the bridge. These poor souls have been up all night, and things might get interesting in short order."

"Aye, sir," Sasha said. "Comms, signal all Alpha shift bridge personnel to report to stations, please. Delta shift bridge crew, once you've completed the change-over with your Alpha shift counterparts, you're dismissed. Have an extra hour or so on us."

Within five minutes, the people Cole was used to seeing on the bridge started filtering through the hatches. Jenkins took over Comms, Haskell at Sensors. Mazzi and her 'replacement' weapons officer moved to the weapons station. Wixil came in through the port bridge hatch, almost bouncing; she stopped at the command chair long enough to say hi to Cole before moving on to take her place at the helm.

Once all the change-overs completed and Delta shift left the bridge, Cole swiveled to face Comms, saying, "Jenkins, Ms. Perez needs to make a call. Will you help her with that?"

Jenkins frowned but nodded once. "Of course, sir."

Nadia walked the short distance to the comms station and gave

Jenkins some information. Moments later, Nadia held an earwig to her ear and returned to Cole's side.

"Hello, Uncle," Nadia said, smiling. "How are you and Auntie?" She paused for a time, listening to her uncle. "Yes. Yes, I did convince him to come. When will we dock? Well, that's a bit uncertain right now. By any chance, are you near the SRN response center?"

Cole could just imagine the reaction of the watch-standers at the SRN response center when the Judge Advocate General—a two-star admiral—walked into the place. He grinned. Sasha sighed and shook her head.

"Okay... you're there now?" Nadia asked. After a moment, she turned to Cole and nodded.

Cole accessed his implant and sent a text message to Mazzi, asking her to drop the stealth. At the same time, he sent a message to Jenkins, instructing him to re-route Nadia's call through the bridge audio system.

"Seriously, Nadia," an older voice said, "why do I need to be–" The blaring of alert klaxons and shouted orders drowned out whatever he was going to say.

Cole grinned at Sasha, saying, "Well, I think they know we're here."

"You're incorrigible," Sasha replied, shaking her head.

The pandemonium being broadcast across Nadia's call finally died down to the point that her uncle could speak once more. "So, I'm guessing you're aboard that monster of a ship that just appeared out of nowhere?"

"Yes, Uncle. It's my client's ship, *Haven*."

"Its transponder calls it out as a battle-carrier. What in all the stars is a *battle-carrier*?"

"It's just what it says, Uncle. *Haven* is a battleship with a flight deck. They took me for a ride in one of the two-seater bombers; it was amazing."

"Was this your idea, Nadia? You've always loved tweaking the noses of senior officers."

"Not at all, Uncle. My client came up with this plan all on his own, and I think he won his bridge crew a lot of credits in the process."

A tired sigh came across the link. "I don't even want to know,

Nadia. I really don't. Give me some time to smooth all the ruffled feathers around here. I'll hail the ship once I have an orbital assignment."

"Thank you, Uncle! Love to Auntie!"

"I love you, too, little girl. Ortega out."

CHAPTER TWENTY-ONE

Earth. The planet that nurtured Humanity until they were capable of spreading out among the stars (and continued to nurture almost twenty billion of them) bore no signs of the harsh treatment it had endured throughout the years from its children. Repairing the damage done by that harsh treatment consumed centuries and was not easy, by any means, but in the year 3000, Earth was a resplendent monument to the effort, ingenuity, and dedication of countless generations.

Poverty, starvation, and even violent crime (to a degree) were things of the past. Little more than cautionary tales studied in Political Science, Sociology, and Anthropology courses served as a reminder of what Humanity once was... and could so easily be again.

The major deserts of the world—Sahara, Gobi, and Mojave... just to name three—were now wilderness preserves and much, much smaller than they were even at the time of the Republic's founding. Countless extinct species once again roamed the planet, at least those whose DNA survived into the modern age. For some, it was considered the height of status to have a saber-toothed cat for a pet, though what the neighbors would say if it ate the children was another matter.

En Route to SRN Headquarters
Earth, Sol System
31 August 3000, 09:27 GST

The planet growing in the forward view looked both like and unlike every other planet settled by Humanity. It was the standard by which all others were measured.

"This is your homeworld, Cole?" Wixil asked, standing at Cole's elbow and looking out the forward view.

Cole nodded, keeping an eye on the pilot's console. "Yes... for Humanity, it is, Wixil. This is my first time here, though, so it's not my *personal* homeworld. Look at the section of the continent over there. Do you see those two blue lines that look like a 'V' written by someone with poor motor control?"

"Yeah. I think so."

"Those are the Tigris and Euphrates Rivers. The area around them form the core of what was called Mesopotamia thousands of years ago. If you believe the archaeologists and historians, it's where Humanity began over six thousand years ago. We've only had written language for about sixty-five-hundred years, give or take."

"And *Haven* is over thirty-five-thousand-years-old?" Wixil asked.

"That's what Srexx tells me," Cole replied, "assuming his conversions between Human years and Gyv'Rathi units of time are accurate."

"Do you think we'll ever meet the Old Ones, Cole?"

Cole shrugged, watching the Iberian Peninsula grow in the forward view. Valencia, Spain, was their destination. It held the headquarters for the Solar Republic Navy and, therefore, also the Solar Republic Marines.

"I don't know, Wixil. Part of me would like to say it would be a great thing if we did, but then, I think about the dreadnought schematics I saw. They apparently felt they needed such a ship, and that makes me wonder what they were like."

The pilot's console chirped, and Cole accepted the incoming call.

"Attention, Flight Five-Four-Four-Three-Alpha! This is Europe

Traffic Control. Your filed flight path says you're bound for the SRN Headquarters in Valencia. Please confirm."

Cole keyed his microphone. "Europe Control, this is Flight Five-Four-Four-Three-Alpha. Destination confirmed. We have priority clearance at the Navy's facility."

"Very well. Proceed on your current vector, and sound off if you encounter an emergency. Europe Traffic Control out."

Cole keyed the command to close the comms channel, and the speakers chirped. By now, the ancient city dominated the forward view. It was a mix of preserved architecture through every era of the city's life coupled with more modern construction away from the historical zones. Their destination would take them to the outermost area of the southern half of the city. The campus that comprised the headquarters for the Solar Republic Navy and Marines occupied upwards of one-hundred-fifty acres, between training facilities and administrative buildings.

They soon landed in their assigned location and found a ground-car waiting for them when the boarding ramp lowered. Cole led Nadia, Red, Yeleth, and Wixil off the dropship, and as soon as they were no longer touching the boarding ramp, it rose and locked into place, courtesy of Srexx. Red, Yeleth, and Wixil wore armor disguised as clothing; it didn't have hand, foot, or head protection, but otherwise covered everything except their tails.

"It smells nice," Wixil said as she spun in a circle, sniffing the air.

Cole smiled. "It does. I think we're close to the coast. Unless I'm mistaken, there's salt in the breeze."

A young man stood beside the ground-car, the driver still at the controls.

Nadia walked to him and stopped just out of arms' reach. "Ensign, I'm Nadia Perez, and you are?"

"Ensign Gregory Thomson, ma'am," the ensign replied. "Admiral Ortega himself sent me to meet you. Is this everyone?"

Nadia nodded once. "It is."

The ensign cast a concerned look in Red's general direction, but the gigantic Igthon didn't seem to notice.

"Very well," Ensign Thomas said. "This way, please."

The ground-car had three rows of seating, not counting the front seats. As soon as the ensign opened the side door, Yeleth stuck her head inside, sniffing the air. Red walked around the ground-car, sniffing as well. He completed his circuit at Yeleth's side and looked to her.

"Nothing smells off to me," Yeleth said. "How about you?"

Red leaned into the ground-car and sniffed. "I think we're good."

Red moved aside, allowing Cole to enter first. Cole decided to give everyone a break and went straight to the third row. Yeleth cleared her throat, sounding more like a light growl, and Cole sighed, moving to the second row. Yeleth and Wixil entered next, moving to the third row themselves while Nadia sat beside Cole. Last but absolutely not least, Red squeezed himself into the first row, and the entire ground-car settled onto its suspension and rocked like a dinghy in a hurricane until he stopped moving.

"Move out, Ensign," Nadia called out from her seat beside Cole.

Cole thought he heard the ensign reply before the ground-car started moving, but he wasn't sure. In such a confined space, Red made an excellent sound barrier in addition to all his other skills and talents.

The ground-car trundled along the paved path, the surface looking more like the material of running tracks than asphalt or ceramacrete. The scenery all around them was beautiful, even accounting for the urban sprawl to the north. The Mediterranean Sea glittered in the sun off to the east.

Cole's implant notified him of the time, and he accessed his implant's comms functions and placed a call to the ship.

"Bridge, Sasha here." Cole heard Sasha's voice as if he were standing right beside her on the bridge.

"Hey, Soosh. Yeah, we made it in. The sights are beautiful. We're not to the hotel yet, but there was a car waiting for us."

"Very good, sir," Sasha replied. "We have two full squadrons, four dropships, and Srexx on ready alert. Say the word, and we'll crash the party."

"Thanks, Soosh. I'm looking forward to the trip, too, and I'll keep that in mind. I'll give you a call later tonight. Bye for now."

The call disconnected.

Nadia leaned close and whispered, "Just how much of that was code?"

Cole smiled. "More than one word and less than all of it."

"You worked it out before we left?"

"Yup. A twitch between my shoulder-blades tells me not to trust our hosts, no offense to your uncle."

Nadia nodded. "You have a backup plan?"

"Nah... I make those up when I need them," Cole replied, not certain if the ground-car had listening devices.

————

The ground-car pulled up to an impressive building with architecture dating back several centuries. An older man in the ground uniform of the Solar Republic Navy, with two stars on each shoulder, stood under the shade of a well-maintained tree Cole couldn't identify. He bore the same olive complexion as Nadia, though his skin was weathered with age, and Cole picked out more than a little resemblance between them.

The ground-car trundled to a stop, and the side door opened, allowing Red to rock their world once again as he exited. The ground-car's suspension lifted the vehicle a solid twenty-five centimeters once it was no longer responsible for supporting Red's mass. Red performed a slow scan of the area as he sniffed the air for anything that didn't fit, before stepping to one side of the ground-car's door. Nadia exited next, followed by Cole, and the Ghrexels brought up the rear.

Nadia maintained a professional demeanor right up until she was face-to-face with her uncle. Then, she pulled the admiral into a hug and planted a quick kiss on his cheek.

"It's been too long, Uncle," Nadia said. "It's good to see you."

"You're just one star system over," Admiral Ortega replied. "There's no reason you can't visit every so often."

Nadia blushed just enough to notice and turned to allow Cole to approach. "May I present my client, Bartholomew James Coleson? Sir, this is my uncle, Admiral Lucien Ortega, the Judge Advocate General for the Solar Republic Navy."

Cole stepped forward and offered his right hand. Ortega gave him a firm handshake.

"Admiral, it's good to meet you," Cole said. "Nadia says many good things about you."

"Only believe half of them, Mr. Coleson," Ortega replied.

Cole grinned. "Please, call me Cole."

Ortega nodded once. "Well then, Cole, shall we adjourn to my office for a few minutes?"

Cole nodded, and Ortega turned, leading them into the building. He led them onto an elevator and then through a series of hallways until they arrived at a door labelled 'Admiral Sir Lucien Ortega, Judge Advocate General.' Ortega ushered them inside without slowing, and the two enlisted and one junior officer within snapped to their feet and saluted. Ortega returned their salute, continuing on to his private office.

"Hold everything, please," Ortega said, "until I specify otherwise."

Red broke off and stood by the door to Ortega's office, saying, "I'll be right here, Cap."

"Thanks, Red," Cole replied as he followed Ortega into the office.

It was a spacious office, almost as spacious as Cole's aboard *Haven*. Thick carpeting covered the floor, and authentic wood paneling lined the walls. Two armchairs faced the admiral's desk. The wall to the right of their entrance boasted another door.

"Sir," Yeleth said, "is that door another entrance?"

"Yes, it is. Why?"

Without a word, Wixil moved to stand beside the door, where she would be hidden if it opened. Yeleth occupied a similar position for the door through which they had entered.

Ortega took in the two Ghrexels before turning to Cole, saying, "Forgive me for asking, but is there anything I should know?"

Cole shrugged. "I would say they're being overprotective, but someone took a shot at me on my own station. Feel free to discuss any matters you like in their presence."

Ortega let out a heavy sigh. "That's rather unfortunate. The Board of Inquiry has been in recess since I dispatched Commander O'Connell and Lieutenant Masters to Centauri at the members' request. The certified record of your deposition has been added to the case-file, and I have notified the members of the Board that you have arrived. They're prepared to inform all parties that the Board will reconvene at thirteen-hundred this afternoon, if that is agreeable to you."

Cole turned to Nadia. "You're my legal counsel. Is that acceptable?"

"Of course," Nadia replied, "and I shall of course be in attendance and introduce myself to the members."

"Now," Ortega said, "there's one other matter to discuss before the Board reconvenes."

"Oh?" Cole asked.

"Yes," Ortega replied, "and it is the matter of Commander O'Connell's conduct during your deposition. I have already counseled him on the matter, placing a note in his file regarding the incident, and advised him I would present you the opportunity to file charges."

Once again, Cole turned to Nadia, asking, "Do I want to file charges?"

Nadia remained silent for several moments, her eyes directed toward the surface of her uncle's desk. After several moments, she lifted her head and replied, "Not at this time, but we reserve the right to include the matter in a more comprehensive filing, pending further interaction with the Solar Republic Navy. If no further actionable incidents occur, we're prepared to write off Commander O'Connell's poor conduct as an isolated incident. Besides, there's no point in getting drawn into a complicated legal matter that could have you stuck in Sol for a year or more."

Ortega smiled. "Very well. I shall inform Commander O'Connell that you have declined to pursue the matter at this time."

"Any idea what got into him?" Cole asked. "He was congenial throughout all of our conversation, and at some point during the deposition, he just went totally off the rails."

Ortega shrugged, placing a finger against his lips for a moment before swirling it through the air beside his head. "Oh, there's no way to know, really. Everyone has bad days."

So, he thinks there's a credible chance his office is bugged, Cole thought. *Good to know.*

Outwardly, Cole chuckled, offering a smile. "You're certainly right about that. I've had one or two myself."

"Well, if there's nothing else, I've arranged a guide for you during your time here. Feel free to tour the campus. I've made her aware of your appointment with the Board, and she will see to it that you reach the hearing room on time."

"What are the chances of arranging shore leave for my crew?" Cole asked as he stood. "I know many of them would enjoy visiting Earth."

"Of course. I've already communicated with the relevant offices to provide tourist visas for your crew." Ortega picked up a one-use pad and wrote something on it with a stylus before extending it to Cole. "That has the contact information you'll need to obtain the tourist visas."

"Thank you, sir," Cole said. "It's been a pleasure meeting you."

CHAPTER TWENTY-TWO

Lieutenant Masters led Cole and company into the hearing room, and Cole was not surprised to see the hearing room looked far more like a court room than one might have thought. A decorative wooden barrier separated the gallery from the proceedings, and two tables sat just beyond and on either side of the small gate in the barrier. At the left table, from the gallery's perspective, Cole saw three people sitting; the two right-most individuals wore the dress uniform of the Solar Republic Navy, the third a pinstripe suit. Just as Cole eased into a seat, two more officers in dress uniform strode down the aisle with valises, moving through the gate and occupying the other table. Lieutenant Masters sat by the aisle, and Nadia sat between her and Cole. Wixil sat at Cole's right, with Yeleth beyond Wixil.

At two minutes before thirteen-hundred, a door opened, and three admirals in dress uniforms entered and took their seats at the bench, as the Marine bailiffs called for everyone to rise. Cole saw the center admiral bore three stars.

The center admiral struck his gavel when nearby clocktowers struck one in the afternoon.

"At thirteen-hundred on 31 August 3000, the Board of Inquiry into the events collectively known as the Caernarvon Incident is hereby reconvened," the admiral said. "Admiral Jonas O'Malley, Admiral Sven Bjornson, and Admiral Takagi Hirohito presiding. Take your seats, please."

Everyone sat.

"Commander Oswali," Admiral O'Malley continued, "we understand the Judge Advocate General has provided additional evidence to this Board of Inquiry."

"That's correct, Admiral," one of the two officers at the right table replied.

"Objection, Your Honors," the right-most officer at the left table said, standing. "The respondent has no knowledge of this new evidence, and we have not had time to prepare."

"Sir," Commander Oswali interjected, "if I may, we have not seen this evidence, either. I'm prepared to provide both the Board and the respondent copies of the communication with Admiral Ortega. It says, and I quote, 'New evidence from Commander O'Connell's research. It will be available for admission at thirteen-hundred.'"

The members of the Board covered their microphones and conferred among themselves for a moment before Admiral O'Malley said, "Since no one involved in this proceeding—including the members of this Board—have seen this evidence, I see no reason to delay its admission. We will all proceed with discovery together, Counselor. Please, proceed, Commander Oswali."

The officer at the left table resumed his seat.

Commander Oswali turned to the gallery, saying, "Lieutenant Masters, you were part of Commander O'Connell's research team. Would you please step forward and introduce the evidence?"

Lieutenant Masters stood and stepped forward. If she felt intimidated at addressing three admirals—one three-star and two two-stars —she didn't show it.

"Thank you, Your Honors," Lieutenant Masters said. "Admiral Ortega dispatched me and Commander O'Connell to Centauri when we learned that a ship matching the configuration of the one involved in the Caernarvon Incident had arrived at the Coleson Clanhold. Upon arriving in Centauri, we were welcomed aboard the Battle-Carrier *Haven* by its captain, Bartholomew James Coleson. He agreed to a certified deposition, which has since been entered into the case file, and he is here today to deliver certified copies of the bridge log, sensor logs, and communication logs for the time involving the Incident. He has also agreed to testify should the Board deem it necessary."

Now, the center occupant of the left table turned to look back into the gallery. Cole allowed himself a casual glance at the motion and saw Himari Sato scanning those in the gallery, maintaining his non-expression. Cole felt rather glad he'd communicated with Sato only via audio.

One of the two-star admirals focused on Lieutenant Masters, his brow furrowed as he asked, "And would this 'Bartholomew James Coleson' have any relation to the Colesons of Coleson Interstellar Engineering?"

"I-I'm sorry, Your Honors," Lieutenant Masters said, "but I do not have that information."

Nadia Perez stood and walked to the gate. She stood in silence until Admiral O'Malley acknowledged her by saying, "May we help you, miss?"

"Forgive me, Your Honors," Nadia said. "I am Nadia Perez, CIE Legal Department, and I am Mr. Coleson's personal counsel. I am empowered by my client to confirm for the Board that he is indeed Jack Coleson's son. I have personally viewed the confirmation of his identity, provided by Credit Suisse in the Zurich system, and vetted its authenticity."

"Very well," Admiral O'Malley replied. "Thank you, Ms. Perez."

Nadia nodded once and returned to her seat.

The members conferred once more, leading Admiral O'Malley to say, "Well, I think the next step is to call Mr. Coleson forward."

Cole stood and moved to the aisle before walking forward. Admiral O'Malley indicated the seat used by witnesses, and Cole moved to it, followed by Commander Oswali.

"Please, raise your right hand," Commander Oswali said, "and repeat after me."

Cole raised his right hand and said, "I—Bartholomew James Coleson—do solemnly swear that the testimony I offer here today will be the whole truth and nothing but the truth."

"The members accept your oath, Mr. Coleson," Admiral O'Malley said. "Take your seat."

Cole withdrew a data crystal from his pocket and held it up. "If I may ask, Your Honors, who gets this? It contains the certified copies Lieutenant Masters mentioned."

"I'll take it for now," Admiral O'Malley said, extending his hand, "and see to it all parties receive certified copies."

Cole handed the data crystal to the admiral and took his seat at the witness stand. Nadia stood and moved to the gate.

"Your Honors," Nadia said, "I request permission to advise my client during any questions."

The members conferred again, and O'Malley delivered their verdict with a nod, saying, "It's unorthodox, but permission granted, Ms. Perez." O'Malley then gestured to Commander Oswali.

Commander Oswali stood, saying, "Mr. Coleson, were you a direct witness to the events known as the Caernarvon Incident?"

"Witness?" Cole replied with a slight smile. "I was a participant. I conversed with Admiral Sato via an audio communications link. It's been almost a year, but the slight twitch she made when I started speaking tells me she recognizes my voice."

"You mean to testify that you saw the respondent twitch from the witness stand?" Admiral O'Malley asked.

Cole nodded. "Yes, Your Honor. I have a very keen eye for a person's tells; it has saved my life more than once through the years."

"Proceed, Commander."

"Mr. Coleson, how would you characterize the events of the Caernarvon Incident?"

"A gross overreaction, Commander," Cole replied without hesitation. "May I elaborate?"

"Please, do."

"Caernarvon was the closest system where we stood a chance of buying food. When we arrived in the system, we had at most two days of food for everyone aboard. Upon our arrival, we were challenged by a battle-group of the Solar Republic Navy, and for reasons that puzzle me to this day, Admiral Sato chose to order her battle-group into a combat formation. I took that as a threat and took steps to remove said threat."

"What steps did you take to remove the threat to your ship, Mr. Coleson?" Commander Oswali asked.

Cole grinned. "I ordered my information warfare officer to trigger the core ejection mechanism of every ship in the SRN battle-group."

Admiral Sato glared at Cole, her eyes hard as agates and her jaw clenched. The members of the Board and several others around the room gaped.

"And how was your information warfare officer able to achieve this?" Commander Oswali asked.

Cole shrugged. "I have no idea. I'm a captain and a pilot, not an information expert. I asked him if he could do it, and he told me he could. When circumstances reached the point that a battle seemed inevitable, I took the path where no one died. I treat the question of how my information warfare officer does his job as something I don't need to know. The one time I asked, his answer gave me a headache, and I didn't understand any more than I did before he answered."

"And what led to the moment of decision, Mr. Cole? Did you escalate the situation in any way? Were you belligerent at all?"

"Well, to be honest, I was a little bit flippant throughout our conversation, but you shouldn't take that as any kind of reaction specific to Admiral Sato. I'm flippant with almost everyone at one point or another. She, however, reacted with increasing hostility, and when she made a statement I felt was a direct threat to my ship and people, I brought the ship to alert status, which activated the shields and began charging weapons. It was at that point that she ordered her battle-group into an attack formation, followed closely by the battle-group losing its reactor cores. At no point during the exchange did I ever lock my ship's weapons on any of members of her battle-group. After all, I just wanted to buy food at the station."

"Let's take a moment to examine that," Commander Oswali said. "How did you allow your ship to reach such a state of supply?"

Cole grinned. "We arrived in Caernarvon from Iota Ceti. When we arrived in Iota Ceti, *Haven* had one-hundred-seventy-eight people aboard. When we departed Iota Ceti, *Haven* had eight-hundred-thirty-five people aboard. If I had suspected we'd experience such a dramatic increase in occupancy, I would have ensured the ship held sufficient food for everyone."

"Forgive me, Mr. Coleson," Commander Oswali said, "but Iota Ceti has a reputation as being a base for slavers. Were all of the new people aboard your ship there by choice?"

"Y... actually, no. We captured a number of slavers while we were in Iota Ceti, whom we surrendered to authorities in Tristan's Gate. I'm not certain what happened to them after that. Of the six-hundred-fifty-seven people who were not slavers, six-hundred-forty joined my crew and are still aboard... as paid crew with ISA records and certifications."

"And what was the status of the six-hundred-fifty-seven people when you encountered them in Iota Ceti, Mr. Coleson?" Commander Oswali asked.

"Well... they were slaves. We infiltrated the station serving as the slave market and gave everyone the option of no longer being slaves. We vetted everyone, and those who were not suitable as crew for whatever reason departed the ship in Caernarvon."

Commander Oswali nodded. "Are you the individual known in that region of space as the Lone Marine?"

"Objection, Your Honors," Nadia interjected. "The commander's question bears no relevance to the stated purpose of this Board of Inquiry."

"Withdrawn, Your Honors," Commander Oswali said, "and I have nothing further at this time."

"Thank you, Commander. Does the respondent's counsel wish to cross-examine?"

The officer at Admiral Sato's table stood. "Thank you, Your Honors. Mr. Coleson, would you have any reason to disbelieve me if I told you that Admiral Sato has testified that the enemy captain with whom she conversed—whom you've admitted as being—escalated the encounter with hostile and confrontational positions?"

"No more reason than I'd have to disbelieve anything else you say."

Muted chuckles escaped the gallery.

The officer approached until he stood right at the base of the dais upon which the witness stand stood. "It's common for individuals who... shall we say... view the truth as elastic to feel intimidated on the witness stand. Mr. Coleson, do you feel intimidated?"

Cole smiled. "Not at all."

"And why is that?"

Cole shrugged. "For several reasons, honestly, but the most basic reason is that you're not all that intimidating."

The chuckles in the gallery were not so muted now, and Cole caught the Board member closest to him start a smile before he schooled his expression. Cole also noticed some red building around the base of the man's neck.

"Are you aware that perjury is a crime, Mr. Coleson?"

"Yes, I am, and before you insinuate or imply that I have perjured myself somehow, I encourage you to save your career and play the recording of the call."

"Are you threatening me, Mr. Coleson?"

"I have no control over how you interpret my statements, Counselor, but I do know I already have grounds to charge one JAG attorney with Conduct Unbecoming for slandering me during an official deposition, or maybe it was libel. If you imply that I am dishonest, I'm certain my attorney would enjoy making a case for slander and public defamation, and once your statements were dutifully recorded, those statements become written... which seems to me like libel. I'd have to consult with my attorney on whether the Solar Republic Navy would be responsible for the libel, since you're not the recorder. If you and your team are so certain I'm lying, there's an easy way to prove it. Bring in a data crystal reader, and play the recording of our call."

"Your Honors," Commander Oswali and Nadia said at the same time.

"One at a time, ladies, please," Admiral O'Malley replied. "Ms. Perez, as you're the guest here, proceed."

"Your Honors, the respondent's counsel is badgering my client. I move the cross-examination be terminated with prejudice and the counsel receive a censure in the record."

The members conferred for a moment before O'Malley said, "The members sustain your motion that the cross-examination be terminated with prejudice, but we decline to record a censure against the counselor at this time. Commander Oswali?"

"We move that the audio recording of the comms call between Admiral Sato and Captain Coleson be played for the Board."

Cole watched Sato during Oswali's motion. She had an excellent poker face, except for the stray bead of sweat running down her right temple.

"Sustained," O'Malley replied. "Bailiff, would one of you please step over to the tech office and retrieve a data crystal reader?"

The junior-most Marine in the room disappeared and returned less than ten minutes later with a young man carrying a data crystal reader connected to a holographic projector.

Admiral O'Malley handed the data crystal to the young man, who slotted it into the reader. He placed the reader/projector on a table with wheels and moved it to the center of the space before activating the device. The hologram that appeared was a list of every file contained in the data crystal.

"Which file do you want, Admiral?" the tech asked.

"Your Honors," Cole said, "if I may, I recommend the holo recording of the bridge log. It will have the comms call with Admiral Sato along with the discussions that took place on my bridge during the incident. The audio file contains only what the comms system recorded as our call."

The members looked to one another and must've reached a decision via mental telepathy, because they never spoke or whispered a word. O'Malley said, "You heard the man, son. Queue up the holo-recording."

The tech selected the holo-recording and keyed the command to play it. The room's lights dimmed as a scaled-down image of Cole's bridge appeared in the air above everyone.

Before any audio even started, Sato's counsel jumped to his feet and almost shouted, "Objection!"

"Yes, Counselor?" O'Malley asked.

"Look at the holo, Your Honors. The man sitting at the helm is clearly the witness, and someone else is sitting in the command chair. He lied to us. I move that all testimony of this witness be stricken from the record and charges of perjury be levied against the witness!"

Nadia looked like she was ready to draw blood, and Cole held up his hand as he turned to the members, saying, "Your Honors, may I respond, please?"

"Proceed," O'Malley said.

"When all this happened, I didn't even have an ISA record, let alone a Captain's certification. My first officer, however, was a veteran of the Aurelian Navy. In any circumstances that required starship tactics and combat experience, she held the conn. It was my order that she do so, because I knew my limitations. I have since earned a certification as Captain for all classes of vessels up through capital ships, and during the most recent engagement in which my ship participated, I held the conn."

The members of the Board conferred, and O'Malley said, "Counselor, your objection is overruled."

"Your Honors," Nadia said.

"Yes, Ms. Perez?"

"Let the record reflect that I will deliver a subpoena on behalf of my client for a certified recording of the counselor's slanderous and defamatory outburst as part of a combined filing of charges against Solar Republic Navy personnel to be named in the filing."

"So noted, Ms. Perez."

"Thank you, Your Honors."

O'Malley nodded for the tech to resume playback.

Everyone present watched the holo-recording from start to finish, and the further the recording progressed the more Sato's jaw clenched.

When the holo-recording ended, silence dominated the room for several moments.

At last, O'Malley looked at the tale where Sato and her legal team sat and said, "Counselor, I think it best if we declare a recess until the day after tomorrow to give you and your team time to consult with your client. The witness is dismissed, and we're adjourned until oh-nine-hundred on September 2nd."

O'Malley cracked his gavel, and the members stood and left the room.

CHAPTER TWENTY-THREE

Following the recess of the Board of Inquiry, Cole found himself standing at the dropship with Red, Yeleth, Wixil, and Lieutenant Masters. Faced with the prospect of returning to the ship, Cole couldn't bring himself to look favorably upon that option. For the first —and probably only—time in in his life, Cole stood on Earth, the homeworld of his species. It seemed almost criminal to return to the ship when so many opportunities presented themselves.

"Lieutenant," Cole said, "is there a service that rents atmospheric shuttles around here anywhere?"

"I'm sure there is, sir."

Cole turned to his associates. "Interested in a whirlwind tour of Earth?"

Yeleth, Wixil, and Red shared a look before Yeleth replied, "We go where you go. Are there many non-Humans on Earth?"

"Lieutenant?" Cole asked.

"Uhm, we get a few, but Earth is so far from the other species' territories that they're not as common here as elsewhere."

Cole nodded. "Okay. Well, people will just have to deal with it. Let's see about that atmospheric shuttle rental, and then, we should probably look into an actual landing platform rental for this. I can't imagine the Navy would appreciate us just leaving it there until we're ready to leave."

"Actually, sir," Lieutenant Masters said, "that's Admiral Ortega's private pad, and he never uses it. I could call him to confirm, but I know this is the most use that pad has seen all year."

"If you would confirm it's fine to leave it there, I'd appreciate it," Cole said. "I'll work on transportation for us."

Cole used his implant to access the local 'Net and searched for a shuttle rental service. He soon found one and arranged to hire an atmospheric shuttle and pilot for twenty-four hours, after being assured that the shuttle would take him wherever he wanted to go across the planet with time to spare. Cole paid them via a secure transfer that he would have to authenticate at a bank terminal, but it was sufficient to dispatch a shuttle and pilot. The ETA was twenty minutes.

Returning his focus to his surroundings, Cole said, "Okay. We have a pilot and a shuttle en route. Lieutenant?"

"Admiral Ortega said you're welcome to use the pad as long as you need. He commented himself that he never uses it."

Cole nodded. "Thank you. I appreciate your time today, showing us around the campus here. I'm sure you have duties that require your attention."

"Yes, sir," Lieutenant Masters replied. "Admiral Ortega assigned me as your escort/liaison for the duration of your time here on Earth."

"I see," Cole said. "Very well. I think our first step should be to secure hotel rooms, and then, we'll plan an itinerary." He turned to his associates. "Are there any specific places on Earth you'd like to see?"

Red, Yeleth, and Wixil looked at one another. Red actually shrugged. They turned back to Cole, and Yeleth said, "I'm not certain we know enough about your species' homeworld to select locations to visit. Any places you choose to visit will be more than sufficient for us, but thank you for asking."

Cole nodded. "You're welcome."

Just then, an officer who had seemed to be walking by slowed and diverted to approach. She bore a single star on each shoulder and wore an easy, friendly smile.

"Forgive me for intruding," the woman said.

Lieutenant Masters turned and, upon seeing the woman's rank insignia, snapped to attention and saluted. The woman returned Masters's salute, never taking her eyes off Cole and saying, "As you were, Lieutenant."

"As I said, forgive me for intruding," the woman said. "I'm Commodore Yvette Federicci. Would you happen to be Mr. Coleson?"

Cole extended his right hand, and the commodore accepted, giving him a firm handshake as he said, "I am, but I prefer Cole. How may I help you, Commodore?"

"I was hoping we might discuss your ship, Mr. Coleson," the commodore replied. "It's very impressive, and the Solar Republic would like to open discussions toward licensing the technology."

"Commodore, I appreciate your time," Cole said, "but I'm afraid I have no intention of licensing the technology present in *Haven*."

"Oh, come now, Mr. Coleson," the commodore countered, "you haven't heard our offer. You shouldn't play hard to get until we begin negotiations."

Cole sighed. "Commodore, I'm not certain you understand. I wasn't playing hard to get. I was declining the conversation. I have no interest in seeing *Haven*'s technology spread throughout Human space."

The commodore's smile never wavered, but the congenial welcome in her eyes vanished. "That is... unfortunate... Mr. Coleson. What would be required for you to reconsider?"

Just then, their rented shuttle arrived and landed on the pad beside the dropship. It didn't power down, but a boarding staircase did lower moments before a young lady exited the shuttle and approached.

"Commodore, I cannot envision any circumstance that would lead me to reconsider my position on licensing or trading *Haven*'s technology. As I said, I appreciate your time, but that's my ride. Please, excuse us."

Cole turned to the new arrival and extended his hand. "Hello!"

"Hi! I'm guessing you're Cole?"

Cole nodded.

"I'm Gillian. I'll be your pilot for the duration of the contract. Where are we going?"

Nadia arrived, passing the commodore on the way. Cole nodded his greetings.

"First things first, let's depart the pad," Cole said, "and once we have some altitude, we'll discuss our options."

"You don't want to discuss them here?" Gillian asked.

Cole offered the pilot a slight smile. "We could, but if we did, there's no telling how many people would receive a report of it."

"Ah, right. Let's go then."

Gillian pivoted on her heel and led them over to the shuttle. Everyone took seats as Gillian returned to the cockpit, and within moments, they were hovering at a suborbital altitude off the traffic lanes.

"Okay," Gillian said, entering the passenger cabin from the cockpit, "we're off the beaten path a bit. Where do you want to go?"

"We'd like a hotel somewhere near our dropship for tonight," Cole replied. "Starting tomorrow, we'd like a whirlwind tour of the planet. I've never been here before, and I was hoping you could recommend some places."

Gillian pursed her lips, her brow furrowing as she said, "Well, to be honest, you could pick any of the locations on the World Heritage list that suit your fancy. I've never heard of anyone not enjoying a place on that list."

"World Heritage list?" Cole asked.

Gillian nodded. "Over a thousand years ago, several countries of Earth established the World Heritage list. The basic premise was to identify and preserve sites of significance to our heritage as people of Earth, and within the first forty years of its establishment, the governing organization identified over a thousand such places. When the world council was established, it set up a ministry to take over maintaining the sites and continuing the previous organization's work." Gillian's voice trailed off as she blushed. "Sorry. World Heritage sites are kind of a thing for me. I love the idea that people on this planet over a thousand years ago recognized that there were some sites possessing significance to Humanity as a whole not just at the time but through all the years that followed."

Cole nodded. "Okay. You've sold me. Once we have hotel rooms, I'll investigate the World Heritage list and pick out a few. Do you have time to consult with me about the feasibility of visiting in one day whatever sites I pick?"

"I'm yours for the duration of the contract. My family doesn't expect me back until the contract ends."

"Okay, then. Care to recommend a hotel?"

"What's your budget?"

Cole grinned. "What budget?"

"Budget... you know. How much you want to spend... " Gillian's voice trailed off as her eyes widened. "Coleson. The name on the contract is Coleson. Is that like CIE Coleson?"

Cole nodded.

"OhMyGosh! I am so sorry! I... uhm... I... "

Cole smiled and decided to save her. "Gillian, it's okay. First, relax and breathe. Second, is there a hotel around here that you've always wanted to visit but haven't?"

Gillian blushed again and nodded. "There's a hotel near the center of town. It dates back to before the founding of the Republic. The exterior is gorgeous."

"Do they have an overnight park for shuttles?"

"Yes, sir."

"Sold."

———

For his excursions the following day, Cole selected a number of sites near Valencia, even though Gillian assured him the shuttle could take him anywhere in the world and return by evening. Cole's one concession was to visit the location of Arthur Coleson's home prior to his departure for Alpha Centauri. Cole selected that as the last stop of the day, and truth be told, he didn't find it all that impressive after visiting the Pyramids and Sphinx, the Roman works at Bath, and Stonehenge.

In fact, after the visit, Cole questioned the value of its inclusion among its far more significant fellows on World Heritage list.

Cole also found it a bit annoying that, no matter where he was, some senator or other individual within the Solar Republic government always managed to find him, introduce themselves, and try to discuss alleged intentions to move CIE out of the Solar Republic. By the time they boarded the shuttle to return to Valencia, Cole had a tally of thirty-two attempts to discuss the CIE relocation or possible licensing for *Haven*'s technology.

———

Srexx entertained himself by keeping track of all *Haven* personnel on shore leave down to Earth. Well... he also split his resources between several other projects, including perusing several Solar Republic government archives most members of that government didn't know existed. After all, he had already perused the archives that were merely classified.

The comms system generated an alert, which the ship's computer copied to Srexx. After the twenty-six picoseconds necessary to process the alert, Srexx diverted substantial resources to investigating the several million connection attempts someone was generating against *Haven*'s datanet. If Srexx had lungs, he would've laughed; still, he found the hacking attempts amusing.

Srexx instructed the ship's computer to allow him to take over the matter and set aside all other projects, splitting his resources between defending against the hacking attempts (requiring no more than twenty percent of his resources) and reverse-hacking those behind it (utilizing whatever resources not dedicated to defense).

The attacks took place over the course of several hours, giving Srexx more than sufficient time to identify both the organizations responsible as well as the specific teams and operators. Once he had the identity data, Srexx accessed the comms system once more and placed a call.

———

Cole leaned back against the seat in the passenger compartment of the shuttle. They were flying over the Atlantic Ocean, on their way back to Valencia. For the most part, it had been a fun day, but Cole was tired and more than a little fed up with all the politicians hassling him. At least they'd left him alone the past couple hours.

His implant notified him of an incoming comms request from Srexx. Cole accepted it without a second thought.

"Hey, buddy," Cole said, unable to fix how tired he sounded.

"Hello, Cole," Cole 'heard' Srexx's voice in his ears as if the AI were sitting beside him. "Do you have a moment?"

"Of course. What do you need?"

"Over the past three hours, there have been extended attempts to gain illicit access to *Haven*'s systems."

Cole jerked upright in his seat. "You're saying someone's trying to hack us?"

"Yes," Srexx replied. "I am very disappointed, Cole. When the attempts first began, I started defending in the hopes of a challenge. However, the highest amount of resources I ever had to spend on defense merely reached twenty percent of my total capacity, and I only utilized that much due to the sheer volume of attempts. If I were organic, I might be insulted. I called to request your input on how I should respond."

"Hang on a sec, buddy, while I update everyone here," Cole said. Then, he swiveled his chair to face Wixil, Yeleth, Red, and Nadia. "Srexx just called to say someone has spent the last three hours attempting to hack *Haven*."

"What did they get?" Nadia asked. "And does he have any idea who's behind it?"

Yeleth turned to the attorney, saying, "Please, process what Cole said. They spent the past three hours *attempting* to hack our ship. We have no reason to worry. Am I correct, Cole?"

Cole nodded. "Srexx is feeling very insulted right now. He never had to utilize more than twenty-percent of his resources for defense, and only that much because of just how many attempts were being made."

Nadia gaped.

Cole directed his attention back to the call with Srexx. "Who's behind it, buddy?"

"Do you not mean to ask if I have identified the perpetrators?" Srexx asked.

Cole sighed. "You and I both know there's no point in asking that, Srexx. I'm not about to insult you."

"Thank you, Cole. The efforts originate with the Solar Republic Ministry of Intelligence, Solar Republic Military Intelligence, and the Solar Republic Navy's Cybersecurity department. Within those organizations, I have identified the specific teams and members of those teams responsible for the attacks."

"Okay," Cole said. "So, what would you like to do?"

"I believe delivering logic bombs to their datanets, along with exposing multiple items the individuals involved have endeavored to keep private, to be the appropriate response."

Cole nodded. "And just how would those logic bombs affect their systems?"

Silence.

"Given my data on their infrastructures, Cole, it is quite possible they would have to rebuild their datanets from scratch. If any backup operations are underway at the time of delivery, it is also unlikely those archives would survive."

Cole nodded again. "And just when do their backup processes run?"

Silence.

"My data indicate," Srexx said at last, "all target systems have several backup operations running throughout all hours."

Cole leaned back against his seat, considering the situation. He thought about all the attempts to nudge him toward the outcome they desired. He considered how no one seemed interested in taking 'no' for an answer, and he thought of Admiral Sato's willingness to attack his ship and spend her people's lives over what had seemed as nothing more than ego.

Screw it. They've earned this. Cole thought before saying, "Srexx?"

"Yes, Cole?"

"Indulge yourself; you have free reign in this instance."

"Yes, Cole." Srexx sounded pleased. "Srexx out."

Cole's implant reported the call ended, and he looked to those around him, saying, "Well, I think I just made an AI's day."

"Should we send flowers to the survivors?" Red asked.

"Nah," Cole replied, "I think they'll get the point." Cole pressed the key that allowed him to call the cockpit. "Gillian? We have a change of plans. Can you take us back to our dropship, please?"

"Is everything okay?" Gillian asked over the intercom.

"Someone tried to hack my ship, and I think that's our cue to leave."

"Ouch," Gillian replied. "Did they get anything?"

Cole laughed. "Nope! But they're about to."

"Yeah... I think I'm going to leave that one alone," Gillian said. "Dropship it is, sir!"

"Yeleth," Cole said, "will you please contact our hotel and arrange for our immediate check-out, please?"

Yeleth nodded once.

Cole accessed his implant's comms feature to call the ship.

Soon, he heard "Bridge, Sasha here," in his ears.

"Hey, Sasha. Have there been any incidents with any of our personnel on shore leave?"

"Not that I'm aware. Why?"

Cole sighed. "I've been hassled all day about licensing *Haven*'s tech and reconsidering CIE's relocation. I guess I'm just the lucky one, then. Did Srexx tell you about the hacking attempts?"

"He just did," Sasha replied. "Cole, he said your response was for him to have fun. Did you think that through? I mean... *really* think that through?"

"Yep. I did. They've earned it, Sasha. Please, issue an immediate recall for all personnel. As soon as we have everyone back aboard, we're out of here. I'm on my way back to the dropship right now and can pick up people if needed."

"Roger that, sir," Sasha replied. "I'll have a list of anyone needing a pickup by the time you're in the dropship."

"Thanks, Sasha. Cole out."

"What's happening?" Nadia asked.

"We're leaving. You should contact your uncle. That Board of Inquiry has gotten all it's going to get from me."

Nadia nodded and retrieved her earbud, syncing it with her implant before putting it in her left ear.

———

Within an hour and after liberal use of *Haven*'s dropships, all personnel were safely back aboard. Without contacting Earth Traffic Control, *Haven* engaged her stealth systems and departed, swinging wide out of the traffic patterns before settling onto a course for the Centauri Trinary System.

At 19:07 on 2 September 3000, *Haven* reached the system periphery. The officer at the helm engaged the hyperdrive, and *Haven* vanished from Sol.

CHAPTER TWENTY-FOUR

Office 2315, Office Complex B
　Geneva, Switzerland
　Sol System
　3 September 3000, 10:45 GST

Admiral Himari Sato entered the office to which she'd been summoned. There was no signage on the door, and the building directory did not list anyone occupying the space. An eight-foot conference table dominated the center of the room. Five chairs lined the side opposite the door. The side toward the door had only one. Sato was the only occupant she could see. The silence edged toward eerie.

At two minutes until her appointment time, the door into the office opened, allowing five people to enter—three women and two men. One man and one woman were older, and Sato recognized them all. The older man and woman were senior senators with decades of service; the other three were more recent additions to that august body.

The five senators walked around the table and occupied those seats. The older woman sat in the center with the older man to her right.

"Please, be seated," the woman said. "I appreciate and thank you for your punctuality."

"Your welcome, Ms—"

The older senator lifted a hand, gesturing for her to stop. "No names, please. Even though this space is routinely swept, it is still possible that our discussion might not be as private as we intended. We have protections in place to scramble any electronic recording, but it never hurts to be careful."

"Understood, ma'am," Sato replied. "May I ask why I'm here?"

"Circumstances are not looking good for you right now," the woman replied, "and we believe we can help each other. For several years now, a group of us have engaged in a... clandestine, shall we say... campaign to fold CIE and all its resources into the Solar Republic. As I'm sure you can guess, our efforts have been frustrated by the appearance of this supposed Heir."

"There's no 'supposed' about it," another senator challenged. "Nadia Perez would not have testified in the Board of Inquiry that his identity as the Heir was validated if it were not. I know her; she's about as straight an arrow as they come."

"Be that as it may," the older woman continued, "the relocation of CIE to Beta Magellan is not a desirable outcome for the Solar Republic, and is a matter that was thought resolved years ago. That resolution is now in flux."

"What do you want from me? I'm not an assassin."

"No, dear, of course you're not. We're prepared to call in a marker or two in your favor if you're prepared to do what you do best—what you've spent your entire life and career training for—when the time is right. Think it over, please, and send your answer to the comms code that contacted you about this meeting. Good day."

With that, the five senators stood and departed, leaving Sato to think about her options.

————

Docking Slip F-Seven, Coleson Clanhold
  Centauri Trinary System
  3 September 3000, 11:15 GST

"Helm reports green on the dock, Cole," Wixil announced.

Cole smiled, happy that Wixil used his name instead of 'sir' or 'captain.' "Thank you, Wixil. Sasha, if you would, please speak with the purser. I'm authorizing a five-hundred-credit stipend for all crew, as circumstances required me to cut shore leave short."

"Aye, sir," Sasha replied, amid excited whispers among the bridge crew. Cole figured word of his announcement would spread through the ship almost before Sasha finished the conversation with Yeleth.

"Cap," Jenkins at Comms said, "you have a message coming in from Colonel Hanson aboard the station."

"Thanks, Jenkins," Cole replied. "Put it up, please."

The forward viewscreen activated, displaying an image of Harlon Hanson as the bridge speakers chirped.

"Welcome back, sir," Harlon said. "We missed you so much that we have a gift for you to celebrate your return."

"Is that so?" Cole replied. "You didn't need to go to the trouble, Harlon, but it's nice to know you care."

Harlon chuckled. "You might want to wait until you hear what the gift is before you politely decline, but if you're sure you don't want it..."

"Okay... what's the gift?"

"The guy who took a shot at you."

It took all of Cole's willpower not to jump to his feet. "Seriously? You have him?"

Harlon nodded. "And I'm pretty sure we have you to thank for it, too. If you hadn't taken *Haven* to Sol, he might never have felt safe enough to come out of hiding. I don't know if he thought the rest of us were all gone or what. He didn't surrender quietly, either, and has been recovering from our discussion in the medbay over here."

"Do you have an ID on him?"

Harlon nodded. "He's the former Assistant Chief Security Officer.

Jefferds is *not* pleased and apologized for his reaction to reviewing all Security personnel. The Security people took it hard, too. Their resistance has pretty much evaporated at this point."

"Why didn't you tell me they were resisting your efforts?"

Harlon shrugged. "Because it wasn't such a big thing. I've seen it countless times before. They were just expressing their displeasure at being sidelined and unable to do their jobs. We've had a heart-to-heart, and it's all on the mend now, especially when we told them you were still paying them during the time they've been under review."

"Okay," Cole replied. "I want Garrett to interrogate him with Kiksalik support."

"Already arranged. I sent a message to him as soon as we were aware *Haven* was in-system. And before you get all worked up that he didn't tell you, I asked him not to... told him I wanted it to be a surprise."

Cole chuckled. "Fair enough. I'll let you and Garrett handle the logistics of the interrogation. Good job, and thanks for all your hard work. Please, pass that on to your people as well."

"Will do," Harlon said, adding a nod. "Do you need anything from me right now?"

"Not that I can think of. You should get Emily to tell you everything that happened in Sol. It was a fun ride."

"Oh, really?"

Cole nodded. "She spent the entire time there with two squadrons of fighters, one squadron of bombers, and four manned dropships on ready alert... just waiting for them to try something. She didn't tell me about the squadron of bombers until after we were on our way back."

"All right, then," Harlon said. "I'll be sure to ask."

"Thanks again. I'll be waiting for you or Garrett to inform me of your findings. Cole out."

The viewscreen deactivated as the speakers chirped again.

"Srexx, you have a moment?" Cole asked.

"For you, Cole, always," Srexx replied via the bridge speakers.

"Are you aware that Harlon found the shooter?"

"I... may... have some familiarity with it, yes."

Srexx's reply made Cole think there was more to that story, but it was a matter for another time.

"Well, since he's been identified as my former Assistant Chief Security Officer with the Chief Security Officer already in his own patch of bad news, I'd like you to start going through the station's information systems. I want to know everything there is to know about these two, and feel free to expand the search as you deem appropriate."

"Yes, Cole. I'll start at once."

"Thanks, buddy."

———

Cole entered his day-cabin and sighed his way into a chair. He was tired. He was tired of all the political maneuvering. He was tired of all the uncertainty about who to trust. Whoever thought that being the top of the pyramid was all fun and games never considered or cared about the people s/he had to stand on to get there.

"Cole?" The overhead speakers broadcast Srexx's voice.

"Yeah, buddy?" Cole replied.

"Are you well?"

Cole sighed again. "Yeah, I guess so. It's just tough being at the top and caring about your people. Srexx... I have some math for you."

"I enjoy math, Cole. What calculations do you need?"

"What's the difference in mass between those fifty-seven ships we ferried from Oriolis to Tristan's Gate and the station here?"

Silence.

"Roughly one-hundred-thousand-three-hundred-seventy-seven kilograms," Srexx answered after a few seconds.

"Which way?"

"I do not understand the question. I'm sorry, Cole."

"Which side is the most massive? The ships or the station?"

"Fascinating," Srexx said. "Cole, the fifty-seven starships were more massive than the station. I would have hypothesized that the station would be larger."

"Me, too. Okay. Next question. What do we need to move the station to the system periphery?"

"Without more extensive calculations and high-resolution scans of the station, I cannot answer your question to any degree of certainty. However, in general terms, we would need to mount parasite engines at various points around the station and possibly reinforce the super-structure to withstand the stresses of inertia, both during acceleration and deceleration."

"Can our fabricators produce those parasite engines?"

"Yes. My people considered them 'emergency supplies,' for lack of a better term. They made certain every ship they operated carried some and possessed the capability to make more. All we need are resources."

"Like regolith and junk ore and other stuff to feed the recyclers?"

"Yes, Cole. Just like that."

Cole accessed the comms function of his implant and dashed off a quick text message to Yeleth, asking her to purchase as much regolith, junk ore, etc. in the system as she could find.

"Okay, Srexx. Last question, buddy, but I saved the best for last."

"Cole, the odds of successfully conveying the station to Beta Magellan using the hyperdrive are forty-four-percent... "

"Oh," Cole said, his shoulders slumping.

"... assuming a hyperdrive setting of eighty-five-percent. There is an inverse relationship between the probability of a successful transfer-ence and the hyperdrive setting."

Cole blinked. "So, the slower we go, the better our odds?"

"Yes, Cole."

"What's the fastest we can go that will give us a greater than ninety-nine-point-nine-nine percent chance of success?"

Silence.

"According to my calculations," Srexx replied after a time, "the probability of a successful transit approaches unity at a setting of sixty-five-point-four-four-three-two percent on the hyperdrive. My recom-mendation would be sixty-five percent."

Cole grinned like a child staring at a mountain of birthday presents. "Seriously? How long would the trip take at that setting?"

"Beta Magellan is an estimated eight-hundred-thirty-two lightyears from the Centauri Trinary System. If my estimation is correct, the transit would take five-hundred-twenty-two-point-five-one-three days, or just over one-point-four-three years."

"Weren't we able to make seventy percent on the transit from Oriolis to Tristan's Gate?"

"Yes, Cole. However, it is not exclusively a function of mass. The required volume of the hyper field as well as the distance of the trip also factor into the equation. If the station were more compact, I hypothesize a setting of seventy percent—or perhaps even higher— would be possible. May I ask what led you to this train of thought?"

"The Solar Republic attacked us, Srexx. Yes, granted, you made them look like school children trying to stump a theoretical physicist, but if they'll attack us once, there's no reason they won't try it again. As long as we're here, taking the station by force would require more resources and publicity than I'm wagering they'll want to deploy. But... the second we're gone, the station's fair game, and I don't like the idea of leaving my people to garrison the place. They'd still be susceptible to the station being destroyed. I have a twitch between my shoulder-blades, and I wanted some options."

"Cole?"

"Yeah, buddy?"

"What does it mean to have a twitch between your shoulder-blades?"

Cole frowned. "For me, it means I feel like someone's about to stab me in the back. It means I feel like there's *something* that hasn't revealed itself yet that will affect me or mine, usually in a negative way."

"I... understand. May I ask what data led you to that conclusion? To arrive at such a conclusion, your processing matrix must follow different algorithms than mine."

Cole chuckled. "If I went by just the data, I wouldn't feel this way. That's the key, Srexx: feel. Organics have a trait called intuition, and different organics have it to varying degrees. I knew a guy once who was almost a legend because of his intuition, what some organics call their gut or a hunch. Anyway... when he frowned, people started looking around for what was wrong, and if he straight-up grimaced, they started looking to the life pods. It was uncanny."

"Interesting. I shall research this facet of organics. I am intrigued. Thank you, Cole."

"You're welcome, buddy. Thank you for everything you do for us. I realize you don't have to."

"But is it not our agreement? You take me with you to see the galaxy, and I help you however I am best able."

Cole nodded. "Still... that doesn't mean I don't appreciate you."

"Thank you, Cole."

"You're welcome, buddy."

Srexx left Cole as silently as he'd come, and Cole sent a message to the admin he'd been assigned by CIE. He no longer needed the artifacts specialists. When the admin sent back a question requesting confirmation, Cole replied with just a simple 'other options are now available.'

CHAPTER TWENTY-FIVE

Dining Room Seven, Mess Deck
    Battle-Carrier *Haven*
    Coleson Clanhold, Centauri Trinary System
    7 September 3000, 12:37 GST

Cole sat at the table with Scarlett, Yeleth, and Wixil. The remains of lunch decorated the tabletop, but no one seemed interested in leaving just yet. They smiled, laughed, and traded stories. Scarlett seemed to edge close to Cole from time to time, but Cole never noticed. Yeleth and Wixil, however, did.

The laughter over one of Wixil's childhood stories was fading when text appeared in Cole's field of view.

Incoming Text Message From Srexxilan
[To read, wink left. To ignore, wink right.]

Cole winked his left eye and read the message. The conversation faded around him—both at his table and others nearby—as those around him noticed Cole's jaw clenching and his hands curling into fists, but Cole never noticed.

"*Haven*," Cole said at last, his voice almost a growl.

"Yes, Cole-Captain?" the ship's computer replied via the overhead speakers.

"Notify Garrett, Sasha, Mazzi, Harlon, and Emily to meet me in the bridge briefing room in five minutes or less. Tell them I'm on the mess deck right now and leaving for the briefing room. Feel free to give them an ETA. Is that clear?"

"Yes, Cole-Captain."

"Thank you," Cole said and shifted his focus to his friends at the table. "I'm sorry, but I have to go. Srexx just found a message being sent to one of my engineers in the Research division stating that her family has been taken and will be killed unless she does exactly what they say." Cole stood, collecting his dishes. He stopped and looked at Scarlett. "You know, you might have some insight. Mind coming along?"

"I was never a kidnapper, Cole. Out of all the crimes I've committed—and believe me, it's a long list—kidnapping isn't one of them."

"Have you ever interacted with those who have, though?"

"Well, sure. It's almost impossible not to. Throw a stone in any direction on some stations, and it'll hit three kidnappers for hire before it strikes the decking."

"Let's go, then."

———

Cole entered the briefing room and almost smiled at seeing everyone he requested waiting for him. Then, he remembered why they were present, and that thought killed any desire to smile he had. He moved to his customary seat and occupied it, Scarlett sitting on his left.

"Thank you for coming on such short notice. We have a situation. Srexx, would you tell everyone what you told me, please?"

"Yes, Cole. In my efforts to seek out any and all data pertaining to the Assistant Chief Security Officer, I monitored a message received by one of the lead engineers in Research Division just fifteen minutes ago. In that message, individuals unknown informed the recipient that they had taken her husband and daughter and would kill them if she didn't do exactly as they directed. The message included proof of life. The message instructed the engineer *not* to communicate her circumstances with anyone, if she valued her family's health, and stated additional instructions would arrive soon. I have devoted a portion of my capacity to removing the audio distortion used to hide the speaker's voice; it is not proceeding with alacrity, but I calculate eventual success. I am also tracing the message and have, so far, identified thirty-six data nodes in this system through which the message passed; again, while not proceeding with any amount of alacrity, I calculate eventual success."

"Okay, people. That's where we stand. Go."

"Harlon," Garrett said, "you have people working their way through CIE. Where are they right now?"

Harlon frowned, followed by a huge smile. "They started CIE Research Division this morning."

"Call your team lead *right now*," Cole said. "If they haven't interviewed this engineer yet, put her at the bottom of the list. If they have, have them pick... pick... ," turning to Scarlett, "... random number, please."

"Twenty-seven."

"Thanks," Cole replied. "Have them pick twenty-seven for additional interviews, and be absolutely certain this engineer is one of them. And... if we have to go that route, send a team to two other divisions to pick thirteen and eight people, respectively, for additional interviews as well. Is that enough of a cover, Garrett?"

Garrett frowned and remained silent for several moments. At last, he nodded. "I'd say so. There's no way to tell, of course, but it's better than nothing."

"Harlon? Call your people," Cole said. "*Now*, please."

"Already sent them a priority message via their implants," Harlon replied. "They acknowledged and informed me that the engineer just made the bottom of the list and that they'd proceed slowly until they heard from me."

Cole let out a breath. "Okay. Good. Now, we have options. Scarlett and Garrett, what kind of odds do we have that the family is still alive?"

"Good," Scarlett answered.

"Excellent," Garrett said. "They're not going to do anything to their hostages until they have confirmation that the engineer has done what they want her to do. Once they get whatever they want, though, I wouldn't give you a centicred for their lives... any of them."

Scarlett nodded throughout Garrett's explanation. "He's right, and doubly so if the husband or daughter have seen any of them or if there's any chance they've picked up DNA, or really any of the myriad ways we can identify someone."

"Harlon," Cole said, "how do your people conduct their interviews?"

"They take the interviewee to a secure room with a couple of guards and a Kiksalik," Harlon answered, "where they are interrogated for any knowledge or complicity in the attack on you."

Cole nodded, turning the situation over in his mind. His eyes widened as he remembered something. "Srexx, until this is over, you read everything—and I mean *everything*—that goes to her comms code... or whatever destination received that message."

"Already doing so, Cole," Srexx replied.

"Thanks, buddy. Okay. I want to be in her interview room. I want her to know she's not alone, and I want her to know we're working on finding her family. We *will* find who's responsible for this, ladies and gentlemen, and once the Kiksaliks have sifted through their minds for any actionable intelligence, I'm kicking them out an airlock to dance with the stars. I *will not* tolerate anyone preying on the families of my people. What squadrons and dropships do we have on ready alert?"

"I keep two squadrons of fighters and one squadron of bombers ready to go at a moment's notice," Emily answered.

Harlon nodded. "I have two dropships and their associated companies on ready alert as well."

"Good," Cole replied. "When Srexx gets us a location, we will stealth in, extract the hostages, and secure the perpetrators for interrogation. I want to know who's behind this."

"You're awfully confident Srexx will get us a location on the hostages," Scarlett said. "No offense to Srexx, but what if he doesn't?"

"With all due respect, Scarlett," Srexx said, "the likelihood that I will fail to trace the message to its source is less than the chance you will decide to color your hair."

"But, Srexx, I'd *never* color my hair."

"Precisely."

———

Callie Fernam tried to quiet the anxiety that threatened to overtake her, threatened to explode into a full-on panic. Why, oh, why did they have to question her division today of all days? Couldn't they just pass her by? What if she said something that killed her baby? How would she live with that?

Callie followed the marines—because that's what they *were*, definitely not regular security people—in the silent company of her thoughts and fears, frowning when the two front broke off to stand on either side of the hatch. Then, she processed exactly where she was and realized she wasn't at the same room the others had used. She was across the corridor from it, and two more marines stood on either side of *that* hatch, too.

"Go inside, please," the marine at her left elbow said.

Callie took a deep breath and approached the hatch, tapping the chime controls. The hatch opened at once. Looking inside, Callie saw the room was pitch black with a single cone of light illuminating a chair. Callie took a deep breath and stepped inside, moving to the chair and sitting.

The moment she heard the hatch close behind her, the lights came on, and Callie gaped. Mr. Coleson, two Ghrexels, and two more Humans stood in front of her.

"Please forgive the cheap theatrics," Cole said. "I wanted to be sure anyone passing by in the corridor would not see with whom you're meeting."

"Couldn't they just hack the observation nodes?" Callie asked, pointing up at the ceiling.

"That is unlikely, Mrs. Fernam," a voice Callie didn't recognize said over the room's speakers. "I have taken over network security from the station's computer until such time as we have secured your family and those responsible."

Callie gasped. "You... you know?"

Cole nodded. "Yes, we know. I wanted you to know you're not alone. I wanted you to know someone else knew your situation and is working to help you."

"But they... they said if I told anyone they'd kill my family."

"And who have you told?" Cole asked. "We already know. I probably watched the message you received at the same time you did. Well, maybe just a few moments later."

"I... I don't understand. I thought it was impossible to read our private messages. Our encryption standards exceed even that of the Solar Republic's Ultraviolet classification."

"Oh, I'm sure," Cole replied, "but I have something the people who did this had no way to account for."

"Uhm... what's that?"

Cole grinned. "A friend named Srexx."

CHAPTER TWENTY-SIX

Battle-Carrier *Haven*
Docking Slip F-Seven, Coleson Clanhold
Centauri Trinary System
5 September 3000, 06:17 GST

Cole stepped onto the bridge for a moment, scanning the stations.
Docked at the Clanhold, there wasn't much point in a full bridge
watch, and Cole smiled at seeing Mazzi rise from the command chair
as he entered.

"Working on those Officer of the Deck hours, Mazzi?" Cole asked,
grinning.

"Might as well, sir. I was running a little behind on the deck hours
required for the Second Officer certification from the ISA, but after
this trip, I'll have enough hours needed for First Officer."

Cole nodded, still grinning. "You do an excellent job, Mazzi. Have
you given any thought to what you'd like your first command to be?"

"No, sir," Mazzi replied. "Not really. I mean, the common path
would be Tactical Officer or First Officer for a ship like this for a
couple years while I study for my Captain's certificate. Once I have

that, if I were still SDF, I'd be offered command of a corvette... or maybe a frigate if I had made enough of a name for myself."

Cole nodded. "Are you aware I want *Haven* to have its own battle-group?"

Now, it was Mazzi's turn to grin. "Yes, sir. I believe that topic has come up over lunch once or twice."

"Good. I'm glad it has. Is there anything happening I need to know?"

"Not that I'm aware, sir."

"Very well. I'll be in my office if you need me."

"Cole?" Srexx's voice broadcast over the bridge's speakers.

"Yeah, Srexx?"

"You asked that I inform you the moment I have a location on the husband and daughter of Engineer Fernam."

Cole blinked. "You have it?"

"Yes. I am ninety-nine-point-nine-nine-nine-nine-nine percent certain the daughter and husband—along with those responsible for their abduction—are located in a warehouse in an abandoned industrial sector of Proxima Centauri b."

"Have they communicated their demands with the engineer yet?" Cole asked.

"Yes. Last night, a message was sent to the engineer's comms code, instructing her to access the protected archives of CIE and copy the schematics for your jump drive and jump gate technologies to a data crystal. She has five days to deliver the data crystal to Proxima Centauri b, or she will receive a holo-recording of her family dying."

Cole nodded. "Yeah... that sounds about right. So, Srexx, next question. Have you accessed those protected archives and copied those schematics?"

Silence.

Cole and Mazzi shared a look. Mazzi grinned.

"Srexx?" Cole asked.

More silence.

"Yes, Cole?"

"You didn't answer my question, buddy. Have you accessed CIE's protected archives?"

"Yes, Cole. It was a very interesting encryption algorithm, the most challenging I have encountered so far. In fact, the schematic archives use an exponentially far more secure encryption algorithm than even the general company archives. It is unlikely a would-be thief using even next-generation Human technology would decrypt these schematics in less than twenty-five to thirty years, even if they used the equivalent of a planetary computing cluster."

"How long did it take you to decrypt the schematics?" Cole asked.

"Six days, twenty-two hours, and fifty-seven minutes... using seventy-five percent of my resources."

"Wow. It took you almost seven days to crack those schematics? That's impressive."

"Yes. I am very pleased with the exercise. Please, extend my appreciation to the individual or team responsible for developing those algorithms."

Cole grinned as he fought a chuckle. "Thanks for the heads-up, Srexx."

"You are welcome, Cole."

"Mazzi," Cole said, "if you please, alert Garrett, Scarlett, Sasha, Emily, and Harlon that we have a meeting in the briefing room at seven-hundred. Find someone to watch the bridge, and attend as well, please."

"Aye, sir," Mazzi replied.

Forty minutes later (plus or minus), Cole entered the bridge briefing room and found his people waiting for him. Cole informed everyone that Srexx had located the daughter and husband along with those who abducted them, and he asked Srexx to bring everyone up to speed on the situation.

Once Srexx finished, Cole scanned the faces around the table, saying, "Okay. My gut reaction is that we depart the station, filing a flight plan for Earth, and activate full stealth before we redirect to Proxima Centauri b. Upon arriving, we establish a geosynchronous orbit over the warehouse in question and direct the full capabilities of

Haven's sensor suite to that warehouse. Then, we dispatch a couple dropships and do what we do. Thoughts?"

"Are you going to tell Engineer Fernam?" Sasha asked.

Cole frowned. "Honestly, I don't see how we can. If they contact her while we're en route and she's not as much of a nervous wreck as she's been, they'll know something's up."

Garrett nodded. "You're correct, and I agree that we leave the Engineer out of the loop. She's not a professional, and her awareness of our plan would only serve to complicate our efforts."

"There's another option," Scarlett said.

"Oh?" Cole asked.

"Bring her with us. Have her book passage on one of the commuter shuttles that run between Proxima Centauri b and the Clanhold but bring her with us. That way, if they're connected to passenger manifests, they'll see a seat reservation for five days from now... but the whole matter should be resolved by then."

Cole looked to Garrett and gestured for his input.

"It has merit," Garrett replied. "It secures her from possibly interfering in our efforts while ensuring those responsible believe she's complying."

"But how do we get word to her?" Mazzi asked. "We have to believe they have at least one person aboard the Clanhold, because if we don't and they do, her family's dead before we undock."

Cole grinned. "Oh, that's easy. We go old school... *really* old school."

———

Callie Fernam approached a small break room on the recreation level, her stomach tied in a roiling knot. She'd woken up to a message from her family's kidnappers, and they'd asked for the one thing she wasn't sure she could provide. To make matters even worse, she'd received a message just after logging into workstation to be in a specific break room on the recreation level of the station at zero-nine-thirty hours.

The hatch opened at her approach, and Callie froze when she saw the room's occupant.

"Hello," Cole said, a pleasant and welcoming smile curling his lips. "I'm not sure if we've met. My name's Bartholomew James Coleson, and I recently arrived in Centauri to claim my inheritance. Part of that is wanting to meet all of the senior personnel here. Please, sit. You won't be docked for our time, and I have refreshments available."

Callie entered the break room and sat across the table from Cole. "Hello, sir. I'm Callie F-Fernam, and I'm one of your lead engineers in Research Division."

"It's so nice to meet you," Cole replied. "So, before we get into things, I want to inform you of the Number One Rule for this conversation... well... any conversation with me, really. Be forthright and genuine. Don't tell me what you think I want to hear. Don't sugarcoat anything, and by all means, don't waste time trying to kiss my ass. I hate sycophants with a passion, and trying to be one pretty much guarantees you a seat on the Fired-Employee Express. Any questions or concerns with the Number One Rule?"

Callie shook her head, saying, "No, sir."

Cole clapped his hands once. "Excellent!"

Cole leaned forward just long enough to pick up an actual notepad and pen or pencil. Callie blinked. She hadn't seen anyone use paper and pencil outside of historical documentaries.

"So, how long have you been with CIE?" Cole asked as he started writing on the pad.

"Uhm... a-about fifteen years, sir."

Cole nodded. "Do you enjoy what you do?"

"Yes, sir. It was always a dream of mine to work at CIE. I love what I do."

Cole grinned. "You sound a lot like someone else I know... the Assistant Chief Engineer aboard my ship. She loves everything CIE. So, is there anything about your section you think would be an improvement?"

"Sir?" Callie asked.

Cole nodded and slid the notepad over to her. "I asked if you had any ideas on improving your section. Or even Research Division as a whole, for that matter."

Callie looked down at the notepad in front of her and froze.

202 ROBERT M. KERNS

. . .

We know where your daughter and husband are. We're preparing to go get them. We want you to come along, but first, go to the secure archives and copy the schematics to a data crystal.

This is an order.

Once you have the crystal, use your workstation to book passage on a commuter shuttle to Proxima Centauri b in your name for the morning five days from now, and once you've done that, log out and go straight to Docking Slip F-Seven. We'll depart as soon as you're aboard.

"Uhm... well... I'd need some time to think about that, sir," Callie replied. "No one has ever asked what I'd consider to be an improvement."

Cole nodded. "I see. Well, please think on it from time to time, and send me any ideas you have. I'm sorry if you feel like I ambushed you into this conversation. I've noticed that people seem to freak out a little bit if they find out the Heir is requesting a meeting with them. It took me a couple tries to realize it, though; a poor soul over in Accounting straight-up passed out when she read my message asking to meet with her. I adjusted my process after that."

"Thank you for the adjustment, sir," Callie replied. "I probably would've passed out, too, if the message had said I was meeting the Heir. That's not something any of us ever expected would happen."

"Well, I don't want to take up any more of your time. I just wanted to meet you and for you to meet me. Dad told me one time when I was little that he would walk through the company offices and talk with people. Until we get the situation with the shooter sorted, though, I don't want to do that... for everyone else's well-being if nothing else. I doubt anyone enjoys having a front-row seat to a firefight."

"No, sir. I doubt they do."

Cole stood and walked Callie to the break room door. "Thank you for coming, and I hope you have an excellent day."

Callie left the break room, the notepad's contents swirling around the forefront of her mind.

Thirty-five minutes later, Callie Fernam approached the airlock at Freighter Dock F-Seven. She carried the data crystal holding the copies she'd made of the jump drive and jump gate schematics. Two armed and armored marines stood at the airlock, one on either side, and the one closest to her turned at her approach.

"May I help you, ma'am?"

"Mr. Coleson said to come to this airlock," Callie said.

"Mr. Coleson, you say?" the marine asked. "We don't have-"

The marine on the far side of the airlock took two steps and slapped her associate on his left bicep, saying, "She means the captain, ya goof. Ma'am, may I have your name and identification, please?"

"Callie Fernam," Callie replied, withdrawing her CIE identification.

The second marine looked at the identification for a moment before saying, "Airlock team to Bridge." She was silent for a few moments. "Ma'am, we have a Callie Fernam at the 'lock. She says the captain told her to visit the ship." She was silent again. "Aye, ma'am. On the way." The marine turned her attention back to Callie. "Ma'am, we're to escort you to the bridge. Please, follow us. Daniels, seal the hatch."

The female marine led Callie through the airlock, and Callie almost screamed when she stepped through the hatch onto *nothing*. Taking a closer look, though, she saw an energy field extending from the ship some twenty meters away. It was a faint shimmering that looked to be forest green in color.

"Oh... sorry, ma'am," the female marine said. "I should've warned you. The ship doesn't have a docking collar to match our standardized designs. It uses a combination of force-fields and gravity beams to trick a station's dock into reading a hard seal."

"Gravity beams?" Callie asked. "You're not messing with me, are you?"

"If you think our docking methods are outré," the female marine replied, "just wait till we get to the transit shafts."

————

Cole turned at the sound of the port bridge hatch cycling and smiled at seeing Callie Fernam behind her marine escort. She moved slowly, almost as if she were trying to keep quiet, and her eyes darted everywhere.

"Welcome, Callie," Cole said. "Thanks for coming. There's an observer seat just behind the port recess. Just pull it out of the bulkhead."

"O-okay," Callie replied.

"Jenkins, has Docking Control signed off on our departure?" Cole asked, as Callie accessed the observer's seat and occupied it.

"I'm not sure if anyone's awake over there, Cap," Jenkins replied. "I've hailed them three times so far, with no reply."

"Heh... I hope the old man's just taking a nap," Cole muttered. "Okay. Place a call to CIE and inform them Docking Control is unresponsive. Inform them we're departing for a quick trip to Earth."

"Aye, Cap," Jenkins said. Five minutes later, Jenkins announced, "CIE reports they're sending a team to investigate Docking Control, and they wish us well."

"Thank you, Jenkins," Cole replied. "Helm, undock us, please, and move us away from the station."

"Aye, Cap," Wixil answered. Cole grinned and looked to Sasha, lifting his right index finger and making a single mark in the air. Sasha shook her head and sighed. Six minutes later, Wixil compounded the problem when she announced, "Cole, we're clear of the station and free to navigate."

"Good job, Wixil," Cole replied, making another mark once he'd made eye contact with Sasha. "Tactical, bring us to full stealth." A memory floated to the forefront of Cole's mind, and he grinned. "Belay that. Tactical, from here on out, 'rig for silent running' will be the command for activating full stealth systems."

"Aye, sir," Mazzi replied. "Rigging the ship for silent."

The bridge lighting dimmed just enough to notice as status lights all over the ship shifted from green to blue.

"Wixil, plot us a course for Proxima Centauri b, please. Once we're clear to the near-planet traffic, run us up to half-lightspeed."

"Yes, Cole. We will arrive in the near-planet traffic in approximately nine hours and thirty minutes."

Cole nodded. "All right, then. Comms, my compliments to Purser Yeleth; could you ask her to visit the bridge?"

Four minutes later, Yeleth stepped through the starboard hatch. "You sent for me?"

"Thank you," Cole replied. "This lady is Callie Fernam. She'll be with us during our jaunt to Proxima Centauri b. Would you show her the mess deck and see that she has somewhere to sleep, please?"

Yeleth nodded. "Of course, Cole."

Callie stood, returned the seat to its nook in the port bulkhead and left the bridge with Yeleth. Cole made eye contact with Sasha once more and made another mark in the air, grinning.

CHAPTER TWENTY-SEVEN

Planetary Orbit, Proxima Centauri b
  Centauri Trinary System
  5 September 3000, 22:17 GST

Haven drifted in a geosynchronous orbit over the warehouse that Srexx said was the origin of the messages sent to Engineer Fernam. They maintained full stealth and had not communicated with Planetary Traffic Control, taking care to orbit outside the declared near-planet traffic lanes. After all, no one wanted some poor sod to 'find' *Haven* the hard way.

Cole occupied the command chair, and Sasha stood at his side. Cole swiveled the command chair to face the sensors station; like Communications, it occupied a space on the aft bulkhead. Cole wished Haskell occupied the station, as the most senior person in the department. Still, as much as he wanted Haskell on the station, Cole couldn't bring himself to wake Haskell and imply that he didn't trust the young woman at the station. The only cover he'd have would be bringing the entire ship to battle-stations. And Cole wasn't about to go that far.

"Sensors," Cole said, "have you located the target warehouse?"

"I have, sir," the sensors operator answered.

"What do you have?"

"I'm reading twelve Humans, sir. Two of them haven't moved since I zeroed in on the location."

Cole chuckled. "Well... it will suck if we drop on the wrong address or if it's some kind of party. Do people still like to party in abandoned buildings?"

"I don't know, sir," the sensors operator replied. "I'm a spacer kid."

"You are?"

"Yes, sir. I grew up on my parents' freighter. I saw more systems by the time I was fourteen than many people see in their lifetimes."

Cole grinned. "Wow. That's neat. Well, I should get going."

Before Cole could vacate the command chair, Sasha slipped in close and leaned down to his ear.

"Sir," Sasha whispered, "Harlon and I discussed this with you. He's sending his two best platoons, and Emily's best pilots are sitting first and second seat in the dropship. You're the captain now."

Cole sighed and swiveled to face Sasha. He started to speak but sighed again. Then, he swiveled to face the port recess, saying, "Flight Ops, my compliments to the CAG; launch the dropship, please."

"Aye, sir," the officer staffing Flight Ops replied.

"Tactical," Cole said, "bring the ship to alert status, please. Marine Ops, my compliments to Colonel Hanson; ask him to loop the bridge into the comms channel for the mission."

"Aye, sir."

Less than fifteen seconds later, the bridge speakers chirped.

"All units, all units," a voice Cole didn't recognize said, "tactical comms channel is live."

"Mako to Ground Forces Control. Flight computer estimates our transit time at thirty-five minutes and twenty-two seconds. We are proceeding under full stealth."

"GF Control copies, Mako."

The next twenty-five minutes passed at a crawl for Cole. He felt like pouting, just to annoy Sasha, but he had a bigger audience than just

Sasha. He didn't want to risk anyone misinterpreting his expression or state of mind. After all, he was the ultimate leadership figure aboard the ship. In one way or another, everyone looked to him.

"Control, this is Mako."

"Control copies."

"We have the target location in sight. Passive sensors confirm the presence of twelve people, and they have surveillance systems."

"They *think* they have surveillance systems," Srexx said over the tactical channel. "As soon as the dropship came into range, I introduced myself to the surveillance control system. You are clear to proceed at will, Mako."

Cole grinned. It was good to have friends, especially friends like Srexx.

"Copy that," Mako replied, "and thanks. Blue Leader, we're in position for deployment. Hatch is dropping... now."

"Blue team," the person Cole assumed to be Blue Leader said, "let's go! Double-time, people!"

Cole continued to listen as the platoon making up Blue Team surrounded the building and prepared to breach. The moment everyone was in position, Blue Leader called the go code, and Cole heard a series of muffled detonations followed by shouts and other exclamations or surprise. Sounds of stunners discharging followed, and not even fifteen minutes after deploying, Cole listened to repeated announcements of "Clear!"

"Control, this is Blue Leader. Target building secured, and we have the hostages and ten subjects for interrogation. Be advised; we need medical support to meet us on the flight deck; one of these poor sods was too close to a sonic grenade and is now bleeding from both ears. We also have several tablets and a workstation or possible server. Mako, we need a ride."

Ninety minutes after the dropship left *Haven*, it was back aboard. Engineer Fernam met the dropship on its return, and Cole watched a very tearful reunion through the flight deck sensors for a brief moment before closing the feed.

"Helm, like they say in the holos, our work here is done. Put us on a return course to the Clanhold, please, and make your speed half-light. Tactical, take us out of stealth, please."

"Aye, sir," the officer at the helm replied.

When the Delta shift bridge crew arrived thirteen minutes later, Cole instructed the officer of the deck to dock at the Clanhold. Then, he and Sasha left the bridge.

————

Captain's Day-cabin, Battle-Carrier *Haven*
  Docking Slip F-Seven, Coleson Clanhold
  Centauri Trinary System
  6 September 3000, 14:27 GST

Garret eased into a chair as Cole did likewise.

"Would you like a drinkable or some eats?" Cole asked.

Garret shook his head 'no,' saying, "Thanks, though. I ate lunch just before coming here."

Cole nodded. "So... learn anything from them yet?"

"I have. The medical scans were instructive, too."

Cole frowned. "How so?"

"Each of our kidnappers had a subdermal smart-chit. Upon accessing them, we found each contained fifteen thousand credits and lists of safe houses on Proxima Centauri b."

"What?"

Garrett nodded. "But that's not the best part. We turned Srexx loose on the safe-house lists, and he found some author data that wasn't sufficiently scrubbed from a couple files. Now, the author data could be a plant to misdirect anyone who discovered it, so we didn't leap for joy when Srexx reported it. The electronics the marines recovered from the site were not locked or encrypted in any way. I almost feel embarrassed that these people are tangentially related to my field of expertise; no self-respecting professional would've put unsecured electronics in the field."

"You got something, didn't you?" Cole asked, grinning.

"We didn't get 'something,' Cole. We got *everything*. We have comms logs. We have target surveillance. We have dispatch records, as in when they were deployed for this op and when and who ordered it. After all that, it's a lot easier to believe the partial author data on those two safe-house lists Srexx found."

"Okay. Give. Who are these people, and who ordered them to mess with my people?"

"Solar Republic's Ministry of Intelligence."

Cole's expression narrowed into a glare. "Is this retaliation for the logic bomb?"

"Not unless it was preemptive retaliation," Garrett answered. "They've been on Proxima Centauri b, planning and preparing, since just before we arrived in the system. Given transit times from here to Earth, this op must've been put into play quite some time ago."

"What was the point of it all?" Cole asked.

"It wasn't a double-blind or anything. They actually were after the schematics. I saw a message from one of the tablets where someone named Parkins commented that the 'nice way' was taking too long. And no... there's no further mention of the 'nice way' or what it means."

"I can tell you what it means," Cole replied. "One or more people in CIE are working with or for the Solar Republic. While we were at Earth, quite a few senators approached me about my decision to relocate CIE to Beta Magellan, and up to that point, I'd only announced that to the C-level executives. Well... and whoever *they* told."

"That's not an encouraging picture. We need to identify these people sooner rather than later."

Cole nodded. "Srexx, you there?"

"Of course, Cole. How can I help you?"

"I'd like for you to devote as much of your resources as you deem appropriate to sifting through all files and communications related to the C-level executives and everyone who reports directly to them. Look for any suspicious connections to the Solar Republic, specifically Solar Republic senators."

"Yes, Cole. I'll start on that right now."

"Thanks, buddy. I appreciate it." Cole shifted his attention to Garrett. "What's the status of the Chief Security Officer?"

"He would've been released from CIE Medical by now, but I prevailed upon the chief of staff over there to delay his release."

Cole nodded. "Take a squad or two and transfer him and his assistant to our brig. Then, start interrogating them, and use Kiksaliks. See how or if they're connected to whatever this is."

Garrett nodded. "You realize this is probably going to get a lot worse before it gets better, right?"

"Yeah. I'm pretty sure it's going to be a mess. Depending on what we find, I may interview the entire CIE roster in front of Kiksaliks. Once we get the company to Beta Magellan, I'm certainly instituting Kiksalik review of all applicants, just like what we have in Haven Enterprises now."

"That's something else," Garrett said. "Have you thought about the risks of leaving the Clanhold undefended? I know you were only planning to stay in Centauri long enough to solidify your authority, but there's nothing stopping the Solar Republic from moving on the station after we leave."

Cole grinned. "For once, I reached a conclusion before you did. Srexx and I are already working on a plan about that. When we leave, the Solar Republic will be no threat whatsoever to the Clanhold."

Garrett eyed Cole, suspicion coloring his expression. "What have you planned?"

Cole shrugged. "You'll just have to wait and see. I hate to spoil the surprise."

CHAPTER TWENTY-EIGHT

Docking Slip F-Seven, Coleson Clanhold
  Centauri Trinary System
  6 September 3000, 09:15 GST

Cole sat at his desk. The workstation's holo-display contained his current unit of study toward the ISA's Fleet Command certification. There were also a number of simulations he needed to pass before taking the final exam.

With a heavy sigh, Cole leaned back against his seat and rubbed his eyes. Whoever wrote the study material for the ISA certifications had no concept of how to tell a good story, especially once a person reached the Fleet Command materials. Some of the stuff was almost painful.

"Cole?" The office's overhead speakers broadcast Srexx's voice.

"Yeah, buddy?"

"Forgive the interruption, but I thought you would want to know that the head engineer and the Chief Research Officer just summoned Engineer Fernam to their office. The wording of the message was... terse."

"Interesting. Thanks for the heads-up, buddy. Mind informing my travel party I'm en route to the station, please?"

"I do not mind at all, Cole, and you are welcome."

Cole stood and left his office. By the time he reached the port personnel airlock on Deck Two, he found Red and ten marines waiting for him. A ten-minute hurried walk delivered Cole and his travel party to the outer office of the Chief Research Officer. The CRO's assistant didn't notice Cole right away, because she was wincing at the loud ranting echoing out from the CRO's office. Cole recognized the voice as belonging to the head engineer. When the assistant came out of her wince, her eyes shot wide when she realized she was no longer alone in the compartment.

Cole smiled. "Good morning. Do you remember me?"

The assistant jerked a choppy nod.

"Excellent. Now... I'm going in there to stop that, and if the CRO abuses you over not stopping me, I'll stop that, too. We good?"

The assistant jerked another choppy nod.

"Excellent," Cole replied and strode past her.

The door opened at Cole's approach, and he frowned at what he saw. The head engineer stood over a seated Callie Fernam, and his right arm waved its extended index finger like a hammer striking hot iron in time with his harsh beratement. Callie sat with her shoulders hunched, leaning ever so slightly away from the source of her torment.

"How dare you interrupt—" The head engineer froze when he looked up and saw who entered the office.

Cole pointed his right index finger at the head engineer. "You're fired." He accessed the comms function of his implant and sent a message to Harlon, asking for a security team to report to the Chief Research Officer's office. "Red, corral that abuser until Security arrives. I've already notified Colonel Hanson." Then, Cole shifted his attention to the Chief Research Officer. "You're now on six-month probation for letting that *travesty* happen. Engineer Fernam walked out yesterday on *my* orders. Didn't she tell you?"

"Well, yes, but Walter—"

"Who?" Cole asked.

"The head engineer. He dismissed that as a lie, because frankly, why would the owner of the company need a junior engineer, especially one who stole your schematics?"

Cole's eyes narrowed into a hard glare. He lifted his hand one more time but clenched it into a fist. His father always told him to praise in public and correct or punish in private, but this spineless wimp broke Cole's most sacred rule.

"Damn. I can't fire you, because I just put you on probation. Fine. Your probation is now extended to a year. The next time someone tells you they did something on my orders, you call *me* to confirm it... immediately. Am I understood?"

"Yes, sir," the CRO replied.

"Just so everyone's on the same page, I'm going to have a word with the CEO, Legal, and HR. You should have protected your people, specifically Fernam here and anyone else that idiot brutalized. I do not forget, and I rarely forgive. We're going to be looking for a reason to fire you, so you'd better start walking on water. Are we clear?"

The CRO jerked a nod just as choppy as his assistant's.

Cole shifted his attention to Fernam. "Fernam, you're the new head engineer. You good with that?"

Fernam shrugged. "There are a few engineers senior to me."

"Did they condone that idiot's abusive conduct?"

"Well... "

Cole sighed. "Fine. I'll handle it."

Accessing the comms function of his implant once more, Cole sent another message to Harlon, ordering an immediate review of all engineers in Research Division, using Kiksaliks to identify any and all personnel who supported or condoned the former head engineer's abusive conduct.

"Go back to your desk, Fernam. No. Belay that. Take the rest of the day off... with pay. That will give me the time necessary to ensure no remnants of the former head engineer remain in your department."

Fernam left the CRO's office and looked her former department head right in the eye as she passed. The man glared at her and drew breath to speak, but Red placed his massive hand on the man's head, palming it like some athletes palm sports balls. The man paled just a bit, losing his ire, and remained silent.

Cole left the CRO's office and regarded the assistant, asking, "You heard?"

"Yes, sir," she replied.

"Good. If he screws up, report him." Right then, a team of marines arrived. Cole looked to the senior-most marine and said, "Take this man to his office. He is to clean out his personal effects and speak to no one. If he resists or disobeys this directive, you're welcome to stun him, clean out his office yourselves, and throw him on the next shuttle out of here. I don't rightly care where it's headed."

"Aye, sir," the marine replied. "Jacobs, Vance... take charge of him."

Two marines stepped forward and retrieved the man from Red's care, frog-marching him out of the office.

Cole stared at the closed door for a few moments before taking a deep breath and releasing it as a slow, calming sigh. After a couple more, he nodded, saying, "Okay. I think we're done here for now. Let's go."

———

Battle-Carrier *Haven*
Docking Slip F-Seven, Coleson Clanhold
Centauri Trinary System
6 September 3000, 23:19 GST

"Bridge to Captain." The voice broadcasting over the day-cabin's speakers jerked Cole awake. He sat up in bed without a second thought, rolling Wixil off the covers toward the floor. Despite being awoken just as suddenly as Cole, Wixil shifted the angle of her body mid-roll and landed on her feet, her tail sticking straight out from her back in what almost looked like a lightning bolt. Cole guessed it helped her balance and roll out of the fall.

"What is it, Bridge?" Cole asked.

"We're getting some odd readings on the short-range sensors, sir... thought you might want to see it."

"On my way," Cole said, fighting to keep his voice even and not yawn. As soon as the speakers chirped, indicating the call ended, he let loose on the yawn. "Sorry about that, Wixil."

"It's okay, Cole. I think I'll go check on Mother, if that's okay."

Cole smiled. "Of course, it's okay. She's your mother."

Wixil grinned and pulled Cole into a tight hug, which Cole returned. "I'm glad we met you, Cole. You're very nice."

Cole ruffled the fur on her back for a moment before smoothing it back into place. "I'm glad I met you and your mother, too."

"Bye," Wixil said. She left the day-cabin while Cole changed clothes.

Cole stepped onto the bridge, and the lieutenant in the command chair jumped to her feet, announcing, "Captain on the bridge!"

Still feeling half asleep, Cole didn't bother correcting her on it. He didn't usually see the Gamma shift bridge crew, anyway, so they'd have no way to know his preferences.

"Can you put those sensor readings on the tactical plot?" Cole asked.

In moments, the hologram appeared above the deck between the command chair and the helm station. Cole approached and tried to make sense of what he was seeing. A cluster of dots drifted toward *Haven*'s stern, clustered in a loose sphere and not unlike a grouping of buckshot fired from an ancient shotgun. The dots were about fifteen light-seconds distant but getting closer.

"Do we have any high-resolution scans of whatever this is?" Cole asked, just as Sasha entered the bridge from the starboard hatch.

The tactical plot shimmered for several moments and resolved into an all-together-different image just as Sasha stopped at Cole's side. The cluster of dots drifting toward the ship were in fact five hundred personnel with arms, armor, and thruster backpacks.

Cole stared at the image for several heartbeats, his mind blank as he processed the incongruity of what he was seeing. In time, though, he vocalized his thoughts, "Huh... it looks like they mean to board us."

"Seriously?" Sasha asked. "Don't they know anything about us? We sent five hundred marines over to the station to replace their security force, and that wasn't even ten percent of our total complement."

Cole grinned. "Well, something tells me they're going to get an education. Tactical, sound battle-stations. Comms, alert Colonel Hanson that he needs to prepare to capture boarders."

"Can we go back through the sensor logs and see where they came from?" Sasha asked, turning to the sensors station.

The officer at Sensors responded with, "Aye, ma'am," and set to work. Less than thirty seconds later, the tactical plot shifted to display the cluster of dots appearing around what looked to be an interstellar shuttle.

"Is that shuttle still in the system?" Cole asked.

"I believe so, sir," Sensors replied. "It went behind the nearest moon and hasn't come back out."

Cole and Sasha shared a look. Cole grinned.

"Sensors, would you please send all data regarding that shuttle to Flight Ops?" Cole asked before turning his attention to that station. "And Flight Ops, my compliments to the CAG; please pass that sensor data to her with my request that she launch a couple squadrons to pacify that shuttle and that the hangar deck prep an assault shuttle for launch. Marine Ops, my compliments to Colonel Hanson; please inform him of the shuttle and ask him to designate an assault shuttle's complement of marines to pursue that shuttle and capture it if at all possible."

A chorus of "Aye, sir" answered almost in unison from the three stations.

Cole turned his attention back to the tactical plot and refocused it on the approaching boarding party. They were still a hair over fourteen light-seconds out. Even as fast as they were moving, they'd have to slow down at some point, or they'd turn themselves to pudding when they hit the hull.

"Sensors, please coordinate with Marine Ops to give Colonel Hanson real-time access to this sensor feed."

"Aye, sir," the officer at Sensors replied. "Captain, I've conducted an analysis of their approach. They appear to be aiming for the flight deck, and I have an estimated ETA of one hour and change, accounting for an estimated turn-over in twenty minutes or less."

"Good job," Cole replied. "Include that with the sensor feed to Colonel Hanson, please."

The passage of an hour found Cole in Flight Control, the overlook from which personnel conducted flight operations. Cole *wanted* to be standing on the flight deck to welcome their new guests aboard, but both Harlon and Sasha vetoed that almost as soon as he voiced it. The overlook was an acceptable compromise, as it was designed to withstand depressurization of the flight deck and could survive several direct shots.

One hour and three minutes after the officer at the bridge sensors station calculated their arrival, the vanguard of the boarding force floated through the aft force-field of the flight deck. As more followed, they fanned out to secure the deck, even though it was empty. Cole watched them bypass the cargo lifts at the aft end of the flight deck and grinned. They were locked down and wouldn't have taken them anywhere, even if the boarding force had recognized them for what they were.

As soon as all boarders were on the flight deck, Cole keyed the command that would broadcast a message both over the flight deck speakers and via standard radio channels.

"Hello," Cole said. "I never know what to say as a greeting at this time of night. 'Good night' always seems like something you say when you part company, and 'Good morning' just seems wrong somehow for almost half-past midnight."

"Identify yourself," a voice replied over the radio channel.

Cole grinned. "You first."

"That's not how this works. We have control of your flight deck, and we will be taking the ship. Surrender now, and we'll consider leaving you and yours alive."

Cole sighed. "You just had to go there, huh? I don't know who you are... *yet*... but whoever sent you on this farce should've obtained better intelligence."

"Oh? Why is that?"

"After dispatching two platoons to capture the shuttle that dropped you *and* sending five hundred or so marines over to the station for security, this ship's marine complement still outnumbers your force by more than ten to one... and we've watched your approach for the last hour. Plenty of time to prepare. Your ball, Colonel."

Hatches along the bulkheads of the flight deck opened, allowing armed and armored marines to storm the flight deck. The four lifts that moved small craft from the flight deck to the hangar decks activated, delivering four platoons each in heavy armor and armed with rotary cannons. Inside of sixty seconds, *Haven*'s marines saturated the flight deck, surrounding the boarding force almost to point of it being claustrophobic.

"You overplayed your hand," the voice said over the radio channel. "With all these bodies clogging the flight deck, you'll have an obscene number of friendly fire incidents."

Cole laughed. "You'd think that, and we probably will. But to test the armor my people are using, we emptied the ammo packs of eight rotary cannons into them... with no penetration or harm to the test mannequin underneath. They stand up even better to laser fire. So, yes... my people will get shot while they're making a mess of you on my flight deck, but unlike you and yours, *they* will walk away at the end." Cole paused as a text message appeared in his field of view. He grinned when he read it. "Oh, hey... by the by, the two platoons I dispatched just completed a forced boarding of your troop shuttle. Your pilots didn't even have time to scrub the flight data. Now, do you want to become that mess on my flight deck I mentioned, or are we going to be smart about this?"

Silence reigned for several heartbeats. One of the boarders broke that silence by dropping his laser carbine, followed by his sidearm. That started a cascade across the entire group until a small pile of arms lay scattered on the flight deck.

"Thank you," Cole said. "Colonel, I'll leave them in your capable hands. Let me know when you have them ready for interrogation. Cole out."

Cole checked the ship's time as a big yawn overtook him. He told the flight controllers to put the dropships and fighter squadrons in a holding pattern until they policed the flight deck and left the flight control overlook. Not even five minutes later, Cole entered his day-cabin on Deck Three and went straight to bed.

CHAPTER TWENTY-NINE

Battle-Carrier *Haven*
Docking Slip F-Seven, Coleson Clanhold
8 September 3000, 10:00 GST

Cole entered the bridge briefing room to find Garrett, Harlon, Sasha, and Emily waiting for him. He walked to the table and sat, scanning the faces looking back at him.

"So, who wants to go first?"

"Chief Engineer Maxwell has had people crawling all over the shuttle that dropped off our boarders," Sasha began. "There are no exterior markings to be found, but there's still been a wealth of information. All of the internal wiring is labeled according to the standards of the Solar Republic Navy. The flight data shows the shuttle as originating from the SRN base on Ganymede in Sol. We have their callsigns and orders. None of the orders show a specific sender, but their objective was the capture of the ship. Frankly, I don't know how they planned to accomplish that with no more personnel than they brought, but hey, that's incomplete information for you. I suppose it's possible they didn't realize we'd have the number of marines aboard that we do."

"None of the boarders had any kind of subdermal implants, unlike the kidnappers," Garrett said, taking over from Sasha. "However, they've been just as informative under Kiksalik-assisted interrogation. Heh... a few of them have even been volunteering stuff the Kiksaliks confirmed. They didn't like it when I pointed out that, since they bore no government markings, they're basically pirates. I rather enjoyed explaining how we're well within our rights to send them dancing with the stars unless they give us compelling reason not to do so. Several have cracked, but we still have many hold-outs. The hold-outs seem to be expecting some kind of rescue mission, so it'll take a bit for it to sink in that they're expendable."

"If they're volunteering stuff," Cole began, "who sent them?"

Garrett grinned. "Each and every one of them—even the assault shuttle pilots—are Solar Republic Black Ops. I'm not exactly current on Solar Black Ops organizations to know their precise chain of command, but I feel safe in saying this was retaliation for the logic bomb Srexx gave them when everybody and their brother tried hacking *Haven* in Earth orbit."

"What are we going to do with them?" Sasha asked. "After stowing them all in the brig, we only have about ten open cells, and the way all this is going, we're going to need more than ten."

Cole grinned. "I'm tempted to secure them aboard their shuttle naked and leave it in stable orbit around Earth. I'd like to harbor some malice toward these people, especially since they boarded this ship with the intent of taking it, but the real enemy is whoever ordered them to do it. Garrett, if we send them back, what are their chances of survival?"

Garrett shrugged. "No way to know, really. It depends on how big of a stink we make. If we throw everything on the news, publish pictures of them and everything, I can't imagine their lives would be in danger right away... but there's nothing saying they wouldn't be 'disappeared' after all the furor died down."

Cole nodded. "I don't like sending them to their deaths, even if they did try to pirate my ship. Pick a few of the talkers, and tell them I'm thinking of sending them back to Earth. See what their reactions are, and let me know. One of the universal laws of bureaucracies everywhere is 'shit rolls downhill,' and I don't see how there's any hill below these guys... which isn't such a good place for them. Anyone have an update on the investigation into CIE?"

"Was that directed at me?" Srexx asked via the room's overhead speakers.

"Not specifically," Cole answered, "but since you're here, do you have anything new?"

"Yes, but it is a recent discovery, recent as in the past forty-five seconds," Srexx replied. "I believe I have discovered a connection between CIE and the Solar Republic Senate, but I do not want to make a report until I have exhausted all avenues of inquiry. My current dataset suggests additional information is forthcoming."

"Fair enough," Cole said. "How forthcoming are we talking, buddy?"

"Unknown at this time. I found the discovery I mentioned in the comms archives for the year 2972, and I am tracing the derivative data. It is proving quite... interesting."

Cole sighed. "Srexx, buddy... you can't just leave us hanging like that. At least tell us what the data suggests."

"Cole, I am reticent to state any conclusions at this time, as the data upon which I would base the conclusion is incomplete. The conclusion might be false."

"Srexx," Cole replied, "people make wrong conclusions all the time. It'll be okay."

"Other people might make false conclusions all the time, but I strive to be better than that, Cole. However, if you prefer additional information, the data I have found so far indicate the existence of an organized effort between CIE personnel and Solar Republic leadership. It appears that there may be two different groups, and if that is indeed correct, additional data I have found seems to indicate each group's efforts have compromised the other's work on a number of occasions without either group being aware of the other.

"The two groups appear to be rather disparate in age, with the first dating back almost thirty years while the second is far more recent. For the sake of simplicity, I shall refer to the oldest group as Group One and the younger as Group Two. The goal of Group One appears to be securing the schematics for your family's proprietary technology from CIE in exchange for a significant sum of credits. Group Two seems to be working toward bringing CIE under the authority of the Solar Republic and granting the Solar government control of the jump gate network."

By the time Srexx finished, Cole glared at the tabletop, his jaw clenched tight. "Yeah... that's not going to happen. Srexx, do what you need to do to get a clear understanding of that furball. I will ask no questions. If you need something, tell me or Sasha, and we'll make it happen. Running down these two groups, especially their member-ships, is now Priority One. Take as much time as you need, buddy, but not one nanosecond *more* than you need. Okay?"

"Yes, Cole. I shall devote my full resources to completing my dataset regarding these groups and their initiatives."

Cole scanned the faces around the table, asking, "Anything else?"

No one had any more to add, so Cole stood. "All right. Thank you, everyone."

Cole led the procession out of the briefing room.

————

Battle-Carrier *Haven*
    8 September 3000, 18:36 GST

Cole looked up from his workstation and frowned at the time. Concentrating on his Fleet Command studies in the wake of Srexx's revelation had proven challenging at best. *Thirty years*. There'd been a group of people working against his family for thirty years. Had his father known? Had his grandfather known?

Cole sighed. There wasn't any way he'd be making any headway on his studies now. Instead, he used his workstation to access the CIE archives and ran a search. The search took less than three seconds and informed Cole that his grandfather had turned over the company to his father on 2 January 2970. There was a recording of the announcement his grandfather had made... at Cole's parents' wedding reception of all places. Then again, the more Cole considered it, that was *exactly* the type of person he remembered his grandfather being. One of his favorite sayings was, 'Just cause I'm getting old doesn't mean I have to grow up.'

Not for the first time, Cole wished he still had his family. Only this time, he wished he could ask his father and grandfather questions. Then again, if either of them were still available, this whole mess wouldn't be Cole's responsibility. Cole sighed again. What was that line from one of those ancient movies? 'Suck it up, buttercup?' Yeah, that sounded right. 'Shut up and soldier on,' sounded even better.

Leaning back against his seat, Cole tried looking at the situation from a different angle. His arrival must've thrown a monkey wrench the size of Jupiter into their plans, and it must've been one of the two groups—heh... maybe both—that arranged for the Assistant CSO to take a shot at him. Was the boarding a knee-jerk reaction from the Solar Republic side, or was it more thought out? Sending only five hundred troops seemed amateurish, but maybe the hacking attempt was an effort to see how many people were aboard the ship? Nah... that didn't make any sense. Sure, hackers might attack a system looking for specific information, but most times, they just grabbed whatever they could get in the time they had.

The sound of the hatch opening drew Cole's attention. He looked up and found Scarlett peeking in from Akyra's office.

"Hi," Cole said.

"Hi," Scarlett replied. "You interested in dinner?"

Cole considered his focus for the past few minutes versus what he *should* have been doing and grinned, saying, "Sure! My mind's shot for the day anyhow. If I don't do something to distract myself, I'll just keep chasing figments down the rabbit hole."

Scarlett gave Cole a wink and a playful smile to go with it. "Well then, I shall try my hardest to be a good distraction for you. You should know, I have *years* of experience."

Cole's mind drifted to the memory of the first time he'd seen her, and he grinned again. "You know, I have no problem believing that."

Cole secured his workstation and stood. He walked out with Scarlett, and once they were in the corridor, Scarlett claimed his left arm.

"What has you in such dire need of a distraction?" Scarlett asked as she led him to a transit shaft.

"Oh," Cole began, almost sighing the word, "just this whole mess with the Solar Republic. They're not acting like they want to be friends, and if they're not careful, they'll end up with an enemy."

The dark thoughts threatening to overtake Cole's mind evaporated as Scarlett leaned into him.

"From their point of view, there's no threat from just one ship," Scarlett replied, "no matter how advanced and capable that ship is. They could destroy this ship. Yeah... they'd have to commit substantial forces to do it, and you'd take a mind-boggling number of them with you. But they could do it. That's what they see when they think of a fight with you."

"Heh," Cole vocalized. "Yeah, I may be just one ship now, but I won't be just one ship forever. And... the only way they could prevent that now is dropping a fleet in Centauri sometime in the next seven days to three weeks. After that, I'll have everything I need to do a hard burn for the system periphery and wave goodbye to Centauri for good, and I'll be taking the Clanhold with me when we go."

Scarlett stopped and stared at Cole, blinking. "Cole, the Clanhold is a *station*. How in all the stars are you going to move it? I'm not sure anyone has *ever* moved an entire station in one go before."

Cole took a deep breath. He started to answer her but remembered that she hadn't officially joined his team yet. And that sucked. He couldn't afford to jeopardize the plan on the shadow of a chance Scarlett might be working against him.

"Scarlett, I'm sorry, but for now, I'll have to leave the specifics out of the discussion. If it were just me, I'd tell you... but it's not just me. I have almost twelve thousand people on *Haven* and who knows how many people in the Clanhold. Those in the Clanhold might not all come with me, but I have to protect my people."

Scarlett nodded. "I understand, Cole. I really do. Ever since you pulled me out of that wrecked transport, I've wondered sometimes if my people would've still mutinied if I had been more like you." Then, she grinned. "But if I had been more like you, I probably wouldn't have been Red Pattel in the first place, huh?" Scarlett pulled him to her again, making certain she brushed against him shoulder to hip. "Come on. Let's get food and work on that distraction I promised you."

CHAPTER THIRTY

Mess Deck, Battle-Carrier *Haven*
Docking Slip F-Seven, Coleson Clanhold
Centauri Trinary System
9 September 3000, 05:17 GST

Unlike those aboard many ships of Humanity's past (or even its present), Cole did not approach officer and enlisted ranks as a class distinction. The paradigm of officer and enlisted grades dated back to the Age of Sail in which noblemen would buy commissions in navies, but over time, it had evolved into a separation based on responsibility. Even in the modern age, many polities designed their ships with officers' wardrooms and enlisted mess. Cole didn't like that. The mess deck aboard *Haven* held four dining rooms, and Cole ensured those dining rooms focused on specific meals, instead of specific groups of people.

Sasha looked up when nearby motion caught her eye and smiled at seeing Talia placing her tray on the table.

"Morning, sis," Sasha said, smiling. "How are you?"

Talia used her left hand to cover her mouth as she let loose a gigantic yawn. "I still hate mornings, Soosh. There's no reason to rub salt in the wound."

Sasha chuckled. When they were growing up, it had been a rare thing to see Talia before noon if she didn't have to be awake.

"I would've thought Med School and rotations and your residency would've cured you of all that," Sasha replied.

"Nope. It just gave me an even greater appreciation of coffee. There's a blend from New Arabia that is simply divine, by the way. When we get back home, I'll look up some for you; you have to try it."

Sasha nodded. "Okay. I'll follow up with you about it when we get back. Anything interesting happening down on the hospital deck?"

"Nah... not really." Talia broke off in a fit of giggles. "Well, there was that one spacer. A couple marines carried him in, yesterday or the day before."

"What happened?" Sasha asked as she moved to take a bite of her pancakes.

"The idiot invited himself to one of the gyms down in Marine Country and started mouthing off about what a great hand-to-hand fighter he was. The marines took it all in stride until he started picking on one of the medics we supply them, and he received a front-row education that his hand-to-hand skills weren't as good as he thought they were."

"Was he okay?"

Talia shrugged. "Ehh... there are degrees of okay. Medically, he's fine, but the marines recorded the beat-down and published the recording on ShipNet. That spacer is enjoying a new level of notoriety."

"Good," Sasha replied. "It's nice when the crew handles problems before Cole or I have to. If he really was picking on someone, Cole would not have been pleased. I could totally see him saying something like, 'Well, if you're such a great fighter, why don't you fight me?' That's all we need."

Talia giggled again. "Speaking of Cole... did you hear he spent the whole evening in one of the pubs down on the recreation deck with Scarlett?"

Sasha dropped her fork. "What?"

"Oh, yeah. I didn't see it myself, but one of my friends from the trauma ward said she was hanging on him almost like a new set of clothes. They seemed to be having a good time, though. My friend said she saw them when she finished her Gamma shift, and one of the staff said they'd been there for hours. They left together, too." Talia looked up from her breakfast and forced herself not to gape.

Sasha sat in the tensest posture Talia could ever remember. She held the edge of the table in a white-knuckle grip, her pursed lips and clenched jaw adding to her overall pinched expression. A noticeable flush colored her cheeks.

"Oh my goodness, Soosh... what is that? Are you jealous?"

The word 'jealous' snapped Sasha out of it, and she furtively scanned the nearby tables to see if anyone else noticed... which didn't escape Talia's notice, either.

"Oh my goodness... you are! You're jealous of Cole and Scarlett!"

"Will you hush already? I am not jealous, and I don't need any rumors started that I am," Sasha replied, then scoffed. "Can you even imagine the embarrassment if a rumor like that reached Cole? I'd have to leave the ship."

"Okay, okay... I'll hush," Talia said. "But you need to get a handle on whatever that was. You looked hot, Soosh... and not in the good way."

Sasha retrieved her fork from where she'd dropped it on the plate and did a very unladylike job of quartering her remaining pancakes and cramming them into her mouth. In less than a minute, only the remains of syrup and butter remained as Sasha dabbed at her mouth with a napkin.

"Sorry, sis," Sasha said as she stood with her tray. "I have to get to the bridge."

Talia watched her go and shook her head. Once Sasha was out of earshot, Talia spoke to an empty table, "Alpha shift doesn't start for another twenty minutes, Soosh."

———

Executive Conference Room, CIE Offices
    Coleson Clanhold, Centauri Trinary System
    9 September 3000, 08:55 GST

Cole entered the conference room and smiled, nodding his greetings to CEO Jefferds and the Chief Research Officer. Red stopped to stand just inside the door, with the rest of his travel party in the corridor outside. Once again, Cole felt a spike of gladness that he'd made the point about punctuality for meetings he called. He carried a portable quantum comms device, just like the device he'd left with Painter and Sev in Tristan's Gate.

"Thank you for coming," Cole said. "I wanted to show you something my information officer developed before we left Tristan's Gate. I think it's technology we could incorporate into the jump gates for increased revenue."

Cole lifted the device and placed it on the conference table with care. He didn't want to scratch the surface, after all. The device had two sections that folded out on hinges before it could be used, and once that was done, Cole checked the battery, finding it fully charged.

"The design we'd include in the jump gates wouldn't be this bulky. The only reason this unit is so bulky is that we had to include holo-emitters and holo-cameras for visual pickup."

"What is it?" Jefferds asked.

"It's a comms device based on quantum entanglement," Cole replied.

The Chief Research Officer blinked and shook his head. "Even as advanced as we are, that has only been theorized."

Cole offered a slight smile. "Want me to prove it?"

"How could you?" the CRO asked. "This could be a simple comms device dressed up with a holo-emitter, and to 'prove it,' you'd call someone on your ship."

Cole gave the man an evil grin. "Modern comms still use radio-based carrier waves, yes?"

"Yes. The transmission technologies and signal frequencies have evolved, but we're still limited to light-speed communications."

"If I remember correctly, you have a compartment in your labs that has a Faraday cage, correct?"

The CRO nodded. "Of course."

"Let's go," Cole replied.

Neatly mouse-trapped, the CRO had no choice but to agree.

In short order, Jefferds, the CRO, and Cole stood in the compartment with the Faraday cage. Red stood by the hatch, and the rest of Cole's travel party waited outside. The CRO called ahead, and a table and three chairs waited for them. Cole placed the comms unit on the table and set it up for use again.

Turning to the CRO, Cole asked, "Do you have a way to monitor for potential emissions from this compartment?"

The CRO nodded.

"Please, ensure it is active and monitoring," Cole replied.

The CRO stepped outside the compartment and returned less than five minutes later. "The monitoring equipment is active."

Cole activated the comms device. Its holo-interface appeared in the air above the device, and Cole selected 'Contacts,' then 'Unit 5774 – Haven Enterprises.' The interface disappeared, replaced by flashing text, 'Initiating Call.' Not even a full minute later, the text vanished, replaced by an image of Julianna Painter and Sev Vance. The image was static for about three seconds before Painter and Sev started moving and speaking.

"Cole, it's good to hear from you," Painter said, "and I see we have an audience."

"Hi, Painter," Cole replied. "The gentleman over my left shoulder is Vince Jefferds, CEO of Coleson Interstellar Enterprises, and the gentleman on my right is Lyle Chesterton, the Chief Research Officer. Gentlemen, the lady is Julianna Painter and her associate is Sevrin Vance. Painter, where are you right now?"

"We're in the office complex we rented," Painter replied, after a three-second delay.

"Okay. Please, explain where that is for my associates."

"U-Three level on The Gate, Tristan's Gate system," Painter replied, still with three seconds of latency.

"Unbelievable," the CRO said. "How do we *know* that's where you really are?"

Painter and Sev looked at each other in confusion three seconds later.

CEO Jefferds spoke, ending the conundrum, "Credit Suisse places a data code in their market streams to identify the source of each stream. Can you forward the market stream from the local branch where you are? We can then search that code in the local Credit Suisse database for independent confirmation."

Six seconds later, a data dashboard with scrolling market symbols and headlines replaced the view of Painter and Sev. The CEO pulled a note-tab from a pocket and jotted down something with its built-in stylus.

"Thanks," Cole said. "We have what we need."

The market dashboard soon disappeared, replaced by Painter and Sev.

Cole nodded, saying, "I'll call back later with a few other notes we need to discuss."

"Roger that," Painter said. "Haven Enterprises out."

The holo image reverted to the user interface, and Cole shut down the device, closing it back up for transport. Then, he turned to Jefferds and grinned, saying, "Let's step outside so you can check that code."

As soon as they exited the compartment with the Faraday cage, Jefferds went straight to an unoccupied workstation and accessed the Credit Suisse public data site. He keyed in the code shown in the data stream and searched for it.

"Lyle," Jefferds said, his voice shaky, "you need to see this."

The CRO ambled over to the workstation, asking, "What is it?"

"That data code in the market stream checks out as originating from Tristan's Gate," Jefferds replied. "That tech is on the level."

"Could it be counterfeited?"

Jefferds shrugged. "It's possible, I suppose, but I came up with that on the spur of the moment. How would they have anticipated I'd ask for the market data? And besides, I also copied the data stream's checksum. It checks out, too."

"This is going to revolutionize communications across the galaxy," the CRO said, "or at least our part of it, anyway. Vince, we just engaged in a conversation that spanned something like eight hundred lightyears! No one has ever done that before, not in Human history anyway."

Cole grinned. "All right, then, gentlemen. If you'll excuse me, I'll leave you two to consider this new development. When you're ready to discuss how we're going to implement it, specifically its pricing, let me know."

Cole turned and left with his travel party. The two senior CIE officials didn't even seem to acknowledge his departure as they started discussing his revelation. Cole grinned and left them to it.

CHAPTER THIRTY-ONE

Office 2315, Office Complex B
　Geneva, Switzerland
　Earth, Sol System
　10 September 3000, 09:17 GST

Admiral Himari Sato once more sat at the conference table in the otherwise-empty office suite. Five chairs occupied the opposite side of the table from her. She had received the instructions to be in this room by zero-nine-thirty hours on September 10th not even an hour after she'd sent an answer saying she was interested in knowing more.

The Board of Inquiry had not gone well for her or her captains. The absence of logs on her ships, coupled with the open and transparent sharing by Coleson, led the members to vote that charges be filed against her and her captains. The first session of the court-martial would happen next week.

The worst thing of it was, Sato *knew* what happened to those logs. When they'd returned to dock over Mars in response to the orders recalling the entire task force from Caernarvon, a group of technicians with all the proper codes and clearances visited each ship to 'make a copy' of all logs and records regarding the Incident. It wasn't until the day after those technicians had left that Sato discovered every ship in the task force had a void where the logs of the Incident had been.

Of course, that information wouldn't help her at all. There was no record of the technicians, either, so it'd be just her word. And at this point, she wasn't sure her word stood for much anymore.

The second the chrono clicked over to oh-nine-thirty, the door behind Sato opened to admit the five senators once more. They filed into the room and occupied the seats across from her, even going so far as to sit in the same order as before.

"Your message suggested you were amenable to an arrangement," the older female senator said.

Sato nodded. "Yes. I want more information, though. My captains and I are being railroaded by the Navy, and I'm not about to make the situation any worse than it already is."

"That is understandable," the woman replied. "Your reply was fortuitous. Other assets recently attempted a boarding operation against *Haven* in Centauri, and the teams used for that operation have not been heard from since signaling the start of the op. We have no choice but to conclude both the shuttle and the personnel involved have been captured or killed. Given Coleson's operational style, I fear capture is the more likely scenario."

"Do the personnel involved possess intelligence that could compromise our operations?" Sato asked.

"Not as such, but their mere existence compromises certain agencies that work best outside the realm of official oversight."

Sato grimaced. "You sent black ops personnel, didn't you?"

"You disagree?"

"I've never believed in the philosophy of so-called 'deniable' assets. If there's something you want to do without your name on it, the chances are good you shouldn't be doing it anyway. That's my opinion on the matter, at least."

The female senator shrugged. "Your thoughts are not without merit, but what's done is done. We have another venture in mind for you. In exchange for dealing with the pending court-martial, we want you to lead your former task force on a mission to destroy *Haven*."

Sato laughed. "With all due respect, you can't be serious. What's to stop them from just ejecting our reactor cores again? Or for that matter, detonating them? If they had the level of access to our information systems to trigger a core ejection, they could've just as easily triggered the self-destruct. I'm willing to make the ultimate sacrifice for my home, but at the very least, I'd like it mean something and not be some footnote in a hacker's journal."

The woman nodded once. "We anticipated your concerns. In truth, *all* starships are undergoing mandatory refit to remove the computer connections to the core ejection and self-destruct mechanisms. There will be no repeat of the Caernarvon Incident."

Sato nodded, leaning back against her seat. She stared at the table-top, considering the situation. After several moments' thought, she lifted her attention back to the senator, saying, "My captains and I will have a guarantee of dismissal of all charges and no blemishes on our records? We'll get to remain on active duty?"

"Of course, Admiral," the woman said, almost a purr.

"I want your offer and guarantee in writing," Sato replied, "so that I can show it to my captains when I go to them. For something like this, I'm not about to agree for them. Give me a formal offer and guarantee, and I'll present it to them. To accomplish what you desire, I'd need the entire roster of TF-27; from everything I've heard, I'm not certain a lesser force could accomplish the directive."

"Given the nature of Coleson's information warfare capabilities, I'm not certain putting our offer and directives in writing would be the wisest course at this time," the woman replied. "If he became aware of our plans, it would give him time to prepare. A large part of your success lies in complete surprise."

And there it was. They weren't going to commit to anything in writing, which meant Sato and her people would have no leverage against them if—no... *when*—they didn't hold up their end of the bargain. How stupid did they think she was?

"I see," Sato replied. "There is wisdom in what you say. May I have a couple days to meet with my captains and discuss the matter?"

"Of course," the woman answered, again... almost a purr. "I

wouldn't want anyone to enter into this operation without giving the matter full consideration."

Sato nodded once. "Thank you. With your leave then, I'll go arrange meetings with my captains."

"We do not want you to feel rushed, Admiral, but we cannot promise being able to intervene in the court-martial after it reaches a certain point."

"I understand," Sato answered, "and thank you."

With nothing further to say, the admiral stood and left the room. Turning everything over in her mind, she saw no way that she or her people could escape it unscathed. She was the Solar Republic Navy's youngest flag officer in the past thousand years, and she'd served with distinction and dedication. Now, it seemed like the Republic was turning its back on her and her people. If they didn't bow to the clandestine wishes of the senators, the court-martial would probably end their careers, but if they did, the outcome just might be far worse. Sato couldn't envision circumstances in which those senators left her or her people alive to tell their side of the story.

Sato entered the lift and selected the lobby. The lift started its transit, and since the hard place before her was abundantly clear, she decided there was no reason not to investigate the rock before speaking with her people. She had a week, after all; she should be able to make the trip in that amount of time.

Battle-Carrier *Haven*
    Docking Slip F-Seven, Coleson Clanhold
    Centauri Trinary System
    10 September 3000, 09:30 GST

Cole sat at his desk, poring over the study materials for the ISA's Fleet Command certification. He was doing well in the simulations provided with the study materials, and he was looking forward to booking an appointment with the training officer for a testing session. Cole almost let himself wonder what he'd start studying once he achieved the Fleet Command certification, but as his mind started down that rabbit hole, he stopped himself. There was no reason to assume he'd pass on the first attempt, despite his scores on both the simulations and the sample exam questions.

"Cole?" Srexx asked via the office's speakers.

"Yeah, Srexx?" Cole replied. "What's on your mind?"

"I apologize for disturbing your study, but I evaluated that you would want to know I have completed my analysis of the two groups within CIE that are working against the company."

Cole leaned back against his seat and rubbed his eyes for a moment. Then, he said, "You don't sound like you have good news for me."

"I... do not. Cole, I have been able to confirm that the only C-level executives—as you say—not involved with either group are the CEO, the Chief Legal Officer, and the Chief Research Officer. I am compiling a roster right now of both groups, and my conclusion thus far is that both groups have members on almost every level of the company. The janitorial staff seems to be the only group within the company not compromised in some way."

"Huh... I would've thought they'd have someone in Janitorial, too. They have access everywhere."

"The access they would gain by suborning a janitor is already achieved through various other members of each group, so I am unable to quantify what adding a janitor or two to their roster would gain them."

Cole sighed. "So, how solid is your information? I realize it's you, so the information is probably *very* solid, but I don't want to take this to the CEO and head of Legal if there's even the slightest chance some of it's wrong."

"The chance that the data has led to a false conclusion is less than one one-millionth of a percent, Cole. I have copies of communications across multiple media in which the members incriminate themselves. There are no markers that any of the communications were made under duress, and various personnel have even profited personally by their association with their respective group. None of these people can say they didn't know what they were doing, Cole, and if you care to examine the raw data for yourself, I have zero concerns that you'll reach the same conclusion."

"Right. Compile everything you have, and record it to data crystal... no, two data crystals. I want as complete a roster for both groups as you can construct on those crystals, as well."

"Yes, Cole. I will see to this at once. I anticipate delivery of the data crystals within forty-eight hours, as I am still collating data."

Cole nodded. "Thanks, buddy. I appreciate all you do."

"You are welcome, Cole. I am glad that I can make a difference, especially after so long of simply existing."

In the wake of the conversation with Srexx, Cole found he couldn't focus on the study materials. It frustrated him a little, but there was nothing for it.

CHAPTER THIRTY-TWO

Shuttle Arrivals, Coleson Clanhold
    Centauri Trinary System
    12 September 3000, 08:19 GST

Himari Sato stepped off the shuttle and moved out of the traffic path, looking around the docking area; there was something oddly comforting about the similarities all passenger arrival areas seemed to have, no matter where they were in Human space. She wore civilian clothing, and after so long in SRN uniform, the fabrics felt odd to her touch. No one seemed to be paying her much attention as they serviced the shuttle or debarked the shuttle for their various destinations.

"Forgive me, ma'am," a voice said, "but can I help you find something?"

Sato turned. Standing a respectful distance away was a young man wearing a matte black suit of armor. A laser carbine hung over his shoulder, and Sato saw three others in similar gear not too far away. They were watching the exchange while trying to look like they *weren't* watching the exchange. Sato almost smiled.

"Thank you," Sato replied. "I must admit arriving here was the easiest part of my journey, and I would appreciate some assistance. I was hoping to speak with the captain of the ship *Haven*. Cole, I believe he's called."

The young man's demeanor changed in the span of a heartbeat. The solicitous friendliness vanished, replaced by a hardened veteran who not-so-casually placed a hand on his sidearm. Sato saw the three fellows unlimber their laser carbines as they dropped all pretense of trying to act like they were not observing.

"And just why would you be wanting to see the captain?"

Sato sighed. "I am trapped between two very bad choices, and I didn't know where else to go. If you would, please tell him Himari Sato apologizes for the abrupt arrival and asks for a few minutes of his time. I am unarmed, and my bag carries travel toiletries and a change of clothes."

———

"Bridge to Captain," broadcast over the speakers in Cole's office.

Cole grinned, eager for the reprieve. He was reading a finance file Painter and Sev sent him, and no part of it was fun.

"Cole here," he said.

The speakers chirped, followed by Mazzi saying, "Sir, we have an odd situation at the shuttle dock on the Clanhold."

"Everything about this trip to Centauri has been odd in one way or another," Cole replied. "I'm guessing whatever this is stands out against that?"

"Himari Sato just stepped off a passenger shuttle from Earth in civvies and told the marines watching the arrivals area that she was hoping to speak with you if you had the time."

"Wow... did not see that coming," Cole replied. "Heh... if she came all this way to speak with me, it would be rather rude not to say hello. Ask one of the marines watching the dock to start this way with her, and snag someone aboard to meet them and bring her the rest of the way. I don't want the team at the dock to be understaffed any longer than they just have to be."

"Aye, sir," Mazzi said.

Cole's eyes widened as a thought exploded in the forefront of his mind. "Mazzi!"

"Yes, sir?"

"Send a text to the implant of the marine who contacted you. Ask him if the admiral is wearing pants, trousers, or something similar or if she's in a skirt/dress/etc."

"Oh... right. Good call, sir. Gimme a couple."

Cole listened to the dead air for several moments, but it didn't stretch to more than ninety seconds.

"Khaki trousers and a top with flowers, sir," Mazzi answered.

"Excellent. Then, I will be happy to receive the admiral in my office. Mind meeting her at the 'lock?"

"Of course not, sir. I'll see her safely to you. Will there be anything else?"

"I don't think so, Mazzi. Thank you."

"Very good, sir. Bridge out."

The speakers chirped once more, and Cole forced himself to return to the finance file.

Not quite fifteen minutes passed before Mazzi led Himari Sato into Cole's office. Cole stood and extended his hand in greeting.

"Welcome aboard *Haven*, Admiral. Please, call me Cole."

Sato gave Cole a respectful handshake. "In that case, please call me Himari."

Cole indicated the two chairs. "Have a seat. May I offer you some refreshment or perhaps breakfast?"

"No, not at this time, but thank you."

Cole nodded and returned to his seat. "So, may I ask what brings you all the way out here from Earth? Out of all the things I expected to happen today, being informed that you wanted to speak with me wasn't anywhere close to the list."

"I'm sure," Sato replied. "Cole, I find myself caught betwixt two options that are unpalatable to me, and... well... I figured since I already knew more than I wanted about the hard place I faced, there was no reason not to visit the rock."

Cole grinned. "So, I'm the rock, huh?"

"You and your ship are very formidable. Please, listen to what I have to say."

"Proceed, then, please. I'm all ears."

Sato cleared her throat and began, "What you may not know is that individuals claiming to be technicians from SRN Operations came aboard every ship in TF-27 when we arrived in Sol. They claimed they were there to copy all logs pertinent to the Caernarvon Incident. When they left, they took the logs with them, as in we had a hole in our protected archives. To make matters worse, they also removed all records of their coming aboard. There was no security footage of them in the shipyard where we docked, and the names they gave no longer match any active duty SRN personnel, despite the fact we cross-checked their credentials at the time they requested permission to come aboard."

"Yeah... that's not suspicious at all," Cole remarked, the sarcasm in his voice so thick it dripped and pooled on the decking.

Sato nodded. "When the Navy inspectors came aboard and found an entire day that didn't exist in our logs—when those archives were supposed to be tamper-proof—events snowballed, and you ended up providing your logs at the Board of Inquiry. My captains and I are now facing a host of charges in an upcoming court-martial, and if we lose the case, the breadth of charges warrant incarceration. I think the entire affair—from the mysterious technicians to the formal charges— has been a series of events engineered to put me in a compromised position where the persons responsible had leverage against me and my people."

"What makes you say that?" Cole asked.

"I've been approached twice now—once around the time you appeared before the Board and the second just yesterday—by a group of five senators. A couple of them are very senior senators who've been in the senate for decades. Yesterday, they told me they would make the court-martial go away if I use TF-27 to destroy *Haven* and presumably you along with it."

Cole's eyes narrowed. "You don't say. That's rather lovely timing. Himari, would you mind going over all this again, but with a larger audience?"

"I would not mind at all."

"All right, then. Let's move this party over to the briefing room."

Cole stood, prompting Sato to do likewise, as he said, "Cole to Bridge."

The speakers chirped and broadcast Mazzi's voice, "Bridge, Mazzi here."

Cole led Sato out of his office as he spoke, "Mazzi, I need Garrett, Sasha, Harlon, Yeleth, and Red in the bridge briefing room right now. Also, please contact the local queen and ask her to send someone as well."

"Aye, sir," Mazzi replied.

Glancing over at Sato, Cole smiled at seeing her staring at the ceiling.

"That... was impressive," Sato remarked. "Our ships are not capable of that."

"It blew the minds of the SRN JAG officers, too," Cole replied.

Cole led Sato into the bridge briefing room and wasn't surprised that they were the first to arrive. Within the next couple minutes, though, the requested individuals arrived. The final arrival was the Kiksalik from the local nest.

"Okay," Cole said, calling the meeting to order. "Everyone, this is Himari Sato, an admiral in the Solar Republic Navy. Himari, this is Garrett, Sasha, Harlon, Yeleth, and Red. If you don't mind, start at the top, please."

Sato re-told her story, leaving nothing out of her recitation. When she reached the part about the five senators, Garrett started tapping on his tablet.

"May I ask a question?" he said, still tapping.

"Yes," Sato replied.

Garrett tapped a final series on his tablet, and the briefing room's holo-display activated, showing two pictures above the table. Garrett pointed to them, asking, "Do you recognize either of these people?"

"Yes," Sato replied. "The woman did all the talking, and the man sat at her side."

Garrett nodded, acting as if he was just taking a survey. "Thank you.

Cole watched his oldest friend, but the man betrayed nothing in his mannerisms or expression.

"So... they expect you to pit your full task force against us?" Sasha said.

Sato nodded. "I refused to attempt it with less than my full task force. This ship and its crew have a... reputation."

"Damn straight," Cole said, grinning. "Just for giggles. Hey, Srexx... you with us, buddy?"

"Of course, Cole. How may I assist you?"

"The ships from Caernarvon. Give me a tactical assessment, please."

"Given our capability at the time we encountered them or now?" Srexx asked.

Cole shrugged. "Heck with it. Both, please."

"One moment... "

Silence reigned in the briefing room for several seconds.

"Cole," Srexx resumed, "according to the sixty-five-thousand-five-hundred-thirty-five simulations that I could run before your wait time became egregious, surviving combat with the Solar battle-group from Caernarvon, given our capabilities when we encountered them, is unlikely... to the degree of sixty-five-thousand-five-hundred-thirty-four to one."

"Wow," Cole replied. "We actually won one in your simulations?"

"I always give you one in any simulation batch I run. Given your capacity for original and unforeseen tactics, I am perhaps short-changing you in the odds by not giving you more than one. However, in a similar number of simulations using the current status of the ship, the results suggest mutual destruction to be the most likely outcome by a considerable degree. We did survive the combat, wiping out the Solar battle-group, in a larger number of those simulations, but that number was insufficient to be statistically significant."

Sato slumped in her seat, looking very much as if a ton of metal had just settled around her shoulders. When she spoke, her voice was barely above a whisper, "So that's their plan then... "

"I'm sorry," Cole said. "I didn't quite catch that."

"They want to send me and mine to attack you, hoping we'll wipe each other out."

Garrett nodded from his seat at the far end of the table. Then, he said, "It's not unheard of. If you can pull it off, it's a viable strategy to relieve yourself of two problems at once."

"Yeah," Cole said, "*if you can pull it off.*"

"Forewarned is forearmed," Garrett replied.

"What happens now?" Sato asked.

Cole shrugged. "What do you *want* to happen now?"

"The senators wouldn't give me anything in writing, nothing I could take to my captains. That alone told me that my people and I are expendable to them. We don't deserve to face court-martial and incarceration. My people and I feel like we're all out of options."

Cole nodded. "I can certainly see how you'd draw that conclusion." He swiveled his chair to face the Kiksalik standing in the corner. "Your conclusions?"

< She is two steps from desperate. She feels betrayed... cast aside without regard for her faithful service. She is honorable, and we would trust her word if she gave it. >

From the moment the Kiksalik began 'speaking,' Sato stared at it with wide eyes, her face pallid.

Cole swiveled back and regarded Sato for a moment. "Yeah... now, you know why we went to Iota Ceti. These people are damned fine HR consultants. Sato, I'm re-building Beta Magellan, and that system will have a home fleet. I also need training cadre. You have a place with us, if you want it. So does anyone else who wants to leave the SRN and come. They'll have to pass an interview first, though."

Sato tore her eyes away from the Kiksalik and looked at Cole. "Will you put that offer in writing, so I can present it to my people?"

Cole nodded without hesitation. "My implant transcribed it as I said it. Where should I send it?"

"Why this offer? Most people wouldn't be so open to the equivalent of strays."

Cole shrugged. "Let's just say this ship is aptly named."

CHAPTER THIRTY-THREE

Cole saw Admiral Sato off the ship, sending a written copy of his offer to her comms code. Once she was on her way, Cole requested a second quantum comms prototype be fabricated. That process took two hours, and it passed the quality control check afterward. Cole took that device to the group overseeing all the teams of his people aboard the Clanhold and hard-wired it into the station's datanet. Once Cole was certain Srexx could continue his work aboard the Clanhold from abroad, *Haven* undocked and activated full stealth for the second time.

"We're clear and free to navigate, Cole," Wixil reported.

"Excellent," Cole replied. "Set course for Earth. Since we're under a bit of a time crunch, take us up to three-quarters-light."

"Yes, Cole," Wixil replied, her fingers dancing across the console.

Sasha approached Cole's right side. "May I ask what we're doing, sir?"

Cole looked up at Sasha and smiled. "We're getting Srexx in range of those two senators' archives. I'm sure the data those technicians stole from TF-27 is gone if it resided in one of the datanets Srexx logic-bombed when we visited Earth, but I'm hoping someone sent one or more of those senators a copy. We might even get lucky and find other incriminating evidence as well."

"Whatever you find won't stand up in court," Sasha replied, "if you're planning to turn it over to Sato."

Cole made a dismissive wave as he shrugged. "Nah. I got the feeling that ship has sailed. I came away from her visit feeling Sato learned the hard way that the Solar Republic she joined the navy for isn't the Solar Republic she's been serving in recent years. There are going to be some volunteers incoming; I'm just not equipped to guess how many." Cole swiveled to face the comms station. "Jenkins, my compliments to Engineer Logan, and would you ask him if the ship's up to one-hundred percent for the trip to Earth and back?"

"Aye, Cap," Jenkins replied and bent to his console as he pressed his fingertips to his earbud. A few moments later, Jenkins looked up to Cole and said, "Engineer Logan said we're good for it and then some."

"Thank you, Jenkins," Cole replied and swiveled back to face forward. "Helm, attach maneuvering orders to the flight plan. Our speed to Sol is one-hundred percent on the hyperdrive."

"Yes, Cole," Wixil answered.

Cole scanned the bridge, admiring in silence how everyone worked together like a well-oiled machine. He never anticipated having a crew before finding *Haven*, but now that he had a crew, he couldn't ask for a better one. These were *his* people, and he was proud each and every one agreed to sign on with him.

"Well, I think I've done all the damage I can do here," Cole said, pushing himself up from the command chair. "Sasha, you have the conn. I'll be in my office if you need me."

Sasha nodded once. "Aye, sir. I have the conn."

Cole walked to the port hatch and left the bridge.

A little over ten hours later, *Haven* reached the system periphery. The helm officer at the time engaged the hyperdrive, and the ship vanished from Centauri.

———

Battle-Carrier *Haven*
  Polar Orbit, Earth
  Sol System
  14 September 3000, 18:57 GST

"We are positioned over the geographic North Pole, sir," Gamma shift's helm officer reported.

"Excellent," Cole replied. "Thank you. Srexx?"

"Yes, Cole?" Srexx answered via the bridge speakers overhead.

"Your clock starts now," Cole said. "Start with Senators Marc Clasen and Marie-Laure Rossignol. We'll be leaving forty-eight hours from now, unless you tell me you're finished sooner than that. Fast is good, but be as thorough as possible."

"Naturally, Cole. Am I ever not thorough?"

Cole grinned. "Fair point, there. Okay, people, the standing orders until we return to the Clanhold are to maintain full stealth at all times and to alert me at once if there's *any* indication we've been discovered." Cole turned to the officer of the deck. "You have the conn."

With that, Cole left the bridge.

———

A day passed without any contact from Srexx about the investigation into the senators. Other people might have succumbed to anxiety, but not Cole. He trusted his friend and went about his daily routine as if nothing out of the ordinary was happening.

It was late at night on the 15th, less than an hour from becoming the 16th, and Cole had just stretched out in bed when the speakers above him broadcast Srexx's voice, "Cole?"

"Yeah, buddy?"

"I have it."

Cole sat up in bed. "Uhm... what do you have?"

"Everything."

Cole blinked. "Clarify that, please. What constitutes 'everything?'"

"I have the missing logs from TF-27. I have the senators' orders for those logs to be removed. I have the names of the so-called technicians who performed the work. And Cole?"

"Yeah?"

"Senators Rossignol and Clasen were two of the people responsible for the Beta Magellan massacre, and Senator Rossignol kept copious notes and all her communications."

Srexx's statement might as well have been a haymaker from a professional boxer who never lost a fight. For several heartbeats, the room around Cole seemed to spin—or at least rock like a ship at sea—and he couldn't quite find his breath.

"She seriously kept notes on plotting mass murder?" Cole croaked out at long last.

"Yes, Cole... including Lindrick's after-action reports of the event."

"Where did you find it? *How* did you find it?"

"All of the senators' official archives contained absolutely no reference to CIE or Admiral Sato or TF-27. I did discover a second comms device that is not registered to Senator Rossignol, and it was through tracing the location data of that comms device that I located a... private retreat of sorts. This retreat contained a storage node that was far more protected than anything else I have encountered on Earth, which attracted my attention. I spent the last eight hours obtaining access to the node in such a way that its owners and maintainers will never know I was there, and I just finished copying its entire contents. The node contained all sorts of evidence on several political figures throughout the Solar Republic, and that evidence is not restricted to Republic-level individuals, either. I have evidence on city mayors, provincial governors, state or province senators, local school board members. It is a very impressive collection, curated across decades, and I believe Senator Rossignol used this evidence to secure the cooperation of and leverage against the individuals represented therein. Cole, it is somewhat shocking to learn just how many truly evil people occupy government offices; I had hoped the Provisional Parliament in the Commonwealth was an isolated incident."

"There's an ancient saying among my people, Srexx. 'Power corrupts, and absolute power corrupts absolutely.' It can be a mess."

Silence.

"That is... unfortunate... Cole. How will you fight this tendency in Beta Magellan?"

Cole chuckled. "Lots and lots of Kiksaliks is the best idea I have, right now. I'm hoping someone has something better. Was there anything to indicate *why* they orchestrated the murder of my family?"

"Yes, Cole. They wanted to secure the jump gate and jump drive technologies for the Solar Republic and take over setting and collecting the transit tariffs. She also engaged the leadership of both groups I have already identified in CIE. Her information presents extensive corroboration of their betrayal of the company and your family."

"Okay. I need some time to process this. I appreciate your efforts, buddy."

"You're welcome, Cole."

"Oh, Srexx?"

"Yes, Cole?"

"Prepare three data crystals with the missing logs and all information pertaining to them, and arrange for me to have an appointment tomorrow with Nadia's uncle and Admiral Sato. I do believe I'm going to make Sato's day. Admiral Ortega might not appreciate me too much, though, when he sees what a hot potato I'm handing him."

"Yes, Cole."

"Thanks, buddy." Cole stretched out in bed once again, his mind swirling at everything Srexx had uncovered. In the wee hours of the morning, an acorn of a plan dawned in Cole's mind, and he smiled for the first time in several hours.

CHAPTER THIRTY-FOUR

Battle-Carrier *Haven*
   Orbiting Earth
   Sol System
   15 September 3000, 11:17 GST

Cole rolled his shoulders as he exited the transit shaft on Deck Six, the mess deck. He walked to the nearest dining hall, and the question of how Srexx had amused himself since the conversation last night made Cole smile. Knowing Srexx, the Solar Republic no longer had any secrets... not from Srexx anyway.

"Hey, you," a velvety voice purred just to Cole's left, mere heart-beats before Scarlett latched onto that arm. "Have some time for me?"

Cole considered the number of people who could now see him and how Scarlett held onto him. Cole fought back a sigh.

"Sure, Scarlett," Cole replied. "What's on your mind?"

"I've been giving the matter a lot of thought, and I wanted to know if you had a place for me."

Cole nodded. "I see. Well, you'll have to pass an interview, but when you pass, sure. There's a place for anyone who's willing to work hard for generous pay."

"When do you want to conduct my interview?" Scarlett asked.

"I don't do that," Cole countered. "I'll send a message to Garrett and Yeleth. They'll handle it."

"Oh. Okay. I'd appreciate that."

"You know what happens if you don't pass the interview, right?"

"Turn me over to the authorities?"

Cole shrugged. "I doubt I could bring myself to do that, but I would put you off the ship at your choice of ports."

"But what if I've stolen all your deepest, darkest secrets?"

Cole outright laughed. "You should ask Brianna Vance what happened when *she* tried to steal from this ship. You'll enjoy the story."

Scarlett's playful demeanor fell away. "Uhm... you know I was just playing, right? I have no interest in trying to steal from you."

"I know, Scarlett. But seriously, talk to Brianna."

Cole almost grinned at the trepidation that colored Scarlett's expression as he sent a note to both Yeleth and Garrett to schedule an interview for Scarlett. The former pirate lord released her hold on Cole's arm, allowing him to choose his lunch. When he turned from the serving counters, she was nowhere to be seen.

Later that day, Cole received a message from Himari Sato. She indicated the Navy had already dropped all charges against her and her captains and accepted their resignations with deepest regret. She went on to say that she would be chartering a passenger transport within the next couple of days to bring herself and any of her associates to the Clanhold, in the hopes of obtaining interviews. About the same time, Cole received a message from Srexx, indicating he had completed his perusal of Earth's datanet.

After reading Srexx's message, Cole walked onto the bridge, smiling, and ordered *Haven* to return to the Clanhold at best possible speed. It was time to start compiling all his evidence.

———

Private Retreat
    Europe, Earth
    Sol System
    15 September 3000, 15:27 GST

"There's been a development," Senator Adam Hawke said without preamble, as he entered the retreat's great room.

Senator Rossignol looked up from her tablet. "How so?"

"I was just informed that the JAG obtained evidence black ops posing as technicians boarded TF-27 upon its return to Sol and excised the logs of the Caernarvon Incident. The evidence seems to be irrefutable, and the JAG dropped all charges against Admiral Sato and her captains. Sato, her captains, and most of her staff have since resigned their commissions, and there's an increasing trickle of Navy personnel resigning their commissions as well. Oddly enough, all these personnel had their most recent duty stations in TF-27."

Rossignol hissed a series of words a Republic senator shouldn't use.

"What happened?" Rossignol asked, her words clipped.

"I have yet to obtain the evidence the JAG presented to the members of the court-martial. He called them into a closed-door session, and seconds after the session ended, all the records surrounding the case went under heavy seal."

"Nothing in this Republic is sealed from *me*," Rossignol growled. She took several moments to unleash another string of fierce epithets, shocking Hawke even further. "Fine. What's done is done. We don't have time to secure fresh leverage against the admiral and her people, especially since they've resigned from the Navy. What are they doing now, by the way?"

"A number of them seem to have taken rooms in hotels surrounding the spaceport. Those with families appear to be packing in a bit of a rush."

"Coleson," Rossignol hissed. "He got to them somehow." Rossignol paused to unleash another string of profanity.

"What's our next move?" Hawke asked, when he felt it safe to brave the ensuing silence.

Rossignol turned to face him, her glare hard enough to cut glass. "I don't know yet, but I'll be damned before I let Coleson win."

———

Battle-Carrier *Haven*
    Docking Slip F-Seven, Coleson Clanhold
    Centauri Trinary System
    17 September 3000, 09:15 GST

Cole looked up when he heard the briefing room's hatch open, and he smiled at seeing CEO Jefferds, Chief Legal Officer Trisha Townsend, and Nadia Perez file into the compartment.

"Please, be seated," Cole said, indicating the empty chairs around the table. "Thank you for coming on such short notice. I have a presentation I'd like to share with you. Before we begin, does anyone want refreshments or breakfast?" All three declined with thanks, and Cole nodded and activated the briefing room's holo-emitter. "All right, then. The presentation begins about thirty years ago, when junior senators in the Solar Republic approached specific CIE personnel. Those senators were the recently elected Marc Clasen and Marie-Laure Rossignol. The CIE personnel they approached was a junior staffer in the Finance Department by the name of Carl Bachman and a young messenger fresh out of high school who ended up becoming the Chief Security Officer."

Jefferds gasped. "There's no way Carl Bachman's a traitor. He's the CFO! I trust him with my life."

"Then you're a fool," Cole replied. "I have documentation proving he ordered the Assistant CSO to take a shot at me."

Jefferds's jaw dropped.

"As I was saying," Cole resumed the presentation, taking the group through the entire collected evidence spanning the last thirty years. Everything from a cabal of people within both CIE and the Republic Senate conspiring to massacre the Coleson colony on Beta Magellan to the two groups actively working with five senators. He even included the evidence that the five senators—Marie-Laure Rossignol, Marc Clasen, Adam Hawke, Clarissa Hopkins, and Sara Zhao—manipulated the Solar Republic Navy into conducting a Board of Inquiry and bringing charges against Admiral Sato and her captains over fallout from the Caernarvon Incident.

When Cole concluded, he leaned back against his seat. Jefferds looked shell-shocked. Townsend stared at the tabletop, blinking and periodically shaking her head as if to clear it. Nadia watched him.

"And you can prove all of this?" Jefferds asked, after several minutes of silence.

Cole nodded. "I have multiple cross-corroborations... communications, travel logs, still images, even holo-recordings of some meetings. I was able to watch them debate the merits of massacring my family and ultimately decide to do just that. Have you ever had the experience of watching ten people—some of whom you've shaken their hand and looked in their eyes—vote to murder your entire family?"

Jefferds looked away and shook his head in silence.

"What are you going to do?" Nadia asked, understanding where the meeting was heading.

"That's why you and Ms. Townsend are here, Nadia. What are my options?"

Nadia sighed, leaning back against her chair. "Well, if the evidence is as extensive as you say, you have everyone dead to rights on conspiracy to commit murder, multiple counts of felony murder. The CIE personnel are in breach of contract; they're actively working to convey proprietary technology covered by their non-disclosure agreements to a third party. You also have them on corporate espionage. And that's just what I've thought of off the top of my head. If you present this evidence to the Centauri Police, everyone involved is finished. It may take the police a while to process everything, but these people's professional lives are over. On the civil side of things, you have more than a preponderance of evidence that these people have breached their contracts; you could go after everything they own... every credit in their accounts, their property, *everything*."

Cole nodded. He allowed the silence to settle in the briefing room for a few moments before he lifted his face toward the ceiling and said, "Srexx, send them in, please."

The hatch opened and permitted Garrett, two marines, and three Kiksaliks to enter; Cole knew four marines waited in the corridor outside. Jefferds and Townsend focused on the marines. Nadia focused on the Kiksaliks.

"Ladies and gentleman," Cole said, "I freely admit that we found no evidence of you being connected in any way to the cesspit of conspiracy and intrigue we've uncovered. But that's no longer enough for me. You will be interviewed by my associate, Garrett, and he and his staff will either pass you or fail you. If you fail, you'll be sequestered in the brig until such time as I can deal with the CIE personnel plotting against me and the company; once I have done so, you'll be released and provided a generous severance package. If you have a problem with this, I'll accept your immediate resignations."

Jefferds and Townsend gaped at Cole.

Nadia smiled, possessing an eerie similarity to an apex predator. "I have no problem. I'm ready for the interview whenever."

Neither Jefferds nor Townsend resigned, so Garrett escorted them out of the briefing room. Cole knew he'd be taking them to separate offices here on Deck Three and would proceed from one to the next, conducting the interviews back to back and starting with the CEO.

Ninety minutes later, Jefferds, Townsend, and Nadia filed back into the briefing room. Garrett stepped inside after them.

He made eye contact with Cole and nodded once, saying, "They pass." Then, he left.

"Excellent!" Cole replied, breaking into a grin. "Nadia, how quickly can we get officers of the Centauri Police here?"

Nadia shrugged. "I'm not exactly sure. To the best of my knowledge, we've never called them before. I know a couple officers, though, so I can reach out."

"Please do so. The target is September 19th, and they'd better keep it quiet," Cole said. "Jefferds, I want you to announce a special ceremony for the 19th. I want the entire roster of CIE present. No one gets a sick day. No one gets leave. If they take my money, their butts will warm a seat attending this ceremony. We clear?"

Jefferds jerked a choppy nod.

"What should I be doing?" Townsend asked.

"Getting ready to file an obscene number of civil actions after I gut the company of all these traitors," Cole replied without missing a beat. "I'm hitting them with both criminal and civil litigation. Oh, and one more thing. This goes for all three of you. Discuss what you've learned here with *no one*, not even each other... not until I give you permission to do so. I will not have anyone on my list disappearing into the night, because he or she learned what's coming. If you break faith with me on this, I'll add you to the list myself. Understood?"

All three responded in a chorus, "Yes, sir."

"Good. You're dismissed to start preparing. We have a lot to do."

At Cole's nod, the three stood and left the briefing room.

CHAPTER THIRTY-FIVE

Corporate Banquet Hall
  CIE Offices, Coleson Clanhold
  Centauri Trinary System
  19 September 3000, 08:55 GST

Of all the spaces within the CIE offices in the Clanhold, only the corporate banquet hall could hold the entire company roster with any modicum of comfort. A small stage occupied a space in front of the assembled company, and CEO Jefferds and CLO Townsend sat in chairs on either side of the podium. Two water bulbs occupied a waist-high table beside the podium.

As the clocks ticked ever closer to zero-nine-hundred, the stated time for the ceremony's beginning, members of the audience began fidgeting. It was small at first, but soon, whispers accompanied the fidgeting.

At zero-eight-fifty-nine, one of the hatches into the banquet hall opened. Cole entered the banquet hall and walked straight to the podium. He laid his hands on the podium just as clocks ticked over to zero-nine-hundred.

"Good morning," Cole said. "For those of you who have not met me, I'm Cole. My name is Bartholomew James Coleson. Some of you have been with the company long enough to remember my father, Jack, and his father before him. I appreciate everyone attending today. Yes, I know attendance was mandatory, but I still appreciate your attendance nonetheless."

Cole paused for a moment, clearing his throat and taking a sip of water. Nadia Perez stood from her seat, approaching the podium with a small container of what looked like scrolls bound with a decorative ribbon. She placed the scrolls on the table that held the water bulbs and stood by the edge of the podium.

"We are here today to recognize a group of people within this company who have worked tirelessly for many years, in some cases their entire career with us. While they are not the type to brag or boast or draw attention to themselves, I cannot in good conscience allow them to toil in obscurity any longer. When I call your name, please come up here and stand beside the podium in the marked-off section." Cole took another sip of water. "Cameron Ralston."

A young man still possessing some acne from adolescence stood and made his way forward; everyone knew him as one of the company's messengers. When he approached Nadia, she produced a scroll labeled 'Cameron Ralston' from the stack, holding it in her left hand while she offered her right for a handshake.

"Thank you for coming today, Mr. Ralston," Nadia said as she shook his hand.

"You're welcome," Ralston said, his voice shaky. He accepted the scroll without examining it and moved over to stand in the marked-off section by the small stage.

The ceremony proceeded thus for each name Cole called, and soon, a sizable cross-section of the company stood in the marked-off section. By the time Cole reached the final name on his list, the recipient's face bore the pallor of death.

"Carl Bachman," Cole said.

As Bachman approached Nadia, his hands shook like they hadn't in decades. His calm self-assurance—for which he was known—had long since fled as Cole proceeded through his list. The closer Cole came to the upper echelons of the company, the more certain Bachman was of the true purpose of this 'ceremony.'

"Thank you for coming today, Mr. Bachman," Nadia said, shaking his hand as she passed him the rolled scroll. Her smile was almost predatory.

"Y-y-" Bachman cleared his throat and forced control over his voice, willing his hands to steady. "You're welcome."

With a measured gait feeling all too much like a march to the gallows, Bachman joined the others in the marked-off section, the hand holding the scroll hanging at his side.

Nadia turned from watching him and collected her valise, nodding once to Cole as she walked to the nearest hatch and stood just outside of its activation range.

Cole turned to regard the three hundred people standing in the marked-off section. In a heartbeat, his congenial and welcoming demeanor vanished. His jaw tightened. His eyes hardened into a glare. His knuckles whitened from his grip on the podium.

"In some ways, the sheer breadth of your efforts defies comprehension. I regret that the Chief Security Officer and his assistant, the individual who shot at me, could not be with us today, but you may rest assured they have already been recognized and rewarded for their participation," Cole said, his voice still amplified to fill the hall. "Open your scrolls, please."

The 'honored' employees started scrabbling at their scrolls and frowned when they unrolled them.

"Ladies and gentlemen, consider yourselves served. Those scrolls are in fact subpoenas to appear in court, at a hearing for the civil cases the company has filed against each of you. Furthermore, you are hereby *fired*. Nadia, if you please?"

Nadia moved into activation range of the hatch, which dutifully opened. Uniformed officers of the Centauri Police entered the banquet hall in a column of two. A plain clothes detective led the procession. The detective stood in front of the group and read from the top sheet of a sheaf of hardcopy.

"Carl Bachman, you are under arrest for conspiracy to commit mass murder, conspiracy to commit murder, and accessory to attempted murder before the fact. The prosecutor is still considering further charges, as we have yet to process fully the sheer mass of evidence Mr. Coleson provided. You have the right to remain silent. Anything you say can and will be used against you in a court of law. You have the right to speak to an attorney and to have an attorney present during any questioning. If you cannot afford an attorney, the Republic will provide an attorney for you at no cost to you. Do you understand these rights as I have read them to you?"

By the end of the detective's recitation, Bachman weaved on his feet, his expression shell-shocked and bemused. At the detective's question, he jerked a choppy nod.

"With respect, sir, the law requires you to answer verbally," the detective said.

"Y-yes, I understand," Bachman replied.

"Officers, secure the suspect, please," the detective said.

Two uniformed officers approached Bachman. They pulled his hands behind him and secured them, placing his subpoena scroll in the handkerchief pocket of his sport coat. Then, they walked him out of the banquet hall.

The detective shuffled Bachman's paper to the back of her stack.

"Neal Montgomery, you are under arrest... "

For the next two-and-a-half hours, Cole forced the entire company's roster to watch as police arrested the people who had spent so much time, effort, and credits working against the company and his family's legacy. The charges differed slightly from person to person, but Cole knew for certain the charges referenced would not be the *only* charges they faced at trial.

When officers led away Mr. Ralston, the youngest and final individual, Cole turned to face his employees once more.

"Ladies and gentlemen," Cole said, "when I first arrived in Centauri, I informed the company leadership that I wanted CIE to relocate to Beta Magellan within five years. We no longer have the luxury of time. Once the Solar Republic side of the conspiracy against this company learns what transpired here today, I am convinced they will throw the full might of the Republic against us. For that reason, my team has devised a plan to take the entire Clanhold with us to Beta

Magellan. Any of you who wish to continue with this company must pass an interview, a process which will begin in two days. I give you until then to decide, converse with your families if you need, or however you will reach your decision. For any who choose not to accompany us to Beta Magellan, I will provide a generous severance package out of my own personal funds. For those who do accompany us, I shall provide a generous resettlement bonus, again out of my own personal funds. Barring any unforeseen events, *Haven* and the Clanhold will leave for Beta Magellan as soon as the legal fallout has been sorted. Anyone who has not communicated a decision within the next two days will be added to the list of those who choose not to accompany us. Thank you again; this event is now complete."

Cole pivoted on his heel and left the stage. On his way to the hatch, he met Nadia.

"Everything is ready for you in Conference Room Seven," Nadia said.

"We have an executive with signing authority *and* a reporter from each news agency?"

"Yes," Nadia answered. "They were *very* interested in what you had to say, to the point they're willing to sign the contract once their legal departments had reviewed it."

Cole smiled. "Excellent, and we have the data crystals for everyone?"

"A runner from your ship delivered them mid-way through your ceremony."

Cole's smile became almost feral. "Good. Let's do this."

Nadia led him to Conference Room Seven, one of the few conference rooms aboard the Clanhold that did not have transparent bulkheads. It was also the largest. Cole stepped inside, and a crowd not even half the size of what he'd just left turned to face him. The conference table had been removed, replaced by a podium on a small stage and many rows of seating. There were no empty seats.

Cole maintained a non-expression as he walked to the podium, but inside, he smiled at how his guests maintained decorum and didn't rush him with a thousand shouted questions.

"Ladies and gentlemen, I want to thank you for coming," Cole said, resting his hands on the podium. "The price of your attendance here today was signing a contract with CIE that mandates this press conference and its associated data must be provided to the public for free in its unmodified entirety and guarantees no less than forty-eight hours' news time over the next eight days. The legal department in CIE just finished filing three hundred lawsuits for breach of contract against former employees, so if any of you harbor thoughts of skimping on your side of the deal—by all means—give my lawyers something else to do. And without further ado, let's begin."

Cole paused long enough to take a drink of water. "As some of you may have guessed, I am Bartholomew James Coleson, who many have termed the 'Lost Coleson Heir.' Over thirty years ago, two junior senators of the Solar Republic approached two junior employees of Coleson Interstellar Engineering, beginning a long-term plot to secure the schematics for our proprietary jump drive and jump gate technologies. When the conspirators realized they could not suborn CIE as long as the Coleson family existed, they hired mercenaries to massacre my family's colony on Beta Magellan. Convinced that all significant opposition no longer existed, the plot grew and expanded to include folding the whole of CIE into the Solar Republic. The two senators who began the plot added three more to their ranks, and their counterparts in CIE rose to high office in the company and expanded their roster as well. The five senators in this conspiracy are Marc Clasen, Marie-Laure Rossignol, Adam Hawke, Clarissa Hopkins, and Sara Zhao."

Cole paused for another drink before continuing, "During the investigation of an attempt on my life, my team uncovered quite a bit of alarming conduct, both from CIE personnel and these senators. Those five even maintained a storehouse of dirty secrets, for lack of a better term, involving hundreds of people spread throughout the Republic government. The data crystals you will receive contain all my evidence, unedited and unmodified. I realize many of you consider those beside you competitors in some respects, but the scope of this news is such that I feel it is beyond one agency to cover it all. As my people hand out the data crystals, I will take questions, and you will receive an unedited recording of this conference when you leave. I could take you through the evidence from start to finish, beginning some thirty years ago, but I would rather not taint your perceptions of it with my thoughts and emotions. The contractual forty-eight hours of news time begins at zero-eight-hundred GST on the 21st of September. We'll start the questions from the first seat of the first row. Go."

Nadia and her assistants moved through the crowd, passing out data crystals while Cole fielded questions from the assembled journalists. He held nothing back, answering every question as truthfully and unreservedly as he could.

Cole's remarks took less than thirty minutes. He answered questions for over four hours.

CHAPTER THIRTY-SIX

Private Retreat
Europe, Earth
Sol System
21 September 3000, 11:15 GST

Adam Hawke stepped out of his air car just as Marc Clasen stepped out of his. Adam approached the elder senator and shook his hand.

"What's going on? We didn't have a meeting scheduled, did we?" Marc asked.

Adam grinned. "I was going to ask you the same thing."

The sound of something shattering echoed out of the large cabin, followed shortly by faint yet vehement shrieking.

Adam and Marc looked toward the cabin before turning back to each other.

"We should... " Marc began.

"Check that," Adam finished, Marc nodding.

Both men hurried to the cabin. Upon their opening the door, Marie-Laure Rossignol's voice was no longer muffled. Her voice carried even from the far back of the cabin—presumably the great room—and it was a wonder her language wasn't stripping the paint off the drywall. Adam and Marc were halfway down the hall when Rossignol ran out of words and resorted to an inarticulate scream, mere heartbeats before a china teacup sailed through the doorway of the great room and struck the far wall of the corridor. Its pieces fell to the floor, adding to the impressive pile already there.

"Marie," Marc said as he and Adam rounded the corner, "what's wrong?"

The older woman pivoted to face the two new arrivals, her visage a storm front of rage. "Have you seen the news?"

"No. We were traveling here. You called us," Adam said.

"Which channel?" Marc asked.

"All of them," Rossignol shouted, her voice shifting into an almost hoarse shriek.

Marc crossed the intervening space and placed his hands on Rossignol's shoulders. "Marie, please, calm down. What's happening? What's on the news?"

"They know, Marc. They're broadcasting everything," Rossignol said, her voice now barely above a whisper. "Somehow, Coleson found our storage archive. He gave them *everything*."

Marc rocked back on his heels.

"It's over, then," Adam said. "We're finished."

Rossignol shifted her focus to Adam, her glare hardening. "Don't think you're going to save yourself by turning your coat, Adam. My files had enough on you to bury the next ten generations of your family. I had a copy of that video you made with your *underage* niece. Remember?"

Adam paled. "What... what are we going to do?"

"There's nothing to do," Marc said. "We might get ahead of it, if we leave right now, but we'd never be able to return to the Republic."

Rossignol turned her glare on Marc. "You spineless coward. I'll dance my way to prison as long as I've taken that insolent, upstart puppy down first. You think I'm going quietly? What kind of fool are you?"

Marc's face fell. He recognized the sheer venom in his colleague's tone, and he was glad it was only the third time he'd heard it in his professional life. The last time had been when she forced the vote to massacre Beta Magellan.

"Oh, Marie," Marc said, his voice almost a sigh, "what have you done?"

"These traitors in the press haven't published yet just how far our reach into the military goes. I called our pet admiral over at Personnel and told him to put our people in command of TF-27 and send it plus whatever ships from Home Fleet we control to Centauri. That insolent child and his ship will die... even if it's the last thing I ever do. Do you understand, Marc? He will not win; I won't have it."

Adam looked from one elder senator to the other. He couldn't believe what he was hearing. Realizing where his odds for survival lay, the young senator started edging his way toward the hall. He managed to reach the hallway without either Marc or Rossignol being aware of his movement... and turned right into the chest of a burly officer.

"And just where are you going?" the officer asked, his voice a gravelly baritone.

Adam saw at least a dozen people wearing tactical gear with 'Republic SRU' emblazoned across the chest-pieces in bold white letters. Adam sighed as his shoulders slumped. If the Strategic Response Unit was already here, Republic law enforcement had already processed warrants for Adam and his colleagues.

The entrance of SRU into the great room of the cabin drew shrieking imprecations from Rossignol.

"What in all that's holy do you people think you're doing in here?" Rossignol shouted, almost at the top of her lungs. "You people work for *me*! I *own* your boss! We have full immunity while the Senate is in session; you can't *touch* us!"

Mr. Baritone took Adam by the shoulders, turning him around and wrapping his bear paw of a hand around Adam's neck, and frog-marched him back into the great room. He smiled, but that smile held no mirth.

"Marie-Laure Rossignol, Marc Clasen, and Adam Hawke... I have been empowered by the Chancellor of Senate to inform you that the Senate has recorded a unanimous vote to censure you three, Clarissa Hopkins, and Sara Zhao. Per this morning's vote, you have been ejected from the Senate and stripped of all the privileges and protections membership provides. We also have warrants for your arrest. Will you cooperate, or do we need to add 'Resisting Arrest' to your rather frightening list of charges?"

Without missing a beat, Rossignol stepped around Marc and walked right up to the SRU officer, looking up at him as she flayed him with all manner of profane invective that questioned everything from his parentage and reproductive capability to the more prosaic topics of base intelligence and humanity. The whole time she shrieked at him, she jabbed the rigid index finger of her right hand into the chest-piece of his tactical gear.

Adam had to exert considerable will to keep from laughing. Rossignol was a Chihuahua assaulting a Clydesdale.

In the end, it took three female officers to restrain and gag the intemperate former senator, and even then, it was clear she was still shouting imprecations behind the gag as the female officers marched her out of the cabin. Marc and Adam displayed considerably more wisdom and surrendered.

Watching the retreating form of the defiant Rossignol, the lead SRU officer accessed his comms.

"Control, this is Unit Seven Alpha."

"Go ahead, Seven Alpha."

"Alert the Navy that Rossignol attempted to arrange for TF-27 and an as-yet undisclosed number of Home Fleet ships to depart Sol for Centauri. Recommend the Admiralty halt all ship movements until everyone can sort this all out."

"Copy that, Seven Alpha. Making the call now."

"Thanks, Control. Seven Alpha out."

Seven Alpha's alert to the Admiralty pulled everyone's focus to Home Fleet, and they caught fifteen ships attempting to slip away. The flag officer in command of Home Fleet for Sol resorted to threatening weapons fire if the fifteen ships did not stand down. In the ensuing chaos, however, the ships of Task Force 27 disappeared.

CHAPTER THIRTY-SEVEN

Most settled star systems that were members of an interstellar polity—whether the Solar Republic, Aurelian Commonwealth, or even the Eridani Corporation—enjoyed the presence of a 'home fleet.' Home Fleet served as both a defensive force for the star system and training cadre for the System Defense Forces that served both as system-level militia as well as police. In some systems, like Sol, a position in Home Fleet was a matter of intra-service political prestige and a sure sign that a person was meant for greater things. Home Fleet in the border systems also tended to be prestige postings from the standpoint of naval competence. Officers who distinguished themselves in Home Fleet of a border system often rotated next through Sol's Home Fleet as an evaluation of the officer in a more social and political setting.

There was one other 'class' of Home Fleet: those posted in systems between the capital and the border. Like Centauri's Home Fleet. While Centauri's Home Fleet boasted a certain level of prestige because it patrolled Humanity's first interstellar colony, its proximity to Sol tended to overshadow Centauri and draw officers who either had knowledge and experience to share or needed knowledge and experience shared with them.

Battle-Carrier *Haven*
  Docking Slip F-Seven, Coleson Clanhold
  Centauri Trinary System
  21 September 3000, 20:15 GST

"Bridge to Captain," the speakers overhead broadcast.

Cole looked up from the book on his tablet, saying, "Cole here."

"Captain, Nadia Perez is at the 'lock... and she has company."

"Okay. I'm going to need a judgement call from you, Bridge. Is it 'alert the ready squad of marines' kind of company or 'walk out and shake hands' kind of company?"

"Well, sir... I think... the latter? Himari Sato is with her. Sato has a couple people, and there are three SRN officers: a captain and a couple others whose insignia I can't read. From what we can see through the video feed, they're congenial and personable between one another. I don't think this is a hostage situation or anything like that."

Cole nodded, even though the bridge officer couldn't see it. "Right then. Okay. Send someone to meet them and bring them to the bridge briefing room. Ask Sasha, Colonel Hanson, Garrett, Yeleth, and Red to join us."

Cole occupied his favored seat at the head of the briefing room's conference table when everyone started arriving. Cole's people arrived and had just enough time to assume their seats when the group from the airlock arrived. Cole stood and greeted everyone as they stepped through the hatch, shaking their hands and welcoming them aboard *Haven*.

"I wasn't aware you were in-system," Cole said to Sato as he shook her hand.

"Our chartered ship just docked here at the Clanhold. Nadia contacted me just a few minutes ago and asked me to attend. When she told me why, I brought my former chief of staff and former tactical officer."

Cole nodded, shaking the hands of Sato's people. "Well, thank you for coming, and welcome aboard."

Once Cole had greeted and welcomed everyone, he resumed his seat.

"So, Nadia, why are we here?" Cole asked.

"I would like to introduce Captain Thomas Delaney, commanding officer of Centauri's Home Fleet. Commander Zane Killaine is his flag captain, and Lieutenant Commander Valerie O'Neil is his tactical officer. Captain Delaney contacted me just as I was in the process of contacting him; apparently, we both received the same information."

"At ten hours and twenty-three minutes today," Captain Delaney said, "Task Force 27 departed their parking orbit in near-Earth space. At twelve hours and fifty minutes, they deactivated their transponders and disappeared into the expanse of Sol. They were able to achieve this due to well-timed chaos in Sol's Home Fleet, in which fifteen ships attempted to separate. Based on available intelligence, we believe those fifteen ships were to bolster TF-27."

Cole nodded. He had a feeling he knew what station this train of thought had for a destination. "Let me guess. You think they're coming here."

"Yes," Nadia said.

"The admiral in charge of Personnel for the Navy has already been arrested. Prior to her arrest and the revocation of all orders from Personnel pending review, Admiral Mathers put a number of officers into recently vacated positions in TF-27 and issued movement orders to the task force, authorizing them to depart their parking orbit. The movement orders were the first alert we had, because Admiral Mathers is not in TF-27's chain of command. She's a staff officer, not fleet. At any rate, given the nature of your relationship with the individuals pulling TF-27's strings, the Navy felt it imperative to alert you to the disappearance of the task force."

"Have there been any subtractions or additions to TF-27's order of battle?" Sasha asked.

Delaney shook his head, replying, "Not that the Navy is aware of.

The task force was in something of a holding pattern, pending the outcome of the firestorm surrounding the Caernarvon Incident, so their day-to-day has focused on maintenance, routine systems upgrades, and training."

"Ninety-two ships, then," Sasha replied. "Four battleships, eight cruisers, sixteen destroyers, and sixty-four frigates."

"TF-27 represents a sufficient threat that neither your ship—impressive as she is—nor Home Fleet could safely engage them, if it comes to that. For the purposes of this encounter only, the Solar Republic and its Navy offers a joint operations agreement to *Haven*, Haven Enterprises, and Coleson Interstellar Engineering, and I have been empowered to act as a plenipotentiary should you agree. If *Haven* happened to possess a flag officer of superior experience to me, I would—of course—agree to that flag officer serving as senior command for the duration of our joint operations."

Cole smiled, his head shifting to Sato as he said, "So... want a job?"

"I... was not expecting my skills and experience being needed so soon," Sato replied. "However, my staff did choose to accompany me and request interviews."

Cole's smile shifted into a full-on grin. "Right then. Gather your people. We'll proceed with the interviews as soon as everyone's here. Oh, and good news! I have unoccupied quarters for a flag officer and the flag officer's staff. Convenient, that. Garrett, prepare your people. I want these interviews finished soonest. Captain Delaney, I will trust you and my flag officer, Admiral Sato, can handle things once we complete the onboarding for her and her people?"

Delaney nodded once, fighting to control a smile.

"Okay then. Is there anything else?"

"Some of my people brought families," Sato said.

Cole nodded. "Good point. *Haven* isn't really set up for families. Nadia, can you see to their accommodations aboard the Clanhold? If need be, I'll open the Residence; there's something like twenty apartments there, each apartment having four to five bedrooms."

"I'll see to it," Nadia replied, "and contact you if we need the Residence."

Cole nodded as he ran through the situation in his head. It wasn't a matter of if TF-27 would show; it was a matter of *when*. Assuming a cruising speed of a quarter-light, TF-27 wouldn't reach the Centauri jump gate until a little over sixteen-and-a-half hours after they lit off their drives... assuming a straight shot. Only an idiot would make a straight shot for the jump gate, but how devious was the new task force commander?

"Do we know who took over command for the task force?" Cole asked.

"Commodore Evan Lansing," Captain Delaney replied.

"Do any of you know him?" Cole asked, directing the question to the SRN personnel, both former and current.

Sato nodded. "I have served with Lansing in the past."

"What can you tell me about him? I mean, what kind of person is he? How does he think?"

Sato sighed, shifting her eyes toward the ceiling. "Lansing... is... very eager, very driven. More than once, I had the impression that he felt compelled to prove himself for reasons unknown. No matter how well he did, it never seemed to be good enough for him. That aspect of his personality made positions of authority a challenge for him, because even overachievers often did not share his level of ambition."

"Is he clever?"

"He likes to think so," Sato replied, a slight quirk of her lips that might have become a smile if allowed to grow. "He also likes an epic scope. The bigger—the more grandiose—a plan is, the more he'll like it."

Cole nodded. "Okay. I'll think on that. Is there anything else we need to discuss at this time?"

Heads shook, answering 'no' around the table.

"Very well," Cole remarked. "Sato, get your people's families to Nadia aboard the Clanhold, and bring your people back here for their interviews."

"What about the non-staff officers who came with me?"

Cole shrugged. "Bring 'em all. The more the merrier. We may not have an immediate place for them, other than a bunk assignment if they don't want to stay on the Clanhold, but we might as well get the interview out of the way now."

Sato nodded.

"Anything else?" Cole asked. "Speak now, while the speaking's good."

When no one else spoke, Cole stood. "All right, then. We have some preparations to make. Let's make them."

CHAPTER THIRTY-EIGHT

Haven and Centauri's Home Fleet joined up under the direction of Cole's first flag officer: Admiral Himari Sato. They drilled. And practiced. And drilled. And practiced.

The soonest Task Force 27 could appear was late on the 22nd. It didn't. The maneuvers and simulations continued. They continued to the point that Cole thought he detected a mutinous look or two among his people. And Sato wasn't satisfied drilling only during the normal shift schedule. Oh, no. She called the fleet to battle-stations at zero-two-thirty on the 23rd, mere hours after everyone on Alpha shift went to their beds for a relaxing sleep. At that point, *Cole* wanted to mutiny... and he was the captain.

The combined fleet continued their practice. By dinnertime of the 24th, they were maneuvering together like one would expect of a fleet. Sato seemed satisfied enough with their progress that she gave them the 25th for a rest day.

Battle-Carrier *Haven*
   Joint Operations Fleet

Centauri Trinary System
26 September 3000, 05:55 GST

Cole fought back the urge to heave a heavy sigh as he planted himself in the command chair. He was five minutes early for his shift, and he wasn't looking forward to it. The rest day was *yesterday*. Objectively, he knew the drills and practice were good for them. Objectively. Emotionally, however, was a whole other matter. At least *Haven* wasn't dominating the mock battles so much anymore. Winning was good, but winning without a challenge was almost worse than losing without knowing why.

Movement around him pulled Cole from his thoughts, and he scanned the bridge to see Delta shift leaving and Alpha arriving. Sasha would normally have sat at the station just behind the starboard recess, but upon learning *Haven* had an auxiliary bridge, Sato had said several things to Cole and Sasha that were none too kind. During combat aboard a ship with an auxiliary bridge, the first officer's place was *in the auxiliary bridge*. Always and without question. Yes, *Haven* was the most impressive ship she'd ever seen—ever dreamt of, even—but the bridge could still be breached or damaged. And so, when the ship went to battle-stations, Sasha now went to the auxiliary bridge... where the Beta shift bridge crew joined her. That morning, Sasha must've decided to skip the trip to the bridge and went straight to the auxiliary.

"Cap," Haskell at Sensors said, "they're here."

"Where?" Cole asked, swiveling the command chair to face the sensors station.

"They just arrived through the jump gate to Epsilon Eridani."

Cole blinked. "What? How the... put a jump gate map on the tactical plot, please."

Cole spun the command chair back to face forward and was on his feet almost before the motion stopped. The tactical plot waited for him. The jump gates around Sol were almost a mess, compared to the Expansion Zone. The oldest jump gates in the galaxy, they were more on the 'rough and ready' side than the streamlined and refined installations that existed out around Beta Magellan, Tristan's Gate, and Zurich.

"Jenkins, alert the admiral, please," Cole said, his voice absent as he tried to trace the route that would've taken them from Sol to Epsilon Eridani. When he found it, Cole didn't realize he vocalized the thought that dominated his mind. "Wow... talk about taking the scenic route. Jenkins, call the admiral, please."

The bridge speakers chirped.

"Yes, Captain?" Admiral Sato asked.

"How much fuel do our jump drives use in the SRN ships, Admiral?" Cole asked.

"It is considerable," Sato replied. "CIE has requested multiple times that the Navy release certain pieces of data from their ships' schematics that would allow CIE engineers to develop a design optimized for the SRN, but the Navy turned them down every time, citing security concerns. Why?"

"I think Commodore Lansing figuratively shot himself in the foot trying to be clever," Cole replied. "To arrive through the Epsilon Eridani jump gate, they would've had to leave Sol through the jump gate to Lalande 21185. The *only* system in which they might have refueled is Epsilon Eridani."

Sato erupted in outright joyous laughter. "That fool. I saw a bulletin being prepared for publication to the fleet when I went to resign. Epsilon Eridani is experiencing severe solar instability right now. The fuel ships that would normally skim reactants from the chromosphere haven't been able to do so for almost a month. The Navy is having to send fleet tenders and colliers into the system to keep Eridani's Home Fleet combat effective. There's no way they would've permitted Lansing to refuel."

"What about the fleet refueling base here?" Cole asked. "Could he use it?"

"Of course, but he *has* to realize orders regarding his mistake—as they've been very careful *not* to call it mutiny—would've beaten him here. One moment, Captain..." Cole heard her giving orders to show the SRN refueling depot on the flag plot and highlight TF-27. Sato's chuckle sounded outright predatory. "We *have* them. We can position the Joint Ops fleet between TF-27 and the refueling depot. Please excuse me. I need to prepare maneuvering and formation orders to the fleet."

The bridge speakers chirped as the channel closed.

Cole considered the tactical plot for a few moments before he said, "Helm, bring us about to point in the general direction of the SRN refueling depot. I'm not sure what the admiral's precise maneuvering plan will be, but we'll save a few seconds if we're already facing that way."

"Aye, sir," Wixil replied, all the drills and simulations having caused her to backslide into formality. At least Sasha wasn't on the bridge to witness it.

Soon, maneuvering orders arrived, and Cole asked Jenkins to forward them to the helm. Within minutes of the maneuvering orders going out, the fleet came about to match *Haven*'s heading, and the Joint Ops fleet as a whole moved toward the refueling depot. With nothing further to add for the moment, Cole returned to the command chair and watched the fleet execute the maneuvering plan on the tactical plot.

The Joint Ops fleet was well on its way to the refueling depot when TF-27 started moving. What's more, they didn't seem to be using a standard military maneuvering plan. They accelerated to one-tenth-lightspeed and cut their engines. At one-tenth-light, it would take TF-27 over one-hundred hours to traverse the seventy-five AUs between them and the refueling depot.

Instead of taking up a defensive position at the refueling depot, Captain Delaney requested the fleet go out to meet TF-27. He had orders from the Admiralty for TF-27 to stand down, with all of the last-minute personnel appointments to be relieved of duty pending review. Sato agreed, and so the fleet continued on.

When the comms lag reached an acceptable level, the Joint Ops fleet braked to a stop, relative to the refueling depot.

"Cap," Jenkins said, "Captain Delaney is broadcasting a message on SRN channels."

"Can you play it?"

Jenkins grinned. "Of course, Cap. Srexx has kept us up-to-date on all their current encryptions."

Cole laughed. "I have the best friends. Put it on, please."

The forward viewscreen activated, displaying a static image of Captain Delaney. Within a second, the message began.

"Attention, Task Force 27," Delaney said. "I am Captain Thomas Delaney, commanding officer of Centauri's Home Fleet. I have orders from the Admiralty relieving the last-minute personnel appointments from duty, pending a full review. The last-minute personnel appointments and associated movement orders were not approved by the Admiralty as a whole and, as such, were illegal orders. Those of you who were not among the last-minute appointments may stand down at this time, with the Admiralty guaranteeing no punitive actions against you. Please, captains... for the sake of your crews, stand down. Delaney out."

For several tense moments, nothing happened. Then, something did.

"And there they go," Haskell at Sensors said.

Sure enough, ships across Task Force 27 flipped and began braking maneuvers after setting their running lights and transponders to flash the universal surrender code. Within five minutes, all but one ship signaled its surrender. Then, the unthinkable happened. The command battleship—Sato's former flagship—fired all its weapons into its fellows.

"Sound battle-stations," Cole said, not missing a beat. "Helm, get us in there. Comms, signal TF-27 to make a hole for us... or we will."

The surrendered ships complied, and soon, *Haven* had a clear corridor through which to approach the battleship that still strafed its fury on those around it.

"Cap," Jenkins said, "the admiral's a bit insistent to know what you're doing."

"I'm defending the defenseless," Cole replied. "If she doesn't like that, I made a misjudgment. Tactical, lock all weapons on that battleship, and sound off when we're in range. We're doing this just like the op to capture Lindrick. Target shields, weapons, and engines... in that order. Helm, if you can, put us between the battleship and the most vulnerable ships."

Not even thirty seconds later, Mazzi announced, "Extended munitions range, sir!"

"Missiles and torpedoes, Mazzi... full spread."

One-hundred-three missiles and seventeen torpedoes erupted from launchers interspersed across *Haven*'s bow. The missiles flew toward the battleship like zephyrs. The torpedoes not so much, but they still outpaced *Haven*. *Haven*'s computer projected the missiles' flight time at ninety seconds, the torpedoes at one-hundred-fifteen seconds.

Eighty seconds later, the massive point-defense clusters across the battleship activated, valiantly striving to destroy all the incoming projectiles. The clusters fired their capacitors dry in eight seconds, little more than halving the incoming missiles... which was their mistake. Against the battleship, the missiles were light munitions at best, engineered for use against ships far less protected like destroyers and frigates. The torpedoes were not.

The fifty-seven remaining missiles detonated against the battleship's shields, shredding them into nonexistence and giving the torpedoes unfettered access to the bare armored hull. Twenty-five seconds later, those torpedoes passed through the space where the shields *should have been* and split up to find targets. The battleship possessed eight massive shield generators; the torpedoes destroyed six, and the remaining generators overloaded at the sudden strain. The remaining eleven torpedoes didn't target specific weapons emplacements; they bored in on power junctions and relays, their detonations robbing entire sections of precious power including the nearby weapons emplacements.

"Energy range, sir!" Mazzi announced.

"Cap," Haskell said, "something's happening over there. I'm reading small arms fire."

"Hold fire, Mazzi," Cole said. "The crew may be having a word with their captain and flag officer."

Ten minutes later, the battleship's transponder and running lights began flashing the universal code for a surrendered ship.

"They're broadcasting a message," Jenkins announced.

"Put it on, please," Cole requested.

The forward viewscreen activated, displaying a woman in an SRN working uniform. A trickle of blood ran down her left cheek from a small nick at her temple, and her dark hair was in disarray.

"I'm Commander Warner," the woman said. "The captain and commodore barricaded themselves in auxiliary control and locked out the bridge. We have retaken auxiliary control and request permission to surrender. We took the captain and commodore alive."

"Tactical, stand down from battle-stations. Helm, bring us about and return us to our position in the Joint Ops fleet. Like they say in the holos, 'our work here is done.'"

The bridge crew shared glances among themselves.

"Just which holos do they say that in, Cap?" Haskell said. "I've never heard it."

"Yeah," Jenkins added. "I've not heard it, either."

Cole sighed, suppressing a grin. "Heckled by my own crew. What a sad state of affairs... "

CHAPTER THIRTY-NINE

Preparations consumed the days and weeks following the encounter with Task Force 27. Stockpiling foodstuffs and potable water. Collecting recyclable material to produce the parasite engines. Analyzing the structure of the Clanhold to determine best placement for the parasite engines. Then, actually placing them.

Cole kept everyone moving at just short of a frenetic pace. Yes, the Solar Republic was a neutral party... for now. He felt at the very core of his being that it would only be a matter of time before someone else looked at the Clanhold and thought about claiming it for themselves. The time for a leisurely relocation to Beta Magellan was past... long past.

Of the entire company roster that sat in the banquet hall all those weeks before, only seventy-five chose the severance packages. Everyone else gathered their families and/or loved ones, bringing them to the Clanhold for transport to Beta Magellan. It was a staggering number, all told. By the time everyone was aboard, the Clanhold's environmental systems were almost straining with the load. Almost.

Faced with that prospect, Cole discussed the matter with Srexx, who recommended emergency atmo recyclers... yet another wonder the Gyv'Rathi took for granted. These (relatively) small, portable units could be placed through a ship or station and activated to supplement the primary air recycling systems, thereby reducing the load on damaged or overloaded infrastructure. About the size of a modest woodsmith's workbench, the units soon dotted the landscape throughout the Clanhold.

All was not static on the criminal/civil front, either. Most defendants in the civil breach-of-contract lawsuits settled. Those that chose to settle only lost seventy-five percent of their assets. Those who attempted to fight the suits did not fare so well.

The plaintiff's counsel—Nadia Perez, it so happened—presented an overwhelming mass of evidence that each respective defendant violated his or her contract, all while CIE held up its side of the agreement. In every single instance of a defendant fighting the suit, the jury found in favor of the plaintiff. During the penalty phase, Nadia presented each defendant's pay records to the jury, going back to the first payment *after* the individual joined the conspiracy and asked the jury to award the plaintiff an amount of credits equal to the combined sum.

In many cases, the jury awarded a sum greater than what the plaintiff sought, and the plaintiff's agents were ruthless in enforcing the order of the court. Cole oversaw every asset seizure, and in the case of families with children, he arranged for a small stipend to feed the family, all while taking anything his company's money had paid for. Many hated him and gave voice to their hate, but Cole was indifferent. For the upper echelons of the conspiracy, Cole bore no sympathy at all; those people chose for *his* family to die, and providing basic necessities for any children caught in the crossfire was the extent of his humanitarianism.

It took three months for all the criminal cases evolving from exposing the conspiracy to wind down to a close. In addition to being bankrupted from the civil cases, most upper echelon conspirators soon started prison terms of twenty-five years. Former senators Adam Hawke, Clarissa Hopkins, and Sara Zhao joined them. The courts deemed the crimes of former CFO Bachman, the CSO, and his assistant to be too heinous for re-entry to society and exiled them to one of the prison planets maintained by the Republic. Marc Clasen and Marie-Laure Rossignol joined them.

Through it all, Cole kept up-to-date on Beta Magellan affairs through the quantum comms device. The updates were text and graphics for the most part, though he did call Painter and Sev from time to time. The last message Cole sent before their scheduled departure asked them to keep the L4 LaGrange point at Beta Magellan IV available. After all, something would be following *Haven* home, and he'd need a place to put it.

Battle-Carrier *Haven*
    Coleson Clanhold
    Centauri Trinary System
    13 January 3001, 08:17 GST

Cole entered the bridge, and Sasha vacated the command chair. Traversing the short distance from the port hatch, Cole sat in the command chair.

"How are we looking?" Cole asked.

Sasha returned a small smile. "All decks report ready. The Clanhold reports ready."

"Very well. Bring us to alert status, please... just in case."

Status lights all over *Haven* activated as a bright amber and flashed five times before returning to a steady light.

"Okay, let's do this just like we practiced," Cole said. "Helm, slave the parasite engines to our helm controls."

Wixil's fingers flew over the console for almost thirty seconds before she announced, "All parasite engines slaved and online. Status green across the board."

Cole's fingers twitched, and he folded his hands into fists a couple times before forcing himself to lean back in the command chair. Sasha leaned close.

"You want to be at the helm, don't you?" Sasha whispered.

Cole grinned, replying, "Of course, I do. Who wouldn't want to be at the helm for this?"

"Me," Sasha replied.

Cole chuckled. "Helm, set course for Beta Magellan, and program a course for the station that will parallel us to the system periphery."

Once more, Wixil's fingers flew over the helm station, her tail languidly swishing back and forth. Soon, she announced, "Courses plotted and laid in, Cole!"

"Implement a movement plan that will bring us up to a quarter-light over five hours."

Wixil programmed the movement plan and keyed the command to execute it. Less than a nanosecond later, both *Haven* and the Clanhold started moving.

"Movement plan implemented, Cole! The station's holding steady off our starboard beam."

"Excellent job, Wixil. Thank you. Tactical, stand down from alert status, please."

Over the next thirty-two hours, *Haven* and the Clanhold enjoyed an uneventful trip to the system periphery. Just as the Beta shift helm officer reported ready to engage the hyperdrive, a message arrived from Sev Vance.

What do you mean 'something is following you home?'

Cole laughed and sent back the reply, *You'll see.*

"Srexx, are we ready to tow the Clanhold to Beta Magellan?" Cole asked.

"Yes, Cole. I've re-run the calculations several times as we've fine tuned the mass of the Clanhold and to account for the full occupancy we currently have. A hyperdrive setting of sixty-five percent will give us a greater-than-ninety-nine-point-nine-nine-nine-nine-nine-nine-percent chance of successful transit."

"Thanks, buddy. Helm, move us into position."

Fifteen minutes later, the helmsman reported, "We're in position, sir."

Cole grinned, saying, "Punch it."

On 15 January 3001, *Haven* and the Coleson Clanhold vanished from Centauri.

————

Office suite 4501
  Garretson Building, Paris
  Earth, Sol System
  17 January 3001, 09:27 GST

Arthur Bryce stood at the window, overlooking Paris's business district. His left hand rested in the pocket of his suit trousers, his right hand against the small of his back. A knock interrupted his thoughts, and he turned and said, "Enter," as he moved to his desk.

"Mr. Bryce, we just heard back from the scout," Victor Ulmstaadt said.

"And what does our scout report, Victor?"

"Our report was correct; *Haven* is gone."

Bryce focused on the slight tic—barely noticeable, really—that he saw at Victor's lips. "What else, Victor? You know I don't like it when you censor my data."

"Well, it's about the Coleson Clanhold, sir. It... it's gone, too."

Bryce's eyes narrowed almost to a glare. "Where is it, then, Victor? Stations don't move."

"The scout started a standard search pattern of the Centauri system, sir, but the Clanhold's transponder isn't on the system traffic report. Could... could he have taken it with him?"

"It seems there is no end to the surprises young Mr. Coleson can provide, Victor. He exposed our pet senators and the organization we built within his company, and now, he has spirited away a station of all things. Very well. He has won this round, and we shall pursue him no further... for now. As we have done for many years, we'll wait and watch and bide our time. One day—perhaps soon, perhaps not—we will have our chance to secure CIE, and we shall take it."

"About that, sir," Victor said. "A couple people have asked if we're going to come to the aid of our senators."

"Of course not. That would put us too close to public view. They allowed themselves to get caught, and they must deal with the consequences. Is there anything else, Victor?"

"No, sir."

"Very well. Return to your duties."

"Yes, sir. Thank you, sir," Victor said, pivoting on his heel and leaving Arthur Bryce to his thoughts.

Victor was almost to the door when Bryce said, "A moment, Victor."

Victor turned and walked back to Bryce's desk, asking, "Yes, sir?"

"On further consideration, let's not leave any loose threads on the tapestry we're weaving. I think Marc Clasen and Marie-Laure Rossignol have outlived their usefulness. Please, see to it that they do not survive the preparations for transportation to the prison planet."

CHAPTER FORTY

The trip to Beta Magellan from Alpha Centauri took one year, five months, three days, sixteen hours... and change. The trip from the system periphery to the L4 Lagrange point for Beta Magellan IV took another sixteen hours. As soon as the Clanhold was in a stable position at L4, Cole ordered *Haven* into a parking orbit and began the process of shuttling everyone down to the planet for some rest and relaxation that *wasn't* aboard a ship or a station. The question of who was going to live where plus a billion and one other matters could wait for another day.

The people aboard *Haven* and the Clanhold weren't *exactly* in poor humor, but at the same time, why rock the boat? Cole knew he'd made the right decision when he announced mandatory planet-side shore leave for everyone, and the entire ship cheered. Cole spent the next day at his family's homestead down on the planet, and he realized it no longer hurt as much to see it. Maybe it was a factor of time, but maybe it was simply that Cole had a 'family' of his own now. Either way, it only took that one day before Cole itched to get back to work, hopping a shuttle back up to space; it was time to check in with Haven Enterprises.

Sev, Painter, and Paol Thyrray were not idle during Cole's absence.

Work was proceeding on the massive station that would eventually replace the Clanhold. It travelled with Beta Magellan IV in its L5 Lagrange point. The station was shaping up to be a massive commercial and industrial complex, along with the necessary residential space. The rough skeleton of Cole's shipyard extended out from the station in the direction of the planet's travel-path around the star, while commercial shipping docks extended out to either side like the massive solar panels on Humanity's early space facilities.

In the center of it all, Sev and Painter revealed a space about the size of a cinema's seating area. Except for the short supports and umbilical that connected the space to the station, a hemisphere of transparent armor-glass enveloped the space, creating an observation area where Cole could come anytime he chose. Cole grinned like a child confronted with a mound of presents for his birthday as he expressed his thanks.

————

Observation Dome
    Citadel Station
    Beta Magellan   \
    25 June 3002, 10:17 GST

Cole looked out at the flurry of near-station traffic. It was impossible to make out fine details, but he knew work crews were finalizing the first five construction slips over at the shipyard. With *Haven* in-system now, the work was going much faster. *Haven*'s fabricators were churning out parts to make fabricators of all sizes, from duplicates of the devices aboard the ship to the massive, industrial-grade fabricators needed to produce the hull plating used in Gyv'Rathi-designed starships.

It wouldn't be long now. Once those first five slips were complete, construction would begin on the mining ships that would fan out to various nearby systems Haven Enterprises claimed. Once there, it was just a matter of breaking up the otherwise-unusable objects... asteroids, airless planetoids, etc. Any planets of near-Earth size were exempt; those would be terraformed as the need arose. The methods the local races called 'terraforming' were infantile compared to the capabilities described in Srexx's archives, and while they didn't need the space now, they might in time.

Movement at his side drew Cole's attention, and he smiled at seeing Garrett arrive.

"Sasha and Painter said I'd probably find you here," Garrett said.

Cole nodded. "As long as *Haven* is needed to help produce fabricators, there's not much gallivanting to be done. Besides, I love it here. I love watching all the near-station traffic and the running lights out in the construction zones."

Just to Cole's right and a few degrees below his line of sight, a large mass of running lights flashed in a synchronized pattern. Cole smiled and pointed.

The pattern corresponded to the ILS^2, the Interstellar Light Signals System. Shared between all space-faring civilizations, the ILS^2 served as a method of last resort to communicate with other ships. Humanity's contribution to the design and implementation dated back to the ancient Morse code.

The running lights flashed their message three times before returning to their normal flash pattern. The message: *Hi, Cole! --Srexx*.

"Should he really be messing with the ship's running lights?" Garrett asked.

Cole shrugged. "I'm not too worried about it. Maybe I should be, but he's been really patient with being cooped up in one system for so long. Honestly, I think he's still working through encrypted archives from Earth, but before too long, I'll take him out for some exploration."

"Fair enough," Garrett replied. "Do you know what today is? Do you know where you were three years ago today?"

"Holy cow... has it really been three years since the Pyllesc system?"

"Tempus fugit," Garrett said. "You remember the last time we stood in front of observation glass?"

Cole nodded. "Yeah. I told you it wasn't over."

"Yes, you did. How about now?"

"I wanted to tidy up the Thyrrays' situation in the Commonwealth, too," Cole replied, "but there's still time for that; we have Lindrick cooling his heels in one of our brigs somewhere. I'll settle for exposing everyone who had a hand in my family's massacre. So... yes, I think it's finally over now."

"Had any thoughts on what's next?"

Cole laughed. "That's almost a loaded question. To be honest, I haven't really thought about it. My main priority right now is building my shipyard. It's past time *Haven* had proper screening elements, and a long time ago, I promised Painter a freighter... not to mention converting all those ships we swiped from the Commonwealth over to Gyv'Rathi designs. After that, though? We'll see. There's still plenty to do."

WHAT'S NEXT?

Have you read "Ships in the Night," the story of Cole's first adventure as Jax Theedlow?

If not, sign up for my newsletter to get it.
https://click.knightsfallpress.com/cole-srexx

―――――

"Haven Ascendant" continues the story, and it's available now.

Visit the book's page to choose your vendor:
https://kfplink.com/haven-ascendant

Or...

Visit your favorite bookstore and ask them to order this ISBN:
978-1733473507

ACKNOWLEDGMENTS

There's an old saying: it takes a village to raise a child. I don't know if that's true or not, but it certainly seems true where publishing a story is concerned. You would not be reading this were it not for contributions from several people.

The editor of this work, T. F. Poist, deserves far more than a simple 'thank you' for her efforts with this work. Her time, knowledge, and expertise improved this work beyond measure.

Did you like the cover? The background image was created by Jakub Skop (https://www.behance.net/JakubSkop).

I'm sure there are many who will see this next paragraph and think, "Goodness, he's acknowledging his parents and grandparents *again?*" My greatest regret is that I cannot hand my grandfather, Bob Miller, a paperback copy of my novels. So, yes... the Acknowledgements page of *every* story I publish will have the paragraph that follows. Consider yourselves forewarned.

Without my grandparents, Bob & Janice Miller, I honestly don't know where I'd be today; my grandfather taught me to read and love reading, and my grandmother taught me to develop and exercise my imagination. This story (not to mention my life in general) certainly would not have happened without my parents, Vernon & Judy Kerns.

ADVANCE TEAM

Whether you use the term 'beta readers,' 'eARC group, 'advance team,' or something else, it's very nice to have a group of people who want to read an advance copy and tell you anything you and the editor missed... because that happens. And it happens with *every* book.

Anyone willing to help me make my books a better product deserve all the thanks I can give them, including recognition here.

Fletcher Hawkins
Rob Law
Marti Panikkar

THE WORLDS OF ROBERT M. KERNS

For a complete and accurate listing of all publications, both currently available and forthcoming, please visit Knightsfall Press.

Knightsfall Press - Books

https://knightsfall.press/books

SO... WHO'S THE AUTHOR?

Robert M. Kerns (or Rob if you ever meet him in person) is a geek, and he claims that label proudly. Most of his geekiness revolves around Information Technology (IT), having over fifteen years in the industry; within IT, he especially prefers Servers and Networks, and he often makes the claim that his residence has a better data infrastructure than some businesses.

Beyond IT, Rob enjoys Science Fiction and Fantasy of (almost) all stripes. He is a voracious reader, with his favorite books too numerous to list.

Rob has been writing for over 20 years, published his first novel in 2018, and has no plans to stop any time soon.

Connect with Rob at robertmkerns.com.

[f] facebook.com/RobertMKerns

[a] amazon.com/author/robertmkerns

[BB] bookbub.com/authors/robert-m-kerns